El Shaddai

**Almighty, most powerful God.
I am God All-sufficient.**

Armour

JO WANMER

El Shaddai
© Jo Wanmer 2024

Published by Armour Books
P. O. Box 492, Corinda QLD 4075 Australia

Cover Images: Alisha Bube | iStock: Max Patch in the Smoky
Mountains in North Carolina; Whimsy Girl | Creative
Fabrica. Interior glyph: Jacpot07 | Creative Fabrica

Cover design, interior design and typeset by Beckon Creative

ISBN: 978-1-925380-79-8

A catalogue record for this
book is available from the
NATIONAL
LIBRARY National Library of Australia
OF AUSTRALIA

Contents

Part 1: The Rescue   5

Chapter 1	7
Chapter 2	13
Chapter 3	23
Chapter 4	39
Chapter 5	53
Chapter 6	71

Part 2: The Restrictions   85

Chapter 7	87
Chapter 8	103
Chapter 9	121
Chapter 10	141
Chapter 11	157

Part 3: The Refuge — 173

Chapter 12 — 175
Chapter 13 — 193
Chapter 14 — 209
Chapter 15 — 237
Chapter 16 — 255
Chapter 17 — 279

Part 4: The Recompense — 295

Chapter 18 — 297
Chapter 19 — 311
Chapter 20 — 327
Chapter 21 — 347
Chapter 22 — 359
Chapter 23 — 369
Chapter 24 — 375

Epilogue — 379
Author's Note — 387

Part 1

The Rescue

Chapter 1

THE BIRDS STOPPED SINGING.

Milly's spoon hung, suspended over her muesli. Their chorus had woken her this morning. Why this sudden silence? The wall of water from her nightmare pushed up to her carefully erected barricades. She shoved the picture down. 'Hosea. Can you hear any seagulls?'

Her five-year-old left the breakfast table and raced to the front door. 'I'll go see, Mum.'

'Me too.' Determination etched Lily's chubby face, as she wriggled off her chair.

'It's okay, Lily. We can go too.' Milly grabbed a wipe and cleaned vegemite from sticky fingers. *Is it today, God? Why else would the birds disappear?* 'Dan...' Milly poured his coffee as she called down the hall. 'We'll be in the front yard.'

'Okay, Beautiful. Is my lunch ready? I don't have long and I want to tell you something before I go.'

'Everything's waiting.' She left his coffee beside his hot toast.

'Thanks, Hon.' His electric shaver hummed from the bathroom.

Lily hammered on the screen door, unable to reach the latch. Hoisting the two-year-old on her hip, Milly went out to the garden and scanned the sky. Seagulls were constant in their life, always squawking and soaring over the nearby ocean. But there were none—not one. No pelicans perched on the esplanade street lights. No noisy minas fighting in their garden. No magpies or parrots in the native trees.

The door banged and Dan dumped his lunch and briefcase on the patio chair. His toast balanced on top of the red coffee mug. 'Sit with me, Milly...'

Lily climbed over to his knee. 'Daddy, there's no birdies.'

'Maybe they're playing hide and seek. You go look while I talk to Mummy.'

'Dan, I'm...'

'Milly.' He squeezed her hand, his blond hair flopping in his eyes. 'My God, El Roi, talked to me in the middle of the night. I'm excited about what He said.'

'That's good.' She dragged her gaze from the sky. 'Dan, the birds are gone.'

'Are they?' He chomped his toast. 'I had a vision. El Roi, my God who sees, showed me a property. It was vast. Cattle and fences and water... I think our dream is about to happen. We can develop a healing home. Isn't that exciting? He talked to me about details and gave me plans and...'

'Is God paying?' Milly turned to glare at her husband. 'We've talked about this. We can't afford a property.'

'Milly! You know I've had this vision several times now. He said He'll do it and I believe Him. You wait and see. The Lord has never failed us.'

'You're such a dreamer.'

El Shaddai

Dan pulled her close, his sapphire eyes twinkling at her. 'You are the dreamer in the family, but I'm sure God gave me this dream. I'm not talking about a nightmare. This is about a hope and a future, Milly. *Our* hope and *our* future.' He kissed her hair, jumped to his feet and picked up his bag.

Fear pricked the back of Milly's throat. 'Dan, I'm...'

'Dad.' Hosea raced around the corner. 'The mother pigeon isn't on her eggs. Is she a bad mummy?'

Dan scooped his son up on one arm. 'I'm sure she'll come back, Hoey.' He gulped his coffee.

Milly's heart sank as he carried their son towards the car. 'Dan, there's something wrong. I feel it in my bones. In my dream last night...'

'Milly. Shh. Little ears are tuned.' Dropping the mug on the roof of the car, he spun Hosea upside down, before lowering the laughing boy to the ground. He grabbed Lily and threw her in the air, caught her, kissed her and slid behind the wheel.

'Dan.' Milly grabbed his arm before he could shut the door. 'Stay with me today. Please. I'm frightened. What if...'

'You're what?' His soft eyes touched hers. 'C'mon, Honey. It's not like you to stress.' He clasped her hand. 'Look at my cup, Amalya.'

The red mug, perched on the dash, reminded her of the absent birds. The words *El Shaddai* decorated the cup, his favourite. It rode to work with him most days. 'God Almighty, El-Shaddai, is still in control, Honey. We can trust Him.'

She clung to him, absorbing his strength and faith. If only she could trust in God as strongly as Dan.

'Mummy. No birdies.' Lily pulled at her shorts.

Bending, she lifted the two-year-old onto her hip. 'Dan...'

He blew her a kiss. 'Trust, Honey. Why don't you take a day off? Head up to the hut and relax.' He grinned. 'See you all tonight.'

Fear rose in her throat. 'Unless... unless the earth moves first.'

'In which case, I'll find you at the hut.' He started the engine and rolled down the window, his blue eyes boring into hers. 'Neither hell nor high water will keep me from the most beautiful girl in the world. Look after Mum, Hosea.' He lifted his red mug in salute. The slogan jumped at her—*El Shaddai, God Almighty*.

Dan accelerated down the hill, turned and disappeared. She tried to swallow the lump in her throat and hold the tears. They escaped and tracked down her cheeks, leaving a salty taste in the corner of her mouth.

❧ ❧

'Milly.'

She spun around at the voice. 'Ky. I... I didn't know you were there.'

Her friend walked down the footpath. 'How long's Dan going for? A month?'

Milly plastered on a smile. 'I'm just being silly, Ky. Sorry.'

Ky squeezed her arm. 'Guess I'm jealous. All I got was a bellowed instruction to make sure the kids were ready for bed before he's home.'

'What's eating the mighty Mal?'

'Let's just say, today I'm over him.' Ky's gaze dropped to the ground. 'Can we have coffee, or take the kids to a park today? I need a diversion.'

El Shaddai

'Talking about kids. Where are yours?'

'I snuck out for a few minutes. I put Bethie back to bed and left Johnno with the television.'

Hosea barrelled around the corner of the house. 'She hasn't come back, Mum.'

Ky ruffled his hair. 'Who've you lost, Hoey?'

'The mummy bird. She's left her eggs. I thought mums were supposed to watch their babies.'

Milly's pulse jumped. 'Ky, let's go up the mountain. You haven't seen our new hut yet. The kids can play and we can chat. Pack a picnic lunch.'

Hurrying inside, she slapped cheese on bread and threw last night's leftover salad into a container. In the garage, she packed her Commodore with camping gear and her hoarded emergency stash. After every devastating nightmare, she'd shopped for more supplies. Embarrassed, she'd hidden the panic buying from Dan. She'd spent a lot, telling herself it wasn't a waste. They would use everything, the rice, tinned food and toilet paper even if it took ten years.

Ky stopped her car across the driveway. 'I'm going to the shops, Milly. Can I meet you at the lookout?'

Milly dropped the big bag of flour on the floor of the car and waved. 'Okay. I'm about to...' Water rose in a wall in front of her eyes. Rolling, churning, foaming, its tentacles reached for her, seeking to devour her and her children.

'Milly. What's wrong?'

She shook her head. The vision evaporated. Her heart pounded. Her mouth felt like sandpaper.

Everything seemed normal... except there were no birds.

Chapter 2

THE OVERLOADED COMMODORE   coasted down the hill towards the beach, Milly's knuckles white on the steering wheel. *Lord, please let me see a bird. Even one seagull. Anything to quell this rising dread.*

No gull squawked over the ocean. The calm green-blue water winked in the sunlight. Small waves ambled up the sand.

'Let's go to the beach, Mummy.' Hosea bounced in his booster seat. 'It's hot. Let's swim.'

'Not today, Hoey.'

'But Mum...'

'Don't argue, Hosea.' She spun the car through a roundabout. The wheels squealed as she stamped on the accelerator. As the distance from the water increased, her body calmed. She sped towards the freeway.

Waiting at the lookout for Ky, she pushed Lily on the swing, the pulse in her throat settling. Ahead she could see the hills where Dan had rented a rundown hut. He claimed it was the first step towards his dream of owning cattle. But

Milly knew he'd rented it so she felt secure, hoping to stop the nightmares that had plagued her sleep for months. 'Got to go, Lily.' Stopping the swing, she bundled the kids back in the car. She longed to be high in the hills, safe.

Ky's little red Mazda turned into the car park. 'Sorry I'm late, Milly. I won't get out. Bethie's asleep.'

Milly squatted beside the window. A young, blond woman sat in the passenger's seat; her green eyes unsettled.

'You remember Caroline?' Ky waved at the young woman. 'We started chatting at the shops so I invited her. Hope that's okay?'

'It's lovely to see you, Caroline.' Milly's greeting was met by a half smile. It didn't reach the woman's eyes—eyes reminiscent of the ocean. Did they hide the same treachery? 'Let's go.'

Their cars descended into a lush green valley, gliding onto the low bridge over the Wambo River. Unbidden, Milly was confronted by brief images of her nightmares falling into the landscape. A wall of water rushed up stream, picking up cars and people like bath toys. Jamming a hand over her mouth, she shook her head. The wheels on the Commodore sprayed gravel as she accelerated off the bridge and up the hill.

With relief she negotiated the bends on the sleep incline. Why did Ky bring Caroline of all people? A rich, stuck-up, arrogant student—though an unexpected baby interrupting her university career may have changed her. Typical Ky. Her heart was pure gold and she often befriended the lonely. Milly tried to find some compassion but couldn't get past the invasion of her time with Ky.

El Shaddai

The road climbed higher and the trees' fingertips kissed above the car. Peace began to permeate her unsettled heart. *If only Dan had come.* She could cope with anything when he was with her, even Caroline.

At the tiny village of Pine Mountain, she parked outside the local shop. Hosea unclipped his belt. 'Can I have an ice cream, Mummy?'

'Not today, Hoey. I only want to ring Daddy before my phone loses reception.' Selecting Dan's number, she watched Caroline pulling herself from Ky's car. Her bleached blonde hair swept across her immaculate pink blouse as she ran up the kiosk steps. Ky, always the attentive mother, twisted behind the wheel to check her children. Johnno and Bethie were sleeping. An extra car capsule crowded the back seat. Milly blinked. *Of course.* Caroline's baby.

Dan's recorded voice asked her to leave a message. 'Hi, Darling. We're at Pine Mountain. Ky and a friend are with me. I loaded all the supplies. Poor car's grunting a little. Still no birds. I'll leave the hut at four if... if the earth hasn't moved.' She hung up and then hit the redial button, hoping he'd pick up. He didn't. Her second message was brief. 'I love you, Honey.'

The road snaked through white-trunked gums rising out of the deep green undergrowth. They dipped onto the rocky crossing over Dead Man's Gully. A chill shimmied down her spine. *Why would anyone give the dip such a name?*

'Birdie, Mummy.' Lily's pudgy finger pointed out her window. A bush turkey ran across the track, its yellow wattle flailing under its red neck.

Her heart skipped a beat. *A bird*. Even a turkey was better than no birds. Then a willy-wagtail flew past. In the distance a crow squawked. *Safe. Thank God, we're safe... for now.*

Tall trees thinned to open eucalypt country. A sharp rocky escarpment rose in front of them. Light bounced off the rock walls and for an instant the escarpment morphed into a panoramic movie screen. Milly blinked, astonished. It vanished. But the image of rolling pastures was seared into her brain. She stopped the car under a tree near the hut and closed her eyes. It was fainter but still there. Acres and acres of land with cattle, fruit trees and sheds. And people walking with her and Dan.

Ky's car pulled in beside them. Milly shook the pictures away and focused on her surroundings. To her left, hidden behind thick shrubbery, the plateau plunged to the valley. Dan was still down there, sitting in his meeting.

Caroline wound down her window and pointed to the corrugated iron structure. 'Is this the cow shed?'

Milly flushed as she shook her head.

'Are you telling me this is the hut? It's not as big as a caravan.' Caroline glared. 'This is it, Ky. You can't expect me to take Bea in there.'

Ky got out of the car and surveyed the scene. 'I love the bush. Let's wait until we look inside, Caro.'

Milly carried a sleepy Lily and strode towards the dirty orange door. A pot of teal-blue paint waited in the car. Soon the door would look brighter. For now she lowered Lily and grabbed three folding chairs from the hut. 'Picnic, anyone?'

El Shaddai

Caroline swallowed the last bite of sandwich and laid her baby in Ky's eager arms. 'I need to use the bathroom. Then I'll feed Bea and we'll head home, won't we?' Hostile green eyes focused on Milly. 'I'll need a large cup of tea while I'm feeding.'

Milly munched her salad. 'Can I finish my lunch first?'

Caroline stretched her tanned legs and stood. 'In an establishment as small as this I guess I can find the toilet myself.' Without waiting for an answer, she headed towards the hut.

'Put the kettle on while you're there, Caroline.' Milly winked at Ky as Caroline opened the orange door. 'Wait for it. Ten, nine, eight, seven...'

Caroline screamed. She exploded out the door, her face as white as her hair. Ky jumped to her feet and ran to her. 'What happened?'

'Spiders. Huge spiders. One attacked me from the roof.' Caroline turned blazing eyes on Milly. 'Why didn't you warn me?'

'You seemed to know what you were doing. I assumed you were a bush girl. Calm down and I'll show you the loo.' Milly retrieved a roll of toilet paper from a hook beside the door. Handing it to Caroline, she led the way past the water tank behind the hut.

'Where are you taking me, Milly?'

'It's called an outhouse, traditionally known as a dunny. I'll check for creepy crawlies before you go in.'

Caroline gaped as she surveyed the quaint structure with its little chimney leaning at a jaunty angle. The door opened to the escarpment, offering occupants a wonderful view.

Breaking a little branch off a bush, Milly entered the cubicle and swept all spiders and cobwebs away. 'There you go. All spic and span.' She left Caroline peering around the door and headed back to Ky.

Baby on her arm, Ky was wandering inside the hut. An ancient three-door wardrobe separated the kitchen from the double bed. 'Milly, where will the kids sleep?' She waved her arm. 'An old wrought iron bedstead, a lumpy sofa and one over-stuffed chair.'

'There are two camp beds in the car.' Milly crossed the threadbare carpet square. She knelt on the couch, lifted the window and swung open the old brown shutters. Light flooded the room.

Ky turned to the window and gasped. 'Diamond-studded hills. How beautiful! The view is worth a million dollars, but...' She shuddered. 'But I can't believe you'd choose to sleep here, Milly.'

'Me either.' Caroline held her hands out as if contaminated. 'That is the most disgusting loo I've ever seen. Where's the bathroom?'

'You'll find soap beside the tap on the tank.' Milly took an old towel from the cupboard and tossed it to her.

Ky leaned against the worn timber table that backed onto the wardrobe. Bea rewarded her with a loud burp, as she lifted the baby over her shoulder. An ancient wood-burning stove filled an alcove jutting out of the room. Blackened saucepans and a large frypan hung from wire hooks. 'Milly, this place isn't anything like you. How does the stove work?'

'It burns wood. There's plenty of timber, but no power.'

'What?' Ky spun around. 'How do you charge your phone?'

'There's no phone reception.'

'And no running water?'

'As Dan says, we run outside to get it.'

'That's not even funny, Milly. Mal would have a fit if I asked him to come here.'

'Talking about Mal. You wanted to share something.'

Ky turned away. 'No. I just wanted a diversion. Something to calm me. This is perfect, Milly. Thanks.' They wandered out the door, passing boxes of tools. Above their heads an old rifle balanced on two rusty nails. The chairs beckoned them. Ky sighed as she sat. 'Pity I don't have a tent. This place reminds me of my early childhood.'

'Where, Ky?'

'Kyogle in the Byron Bay hinterland.'

'Ky from Kyogle?'

Ky pulled out a handkerchief and blew her nose. 'I don't tell many people but my name is Kyogle. Dad named me after the place where I was conceived.'

Milly chuckled. 'Oh, Ky. How romantic!'

'It may seem that way. Mal sees it differently. He loves to call me Ogle or Olga. Ugly Ogle is his favourite at the moment.'

As though upset on Ky's behalf, Beatrice screwed up her baby nose and cried. Caroline rushed from behind the tank to take her. 'Can I move the car into the shade, Ky? I'm not feeding her in that hovel.'

Ky pressed a kiss onto the baby's forehead before handing her to her mother. 'Sure, Caro. Did you see the kids?'

'Yes. They're playing back there.'

Ky glanced at them before taking in the hut once more.

'It's quaint, Milly, but completely inconsistent with your beautifully decorated home.'

'Dan's always wanted land. He dreams about owning a place where people can come and find God, be healed and restored.' She stopped herself from sharing the vision she'd just seen.

'Yes. I know Dan's passionate about God's call and promise. But the Milly I know reminds him it's impossible. I'm worried about you. Won't you miss your comfortable king-size bed?'

'A bed of nightmares.' Milly had told Ky about her dreams, but she'd dismissed them as carrying a spiritual message. Milly hoped Ky was right, but the wall of water rushing up her street didn't feel spiritual. It was terrifying, wet and cold. 'Ky, it's like when you're pregnant and your time is close. The pressure is so strong something has to give. Today I woke after another dream and, when I realised there were no birds, I had to get away.'

'They're only dreams, Milly.'

'As I crossed the river today, I saw a wall of water rushing up towards me.' Milly rubbed her eyes trying to erase the memory. Her fists clenched. 'Why, Ky? Why's this happening to me? Night after night a wall of dirty water rolls up our street in slow motion. It sucks up everything. Closer and closer. Higher and higher.' She unclenched her fists and threw up her hands.

'Steady, Milly.' Ky stepped over to hug her. 'What does Dan say?'

'Suck it up. Control my thinking. Trust God. As if! I wish...' She dropped her face onto Ky's shoulder. 'Last night,

Dan explained a tidal wave needs a trigger. A storm or an earthquake.' She pulled away from Ky, quivering.

'This isn't normal. The Milly I know is calm, strong and capable.'

'Nothing's normal.' Milly slumped onto the grass and leaned back against a tree trunk. A magpie landed close by, fixing a beady eye on them. Above her head a crow squawked. Her pulse slowed. 'I love it here, Ky. Somehow it seems... secure. We are safe and happy here. I just wish...'

'Wish what, Milly?'

'I want Dan with me. He's still down there.' Milly looked out over the trees to the rolling hills. 'He says warnings are always issued before any tidal wave.'

Ky squeezed her hand. 'We never have earthquakes in Wamberoo, Milly. Or tidal waves.'

'You're just like Dan.' She stared at the magpie. 'I told him unless the earth moves under my feet I'll return at four.' Again, before her mind's eye, she saw the wall of water devouring everything in its path. She shook her head, trying to erase the picture.

Chapter 3

CAROLINE ROUNDED THE CORNER of the hut, eyes blazing. 'Ready to go yet?'

'Sorry, Caro. Milly hasn't unpacked yet.' Ky turned to Milly. 'Can you move your car closer? It would easier to unload. The boys and I can carry. You can put things away.'

Milly walked towards her car, her legs like lead. A bubble of pressure exploded somewhere between her belly and her heart. She doubled over in pain, holding her breath until the spasm passed.

Don't move the car

Shaking her head, she dismissed the thought. Ky was cuddling Bethie as she returned. Caroline had gone again. 'Let's grab a moment to talk about Mal. I'll unload later.'

'Helping you is much better than talking about Mal.' Bethie grabbed Ky's t-shirt and pulled it down. 'She's hungry. I'll give her a little drink while you move the car.'

Hoey ran from behind the water tank, a streak of dirt across his excited face. 'Mum, I'll help you. Can I steer?'

'I guess so. Lily, you stay with Bethie.' Hoey skipped beside her as she forced her feet towards the car. *Whatever is wrong with me?*

~~~ *Let the peace of God rule your heart* ~~~

Peace, God? I have no peace.

She froze.

A shiver raced from her feet to her brain. 'Ky. Did you feel anything?' *Did the earth just tremble?*

Caroline raced past, pushing a pram. 'C'mon, Ky, let's go home. It's spooky up here.'

'Calm down, Caro. It could have been anything. But, yes, let's all go home.'

'Listen, Mum.' Hoey pulled on Milly's hand. 'Is that a bunyip?'

The distant yowl was eerie, sending another shudder through Milly's body. It grew louder and louder, more and more terrifying. Milly yelled for Lily. She needed her kids close. Lily ran. She leapt into her mother's arms and flung both arms around her neck.

The earth heaved.

Up and down.

Again, and again.

Giant hands twisted her intestines, squeezing all the air from her. Her feet left the ground, tossed upwards as the earth flexed like a trampoline. Everything moved in slow motion. Even the unmovable shook.

Milly hung in the air. Lily's feet flew out but her arms gripped her mother's neck. Her terrified screams joined the bunyip's growl. 'Hoey. Where are...' She belted into the ground. Hoey tumbled from the sky, falling on top of her and Lily. Heart pounding, she grabbed his wrist with one hand and a weedy sapling with the other. The earth threw them heavenwards again. Lily screamed. Fingernails bit Milly's neck.

'Jesus. Lord, Jesus, help.' With a mighty yank she pulled Hoey in beside Lily. With them under her wings, Milly clung to the sapling as it danced to the beat of the bunyip. She clamped her eyes shut and waited to die. The noise and wild motion vibrated through every part of her. Bile rose to her throat. She gasped for air, coiling her head and shoulders over her children to take the brunt of the avalanche of sticks, leaves and branches.

A dynamite boom cut the air. The earth convulsed once more and settled. A mighty rumbling roared from the direction of the escarpment. She clung to the sapling and her children.

Silence.

Stillness.

Waiting, waiting.

Not daring to move or even breathe. Her children shook with voiceless sobs. The world hung, suspended in eerie silence.

Hoey pushed out of her iron grasp. 'I'm glad the… the train missed us, Mum.'

'Train… train… Oh, it did sound like a train. I think it went under us, Hoey.' Milly opened her eyes. The world spun, slowed, stopped. Every organ felt misplaced and twisted.

Caroline's scream cut the silence. 'My baby? The baby's gone…'

'I. Have. The. Baby.' The stilted voice sounded like Ky, but Milly couldn't see her anywhere.

'Ky. Are you okay?'

'Okay, okay.' A robotic laugh morphed into a broken sob.

Milly shoved a few small branches aside and pulled herself onto her knees. Ky huddled a few metres away, her body curled forwards into a shell, her arms encasing her children. But where was Bea? Caroline's hysterical sobbing receded as she ran further away.

Milly pushed herself to her feet. Lily still clung to her neck. Hoey threw aside branches and kicked twigs away. 'Johnno, did you hear the train?'

Ky lifted a white face. Johnno plopped out of her grasp, revealing a sleeping Bea, cocooned between Ky's crossed legs. Bethie clung to her mother's side, eyes shut, her little body shaking. 'Lily, can you hug Bethie?'

Lily released her iron grip and slipped to the ground. Milly scooped the baby from Ky's knees just before Ky emptied her stomach into the leaf litter.

'Boys, can you see Caroline?'

Hoey pointed down the hill.

'Bea. Bea. Where are you?'

'Caroline.' Milly started to carry the baby towards her but stopped. She couldn't leave her children ever again.

'I'll get her, Mum.' Hoey started to jump over branches.

'Hosea, get back here.'

'Mum?' The eagerness fell from his face.

'Sorry, baby. But you must stay close.'

'In case the train comes again?'

'Yes… the train…' Milly sank to the ground beside Ky. They clung to each other, pulling their girls close.

Ky whispered over and over. 'You're our refuge, God. Our refuge and strength.'

El Shaddai

Caroline stormed back, kicked aside a couple of branches and snatched the baby from Milly. Startled, Bea screamed. Caroline rocked and jumped in circles. 'You're okay, Bea, you're okay. Mummy's got you now.' The wails increased.

Lily started to cry. 'I bleeding, Mummy. My leg hurts.' She pointed to a scratch on her thigh.

'Sorry, baby. I'll find you a band-aid soon.'

Ky scrambled to her feet and stumbled to the nearest tree. She emptied her stomach again. It triggered Milly to action. Groaning, she felt as if she'd battled the earth and lost. They needed a safer place. But was anywhere safe? Around her lay a disaster zone. Half a dead gum tree lay between them and the hut, its roots surrendered to the sky. A large branch pinned Ky's chair to the ground. The hut still stood, under a cover of twigs and small branches, but it leaned at a strange angle. Half-naked trees stood, stark against the dark red backdrop of the escarpment. Gaping scars showed where limbs had been ripped from them.

Caroline ran in circles, eyes crazed. 'Where's the car? I can't see the car. I need the car. I've got to go home…'

'Caroline! Stop. It's there.' Milly pointed down the hill.

Ky's little red Mazda rested against a tree, its wheels groping the air, like a stranded Christmas beetle. Caroline's screeches were edged with hysteria. 'Get me out of here, get me out of here. Get your car, Milly. You gotta get me out of here.'

'Caroline. Pull yourself together. I can't even see my car.'

'It's there, Mummy.' Hosea pointed towards a large pile of branches. The cream duco cowered under a pile of smashed greenery.

Hugging Bea to her chest, Caroline ran to the Commodore. 'It's on its wheels. It's okay.' Wild-eyed, she started to pull at broken branches with one hand. 'Help me. You must help me.'

Ky slumped back to the ground, hanging her head. Bethie crawled under her knees and peered out, thumb filling her mouth. Milly sat beside them. 'I'm sorry, Ky. Are you okay?'

'When I look up, everything starts to spin. It turns my stomach.'

'Let's sit for a while. My body's all funny, discombobulated.'

The world hung still, not even a leaf moved. A crow squawked above them. Sun blazed from clear blue sky, as though nothing had happened. In contrast, Milly's thoughts raged. They chased each other in circles. She couldn't go home now. The earth *had* moved. What if Caro dragged Ky back to the valley? What if they were caught in the tidal wave? But what would they do here? They couldn't all fit in the hut.

'Mum.'

Hoey dragged her back to the present. 'I need to go to the toilet.'

Milly jumped to her feet, the 'what ifs' banished by the reality of *now*. 'Go behind a tree for now. I'll need to check the dunny is safe.'

At the car, Caroline waved her arms above her head, yelling.

'Lily, you look after Ky and Bethie. Mummy will go to Caroline. Johnno, I need you and Hoey to help me.' Together with the boys, she navigated a path to her car, pushing branches to one side. Caroline pointed to the pram. It lay on its side against a tree, one side bent. She clutched blankets, toys and clothes.

El Shaddai

Milly retrieved a baby's bottle from under a log. 'Boys, see if you can find baby Bea's things and take them to Caroline. I'll get the pram.'

Caroline dropped the baby in the pram as soon as Milly straightened it. She yanked at branches covering the car. Milly surveyed the leafy web. Around the other side, the mess didn't look as hopeless. With the help of the boys, they dragged some branches from the driver's door. It opened, giving her access to the supplies. Relief flooded her. Selecting a few bags from the car, she turned towards the hut.

Caroline blocked her. 'What are you doing? Stuff your stupid shopping. We have to get the car out. I've got to get home.'

'How are you going to get in the car if we don't empty it, Caroline?' Milly stepped around her and carried the bags close to the hut. Not trusting Caroline's erratic behaviour, she returned to retrieve the keys from the ignition. Grabbing more bags, she left Caroline struggling with the tangle tethering the car to the ground. Ky watched from her chair, both girls snuggled on her knee.

'How're you doing, Ky?'

'Better. Tummy's still complaining.' Her shaky hand pointed to the branch pinning another chair to the ground. 'Milly, this chair. What if... what if I'd still been sitting there? If you'd moved the car it'd be squashed under that tree.' Her body started to tremble. 'And... and... what's happened at home? Our house doesn't have earthquake rating. If it slid down the hill it'll be on top of your place.'

Milly stroked Ky's shoulders, pulling twigs out of her blond curls. 'Ky, we don't know...'

'I've tried to ring Mal, but the phone won't work. He'll be furious with me. I didn't even leave a note. Can I take your car and we'll go back to the shop? I can phone from there, can't I?'

'Yes, but both cars are stuck. Track is blocked. I need tools and they're in the hut.'

Ky pulled out her hanky and wiped her face. 'I think I can help now.' She lowered the girls to the ground. Bethie wailed. Ky fell back to the chair, the little colour draining from her face.

'Sit a little longer. I'll check the hut. I want to get the kids protected in case...'

'In case what?'

'Aftershocks. Best we're prepared.' As the words left her mouth she shuddered. She never, ever wanted to feel the ground move again. *Dan, I need you. Please hurry.*

She sat on a dead log. Picking up broken sticks, she threw them into a pile beside the hut. Soon she'd cleared a pathway to the door.

The hut leaned forward, staring towards the hills like a sentinel on watch. Milly shoved all four walls. They seemed solid. She pushed the door. It didn't open. She shoved it with her shoulder. Not even a slight shudder. She kicked the bottom of the door. It moved a little, but the lean trapped the top.

'What about the window?' Ky stood at the log. 'It was open before the quake.'

'Good thinking.' Encouraged, Milly went around the hut. She picked up one shutter from the ground and leaned it against the wall. The other hung by a hinge. The window she'd left up was shut but intact. With both hands on the dirty glass, she pushed up, but it wouldn't budge.

El Shaddai

The furniture huddled together in the middle of the room. Everything from the shelves was scattered on the floor behind the door. Even if it opened, the mess would make access difficult. Johnno barrelled around the corner. She picked him up and he buried his tear-stained face into her shoulder. 'Milly, I thirsty. Mummy... Mummy says wait.' Little sobs shook his frame.

His weight on her shoulder felt lighter than the fear squeezing her heart. They were stranded. Even if she could fit everyone in her car, she wasn't willing to drive into the valley until she knew there was no danger of a tidal wave. Her brain raced. It would take ages to disengage the car from its cage of branches. Ky's vehicle was useless. She couldn't get into the hut. As she grappled with these thoughts, shadow engulfed her. Panicked, she looked up. The sun had dropped below the escarpment.

She took long, slow breaths. *C'mon, Milly. You can do this. What is the most important? Water, shelter and food. Focus on them.* She lowered Johnno beside Ky's chair. 'Have you seen Hosea?'

Ky's cheeks were pinker. 'No. I thought he was with you. Any luck with the window?'

'Shut tight. Johnno, do you know where Hoey is?'

The little boy nodded, lifting his brown eyes.

'Where did he go, Honey?'

'I sorry, Milly.' Tears began to pool in the brown depths.

'Johnno, you're not in trouble. Tell me where he went. I need his help.'

'Caroline said he had to help her. She said I'm too slow.' A big tear escaped and tracked down to his chin.

Pulling him in close, Ky hugged him. 'What did Caroline want Hoey for?'

Milly's eyes scanned the area, her stomach churning. 'Hoey. Hosea. Come here.'

There was no response.

Ky turned Johnno's face to hers. 'Johnno. This is important. Where is Caroline?'

'Gone to the shop. I wanted to go but she said I couldn't, but she needed Hoey.'

Milly squatted down beside the boy. 'Why did she need him?'

'He had to move the branches so she could push the pram.'

She'd heard enough. Running, dodging branches and jumping logs, she passed her car, then Ky's stranded vehicle. She followed the track towards the road. The pram's wheel tracks were visible between smashed greenery. 'Hoey. Hoey. Wait for Mummy.' Her voice echoed off the escarpment.

Abandoned, the pram was parked in front of a pile of twisted branches. Heart racing, she pushed her way past. A scream, a gut-wrenching guttural scream, cut the air. It dissolved into a long wail. Milly ignored her bursting lungs and broke into a sprint. 'Hoey! Hoey!'

As she rounded a boulder, he crashed into her stomach. She pulled him close. 'Hoey, don't you...'

'Mum. There's a... a... big hole in the road.'

Milly doubled over, panting. 'Are Caroline and Bea okay?'

'Car'line's crying.' He pulled her hand. 'Come, Mummy. Come and look.'

Milly allowed herself to be dragged along, her hand pushing the stitch biting her side.

El Shaddai

'Help! Help!' Caroline's frantic yells filled the air. Milly swallowed her impatience. Still puffing, they followed the littered track. The distraught girl knelt on the ground cradling her baby, sobbing and yelling.

'Don't fall in the big hole, Mummy. It's gi-normous. It could swallow a whole house.'

Milly ruffled her son's hair, amused by his exaggeration.

Then she saw it.

The earth had opened up. Dead Man's Gully now resembled a gorge. She stood beside Caroline's dejected figure and stared. The yawning slash in the ground went as far as she could see in both directions. In the lengthening shadows she couldn't tell its depth. But any crossing was impossible. There was nowhere to go. Not tonight. Not tomorrow. They were stuck. Stranded. A choking ball lodged in her throat.

Coming to life, she shook Caro's shoulder. 'Caroline. Get up. We must get back to the hut before dark.'

Ignoring her, Caroline yelled across the gorge. 'Help. Help. Someone, please help.'

Milly turned. 'Come on. There's no one to hear you.'

'The shop people will come.'

'Even if they did, they can't reach us tonight. I must go back to Lily and Ky.'

'Can you carry the baby? I'm so tired.'

Milly went to take Bea, but something rose up within her. Others needed her too. 'No, Caroline. I've got to get the hut door open before dark.'

'Don't leave me here.'

'I'm not leaving you. It's your choice. Come or stay.' She took Hoey's hand and jogged back, jumping branches as they went.

Ky and the children were at the car. Ky handed Milly a couple of bags and found a smaller one for Hoey to carry. 'Pleased to see you, Hoey. Where's Caroline?'

Milly sighed. 'Coming—I hope. Did you hear her scream?'

'I wondered if it was a scream or a bird call.' Ky winced as she moved Beth to the other hip and picked up two bags of shopping.

'Ky.' Hoey sounded full of importance. 'We found the biggest hole you've ever seen.'

'Did you, little man? You can tell me later.'

'Later, Hoey.' Milly shuddered at the thought of the road dropping into the earth. 'We won't be going anywhere tonight, Ky. I reckon we've got about an hour before dark. We must get the hut door open.'

Ky didn't falter. 'I figured as much. That's why I've been emptying the car. If all else fails, we'll spend the night in it. Do you have any idea how to open the hut door?'

'A battering ram?'

'What do you mean?'

'We'll get a strong log, hold it above our heads and punch the top of the door.'

Ky threw a doubtful glance over her shoulder.

Milly shrugged. 'Do you have a better idea?'

'Only the car.'

'Let's try to get into the hut. If the lantern hasn't broken, we'll have light.'

El Shaddai

Milly selected a log from the pile of debris, while Ky found muesli bars and a bottle of water. She settled the children in a group on the ground. Johnno held Bethie on his lap, promising to look after her.

Their first attempt missed the dirty orange door, leaving a dent in the corrugated iron wall. After several attempts, they managed to hit the top corner of the door, but it didn't budge.

'Mum?' Hoey stood behind Milly.

'Hoey, I told you to stay with the kids.'

Shoulders dropped, he turned. 'I just thought Dad's crowbar might help.'

Milly grabbed him and kissed his head. 'Sorry, Son. Where is it?'

'He left it near a big rock the other day. Remember. He tried to move the rock. It's still there. Dad said I can't touch it 'til I'm seven.'

Using a log as a fulcrum, the women cracked the door open with the crowbar. Excited, Milly leaned against it. A small gap opened but it barely budged when Milly shoved it further. 'All the stuff from the shelves must be blocking it.' In the deepening shadows she could only make out shapes. 'Hoey. Can you squeeze in and shift the things behind the door?"

He peered through the opening. 'I... I can't Mum. It's too dark.' His bottom lip wobbled.

'Hang on. I think there's a torch in the car.'

As she neared the Commodore, Caroline yelled. 'Milly, help me. The pram's stuck and I can't see.'

'Caroline, everyone's stuck. If you can't keep going, sit on a log and wait. I'll come when I can.' Leaning through the car she located the dynamo torch in the glovebox. Dan mightn't be here, but his efficiencies were still equipping her. She jogged back to the hut, winding the handle on the torch to charge the battery.

Ky took the torch and shone the light through the window. Encouraged, Hoey squeezed through the gap. He moved sufficient debris for Milly to push the door open enough to squeeze through. The lantern still hung from the wire hook in the ceiling. *At least it's intact.* It flared in response to a match. Ky cheered, and the children rushed into the light. As each one squeezed through the door, Milly lifted them onto the bed. With Hoey's help she cleared enough space behind the door so Ky could get through and join them. Together they worked to relocate furniture. Milly swept broken crockery, spilt cutlery and other scatterings into a corner. Tools, screws and bullets were pushed behind the door. Ky attended to the children. She wiped their hands and faces, using a rag and one of the bottles of water she'd found in Milly's shopping.

'Mummy, I want my 'jamas and Booboo.' Lily's bottom lip started to tremble. 'I want home with Daddy.'

'So does Mummy, Darling.' Milly picked up her crying girl and sat in the lumpy chair. Her own tears fell unchecked on her daughter's messy hair. *God, where is Dan and where are You? I asked You to save us. Is this Your idea of rescue?* All she could hear was her daughter's sobs.

Ky curled around her children on the bed pulling them close. She caught Milly's eye over the two tousled heads. 'Where's Caroline? I'm worried about her.'

'Last I saw her she was down the track and as cranky as anything. I couldn't wait for her. I had to get back to the rest of you.' Milly pulled herself out of the chair and lay Lily on the bed, kissing her cheek. 'Now Lily's asleep, I'll take the torch and find her.'

The interior light of her car shone like a beacon, leading her to Caroline. She sat in the driver's seat trying to feed Bea. The baby was crying in frustration. 'Why won't she feed? I'm so scared, Milly. I hate the dark and I need to get home. I have a date tonight. Is it seven yet? I need to have a shower and...'

Milly passed a bottle of water she'd grabbed from the hut. 'You're too dry and stressed to make milk. Have a drink and try again soon. Where's the pram?' Following Caroline's pointed finger, Milly took the torch and retrieved the pram. In its carrier she found a baby's bottle. Filling it with water, she rinsed the teat. 'Try this. It may satisfy her for a while.'

'Yuk. It's not sterilised.'

'Well, suck it then. There's no way to sterilise it.' *She'll drive me crazy.* 'Now, do you want to come to the hut or stay here?'

'I'm not going in that disgusting place.'

'Please yourself.' Milly turned back towards the hut.

'Milly. Wait.' Caroline bleated like a scared child. 'Can I have the torch? I need it. You're not scared of the dark like me.'

'If you want light, there's a lamp in the hut. Coming or staying?' Milly hoped she'd stay.

'Can you hold the baby while I get out?'

Milly cradled Bea and led her mother to the hut in silence. Hoey sat cross-legged amongst the mess sorting nails and screws into their containers. The others curled together asleep.

'Caroline.' Ky rushed over, hugged her and waved towards the table. 'Dinner's served.'

Milly sank onto an old wooden chair. Chaos surrounded her, but somehow Ky made everything feel calm. She relaxed.

We've survived. We have a roof over our heads and food on the table.

Ky echoed her thoughts. 'Thank You, Jesus, for Your protection and for this food.' She handed out plastic mugs as though serving the finest crockery.

Caroline turned up her nose. 'What is it?'

'My special beans.'

'Cold baked beans. Oh, Ky. You know I can't eat beans. I'm breast feeding.'

Milly swallowed a sharp retort and smiled. 'Thanks, Ky. You're amazing.' Taking a spoon, she escaped through the door before she told Caroline off. Hoey followed, winding up the torch and flashing its light into the bare tree branches. A cold empty ache filled her chest. *Where is Dan? Where is God?* Was it His leading or her paranoia that brought her here and left them in this predicament? She shivered in the warm evening breeze.

'Mum, let's light a fire.'

'Okay, Hoey. We can try. Can you find some matches?' She gathered little dry twigs from around her feet. Every twig she snapped eased her angst. Her little fire ignited bigger twigs until it blazed enough to burn small branches. She pulled up a chair and ate her cold beans. Her little man draped himself across her knee. If only Dan was here. He must come.

Then she remembered the chasm cutting the road. Silent tears snaked down her cheeks. The earthquake had split her family in two.

What about Your great vision and promises now, Dan's El Roi? Where are they?

Chapter 4

A MOVEMENT WOKE MILLY. Disoriented, she sat up. *Why am I on the floor?* In the pitch dark everything trembled. With a start she realised this wasn't a nightmare. Caroline and Lily both started screaming. Milly grabbed the torch. 'Get under the bed or the table.'

Sleepy women grabbed their children, but… all was still. They froze, waiting. Caroline wailed. Ky flopped on the bed and shoved her head between her knees. Bethie cried, clinging to her side. Baby Bea, snug in her pram, slept—unaffected by the tremor.

Milly cuddled both boys and soothed Lily. 'It's an aftershock. It's okay now. Go back to sleep.' She hoped she was right. Comforted, the children fell asleep in minutes, sprawled across the cheap doona separating them from the thin carpet. Behind her, Caroline sobbed.

Ky rummaged in the bags in the kitchen. She threw Milly's new purple towels over the children. 'It's cool. Shame the door won't close. Milly, lie on the bed. There's room for us both with the kids sleeping on the floor.' As Milly sank onto the soft bed, she could hear Ky's gentle tones comforting Caroline. Her own silent tears soaked the sheet.

A strange noise disturbed Milly's sleep. 'Dan...'

But he wasn't there. Heart hurting and pulse racing, memories of the quake rattled her mind. The rhythmic noise got closer, pulling her fully awake. The hut was still dark but faint light peeked through the window. Milly hauled herself over Ky and crept outside. A line of helicopters was coming from the south. She jumped up and down, waving her hands over her head. Unswerving, the army Mohawks continued in the direction of Wamberoo. Slumped on a rock, she watched them get smaller and smaller.

'Was that a chopper?' Ky rushed out of the hut.

'Seven army Mohawks.'

'Did they see you?'

'No.'

'They'll come back... won't they?' Ky sat beside Milly.

Milly blinked. 'Your hair...'

Ky's hands tried to flatten her wild curls. 'Early morning look. I always douse them with conditioner before Mal wakes.' She left in the direction of the outhouse, curls reaching for the sky. When she returned, her damp curls were tied back. 'I've been thinking. Maybe others are missing too, Milly. How bad do you think it is at home?'

'The choppers are obviously needed. I think it's been a big quake. Big enough to spark a tidal wave.'

El Shaddai

Ky's grey eyes reflected her own horror. 'Your tidal wave. Oh, Milly. What... what about our friends, family, Mal, Dan?' She shoved her phone into the pocket of her cargo pants. 'If only we could contact someone... anyone.'

Milly jumped up. Hope rushed into her heart. 'The radio... in the car.'

They ran to the car, jumping the branches and dodging leaf chaos. Ky arrived first. 'The door's open. I hope there's no snake or anything.'

Milly jumped in and turned the key. *Click. Click.* She thumped the steering wheel and tried again. Nothing.

'I guess the open door flattened the battery.' Ky sounded close to tears. 'And my car's useless.' The wheels of her little red car were up in the air, as if in surrender.

'But the radio might still work.'

'My radio never works...'

Milly wended her way down the hill. 'But the battery...' Reaching the car, she pushed up and down on its bottom edge. It rocked back and forth. 'Maybe... if Caroline would help us, we could to turn it over. We'll need the crowbar and a log.'

'Mum.'

At the yell they ran towards the hut. Hoey met them on the way. 'Mum, Caroline yelled at Johnno and told us to get out. She made the girls cry.' He flicked a tear away, pretending he was too big to cry. 'We did nothing wrong.'

Milly grabbed his hand and followed Ky to the hut. Hoey ran beside her. 'I... I had a bad dream...'

'That's no good.'

'Dad drove into the big hole.' A sob racked his body. 'His car went down… down… down. I couldn't even see it at the bottom.' Big tears ran down his face.

'Oh, Baby.' She stooped down to hug him.

'Why didn't he stop, Mummy?'

A shudder ran through her. Nothing marked the hole and she couldn't ring Dan to warn him.

Ky led Lily out of the hut. Little Bethie fed from her breast. 'They need breakfast but this'll satisfy her until I find something for the kids to eat. Can you get a fire going again, Milly?'

'I'll try to light the stove.' Taking a deep breath, Milly pushed open the door into the hut.

'Get out of my room now.' Caroline pulled a towel over her head.

'Caroline. This is not your room. The kids need breakfast.'

Milly waited for an argument, but instead the young woman started sobbing. 'I want to go home. I want to go home.'

'We all do.' Milly left her to cry. She wanted to get to the road, but first the fire. Hoey and Johnno carried in sticks and leaves. A lighter from the pile behind the door helped the fire catch. Soon flames licked the stove top. She filled the kettle from the tank. 'Ky. Are you okay for a while?'

Ky waved her off. Milly left her rummaging in plastic bags of shopping. 'Come on, Hoey. We'll go and see what we can do about the hole in the road.' They left Bethie and Lily dressing sticks with leaves. Ky had told them they were baby dolls.

Pictures of Dan's car plunging into the ravine pushed her to a run. When Hoey complained, she slowed her pace, trying to stop imagination overriding common sense. *What if he'd come and driven into the hole?* Headlights would shine straight over the top. She sprinted the last hundred metres, ignoring Hoey's yells.

The edge of the ravine fell straight down. Warning Hoey to stay back, she lay on her stomach and crept to the edge. She peered down, her gaze following the falling dirt and gravel dislodged by her hands. Pinpricks of horror erupted behind her neck and ran down her arms. A giant's knife had slashed through the earth leaving a bottomless gaping wound about six or seven metres wide. Far below, a large rock was wedged between the two walls. A few tufts of grass clung to its surface like hair on a bald head. Milly could hear running water, but she couldn't see it.

A little hand on her arm alerted her. Hoey had crawled out beside her. 'Careful, Honey.' She gripped his arm.

'Is... is Dad down there, Mummy?'

'No, Darling. Look. There are no car tracks going over the edge on the other side.' She pulled herself back from the precipice. 'We need to find a way to warn anyone who comes.'

Hoey picked up branches and threw them. They spiralled into the ravine.

'Don't do that, Mate.'

'I need to get them on the other side to stop Dad.'

'Good idea. Find some without many leaves. They'll go further.' By the time they'd finished there were enough sticks on the road to stop anyone before they drove into the ravine. Puffing, they walked away.

Ky served hot porridge, powdered milk and weak tea for breakfast.

Lily buried her head in her mother's chest. 'I want toast and vegemite.'

'Sorry, Honey.' Milly ruffled her hair. It needed a comb.

Caroline screwed up her nose. 'This tea is disgusting, Ky. I like strong tea.'

'Sorry, Caro. I thought we could all share one tea bag. We don't have many and I want them to last.'

'But we must get home today. I need a shower and clean clothes. And Bea needs nappies and bottles and...'

Ky cut across the monologue. 'What do you think, Milly?'

'I can only see two ways to get home. We can wait to be rescued. It may happen today, or it may not. Who knows? Or we can find a way out ourselves, which could take days. We can't drive. The road's cut. Let's work out the most important things to do.'

'We need a sign the planes can see.'

'Good idea, Caroline. Can you look after that?' Milly ignored the scowl.

'We need a radio.' Ky shovelled porridge into Bethie. 'Then we'd know if anyone is trying to find us.'

Caro jumped up. 'I'll feed Bea in your car, Milly, and listen to the radio.'

'Can't, Caroline.'

'Why not?' Green eyes sparked daggers at Milly.

'Battery's dead. Seems someone left the car door open all night. Wonder who?'

'Don't blame me. You marched off with the only torch.'

'Girls. Stop it.' Ky glared at them both. 'We'll try to get my car going. Then we can start Milly's. There'll be jumper leads in your car, won't there?'

Hoey's bottom lip trembled. 'I want Dad, Mummy. I don't want to live here forever.'

Milly pulled him close. 'We'll get home somehow. Now we need you and Johnno to help us with the cars.'

Using the crowbar and axe, they released the Commodore from its leafy tomb. Caroline called them for another cup of weak tea. To Milly's astonishment she also produced scones.

'I used some of the big bag of flour, Milly. But they're pretty hard. The oven isn't hot enough and there's no butter or jam or cream.'

Ky gave her a big hug. 'You're so clever, Caro. These are so yummy served hot.' As they munched scones, Caroline led them to the front of the hut. A purple SOS yelled to the empty sky.

'Do you think a plane would see it?'

'I think so. Great work, Caro.' Ky scanned the sky. 'Has anyone heard any planes?'

Caroline shook her head. 'I watched while I fed Bea. A couple of helicopters down the valley, but nothing close. Why aren't they looking for us? Mum and Dad would have reported me missing by now.'

Milly turned back to the hut. 'Why don't we try to get the red car on its wheels? I'll get the ropes, crowbar and axe. We'll need everyone.'

The three women rocked the vehicle back and forth, hoping it would somehow land on its wheels. What they'd seen on television didn't work for them. Milly and Caro pushed the crowbar under the car, and by levering off a rock they could lift it. Ky pushed rocks or logs trying to hold every centimetre. After repeating the effort several times, the car leaned on a drunken angle, but its wheels still pointed to the treetops.

'We need a sky hook.' Milly sat beside the pram with Caroline while Ky went to get the girls from the other car. She pointed above them. 'If we could get the rope over that branch, it may work.'

Caroline studied the trees. 'The branch over there would work better. Better angle. More leverage.'

Milly swallowed her sharp retort. Why was Caroline so stupid at life and so smart with other things? It annoyed her. She grabbed a clothesline and flung it over the branch. Using it, they pulled Dan's tow rope over their skyhook. The rope was secured to the doorpost of the car, threaded through the back and front windows. Seating the kids on a log, the three women grabbed the rope, and pushed their feet into the rough earth.

'One. Two. Three.' Milly could feel the veins bulging in her neck. Twang. She hit the ground. The rope was still in her burning hands, but the car hadn't moved. The knot had come undone. Milly gulped down tears as the boys' laughter rang out. *Why is it so hard?* The sun headed towards the escarpment again. Her body was bruised. Despondent, she sat down, her head in her hands.

Ky jumped up. 'C'mon, girls. We can do it. If we tie a better knot, I reckon it'll work.' The knots were ungainly but solid.

As the women picked up the rope again, the boys counted. 'One. Two. Three. Pull, pull, pull.' Milly wedged her feet against an exposed root and threw her full weight on the rope. Her veins bulged, her hands burnt, but it moved a fraction. Hoey yelled. 'Keep pulling. Pull, Mum. Pull. It's coming.'

She moved her lower hand up the rope and dropped all her weight on it. *Bang.* Her backside hit the ground again. Caroline and Ky tumbled on top of her.

'You did it! You did it!' The boys clapped and cheered.

Sure enough, the battered red car stood amongst branches and leaves but on its wheels. Ky yanked at the driver's door, falling back when it swung open. 'I think I can smell petrol. I won't try to start it yet.'

Milly's whole body trembled. 'Let's leave it 'til later. We're exhausted. We need a drink and a rest. Besides it's getting late.'

Picking up their tools, the weary band were half-way to the hut when the earth moved again. The ground grumbled and vibrated under them. They grabbed at kids and each other, trying to hold anything stable. Fear rose in Milly's throat. Would the ground play toss with them again? Would it open under them as Dead Man's Gully had? Would the car stay on its wheels?

The rumblings faded and all hung still. Caroline rocked Bea, tears streaming down her face. Ky passed Beth to Milly, ran to a tree and started dry-retching. Milly flopped on the ground, gathering in four scared children. 'It's okay, guys. It's over now.'

'Why does it keep happening, Mummy?' Hoey's question echoed her own.

In the privacy of her heart, she threw the question to heaven. *Yes, God. What are You doing? What do I tell these frightened children?*

'I think God is renovating.' Her own words surprised her. 'Remember when we fixed our house and Dad added another room?'

Hoey nodded his little head but his eyes betrayed fear. 'Dad did make lots of noise but it wasn't as loud or scary as this.'

'I guess God is fixing bigger things.' Milly leaned over the girls huddled in her lap and kissed him on the head. 'You know how Dad won't let you help when he does dangerous work. Remember why?'

'He didn't want us to get hurt.' Hoey waited for the nod from his mother.

Ky, looking pale, sat with one arm around Caroline. 'So there is no need for us to be scared. God promises He will look after us and each time He's changed things we haven't been hurt.'

Caroline shook, her green eyes betraying her terror. 'But...'

'Caro.' Milly put up her hand to stop adult fear spewing out on the children.

Caroline glared at Milly. 'I'm going to Dead Man's Gully to see if anyone's been there. Coming, Ky?'

Ky hesitated. 'I'd like to see the hole but I'm thirsty. I'll take this stuff to the hut and follow after I've had a drink. Aren't you thirsty, Caro?'

'I've got water.' She pulled two bottles of water from her bag under the pram. Anger surged through Milly. How much water had Caroline taken? What would happen if they ran out?

Ky took a bottle and passed it to Milly and the four kids to drink first. She drained the bottle and replaced it in the pram. 'Coming?'

Milly shook her head. 'Be careful. The edges of the ravine aren't stable and could cave at any time.' She looped the ropes

El Shaddai

over her shoulder and picked up the crowbar. 'Come with me, Lily and Hoey.'

'Mum, I want to go.'

'No. I need you to help me.' She passed him a rope, ignoring his resentful eyes.

After a couple of seconds, he dropped his gaze to the ground. 'No fair.'

'No, but that's the way it is today.' She grabbed Lily's hand and dragged her feet towards the hut. If she was organised for the night, maybe there'd be time to get the radio working.

❧ ❧

Milly straightened from unpacking the last of the provisions as a car started. Hoey ran out the door. 'It's Daddy.'

'No, Honey. It's Ky's car.' Unable to bear the disappointment in his face, she picked him up and carried him to join the others. His head dropped into her neck. She felt the hot tears running over her shoulder as his lanky body quivered.

Ky drove her red wreck over leaves and around branches to bring it nose to nose with the Commodore. Like two battered soldiers they stood, guarded by a scarred gum whose branches had been twisted off by invisible hands. Ky opened the red bonnet. 'Grab your jumper leads, Milly. Let's get your car going.'

She hesitated, wracked by fear. All day she'd been working to get the radio started and now she recoiled from it. *Why?* The wall of water rose before her. Rubbing her eyes, she opened them again.

Ky stared at her. 'Milly. You're as white as a sheet. Are you okay?'

She leaned against a tree. 'Don't start the car yet, Ky.'

'C'mon.' Caroline pushed past her. 'Where are the leads, Milly?'

'They're here.' Hoey held them high. 'Dad keeps them under the seat.'

Caroline released the bonnet and clipped leads to terminals. Milly froze. *What's wrong with me?* The sun dropped below the escarpment. She shivered as though the shadow of death had passed over.

Ky raised an eyebrow.

Milly's pushed her fear down. 'Caroline, do you know what you're doing?'

Caroline snorted. 'Of course.'

Ky put her hands on Milly's shoulders. 'What's wrong?'

'The radio. There's something not right. The kids... the kids shouldn't hear.'

'Hmm.' Ky turned her towards the hut. 'You go. Light the fire. I'll grab the keys and bring the others.'

Milly grabbed Lily and left.

Later, kids asleep, the three women sat around the cold fireplace. Milly stretched her aching legs. With the boys' help, she'd cleared the area in front of the hut, piling everything in a mountain behind the fireplace while Ky found food. After Ky had taken the keys, Caroline had sulked in the car. Towards dark she arrived with two camp stretchers, claiming one for herself.

The cars, cowering under the grotesque gum, beckoned Milly. But she hesitated, fearful. Another day had passed without any sign of Dan. The news must be bad.

Ky sighed. 'I'd love a shower.'

El Shaddai

'Me too. I stink.' Caroline broke stick after stick and threw them at the dead fire. 'This is ridiculous. Why'd we ever come here, Ky?'

Ky didn't look up. 'It seemed a good idea at the time.'

Milly moved aside a few tools under the tank stand and pulled out an old metal tub. Rolling it into the hut, it filled most of the space between the table and the stove. Returning to the tank she filled the biggest saucepan. Placing it over an open porthole in the top of the stove, she added two more logs. The fire flamed and the water began to sing. Soon every pan crowded the stove top.

All the time the radio attracted and repelled her. She wanted to hear the news, but dreaded knowing at the same time.

The bath wouldn't be deep, but she longed to be washed. She felt filthy. And there were no clean undies. She shuddered. The towel would cover her while her undies dried on the line over the stove. With her new purple bath sheets and face washers piled beside the tub, she paused and sighed. Resisting the urge to hop in, she turned towards the door.

The others weren't there. The faint sound of a male voice from her car sent a shiver up her spine. *The radio. It's working.* Drawn towards the circle of light, she strained to hear over the car motor. 'Earthquake specialists are flying in from New Zealand and Japan. Disaster crews from the southern states have worked tirelessly since arriving this morning. While the entire coastline has been affected, the city of Wamberoo took the brunt of the tsunami. We're crossing now to the Chief of Police.'

The voice faded as she ran back up the hill. She'd have first bath after all. Her feet didn't fit in the tub. She hung them over the edge and used a small saucepan to pour warm water over her shoulders. But a wall of dirty water flashed before her eyes. Her heart screamed for Dan. His office building proudly stood on the esplanade.

The singing kettle mocked her. Wiping her tears away, she lifted herself out of the bath. In the dim light the water didn't look too dirty. To conserve water they'd have to use the same bath. Wrapping herself in a towel, she refilled saucepans. Was this her life from now on?

Chapter 5

EARLY NEXT MORNING Milly and Ky, wrapped in purple towels, sat on a rock. Deep red light on the horizon slanted through the darkness. Ky tried to flatten her hair with her hands. 'I still can't believe it, Milly. It's horrifying. I had to stop listening.'

Milly wrapped her arms around her body, trying to stop the shaking. 'I hoped I was wrong. Wished I was wrong. So many dead. It's awful. I've seen it over and over and...'

Ky held her. Her compassion released Milly's sobs—sobs trapped within her for months. 'Dan and Mal and... old Mary... and...'

Ky rocked her. 'Yet God heard your cry. He rescued your kids and mine. We need to be thankful, Milly.'

'I'm try... trying. But I didn't warn enough people.'

'You did your best. Not even Dan believed your dream...'

'I didn't bring enough food. Or water or clothes or nappies or anything. Why didn't I give it more thought? And I can't live without Dan.' They slipped off the rock onto the grass and clung together, sobbing.

'There you are.' Caroline stormed towards them. 'How can the sun still come up, when the world has ended? I hope you bought suicide pills, Milly.'

'Caroline!'

'Well, it'd better than starving to death in this God-forsaken hole.'

Milly's grief turned to fury. 'Don't you dare speak that way, Caroline! You and Beatrice are alive and well. You're not trapped in a collapsed building. You haven't been washed out to sea. Your baby hasn't been snatched out of your arms by muddy water. God has rescued you, rescued us all. Why would He rescue us and then let us die? He must have a plan.' Milly stood, tightened her towel and strode off. *God. You must. You must have a plan. Your word… It says You give us all we need.* She pushed further into the bush, lifting the towel to free her legs. The further she went, the more the vista opened before her. Sinking onto a large log, she pulled her knees under her chin. *Why did You bring that stupid girl, Lord? She is selfish and childish, painful and pathetic. She drives me crazy.*

꩜ A cord of three strands ꩜

Where did that come from? She pulled her legs closer. *Are You talking to me?* Maybe she'd try again. *Where is Dan, Lord? Is he okay? Will You send him?* She strained to listen—to get an idea, but all she could hear was a distant droning.

A plane! Jumping up, she stood on the log, waving the towel over her head. The plane flew low, dipping its wings before disappearing over the escarpment. As the drone faded, she lowered the towel. Looking down, she realised she was stark naked. But they'd acknowledged her. Was that God's answer?

'Mummy, will they bring a big helicopter? Will we all get in? Can I sit with the pilot?' Hoey danced in circles.

Rescue was coming. It had to be.

Every hour they sat in the car and listened to the news headlines. Caroline wanted the radio playing all the time. It churned Milly's stomach and she worried about the effect of constant drama on the children. She carried the key in her pocket, turning it on once each hour for five minutes. The news became more and more alarming.

An earthquake, measuring 6.9 on the Richter scale, centred below Pine Mountain, had devastated their city. With little time to warn the shocked people before the subsequent tsunami, the community was a disaster zone. Every news bulletin gave different statistics of the number of people dead or missing.

At three o'clock she sat in the driver's seat listening to headlines. 'In the city centre, all buildings still standing must pass an engineer's assessment before rescuers are allowed to enter. Many buildings resemble a box of spilt matches. Police estimate thousands of people are still missing. It is feared many are buried in the rubble, others washed out to sea.'

Milly couldn't bear any more. She cut the motor. The radio went dead. From the passenger seat, Caroline grabbed Milly's arm. 'Turn it back on. I must to know if Mum and Dad are okay.'

'We've heard enough, Caro.'

Caroline dug her fingernails into the flesh of Milly's arm. 'You run away from the truth if you want to. Coward. But leave the keys.'

Lily started to wail.

'Let me go, Caroline. I've got to help Lily.'

Green eyes sparked and her fingernails dug deeper. 'The keys!'

Milly yelled as the fingernails drew blood. Swinging her free arm, her hand connected with Caroline's angry face. As her head jerked back, Caroline released her grip and Milly leapt out. She'd taken three long strides towards Lily when she was knocked flat from behind. Her face jammed in the dirt, the full force of Caroline's fury hit her, pummelling her back and head with piston fists.

Crying. Who's crying? Milly tried to bring order to her befuddled brain. Pushing back the fog, she realised it was Lily. She spat dirt from her mouth and tried to lever herself up.

'Mummy.' Hoey's little hands stopped her. 'Ky says wait. Don't move 'til she gets here.'

A little gasp punctuated Lily's sobbing. 'Mummy. You okay, Mummy?'

Milly's head dropped back in the dirt. A hand lifted her head and pushed something under her face. Hoey's red t-shirt. 'That feel better, Mummy?'

Moved by her children's distress she managed to roll a little. Fear coursed through her body. 'Hoey? Where's Caro?'

'In Ky's car. And she's not allowed out.' He turned to his sister. 'Lily, go and get Mummy a washer.'

Lily hiccupped. 'I tarn't. I got prickles.' She started howling again.

Milly tried to push herself up. Her entire body seemed to ache.

'Don't move, Milly.' Ky's soft hands were on her back. 'Hoey, can you get the prickles out of Lily's feet? Johnno, find a washer for Mummy.' Gentle fingers explored Milly's body, bit by bit, across the shoulders and down her spine.

Satisfied, Ky helped Milly to her feet. Followed by two crying little girls, they limped towards the hut. Ky helped Milly onto the bed. Her body quivered. Her teeth chattered. Lily snuggled in beside her, still whimpering and sucking her thumb. A doona floated around them. Soft hands washed her face, sending needles of pain through her head. The warmth eased her discomfort. The noises faded.

The smell of fresh bread filled Milly's nostrils. She walked through her kitchen to check her breadmaker. Hmmm. Fragrant bread, sliced warm, dripping with butter and vegemite.

Pain woke her. The sharp contrast of the hut and the smell of dirty children assaulted her. Lying still, she struggled to stop her tears.

'Ky?' Hoey sounded as though he was in the kitchen.

'Yes, Hoey?

'Is the damper nearly cooked? Johnno's hungry.'

'Just a little longer, boys.'

'Mummy. Why didn't the big 'copter come yet?'

'There's lots of people hurt, Johnny. Maybe the helicopter needs to help them first.'

'Will it come tomorrow?'

'I hope so.'

'Ky, why did Caroline jump on Mummy?'

'She's upset and she got very angry.'

'But you shouldn't hit, even if you're angry. Mummy says.'

'I know, Darling. It was wrong.'

'I hope she stays in the car all night.'

Johnno's shrill little voice yelled over Hoey's constant chatter. 'She's gone.'

'What do you mean, Johnny boy?'

'She's gone up the hill. She told me not to tell.' The little quiver in his voice betrayed his confusion. 'I sorry, Mummy.'

Milly lifted her head as Ky looked out the door. 'She was in the car but she's gone. Did she take Bea, Johnno?'

'She's in the pram. She told me to watch her, but I needed you, Mummy.'

Milly tried to roll. By clamping her teeth, she quietened the moan in her throat. She was sitting on the side of the bed when Ky returned. The screaming baby slashed the air with tiny fists. Flopping onto the settee, Ky pulled up her shirt. It took a little persuasion, but soon the baby's screams were replaced by desperate sucking. Milly lowered herself into the lumpy chair and nodded at Bea. 'Like her mother. Slashing fists must run in the family.'

'I'm sorry, Milly. You okay?' Ky was doing what she did best, mothering everyone. Yet her eyes were tired and anxious.

A wayward spring made Milly wince. 'Just a few bruises. I'll be fine in the morning.'

El Shaddai

The half-moon hung red in the sky, casting weird shadows on the escarpment. Milly turned off the torch and sank onto a rock. *God, what am I doing here?*

Looking for Caroline

Why? She tried to kill me. I'm bruised all over. She's a self-centred rotten selfish bitch. There, I've said it. What are You going to do about it?

Milly shook, more from anger than cold. She had sworn in front of God. Would she be struck by lightning? Now she couldn't even ask Him for help. A cool breeze lifted and added a shiver to her shaking.

'Why did I come?' Now she spoke to herself. There was no point talking to God. 'Why? Caroline's run away. So what? Stupid bitch.'

When Milly had left the hut, Ky was trying to breast-feed two babies. Only Ky would attempt anything so kind and crazy. Milly would have left the baby screaming in the pram under the trees. *What sort of woman leaves her baby behind?* Ky had left the hut to search for Caroline, but Milly sent her back. She'd rather stumble around in the dark herself than lose Ky and be left with two screaming babies and no milk.

The breeze increased. *That's right, God. I'm sore, tired, beaten up, searching for a needle in a haystack and now You make the conditions uncomfortable.* As if on cue, a cloud covered the moon, leaving her surrounded by darkness. Unable to stop the tears another moment, Milly sat on the rock and sobbed. A bird screamed in the distance. She shuddered and held her breath to listen. Was it a bird? It sounded like a little lost child. A mopoke's gentle cry answered it. She closed her eyes. The wind dropped and the scream faded, receding into the distance.

Caroline? She often sounded like a child. *Is it her?* Using her torch, Milly picked her way between the rocks, following the escarpment around until it split in two. The moon reappeared. Should she go up the narrow gorge into the dark or follow the outside in the watery pink moonlight? The breeze lifted again. She shivered and stepped into the shelter of the gorge. No night cry in there. Back out of the gorge she pushed into the wind, yelling, 'Caroline. Caroline.'

Back and forth, stumbling over the stone-strewn ground, she searched. Sometimes the cry seemed to be in front of her, other times behind her. Then it stopped leaving an eerie silence. 'Caroline!'

The hairs on her arms stood on end.

A twig broke behind her. She swung around. A gaping black hole broke an otherwise moonlit wall. Two eyes blinked at her. A strangled scream escaped her lips. 'Caroline?' Her stomach turned. Her pulse banged in her neck.

'No, Missus. I'm Bobby. Didn't mean to scare you, Missus.'

Every hair on Milly's body stood on end. 'Where's Caroline?'

'White-haired lady, Missus?'

'Yes.'

'She climbed the gorge. At sundown. Stupid. She's stuck.' An edge of a chuckle softened his voice. 'She's okay, Missus. But she cries lots.'

Milly stumbled and grabbed at a branch to steady herself. The dark shape jumped to her rescue. 'Sit down, Missus. You're shaking.'

El Shaddai

Milly sat, trembling. *Who is this person?*

'Here. Have a drink.' A dark hand thrust a dirty flagon at her. 'You'll feel better.'

She pushed it away. 'No. No, thanks. Can... can you show me where Caroline is?'

His black hand scratched through matted curls. She wished he'd turn his face to the moon so she could see him. 'I'll show you in the morning. Meet me at sunup. Bring a rope, please. You go and rest now. I'll go back to her.' He turned and his shadowy form merged with the black hole.

'Wait.' Panic rose at his disappearance. 'Is she okay?'

'Why do you care? She beat you up. You're not okay. Go to bed and don't worry. Bobby'll watch her tonight.' His unexpected sympathy touched Milly. The horror of the pummelling washed over her in waves. Her shoulders shook with silent sobs.

His hand rested on her arm. 'It's okay to cry, Missus. Make you feel better.'

'I'm sorry.' She took her hands off her face to find the moon had gone again.

'Come.' He touched her arm. 'I'll take you home.' He led her by the hand away from the wall, guiding her over fallen branches. She followed, wondering why she trusted him. He held some branches back for her. 'Through there, Missus.'

The hut, ghostly silver in the pale light, beckoned her.

'I'll see you at sunup.'

Milly crept out of the hut, stiff and sore. Ky followed with Bea snuggled against her shoulder, a milky grin curving her cupid lips. 'Caroline? You said she was okay. But she's not here. Didn't you find her?'

'I'm going to get her now. I'll be back soon.'

'You know where she is?'

'Well... sort of.'

'Why didn't you bring her last night?'

'I couldn't rescue her in the dark. I had to wait for light.'

The red sun was just peeking over the valley, still shrouded in smoke. Milly realised she must focus on the moment, take one day at a time, one challenge at a time. She broke into a jog, leaving Ky behind. Once past the crooked outhouse, she slowed to a walk. *What if he doesn't come back?* She wondered if she'd dreamt the whole thing.

'G'day Missus.'

Milly stopped, startled. He stood still, wet hair gleaming in the early morning light. He was only a boy, a tall gangly lad. 'Bobby. You frightened me. I didn't see you.'

'Sorry, Missus. I waited in the shadow. This way.'

'Is Caroline okay?' She winced, her sore muscles complaining about the jog.

'She's scared, I think.'

'Scared?'

'Yes. She's frightened of the dark so I camped with her. But she's frightened of me. Sorry, Missus.' He skirted the edge of the escarpment, towering blood-red in the early sunlight. Milly tried to keep up with Bobby, but her shoed feet weren't as nimble as his bare ones. He waited at the opening of the little gorge. 'This way, Missus.'

Milly heard the same cry as the previous evening. 'Is that her or a bird?'

El Shaddai

'Her, Missus. A grown woman, but she cries like a baby.' He held out his hand and helped Milly climb a boulder blocking the path. He jumped to another and then another. Each time he went higher. 'C'mon. You a strong lady. You no baby. You can jump.'

Milly gulped and focused on the next rock, prayed a desperate prayer and jumped. Four more jumps and Bobby pointed to a ledge about two metres above them. 'You call her. She'll come to you, I think.'

'Caroline?' The wind whispered in the trees. 'Caroline. It's Milly.'

Silence. At the unspoken question, Bobby nodded.

'Caroline. Answer me or I'm leaving.'

'Milly, I need help.' She sounded like a frightened child. 'I'm stuck. I can't get down and I've been terrorised by an aboriginal. I've got frost bite and ant bite and I'm cold and thirsty and… and this rat thingy…'

'Caroline.' Milly felt more agitated by the second. 'Come out to where I can see you.'

'But he might come back.'

'If you're talking about Bobby, he's here with me. He led me to you.'

She waited. There was no sign of her. 'Caroline, what are you doing up there?'

They waited in silence. Bobby took the rope and making a loop in one end he threw it at the outcrop on the ledge above. On the third throw he caught the rock. Pulling hard to test the security he grinned. 'Good and strong, Missus. She can swing down.'

Milly raised an eyebrow. 'How?'

He jumped off the rock and swung out wide. As he came back in, his feet met the rock and he kicked out again. Seconds later, he landed on the ground near the base of the escarpment.

Milly's heart lurched.

'It's okay, Missus. I can climb back.'

A minute later, he hauled himself over the side of the rock and sat on his haunches beside her. 'You climb down and go home. Big baby can come when she's ready. Still too scared.'

'Caroline. If you don't talk to me, I'm going home.'

As the silence lengthened, Bobby tied a few big knots in the rope and handed it to her. Milly drew back as though he had offered her a viper.

'I'll show you.'

She nodded. He lay on his belly and bit by bit pushed his body off the edge, one of the knots wedged between his feet. Using the knots like the rungs of a ladder, he climbed down and then up again.

'Which way?'

He pointed to the rocks they had climbed up. Milly shuddered and picked up the rope.

Back at the hut, Milly and Ky bathed the children. Sun-dried, the boys ran naked as their clothes soaked in a tub of brown water. The clean girls were just wrapped in towels when they heard Caroline's muffled cry. 'Ky, you go. Cooee if you need me.'

Ky looked doubtful. 'Why don't you go?'

'She's scared of me. I expect she's waiting for me to beat her up, and I may if she doesn't grow up! Stop, boys.' She grabbed Hoey's shoulder as he ran to follow. 'Let Ky talk to Caroline by herself.'

Milly retied the towel she wore and returned to the bath of dirty water. She channelled her frustration into pummelling the washing. The clothes were hanging on branches of the log and Milly had lunch ready when Caroline stormed out of the shrubbery. Her face glowed bright red. 'Never, ever, in all my life have I been so humiliated. And what does anyone care? I've suffered dreadfully overnight and Ky's being mean. Where's Bea? I need to feed her.' Caroline grabbed her baby from the pram and kicked the door of the hut as she passed. Utensils and gear clattered to the floor.

Milly gritted her teeth as she served bowls of rice to the children.

'Ky.' Caroline yelled from inside the hut. 'Bea won't feed. I'm bursting with milk and she won't take it. Why won't she suck?'

Ky stopped to spoon rice into Bethie's mouth. 'Maybe she's not hungry, Caro. Why don't you eat yourself? There's rice out here.'

Caroline stormed back, grumbling about the things on the floor behind the door. She snatched a bowl of rice. Milly clenched her fists. Why hadn't Bobby left her on the ledge to rot?

'Caroline.' Ky used her mother voice, the one that allowed no argument. 'Before you eat there are a few things you need to say. Firstly… to Milly.'

'What?'

Ky sighed. 'We discussed this, Caro. We are a team here. Yes, our situation is difficult. But we are all suffering grief and loss. We must work together to survive.'

Caroline picked up her fork and started shovelling rice into her mouth. In one quick move Ky snatched her bowl and handed it to Milly. Her hand shook.

'Hey. Give it back. I'm starving.'

'Team members eat. Mavericks don't.'

Caroline's eyes bugged. For a few seconds Milly thought she would lash out but Ky stared her down. 'Go back to the escarpment, Caroline. When you're ready to be a team player, you may return.' She pointed towards the bushes.

'But... Bea. You can't do that to Bea.'

'You didn't worry about Bea last night. Take her with you. But go! You are welcome here as a team member but not as a diva.'

Caroline turned to Milly. 'I hate you.' She snatched the bowl of rice and stormed off, leaving her baby in the pram.

Ky sank to the ground, tears bubbling in her eyes. Bethie crawled into her lap and Johnno cuddled her leg. Milly railed at God while she cleared the remains of their scant meal. *What was all that about? I go and rescue her and still she can't speak a civil word to me. She comes back into camp without a care even for her own baby. Why? God, why?*

～ℓℓ～ *You need her* ～ℓℓ～

Why?

～ℓℓ～ *Forgive. Milly, forgive* ～ℓℓ～

'I can't.' She didn't realise she had spoken aloud.

'Can't what, Mummy?' Hoey, still naked, pulled at her hand. 'Can I help you?'

'I don't know what to do, Hosea. I wish Dad was here.' She turned the dry sob into a cough.

'Dad would pray.'

'I don't think I can.' Embarrassed at her own words, she wondered what sort of example she was setting her son.

He pulled at her hand. 'Sit with me, Mummy. Come under the tree.' He led her as though she was the child. She sat with him on the ground, clutching her towel. Hoey pushed in under her arm. 'Dear God. We need Daddy but he's not here. So please help us. Mummy needs help. Ky needs a cuddle. And can You make Caroline nicer? Amen.'

Tears coursed down Milly's face. Hoey burst into sobs and buried his face in her bare shoulder. Lily surveyed them with big eyes. Milly held out a hand and pulled her in, closing her eyes and heart to their harsh reality.

A stick poking into her back woke her. Her body was curled around her children, sleeping on the ground. Loosening the towel, she tried to sit up without disturbing the kids. Ky and her children were also curled together on the grass, sleeping.

Retrieving her damp clothes from the line she pulled them over her body, relieved to be covered again. Ky woke. Milly tossed her clothes towards her and, when she was dressed, they retreated to the cream car, sinking gratefully into padded seats. 'What will we do, Ky?'

'You're the one God talks to. Ask Him.'

'I'm angry with Him.'

'But He rescued us, Milly. It's a miracle. He's saved us for a purpose. He won't abandon us now. Ask God, Amalya.'

Tears threatened again at the use of Dan's favourite name. He too would be encouraging her to pray. 'I can't. He won't say anything until I obey the last thing He said.'

'Which was?'

'Forgive the bitch.'

Ky threw her head back and laughed.

'What's so funny?'

'You're swearing. The pair of you remind me of junior high girls.'

'I walked half the night looking for her, Ky.'

Ky took her hand. 'I'm sorry. You did. Extravagant kindness always changes a person.'

Hoey, still naked, ran up to the car. 'Mummy, can we make a cubby house?'

'Sure, Honey.'

'Can you help?'

Ky stretched and lifted herself out of the car. 'A cubby house. What fun. C'mon, Milly. Let's build a cubby.'

They created a great hideout for the kids in the fork of a fallen tree, lacing together branches and sticks. They covered it all with leaves. The sky glowed pink when Caroline crept into the hut. 'Milly. Ky. I...' She dropped her eyes.

Ky stopped opening the can of beans. 'Yes... Caro?'

The young woman studied the floor. 'You're right. We need to be a team.' She lifted her head, fixing her gaze below Milly's face. 'Milly, thanks for looking for me last night, even after our fight. I wanted to die, so I didn't answer. I'm sorry.'

'Die?'

'I climbed up there to jump and kill myself. But I was too scared. And that stupid boy hung around all night.'

El Shaddai

Ky paled. 'Kill yourself? But, Caro, what about Bea?'

'I guess Mum's always looked after Bea. I can do what I like when I like.' She slumped onto a kitchen chair.

'It's not going to work like that here.' Milly glared across the room. 'You have to decide. Are you going to pull your weight or make your own way?'

'I've never had to work as a team before. Ky, can you teach me?'

Chapter 6

'Six days. Almost a week of this horror.' Caroline scowled at her breakfast of boiled rice. 'I wish I could have Eggs Benedict.'

Ky nodded. 'With fresh orange juice and brewed coffee.'

'Juice, Mummy. I want juice.'

Caroline turned on Bethie. 'Stop your whinging.'

'Caro!' Ky glared a warning.

'Well, I'm over it. Over it! Why they haven't sent a chopper? No! Don't give me the usual line.' She mimicked Milly. 'There's lots of people to be rescued, Caro.'

Milly watched the exchange from the lumpy chair and chose to ignore the jibe. Everyone was struggling, changing. In many ways they were different from who they'd been six days ago. Ky's neat appearance had disappeared with the earthquake. Caroline's pink blouse had stains from the night on the ledge. The kids were all grubby.

'I want my daddy.' Johnno picked up on the melancholy atmosphere.

'Me too.' Hoey's bottom lip shook. 'My Dad would know where to get food.'

Food was an issue. Although there were plenty of tins and packets left, they were often hungry. Ky's rationed servings were much smaller than they were used to. They craved meat, longing for anything but rice and beans. Caroline had been repeating the chopper monologue for days. The news bulletins didn't penetrate her thinking.

Milly contained her bubbling fear. They couldn't avoid the truth any longer. Life as they'd known it was gone. *God, help us. Help me.* Pulling deep, she found enough courage to break through the chatter. 'Girls, we need to make plans. Hoey, can you mind the littlies outside for a while, please?'

Hoey glared. 'I'm the biggest kid. I should be at your meetings.'

'Hoey.' Ky squatted down to his eye level. 'You are the biggest kid. We would never manage without you. Can you watch for helicopters for us?'

Anger flashed through his eyes. For a moment he glared at his mother, and then capitulated. 'C'mon, kids. Let's play spot the big bird.' At the door he paused, sad eyes dominating his little face. 'It's too boring to play spot the helicopter. Yesterday there wasn't even one.' With shoulders slumped, he left the room.

Milly wished she could run after him and assure him everything was going to be fine. But she couldn't. She took a deep breath. 'I woke early and listened to the morning news. It's not good.'

Caroline's eyes flew open. 'Did they say anything about my parents?'

'No.'

El Shaddai

Caroline flopped back in her chair. 'Good. They must be alive. My Dad is a Councillor. If he'd died, they'd mention it. There'd be tributes to him. He...'

'Caro, listen. They've stopping looking for survivors. The likelihood of finding any more is negligible. Everyone is being evacuated.'

'Everyone? Evacuated? From where?' Caro glared daggers at Milly.

'The whole of Wamberoo. It will be sealed as soon as everyone has gone.' Milly shook. 'Those who weren't killed in the earthquake or tidal wave... authorities reckon they've died from radiation from the nuclear power plant. No one's allowed to enter the area without full body protection. They're trying to contain the leak to stop a disaster along the entire coastline. I guess... if anyone is still alive, they've been sacrificed to the cause.'

Ky nodded, silent tears running down her face. 'I'm not surprised. It sounded desperate yesterday. The whole thing is unbelievable.'

'What about us?' Caroline grabbed Milly's arm. 'They must rescue us.'

'I think we're on our own. Dan... promised to come but...' Milly's heart constricted. She stood and pushed her shoulders back. Now was not the time for self-pity.

'On our own! What do you mean?' Caro clenched her fists. Veins pulsed in her neck.

Milly watched her, worried she'd snap again. 'We must keep calm for our kids. Let's look at our options.'

Ky wiped her face with her dirty t-shirt. 'I'm sure of one thing. God knows we're here. I've been asking Him to give us strength and wisdom.' She pulled a piece of paper from her pocket. 'If I reduce our food rations, we can survive for about eight weeks, maybe ten. Assuming it rains and fills our tank.' She pushed the paper across the table.

Milly took a quick glance at it. 'The kids will be hungry all the time. And so will you nursing mothers. We need a way to live off the land.'

'I suppose I could start a veggie garden.' Caroline brightened for a moment, then slumped back. 'But we don't have seeds.'

'We could dry the seeds from the last tomato. One of the sweet potatoes is sprouting.' Ky pulled it from the bench and laid it on the table like an offering. 'But gardens need water.'

Milly pulled on her shoes. 'Which is why I'm going to try to find Bobby. The morning I met him he was wet. His hair was dripping. He must know where there's a spring. He might be able to teach us to live off the land. And...' She paused. '... he must know a way out of here.'

'He's not safe, Milly.' Caroline shuddered. 'He can't be trusted.'

'Caro, tell me. How did you get off the ledge? How did you find your way back?'

'I don't want to talk about it.' She crossed her arms and turned away.

Disgusted, Milly filled her water bottle. 'Caroline, you start the garden. I want meat for tea, so I'm going to find Bobby. Ky, thanks for watching our supplies so closely. Can you mind Lily, if I take Hosea?'

'Are you going now?' Ky looked shocked.

Milly looped the rope Bobby had knotted, and threw it over her shoulder. Taking a coil of wire from behind the door, she shoved it, her water bottle and a can of beans into her backpack. 'We'll be back before sundown.'

At the escarpment they turned left. The scrub grew thick. They found no sign of Bobby, so retraced their steps and headed into the gorge. Every few minutes Milly called, 'Bobby.' He'd disappeared. At the cave where he'd first startled her, they sat on a log and shared the can of beans, as Milly told Hoey about meeting him. Wide-eyed, Hoey poked the cold remnants of a fire. Judging by the ashes, it hadn't been lit for days. To one side of the cave, Hoey found the remains of a charred snake, but no sign of Bobby.

Milly wandered outside. They were surrounded by green, but she didn't know if any was edible. She'd looked for berries all day without seeing one. They ventured further along the escarpment into new territory. The sun told her they were heading towards Dead Man's Gully. Maybe she could find a way past this rock face and find people—any people.

The rock face swung to the left. Her heart pounded with hope and her pace quickened. The foliage on her right grew thicker. Step by step the rock wall seemed lower.

'Mum. Stop.' Hoey's warning jolted Milly to attention. The ground fell away just ahead. They crept forwards on their bellies, fearful of landslides. It had to be Dead Man's Gully. She still couldn't see any way to cross it. To their left the escarpment fell away into the gorge. A massive landslide had left a raw gouge in the hillside. Rocks were piled in the bottom of the chasm. With nowhere else to go they turned to follow the ravine. Soon they found the track and returned to the hut.

'Anything?' Ky looked up from stoking the fire.

Milly shook her head, 'Ky, what happened to your hair?' Milly stared at her friend. The long curls were gone. Soft, short waves covered her head.

'You like it?'

'I... it's so different. Who cut it?'

'I tried to do it myself but Caro came to the rescue. Long hair is too hard to look after here and I've always wanted it short but Mal...'

'Mal likes it long? Won't he be upset?'

'He's not here. It's practical and it's cool.'

'It's nice. I mightn't recognise you for a while, though.' Milly turned, hoping Ky hadn't seen her tears. *God. I wish I hadn't brought them up here. Not enough water or hair conditioner. They're isolated, grieving and hungry.*

I brought them here

You did? Why, God?

To save them. To give you companions

'Save them?' The lone face she'd seen in her visions was Hoey. She hadn't seen any other children. Faces of her friend's children now rushed past her eyes. Are any of them alive? Had they been trapped, drowned, washed away?

God! Hidden behind the hut, she slumped to the ground, grief pouring out in strangled sobs. Faces from kindy, faces from church, neighbours, shopkeepers. God. *Are they all gone? All of them? Dan?*

Dan knew of the danger. He would have moved heaven and earth to get to them. Yet there was no sign of any car coming to the other side of the gully. *God, it would be so much easier with Dan here. But no. Instead I'm stuck with five kids*

El Shaddai

under six. Any mother's nightmare. And with super bitch. You
have Dan. I get Caroline. It's not a fair swap.

Ky

The gentle thought slowed her tears. Ky. How would she
cope without her—the ultimate mother, calm nurse, cook,
babysitter and friend? Last night after the kids were in bed,
they'd sat together as Caroline cried herself to sleep. They
talked honestly, openly. Yes, Ky cried quiet tears for Mal, but
she remained calm. *Thank You, God, for Ky.*

You will thank Me for Caroline one day

I don't think so, God.

A cord of three strands isn't easily broken

A scream broke her concentration. *Lily.* Milly raced
towards the hut. Hoey dragged Lily outside. 'Snake, Mum.'

Caroline was on the bed, screaming. 'Get the baby. Get
the baby.' Milly scooped Bea off the floor and gave her to the
frantic mother. 'Where's Bethie?'

'Ky took her for a walk and left me here alone.'

'Is this long enough, Mum?' Hoey dragged a long log
through the door.

Caroline screeched. 'Get that outside. It's probably covered
with spiders.'

Milly put her arm around Hoey. Even in the dim light she
saw the glimmer of tears. 'It's okay, Hoey. What do we need
the log for?'

'To kill the snake.'

Milly gulped. 'It's too big, Honey. Where is the snake?'

'It went under the bed.' Shoulders slumped, he pulled the
log outside.

Milly's heart screamed for Dan. Tears pooled in her eyes. Caroline screamed. Ky raced up with Bethie on her hip and Johnno at her side. 'What's the matter?'

'Snake!'

Together they peered in the door, little girls in their arms, the boys peering around their legs.

'Help me. Please help me. It's going to swallow us.' Caroline danced on the middle of the old bed, holding the baby over her head.

Milly followed her eyes. A large mottled snake slithered up the chair near the end of the bed. Someone pushed past her. 'Hoey! Get back here.' Before she could stop him, a small stick smacked the snake behind its head. It fell from the chair. The stick came down again and again. The reptile lay bent and still.

Hoey tried to pick it up with his stick, but it flopped to the ground. He danced in celebration. 'Wait 'til I tell Dad.'

Milly took the stick and carried the snake from the hut and headed down the hill.

'Wait, Mum.'

'Why, Hosea?'

'Bobby ate snake. We saw burnt bits on his fire. I've seen it on the television. You cook it in the coals. C'mon, Mum. Let's try.'

Milly's stomach turned over as she stared at the serious little man in front of her. She gulped. He was right, but she didn't know if she could swallow snake.

You will, when you are hungry

God, are we going to get that hungry?

Hosea held her arm. 'This is how Bobby eats from the land.'

Ky grabbed the shovel from near the door. 'Good thing we've got a fire going.' She started dragging coals aside. 'Drop him in here, Milly.'

Milly turned her face away and dropped the snake. Ky coiled it in the hole and shovelled more coals on top.

Caroline's white face peered out the door. 'Milly, did you get rid of that thing?'

Ky grinned at her. 'It won't bother us again, Caro. It's safe to come out.'

Caroline edged out the door. 'Hoey, you are so brave. You saved me and little Bea.' Crouching down in front of him, she gave him a hug.

~ ✦ ✦ ~

The group sat around the fire talking while they waited for dinner. Ky produced a pot of large pasta shells. They nibbled from the pot, eating with their fingers, laughing and sharing.

Family

Milly was startled by the thought. Family. Yes, tonight felt like family. Her heart constricted. *But God, I want Dan back. I want my family.*

Yes... but for now, this is family

Ky adjusted the coals in the fire.

'Why are you playing in the fire, Mummy?' Johnno loved fire and was always being told to keep away.

'I'm checking dinner, Johnno.' She straightened, one hand in the small of her back. 'Nearly ready, I think.'

'I thought the pasta was dinner?' Caroline looked confused. 'Is there something else?'

'Meat for dinner tonight.' Ky grinned. 'I'm looking forward to it. Would you mind setting the table inside, Caroline? And can you wash the kids? Hoey, you can be my helper. I'll need a big plate, tongs and the spatula. Milly, you go inside. Hoey and I can manage here.'

With relief Milly left the fire. All the little hands were scrubbed before they sat. Caroline passed out tumblers of water. Hoey rushed in with the pasta shells. 'Ky says you can have some more pasta. We won't be long.' He left again, head up, shoulders back. When he returned, he beamed from ear to ear.

Ky carried the plate high. 'It's a little burned but it tastes delicious.' The dish piled with little chunks of charred meat sat in the middle of the table. All eyes stared. Ky sat. 'Now join hands and we will pray before we eat.' Once hands were linked around the table, Ky prayed. 'Thank You, God for protecting us this afternoon. Thank You for this meat. Please bless it and may it nourish our bodies. Amen.'

'What is it, Ky?' Caroline leaned back.

Ky smiled and passed her a serving. Hoey grabbed his fork and pushed meat onto his plate. He ate with his fingers. Milly went to correct him, but stopped herself. He took a lump of meat, examined it and then chewed with gusto.

'Milly, pass your plate.'

She handed her plate to Ky, but the thought of eating snake made her squeamish.

Ky caught her eye. 'Milly. I believe it was you who said we had to learn.'

Most were now eating without question. Ky diced some for Bethie and Lily. Johnno followed Hoey's lead. Caroline extracted the uncharred bits, chewing as though sampling a delicacy. 'I guess it's not bad for your first attempt at fire cooking, Ky. But I'd prefer you used the oven. Pity so much of it is burned.' She took another delicate mouthful. 'It's hard to pick the flavour. What is it? Where did you get it from?'

Ky caught Milly's eye but, before either of them had worked out way to answer, Johnno replied, 'Snake. Yummy, eh?'

Caroline's hand flew to her throat, her eyes wide as saucers.

Hoey patted her shoulder. 'It's okay. Bobby eats snake and he's fine.'

Caroline jumped from the table, her throat convulsing. She flew out the door and the family heard her dinner hit the ground.

'Poor Caro.' Hoey's hand hovered over the platter. 'Does that mean I can have more, Ky?'

The kids were full and the platter nearly bare when Milly rose to clean up. 'Thanks for dinner, Ky and Hoey.'

'It's okay.' Her little man grinned. 'Isn't it good God gave us meat? I wonder what He'll give us next.'

The mothers decided no one was safe sleeping on the floor. Caro was in one bunk and the boys shared the other. Both girls joined Ky and Milly on the double bed. Overcrowded, frustrated and hot, Milly crept out of the hut with a pillow and purple towel. Outside she laid a folded doona on a plastic tarp and stretched out under the stars. The night noises were now familiar. The stars were vivid, close enough to touch. A peace settled over her. Covering herself with the towel she relaxed and rolled over.

Birds sang in the treetops, waking her. Sucking in great mouthfuls of fresh morning air, she threw back the towel. It was damp with dew, but she felt refreshed.

Day followed day without any sign of aircraft. The women focused on comfort and survival. With the help of a saw, the hut door closed again. The top was jagged, but at least it shut against crawling visitors. Two coats of teal blue paint softened the rough edges. Milly continued to sleep outside, enjoying the privacy and clear air.

The water level in the tank dropped and, with no sign of rain, the bath went back under the tank. Wet face-washers cleaned them all. Milly tossed on her thin bed. *We must find water.* Bobby had vanished. So there had to be a way off the plateau. Every day she explored another area, but the escarpment rose behind them, and the cliff dropped into the valley in front. No one responded when she called across Dead Man's Gully.

'It's two weeks since the earthquake.' Ky put her pen away. 'I think. Some days I get diverted and then I can't remember if I've marked the wall. But there are fourteen lines today.'

Milly nodded. 'Let's go for a walk, Ky.'

'But the kids?'

'Caro.' Milly called through the window. 'Can you keep an eye on the children? Ky needs to get out of the house.'

Ky chuckled as they walked towards the valley. 'House?'

Milly shaded her eyes, peering to the east. 'No movement anywhere. Not even birds flying towards Wamberoo. Even if I could get down to the valley, I'm not sure I'd find anyone to help us.'

Ky eyed a large gum. 'It's too dangerous. Please don't try. I couldn't bear it if you were hurt.'

'Don't worry. The thought of climbing over the edge terrifies me. There must be a way that doesn't head towards Wamberoo.' Milly shaded her eyes and looked to the south where dense scrub blocked further exploration. 'If you don't mind watching both my kids, I'd like to explore tomorrow. I must find water.' She pointed at the thick bush. 'There must a farmhouse somewhere down there. I can't twiddle my thumbs and watch our supplies run out.'

'I'm glad you're so courageous, Milly. I get lost if I turn the wrong way when I leave the outhouse.' Ky chuckled. 'Lucky I'm with you now.' She turned. 'Kids are quiet. I wonder what they're up to.'

Lily was running towards Milly, her chubby legs wobbling with the effort. 'Mummy, look. We made cakes.' Smeared in mud, she held out two round lumps as great delicacies.

Milly smiled, even as her mind raced. *Mud? Had they found water?* 'Show me, Lily.'

The little girl pointed to the tank. Water was pouring onto the ground. Milly sprinted, leaving her crying daughter behind. Before she reached the tap, the stream slowed to a trickle.

Ky allocated a named water bottle to each person. They were half full. The handle from the tap was stored on top of the tank. Milly left the hut and pushed through the scrub. There must be a creek somewhere.

Hearing a noise, she stopped. A bush turkey scratched in the dirt. Taking the coil of wire from her backpack she straightened it and fashioned a hook. Rather than give chase, she lay under a bush and waited. Ants used her as a climbing frame. On the point of giving up, she heard clucking. Head to the ground, the bird came towards her. She held her breath. *Please, Lord, help me.*

She guided her hook through the dirt. With a flick she snared one leg and lifted the bird off the ground. Delighted, she pushed back through the bushes to the hut. Not allowing herself to think of anything except their need for food, she chopped its head off with the axe. She presented it to Ky to prepare dinner.

Before they ate, Ky prayed. 'Father, thank You for this wonderful meat. Please bless it to our bodies and give us strength. Lord, please send rain. We need water.' Their tummies were full but they went to bed dirty. And thirsty.

El Shaddai

Part 2

The Restrictions

Chapter 7

MILLY TOSSED. SLEEP ELUDED HER. A few weeks ago her big decisions had revolved around the right wine to serve with dinner. The freezer had been stocked with cuts of meat, the fridge packed with fresh vegetables. She shared life with Dan, her never-failing problem-solver. Now she lay alone on a thin doona under the stars, worrying about the next glass of water.

Half-asleep and half-awake, Dan's voice replayed in her head. *'God has promised me, Milly. One day we will have a big cattle property with sheds and fences. Fruit trees and a vegetable garden. And God will bring us helpers who need work and healing. We will teach them about the love of El Roi, my God. And El Shaddai will heal them.'*

She rolled over and sobbed into her thin pillow. *God, Your words are empty. Do You give visions for nothing? Do You even care?'*

My words never return void. I rescued you

From what God? For what? So I can watch my children die of thirst?

Be still, Milly

In her dreams, rain pelted on her roof. The downpipe started to drip again and again. The dripping woke her. Darkness enveloped her. There was no rain.

Pushing back the towel, she looked for the cause of the drip. Before they went to bed, Caroline had rigged a sheet of plastic between two trees, funnelling it into a bucket. Milly had scoffed at the idea, but now the dew flowed into a thin layer of precious water.

Some water was better than none, but it wasn't enough. Yet wallabies and bush turkeys must be drinking somewhere. She must track the animals. Sneaking into the hut she retrieved her backpack, the torch, a lump of the turkey and her near-empty water bottle. She shoved several empty bottles in the backpack, determined to return with them full.

The first light of day coloured the horizon as she skirted the outhouse. A purple towel around her shoulders protected her from the cool air and ever-present midges. The leaves were wet. Licking the moisture from leaves satisfied her thirst and saved her precious water. *God, help me find water. We've prayed for rain. Ky says to have faith. Well, I'm here, putting her faith into action. Please lead me.*

I am El Roi. I see you

I hope You see water. She skirted the dense bush looking for a gap, waiting for more light. On hearing a noise, she froze. A little wallaby jumped right in front of her. She tried to grab him. He'd feed them for a few days. But he bounded sideways and crashed through the bush. *God, he must get water somewhere.*

Be still
Be still
Be still

More determined, Milly rushed after him, ignoring scratches from the branches. He outran her but she pushed on in the same direction. Breaking through the bushes, she burst into an open grassy plain. The escarpment rose red to her right, reflecting the early morning light. The valley dropped away to her left.

Excited, she ran across the clearing following a faint track. Did it lead to water? The track was swallowed by rocks at the base of the escarpment. She followed the base, skirting piles of boulders dislodged by the earthquake. Drier land concerned her. Was it taking her further from water? A scrub turkey darted between the sparse, scrubby plants. A lizard scuttled under a rock. The presence of the animals assured her water must be close.

This gorge was much wider than the one where Caroline had hidden. The vegetation was different, the foliage more luxurious. She stopped. Was that water—running water? Heart thumping, she ran towards the sound.

When she stopped, she couldn't hear the water. Panting, she flopped on a rock. Had she imagined it? Her whole body now ached for cool running water, her throat, her skin, her hair. But the sound had disappeared.

'God.'

'He won't help ya, lady.'

She froze. The voice was deep and gruff. Hairs on her arms stood to attention. 'Who... who's there?'

'I tried God. He's never helped me yet. 'Til now.' The gravelly voice taunted her.

She spun but couldn't see anyone. Maybe this was delirium?

'Yup. This place can drive ya crazy.'

Could he read her thoughts?

'Looking for water? Come too far. Go back. Turn at the yellow rock.'

She turned and ran from the voice. Her heart thumped in her ears. What if he shot her from behind?

God help me. Where's the yellow rock? As she slowed, the pounding eased in her ears. Once again, she could hear running water. A wall of rock blocked her way. Tinkling water mocked her. Hearing the man crashing behind her, she squeezed between two rocks.

'Okay, Girlie. I know you're here someplace. I told you to turn at the yellow rock, not the yellow bush. You'll have to learn to listen to Pete. Pete knows best.' His muttering faded into the distance.

She caught a glimpse of long matted hair and dirty clothes. Her gut constricted. Her heart pounded so loud she worried he would hear it. She waited, jammed between the rocks. The tantalising sound of water taunted her. What to do? She couldn't stay hidden forever. Could she get back to the safety of the hut? *The hut?* It couldn't even be locked. What if she led this moron back to the children? She shuddered. *God! Where are You? Why aren't You helping me?*

The water gurgled, teasing her, calling. She inched out of the crevice. No sign of the man. But he hadn't shown himself before. Summoning all her courage, she strode out, ready to face him. However, she determined she wouldn't lead him to the others. The immediate task was finding water.

Exhausted from searching, she sat on a rock, sipped some water and ate a portion of meat. The sun had disappeared. She should go home, but what if he followed her? Although she hadn't seen or heard him again, Milly felt his eyes boring into her at every turn. Her every nerve was on edge. Frustrated she yelled. 'Why are you hiding, man? I know you're there.'

A startled wallaby leapt in fright and bounded up a rock slip. Milly had skirted the rocks several times. Now she tackled the slip. Stones moved and rattled under her feet but she pushed herself upwards. The hill rose sharply on either side as if a giant sledgehammer had bashed through it, pulverising it into hundreds of stones. Panting, she reached the top and gasped. Below her lay water—a large pool of clear running water.

A wallaby track led to the left. She followed it, racing down towards the oasis. Throwing herself down at the edge, she pushed her face into the pool, gulping large mouthfuls of water. Pushing her shoes off, she plunged in. Although gasping with the chill, she laughed. She swam and dived, and drank and drank. Swimming to a waterfall she stood and let the water flood over her hair and down her body. Back in the deeper water she slipped her clothes off and threw them on a rock. It was wonderful to scrub her body clean.

There was no sight or sound of the man. Grabbing her towel, she rubbed herself dry and wrapped herself in the purple softness. She rinsed her water bottle and filled it to the brim.

'Hungry?'

Her heart leapt into her mouth. *How long has he been watching?* She clutched her towel and scrambled for her clothes. The rock was bare.

'I'm drying 'em near the fire.'

Her eyes darted everywhere. She couldn't see the man, her clothes or a fire. 'Give my clothes back now.' She tightened the towel.

'They're still wet.' His voice sounded nearer but she couldn't see him.

'I'll have them wet.' She swallowed the ballooning lump in her throat. 'Pl... please.'

'C'mon in then and get 'em. Meat's cooked. A girl's gotta eat. Arrr. Then we sleep.'

She froze. *Sleep? With him?* Her mouth filled with bile. *God? God help me.*

She sensed the man's presence behind her. Grabbing a rock, she spun to face him. A massive hand grabbed her right wrist from behind, spinning her away from him. Shocked, she released the rock. His other hand captured her left wrist. Standing at her back, he held her still. Filthy stale sweat filled her nostrils. Terrified, heart thumping, she willed the towel to hold.

'I dry yer clobber and cook yer dinner and you turn into a wild cat.'

'Let me go.'

His grip eased. 'No rocks?'

'No rocks.'

He let her hands go. The towel came loose. She grabbed it and yanked it up. With a mocking laugh, he picked up her backpack and shoes and walked off. 'Grub's this way.'

Her head told her to run but her legs gave way and dropped her on a log. He waited. He had her shoes in his hand. He'd hidden her clothes. 'C'mon, Girlie. Arrr.'

Her legs shook. Her heart thumped. Her stomach rolled. Powerless, she followed the matted hair and filthy trousers. A narrow path led around a massive rock. 'Keep close to this wall. Fall off the edge and you'll never get to taste Pete's roast roo.'

She hesitated, her hand gripping the rock. Dusk was closing in. At her feet the mountain dropped into a ravine. To her left, the waterfall still splashed onto the rocks. In front, beyond the ledge, an open spread of country was tinged pink by the setting sun.

'You like Pete's penthouse? Keep coming. Not chicken, are you?'

The path narrowed to less than a metre wide. The drop seemed bottomless and Pete had disappeared out of sight. She backed out, her heart racing. His head appeared around the rock. 'Course, I could carry yer in, if yer like.'

She shuddered. Terror tingles raced down her spine. 'Bring my clothes out here, please?'

'Nup. I'll carry yer in when it's pitch dark. Then yer won't even be able to see if we're going to fall.' His 'arrr' chuckle stood her hair on end.

'How far does the track go?'

'Only a metre and you'll be in Pete's parlour.'

As the darkness deepened, she could see the flickers of light from his fire. Leaning against the rock wall, her thoughts raced. She could retreat and hide but she had no clothes, shoes or water bottle. As soon as she moved, he'd track her. He mustn't know about the kids or the women. A shudder shook her from her toes up. Steadying herself she pressed close to the rock and forced her leaden legs forwards. A few steps and she entered a large cave. Pete crouched over the fire. 'A lady with guts. I like that.'

He faced her for the first time. In the flicker of the fire she saw the outline of a beard and the whites of his eyes. His defining feature was his odour. 'Sit ya self on the mat.' He waved towards a dirty animal hide. 'Hungry?' He passed a metal plate.

She took it and stared at the offering in the dim light. A chunk of charred meat covered the plate, hanging off the sides. He sat on a rock chomping into a similar piece, holding it in both hands. He looked at her and spoke through a mouthful. 'You just gunna stand there? Sit and eat, woman. Don't get tucker every day.'

She sat as far away from him as possible. Picking up the meat she took a nibble. 'Yeesh.' She spat out a mouthful of burnt hair.

His big hand grabbed the charred offering. He attacked it with his teeth, ripping away long burnt strips and spitting them onto the fire. With a clunk her meal landed back on her plate. 'Sorry. Guess I shoulda skinned it for yer. It's good now.'

Her stomach roiled. She stared at the hunk of meat.

'Should skin 'em anyways. Need the hides but was busy watchin' a beautiful gal today. Long time since I seen a lady and God brings me a stunner. Pete's lucky day. Arrr.' He chewed noisily on another big mouthful. 'But I shoulda skinned it. Need more rugs now there's two of us. Still I got couple of little ones stretchin' out on me dryin' rock. You'll need a big one. I'll get you a biggie tomorra.' He snorted. 'Thought I was the only one left alive. Dead people everywhere. Good I was hidin' out here. Then God brings you to me. Maybe we're the new Abraham and Sarah? We can start a new crowd, have as many kids as the stars in the sky. Arr.' His chuckle sent a violent shudder through her body.

'Wh... who are you?'

'Pete. I telled yer that.'

'Pete who?'

'Pete the free.' His laugh made her shiver. 'They wanna lock me up but I too slippery for them coppers.'

She shuddered. 'Have you got family?'

'Fam'ly? What's fam'ly? Me mum was okay. I miss her but dad...' He spat a stream of spittle across the cave. 'He loved the others and hated me. I planned to kill him... but he's already dead.'

Milly searched her befuddled mind. She needed to change the subject, to keep him talking. 'Who taught you 'bout God?' She shook her head. Now she was talking like him.

'Mum loved God. Read me lots of stories.'

'What's your favourite?'

'Abraham. Yup. He was a good fellow. But God gave him bad woman. Couldn't have kids. You betta have kids.' Laughter echoed around the cave.

He made a sudden grab for her towel. She lifted her knee to plant it in his groin but the wrapped towel hobbled her. Her other foot slipped and she fell back, hitting the mat.

He dropped onto her, laughing like a madman. She kicked and screamed, but his size, his strength, overpowered her. Struggling and biting, she fought until he banged down into her. Searing heat blazed through her body. He punched down again and again. All the fight flowed out of her, merging into the filthy animal skin under them.

He screamed as his body shuddered and convulsed. Spent, he collapsed on top of her. Gasping for breath, stomach churning, she beat at his chest, ripping at his chest hair. 'Fiery one, aren't ya?' He grabbed her and rolled, granite arms tight around her waist. She managed to turn her head before she vomited.

'Bingo.' His voice softened. 'Got yer first time. There's a baby comin'. We're married now, firecat.'

She wriggled, desperate to escape but his grip tightened further. 'I like you just here, Wifey. You and me now... 'til death does us part.'

Terrified, she remained still until his body relaxed and he fell asleep so she could slide away from his foul body. Grabbing the purple towel she ran past the rock along the narrow path. Death held no fear. It was welcome.

At the waterhole, she tried to clean her shaking body, but his filth slimed all over her, all through her. She scrubbed her skin with handfuls of sand, embracing the pain. *God? Where are You? I thought You were my refuge? My safe place?* A little calmer, she wrapped herself in the towel and returned. She wanted to grab her things and leave while he slept. But where would she go? She couldn't risk him finding the others.

Back in the cave, she lifted her clothes off the line as he snored. Skirting the fire to reach her backpack, she passed his sleeping form. He lay on his back, arms splayed, a satisfied smirk on his face. A fury rose in her, red hot anger.

His eyes flew open. 'Come 'ere, Baby.'

She turned to run.

El Shaddai

'I said come 'ere.' He rolled and tried to stand. His trousers twisted around his ankles, tripping him. He sprawled face down but an iron fist still gripped one of her ankles.

She grabbed a rock and flung it at his head.

He screamed.

She wrenched her foot free. He slid towards her, kicking, trying to escape his trousers. Without thinking she heaved up a larger rock and banged it on top of his head. The crack of its impact echoed around the cave.

He slumped onto the ground. In a frenzy she let the towel drop and picked up rock after rock, throwing them at him. He didn't move. She didn't care.

When his head and groin were buried, she stopped, puffing. Kicking over his billy, she swilled from her water bottle. Grabbing the plate of meat, she ate. She was ravenous. The food tasted good.

Horror began to seep into her soul as thin moonlight crept across the dirty hide she sat on. *It can't have happened.* She must have dreamt it, surely? But the dried blood on her legs and the pile of rocks were real. Shaking, she snatched her clothes, backpack and towel and limped to the waterfall.

By the light of her dynamo torch she showered again, scrubbing, scrubbing, but never feeling clean. The cold fist of reality squeezed her heart. Darkness invaded her, darker than a moonless night.

She looked at her hands. They had murdered a man. *God! I killed him. How could I?* She forced herself back to his penthouse. The evidence must be buried. In the light of the setting moon she picked up rocks, big ones, and outlined his body, making a base to hold smaller ones.

'Missus?'

She screamed. In the mouth of the cave, an inky shadow stood, outlined by the moon. He balanced on one leg. The other foot rested on his knee. He held a spear-like stick beside him.

'Don't be frightened, Missus. I won't hurt you.' The figure backed away. 'I go now.'

His voice triggered her memory. 'Bobby?'

'Yes, Missus. I didn't mean to startle you. I go now.'

'No, Bobby, no.' She pushed her fist against her racing heart. 'Please, Bobby. I need you. I need your help.'

'Where's Pete?'

Her shaking increased. Now he was a witness. He walked to the pile of rocks. 'It that him?'

She nodded, pulse racing.

'You killed him?' Leaning over, he punched Pete in the stomach. 'Dead as dead. Too rotten to even eat. Yahoo. Pete's dead.' He punched the air and danced in a circle. 'You're one strong lady. You're no crybaby.' He went to the back of cave and started collecting stones. 'C'mon, let's bury him good.'

Milly spied a large pile of rocks to one side and started to collect them. 'No, Missus. Can't use them. Pete's missus under them. Pete's mum is under that pile.' He indicated a cairn at the rear of the cave.

Milly backed away, shocked by a cave of death.

'You sit on the log. I finish.'

She tried to sit but it hurt. 'Is this placed cursed, Bobby?'

'It was. But you broke the curse. Make Bobby very happy. Ladies buried here. Men—he throws 'em to the dingoes.' He threw a few more rocks and stopped to get his breath. 'He was a bad man. World's better without him.'

El Shaddai

The shadows started to hint of colour.

'It's coming light now. Go and sit beside the water. I come when I finish.'

'Bobby, do you know the way home?'

'Yes, Missus. Bobby will take you.'

Milly left the scene of the crime and rested by the cool water.

I lead you beside the still waters

Surely, You're not still leading me, God. I've got blood on my hands.

When they left the spring, Bobby led her along an easy path through the scrub on a wallaby track. Skirting a massive rock, they came out into the open paddock she'd crossed the morning before. She carried her backpack with full bottles of water. It cut into her back. Bobby had a bulging skin slung across one shoulder and two of Pete's billies filled to the brim.

From the waist down, she hurt. Every step shot pain through her groin. She struggled to keep Bobby's pace. He stopped and took her backpack, swinging it over his other shoulder. Billies in hand again, he walked on slower. His soft eyes sought hers. 'He hurt you, didn't he?'

She nodded. A vein bulged in his neck. 'Did he nail you?'

'Bobby!'

'Pete told me you must nail woman to the ground. Then she belong. She do as she's told. But not you. You kill him. You nailed Pete to the ground.' He lifted his dark eyes to hers. 'You... must be a god.'

'No, Bobby. I'm just like you.' *Except for one big difference.* She'd killed a man. Her hands, though clean, were heavy with blood. 'We don't talk about this at the hut, okay? They mustn't know about Pete. Please, Bobby.'

'Bobby promise. Never talk about Pete ever again. He's gone.' His feet did a little jig.

Milly sat in a camp chair cuddling Lily. Ky sliced meat. The boys jumped up and down in anticipation. All their water bottles were full and they were drooling over cold, roast wallaby.

'Wait, boys.' Ky glared at sneaking fingers. 'No one is eating until we have blessed this food. A blessing will make sure it is good for us.'

'Seriously, Ky.' Caroline screwed up her nose. She kept drinking from a water bottle as Bea sucked at her dry breast. 'Do you really think a prayer is going to make such a disgusting mess fit to eat?'

'What did we pray this morning, Caro?'

Johnno started dancing. 'I prayed for lots of water, and we've got lots of water.'

Lily pulled her head out of Milly's chest. 'Mummy home.'

Hoey knelt beside his mother, looking into her eyes. 'Lily asked God to bring you home. I asked God to send Bobby to find you. Which prayer did he answer, Mummy?'

'Both, Honey. God sent Bobby to bring me home. After we eat, he will take you for a swim and get more water.'

Ky called them to the table. 'Gather round, everyone. Let's join hands and thank God for this food.' Before she had finished praying, children's mouths were stuffed with juicy tender meat.

El Shaddai

'This is good, Bobby. Did you cook it?' Ky grinned at the nervous boy at the end of the table.

He hung his head. 'No, Missus. But Bobby will cook special meat for you, when I can hunt him.'

After the meal, the children danced around, impatient to go and see the water. 'Let's take the car.' Caroline rattled Milly's keys. 'It'll be easier for the little ones.'

Milly watched them pile in. Bobby, Hoey and Ky volunteered to walk in front to clear a track for the vehicle. Caro loaded the car with towels, soap and all their clothes. 'Hop in, Milly. There's plenty of room.'

Milly shook her head. 'I've had enough adventure. I'll mind the hut.' She kissed Lily and waved good-bye. As they disappeared from sight, Milly ran into the hut, dragged a chair over and wedged it behind the door. She fell on the bed and let the wailing escape.

God. You answered their prayers. Why didn't You answer mine?

Chapter 8

DISCOVERY OF THE OASIS changed the family's routine. The children waited all day for Ky's call to go for water. Each trip they cleared more scrub so they could drive closer.

Caroline tried to teach the little girls to dog-paddle. Hoey and Johnno already swam like fish. But Pete's presence stalked Milly, pouring condemnation over her tormented soul. She forced herself to watch the children's games and fill containers from the waterfall. Bobby always stayed close.

Hoey loved to hunt with him. One day they caught a lot of quail using Milly's bent wire. Another day they herded fish into shallow water and Bobby threw them on the bank. He shook his head when Ky tried to scale them. 'Scales stop fish burning in the fire.' When they emerged from under the coals, he taught them to peel back the skin and flake the flesh off the bones.

Every night they gathered together to pray. Ky always said the same thing. 'Thank You, God, for protecting us today. Thank You for food and for water. We pray for our daddies.

Keep them safe and help them find us. We ask for food for tomorrow and please show us a way home. Amen.'

The children prayed, expressing their little hearts to the only Daddy they could contact. Caroline watched on, present because Ky insisted, absent in spirit. Milly continued to sleep outside, thankful for the cool air. Bobby lay under a tree not far from her feet. With him close, she felt secure, but nightmares still plagued her. Often, she woke squirming and sweating with Bobby crouched at her head. 'You okay, Missus? You have bad dream. It's all right. Bobby's here to look after you.'

After the nightmares she'd crawl to a tree to empty her stomach. Pete's stench seeped out from her memory and into her gut. His laugh, his chuckling 'arr', even in her head, made her skin crawl. She longed to get up in the middle of the night and scrub her skin to try to remove his filth.

Mornings were difficult. The sun woke her early. Her body was tired and she ached. Nausea never eased. Most nights she determined to ask Bobby to show her the way off the plateau. But in the cold light of day she struggled to get up and often collapsed on Ky's bed after breakfast. One morning as she dozed she smelt coffee. She stretched and opened her eyes. Ky sat on the foot of the bed. 'Ky. Is that coffee?'

'It is.'

'Where did you get it?'

'I found a couple of sachets in my glove box and hid them in my emergency stash.'

'And this is an emergency?'

'Yes.'

'Is one for me?' Milly pulled herself up and held her hand out.

Ky withdrew the coffee. 'There's a condition.'

'Okay, I'll do it. Whatever it is. Can I have the coffee first, while it's hot?' Milly stuffed a pillow behind her back.

'You can talk while you sip.' Ky handed her the cup. 'Milly, we're a team, you and I. But you are hiding something. Spill. Tell me what's wrong.'

Milly let the rich aroma waft up her nostrils. 'I'd rather not talk about it, Ky.' The night of shame boiled in her gut, a dark, putrid block of humiliation and horror. 'It's better you don't know.'

'Not true. Whatever's bothering you, we can carry together, Milly. For the past month you've been reluctant to speak to anyone except Bobby. You hide behind him, even from your own kids. You're no longer hunting or even searching for a way home.'

'Bobby and the boys are hunting.' She savoured the coffee, taking small sips.

'Yes, and I'm thankful. The only time you leave the camp is to throw up. Even Caroline is coping better than you. This is not the Milly I know.'

Milly stared at her coffee. The black reflected the darkness of her secret. Ky deserved an explanation but it was too terrifying to explain. She closed her eyes but the images and smells assaulted her.

'Are you having more dreams?'

'No... no dreams. Nightmares yes, but not prophetic dreams.' Hot tears escaped. 'It's too awful, Ky.' She dropped her head. 'I can't tell you.'

'Have another sip of coffee and start at the beginning. You left one morning to find water for us. You walked down there.'

She pointed south. 'What happened next, Milly?'

Once Milly started, the words gushed out, an unstoppable river. The mug was empty long before the penthouse darkened her story. She stopped, unable to speak of Pete's brutality. She avoided Ky's eyes. 'I can't... I can't...'

'Milly.' Ky grabbed her hand. 'He raped you, didn't he?'

She nodded, pushing her fist into her mouth. She mustn't scream.

Ky threw her arms around her, their tears mingling. 'Oh, my poor darling. I wish you'd told me earlier. And Bobby sleeping so close helps you feel safe?'

After a few minutes Ky sat up, eyes wide. 'Where is the monster now? Will he try to attack you again? What about the kids? Would he hurt them?'

Milly shook her head. 'He's dead.'

'Oh.' She hugged Milly again. 'Saves me having to kill him.'

'I did.' Her face flamed hot. 'I… I…' His disgusting odour filled her throat and then her nostrils. *Will I ever be free of it?* Jumping off the bed she ran outside to throw up.

Ky followed her, and knelt, holding her forehead. 'You killed him, Milly. How?'

Milly wiped her mouth. 'I smashed his head with a rock. He grabbed me for a second go. I think I lost my mind. I pelted him with rocks. I'm sorry, Ky, but what if he found you and the children? He was vermin. A criminal. Filthy. Disgusting.' She retched again. 'His revolting teeth leer in my face in every shadow. He hulks over me in my dreams but I can't scream.'

Hearing Caroline and the children returning, Ky bundled Milly back to bed. 'Rest. We'll talk more later.'

'What if I go to jail for murder, Ky?'

El Shaddai

'No one knows. Just you, me and Bobby. Is he safe?'

'Bobby hated him. He'd been abusing him for years.'

'So how will anyone ever know?'

Milly curled into a ball, her arms across her belly. 'I think I'm carrying his baby.'

After the kids were asleep, Milly lay under the stars. Bobby had gone for a walk and she felt bereft. Weird noises came from all directions. Shadows danced around her. Bushes rustled and her hair stood on end. The door creaked, making her squeal.

'It's only me, Milly.' Ky spread out an old blanket, tightened the towel around her and plonked down with a sigh. 'Took an age for Johnno to drop off. He wants Mal. It's so hard on the kids.'

Milly's heart pounded in her chest. 'It's hard on all of you, Ky. I'm sorry.'

'In a way I'm sorry. Yes, we're stranded and I'm concerned about food, but we're alive and I'm learning so much, Milly.'

'Like how to cook snake in the coals, and toilet train babies, and get prickles out of bare feet.'

'And how to wash hair with sand. Naked children are beautiful and free. And God does answer prayer.' Ky sought Milly's eyes in the moonlight. 'We need to pray.'

'Why? What's wrong with the prayers we pray with the kids?'

'Nothing, but we need to pray about... about your suffering.'

'I'm not talking to God.'

'Milly! You've always talked to God. We're here because you listened to God. He kept us alive.'

'To abandon us.'

'No. He hasn't.'

'Where was He the other night when... when...'

'Which is why I want to pray.'

'Besides I killed a man. Remember, Ky. I killed a man. How can I pray? I'm dirty inside and out. My insides are filled with filth and demons from that disgusting creature and outside...' She held up her trembling arms. 'Outside, there's blood on my hands.'

'God.' Ky's voice trembled. 'God, Your Word says if we confess our sins, You will cleanse us from all unrighteousness. You've heard Milly talk about what happened. I'm claiming Your forgiveness for her. Please take her guilt away.'

'Ky. This isn't just sin. I killed a man. Can't you hear? Killed. A. Man. Cain was banished for killing Abel.'

'David was forgiven for killing Bathsheba's husband.'

'But his children suffered because of his mistakes. Oh, Ky, what have I done?'

'I've been trying to figure something out. Why didn't you run when you first heard him? Why didn't you leave and come home?'

Milly rolled away. Ky's questions hurt. A gentle hand stroked her arm but Ky didn't speak again. A mopoke's soft call calmed her a little. 'I hid in a crevice between the rocks for ages. He couldn't find me. But I had to decide. Make a run for it or risk it. I chose to go on.'

'Why, Milly?'

'I could hear water. I wasn't sure of the way home. And there's no security here. I couldn't risk the kids.'

Ky pulled Milly around to face her. 'You put yourself in jeopardy to protect us?'

El Shaddai

'And we needed water. I had to be sure he wasn't watching before I came home.' A sarcastic chuckle escaped her lips. 'At least I achieved that.'

'You risked your life for us, Milly. You protected us, and you bought us water. You paid such a price.'

'Don't be ridiculous, Ky. I killed a man.'

'You killed an enemy. Just like Jael.'

'Jael?' Milly tried to read Ky's eyes in the dark.

'You know... the Bible story. Jael was minding her own business when an enemy general came into her tent. He asked for a drink and protection from the army chasing him. She invited him in, gave him milk and lulled him to sleep.'

'Great. Just like me. I ate with him and lulled him to sleep alright.'

'But wait. This is the best part. Jael took a tent peg and nailed his head to the ground. When the army arrived, she showed them their enemy, killed by a woman. She protected the whole nation from the evil invader. You, Milly, have protected this whole family. You said he was a criminal.'

She nodded. 'The police were after him. He'd hidden out there for years, I guess. He said I restored his faith in God. He'd been asking God for a woman. He was thanking God for sending him a young and beautiful one. He talked about our future as if... as if we were husband and wife.'

'I'm so glad he's dead. Otherwise we'd all be in danger. I can't believe you were so brave.'

'I'm not brave, Ky. I was filled with rage and hurt, past caring if I lived or died.'

'I think you're a hero.'

They lay in silence for a long time. Milly watched the stars. Their patterns and rhythms fascinated her. Their consistency bought comfort. She tightened her towel. 'I'm not like Jael. I didn't nail him. He nailed me.'

'Milly, what do you mean?'

'Bobby told me.'

'You're not making any sense.'

'Pete taught Bobby about women. He said men have to nail a woman to the ground so she knows who's boss—so she stays with him. If she rebels, the man nails her again.'

Ky shuddered. 'Men! I think I hate them. Was it that bad?'

'It describes how it felt.'

Milly could feel Ky's tears on her hair. 'Thank God you killed the monster. Thank you, Milly. What bravery! It reminds me of Genesis.'

'Ky. What are you talking about?

'You crushed the enemy's head like it says in Genesis. The snake will strike at her heel but she will crush his head. You crushed your enemy's head with a rock. Jesus is the Rock, Milly.' She stroked Milly's hair. 'Wow. Thanks, Jesus, for fighting for us.'

Warmed by love and calmed by a peace she didn't understand, Milly fell asleep with her head on her friend's bare shoulder.

Milly regained some strength, but fear still gripped her when she left sight of the hut. Alone at night, she stretched out under the stars and tried to worship God, but struggled. After all, He didn't protect her. He didn't stop the rape.

ese Pete's not bothering you anymore ese

That's because he's dead. How do I know he doesn't have friends who will come looking for me one day?

ese Trust Me, Milly ese

Trust You? I've tried and it didn't work.

ese Did you trust Me, or yourself? ese

Milly rolled over. Anger surged from deep in her belly into her throat, sending her crawling behind a tree to throw up again. The nausea was more evidence of Pete's crime. Both her babies had caused morning sickness. She hated it. It left her with no energy. But this baby felt like an intruder. She cringed at the knowledge that part of Pete was lodged within her and growing. She retched again.

Back at her towel, she shoved the thoughts away. Tomorrow, she needed enough strength to hunt. Bobby had disappeared. He'd been gone two days.

'Mum!' Hoey ran around the hut, stopped, and doubled over, puffing. 'Mum. Hurry.' He had taken the hook, assuring her he knew how to hunt by himself. She'd let him go and crawled back under a tree, hoping the intense nausea would pass early. 'Mum. I can hear Bobby but I can't find him.'

Milly pushed herself up and held the tree, waiting for the world to stop spinning. 'What do you mean, Hoey?'

He grabbed her hand, still puffing. 'I think he's hurt. His voice came from the valley.'

'Get the ropes, Hosea.'

He raced into the hut. 'Gotta get the ropes.'

Ky and Caroline rushed through the door. 'What's going on?'

Hoey dragged on Milly's hand. 'Bobby. I think he's stuck. Maybe he's hurt.'

Ky looked Milly up and down. 'You can't go anywhere. You're not well.'

'Of course she can. It's time she got off her backside.' Caroline glared at Milly. 'Get in the car. We'll drive as far as we can. And get your stomach under control. The way you're carrying on anyone would think you're morning sick.'

Ky grabbed the children. 'No, Johnno. You stay and help me with the three girls.'

Johnno pulled against his mother's hand, protesting.

'Hoey has to go. He knows where Bobby is.' She hugged him as Caroline bumped the car over the grass.

'Slow down, Caro. Please.' Milly tried to focus on something stationary. *God, please settle my stomach. Please clear my head and keep Bobby safe.*

I love you, Milly

My stomach... please.

Hoey bounced on the back seat, pointing to the valley. Caroline drove until he yelled for her to stop. He flung the door open and ran to the edge of the drop. 'Bobby! We're here. Mum's here.'

Milly pulled herself out of the car. 'Where were you when you heard him?'

'I went down there a bit, trying to get a turkey. I was on that level patch when I heard him.'

Milly threw her head back and yelled. 'Cooee! Bobby! Cooee!'

El Shaddai

The reply sounded distant, but distinct.

'Hoey, how did you get down there?'

He grinned. 'This way, Mum. It's not hard.'

She raced after him as he wove amongst rocks and bushes, lowering himself using tree branches. Caroline followed, carrying the ropes.

'There he is, Mum. I can see him.' Hoey pointed. 'I can see you, Bobby. Mum will get you.'

Milly gulped. She could see him but he lay well below them. 'Bobby. Are you okay?'

'Bad leg, Missus. Can't walk. Sorry.'

Milly searched for a way down. 'How do I get there?'

'Back to big red tree. Drop down there. Follow wallaby trail. Sorry, Missus.'

'I can go, Mum. I'm a good climber.' Hoey turned and raced back the way they'd come.

'Hosea, stop!'

'I'll go with him, Milly.' Caroline dropped two ropes at Milly's feet and shouldered the backpack. 'I can climb rocks... remember. You stay here. He'll need water.'

Milly sank onto the ground. *How can we get Bobby home if he can't walk?* Her son was out of sight and alone. What happened to the scared little kid she'd brought up the mountain? He seemed so much older, stronger, more reliable and even happier.

How can that be, God?

Opportunity

What do You mean?

He's had the opportunity to show his strength, his boyhood. I'm proud of him and you should be too

Will he be okay? Will Bobby be okay? I need him, Lord.

Trust him... and Me, Amalya

'Mum. Mum. Can you see me?'

Moving closer to the edge she looked down. Caroline and Hoey were waving. 'We can't see him anymore.'

She cupped her mouth. 'Keep going. You're nearly there. Bobby, can you call them?'

Bobby called and they ran towards his voice. From her vantage point, Milly guided them past rocks and bushes until they found him. Bobby grabbed the offered water bottle and drank.

Frustrated, Milly watched the action below. To her dismay, Hoey took the backpack and ran away from Bobby, disappearing among the shrubbery. 'Hoey.'

Caroline stood and yelled back. 'He's fine. Just gone to get something for Bobby. Leg's broken, I think. What now?'

'Can you splint it?'

'Never done it before. Milly, you'll have to come down.'

How am I supposed to know how to set a break? Yet she wanted to get to him. Could she do it? Under normal circumstances she would already be down there, but with this woozy head... She shook herself. It was clear, not spinning. She checked her stomach. Even it had settled.

Do I hear a thank You?

Thank You, Father.

'Milly. What can we do to help?' Ky stood on the top level, Lily holding one hand and Bethie on her hip. Johnno was with her, peering over the edge, both arms around Bea.

At the sight of her calm friend, tears sprang to Milly's eyes. After a quick conversation, Ky left in the car to find something to splint a broken leg. Milly turned back to the valley to see Caroline dragging something across the ground. She walked so close to the base of the cliff she disappeared from Milly's view. 'Caro. What are you doing? Are you dragging Bobby?'

'No. It's a gift from Bobby. Join the ropes together and drop one end over.'

Hoey jumped up and down. 'Bananas, Mum.'

'I'm not going crazy, Hoey.' Turning her attention to the ropes, she joined them together, thankful they'd practiced knots. Tying her end to a sapling, she threw the rope over the edge and yelled to Caroline. All she could see was Hoey holding Bobby's hand.

What are they doing, Lord?

A few things for Me

What?

Hoey is loving Bobby. Caroline is helping Bobby loving the family

God, You're not making sense... again. When did God ever make sense?

'Pull, Milly.' The call wafted up over the precipice.

She started to pull the rope, surprised how easily it came. Then it stopped.

'Pull, Milly.'

Hand over hand she pulled up the heavy mysterious object until it stopped with a sudden jerk.

'It's stuck. Let it down a bit.'

Milly eased the pressure on the rope. Her independent spirit struggled with having to follow Caro's instructions. 'Move to your right, Milly... Yes... Now, pull.'

She reeled the mystery object in, coiling the rope near her feet. With a big heave, a whole bunch of bananas appeared with the backpack tied under it. The fruit were scratched and marked but intact. The top ones were yellow, the rest green.

'Try one, Mum. They're yum.'

She broke one off the bunch and split it open.

'Milly.' Ky yelled from above her. 'Are they bananas? Or am I going bananas?'

Peeling back the skin, she took a bite. 'Nectar of the gods, Ky. A miracle gift from Bobby.' Undoing the rope from the tree, she threw it to Ky. 'Pull, Ky. Morning tea is on its way.'

The splints and sheet Ky had ripped into strips were lowered the same way as the bananas went up. Hoey returned to the red tree to guide Milly down to Bobby. How they'd get him up remained a mystery to her. She ran to his side and kissed him.

Tears trickled down his face. 'I sorry, Missus. I sorry.'

She knelt and hugged him. 'Bobby, did you go looking for those bananas for me?'

He nodded. 'You need good food. Sorry I took so long. Not that far, but hard going.'

'Bobby.' She kissed his cheek choking back her tears. 'They are wonderful. Thank you.'

'Did you eat one?' His eyes were fixed on her.

'I have never tasted anything better.'

He smiled and winced at the same time. One leg looked a little bent and swollen. Both legs were covered in scratches.

'When did you hurt your leg?'

'I fell over a log yesterday before sunup. Should've waited for the light. Sorry, Missus.'

El Shaddai

Milly looked at his leg and pushed down her panic. Her medical knowledge came from television shows. She placed her fingers on his shin and traced his bone up to the knee. He closed his eyes as though trying to disguise the pain. When her fingers were below the knee, he winced. She pushed a little harder. He yelled.

God. I need a doctor, a paramedic and helicopter. But the only help at hand was Caro who stood watching, holding two sticks and Ky's bandages.

'He's light, Milly. Maybe we can carry him on a towel?'

'Up over the rocks and trees?'

Hoey tapped her shoulder. 'Mum, we could pull him up the same way as the bananas.'

Milly shuddered. 'They got all scratched.' She slumped down on the grass.

'Sorry, Missus. You leave me here. I'll be okay.'

'Bobby, I'll do no such thing. We'll find a way.'

Caro jumped up and ran back along the track. 'Won't be long.'

Before Milly could protest, she'd gone. Looking in Bobby's pained eyes, Milly shook off her frustration. 'It's you and me, Hoey. Let's bandage the leg. It should ease his pain.'

Hoey grabbed the bandages, his young eyes shining with the adventure.

Ages later, Caro called from the upper ledge. Bobby's bandaged leg looked like something from outer space, but his eyes were less haunted. Hoey's eyes were more haunted. Pain wasn't easy to watch. Caro used the rope to lower a red object.

At the base of the cliff, Milly found the bonnet of Ky's car. *What? Has she gone crazy?* She turned it over. *A sled.* It would work like a sled. *Lord, sometimes this girl amazes me. Mostly she annoys me.*

~∞ You need her ∞~

By the time Milly got the rope off the bonnet Caro arrived, puffing. 'Sorry. It took me ages to get it off the car.' She tossed Milly a purple towel and bent, hands on knees, until her breath returned. Returning to the boys, they manoeuvred Bobby onto the towel.

Milly grabbed the top end of the towel-sling. 'Okay, Bobby. We're going to lift you. Hoey, you hold his leg as still as possible. Ready, Caro? One two, three... lift.'

Bobby grimaced as he landed on the sled, then smiled through tears. 'Thank you, Milly. Thank you, Caro.'

They dragged and lifted until faced with the climb. Pulling his sled into shade under a tree, they argued about how to get him up the cliff. Bored, Hoey picked up the discarded hunting hook and wandered away. Bobby fell into a fitful sleep.

They needed to take him up on the bonnet, but most of the rope was needed to pull the sled up the cliff. There wasn't enough to tie him on the sled. Milly slumped to the ground, clueless. Caro wanted Bobby to hang on to the sled himself but Milly feared he'd let go and fall. They leant back on the tree trunk and munched on bananas. Milly's stomach embraced the food.

'Milly.' Ky yelled from the top. 'Would this help? Packing tape. Found it in the hut.'

'Oh, Ky. Fabulous. Can you throw it?'

El Shaddai

'I'll get it, Mum.' Hoey appeared on the middle level. 'Got to get dinner to Ky.' He held up a small scrub turkey.

For dinner they feasted on turkey and baked green bananas. Bobby leaned against a tree and ate with his fingers. Bands of tape still decorated his torso and he grimaced in pain. They'd taped him to the bonnet and pulled him up without causing any more harm. Milly celebrated his return but worried about his leg. Had she set it right? Would it heal without plaster?

The boys wrestled on the grass. Ky and Caroline chatted as they fed their babies. Milly sighed. *How can it be so peaceful, yet so surreal?* The diminishing food supplies pressed upon her. And now Bobby could neither hunt nor lead them to civilisation.

What about the bananas?

Sorry, Lord. Help my unbelief.

Chapter 9

Ky rationed the bananas, hoping they would keep for three weeks. She covered the bunch with a sack, keeping it wet to cool them as much as possible. 'If we can catch meat every second or third day, Milly, our supplies might last six weeks. I wonder if we can get more bananas.'

'I'll ask Bobby.' Milly pulled her chair over to his tree. This morning he looked a little better. He worked on a large stick with a hammer and chisel, fashioning a crutch. 'Bobby, can you tell me where to find more bananas?'

'Too hard, Missus. When leg's better, I'll go.'

'Could Caro go?'

He snorted. 'Have to sleep out. She too scared.' He shook his head. 'Hard way and dangerous. I had to go through dead land.'

'Dead land? What do you mean?'

'Everything dying in valley. Had to climb high to get good bananas. All others are dead.'

The nuclear explosion. Had that affected the trees and crops in the valley? *God, are we eating contaminated bananas?*

My blesses them
Yes, I know, but what if we are poisoning our children?
Trust Me, Milly

She turned back to Bobby. 'Is there anywhere else we can go? Do you know how to get to a town?'

'Wamberoo down there.' He pointed over the valley. 'But no good. Pine Mountain down the track.' He shrugged as he looked towards Dead Man's Gully.

'How did you get here? Where did you come from?'

Bobby didn't answer. He attacked his stick with renewed vigour.

'Bobby, where do you live?'

Bobby looked up, his eyes puzzled. 'I live with you, Missus.'

She gave him a hug. 'Yes, of course you do. But where did you live before the earthquake?'

He looked confused.

'Before the earth moved, Bobby.'

He ran his fingers up and down his stick. 'Pete...'

At the mention of Pete, Milly spun around to see who could hear. She didn't want Caroline asking questions. She lowered her voice. 'Did you live with Pete?'

Bobby picked up his knife and whittled the stick. Milly's stomach churned from frustration as much as nausea.

Caroline flopped down on the grass under their tree. 'Do you know how to do macramé, Milly? I've been thinking. Could we make a fishing net from this ball of string?'

Milly turned her attention to tying knots. It felt more productive than pumping information out of Bobby. Every time she tried, she hit a wall.

El Shaddai

They caught some small fish in Caroline's net, but no one hunted as well as Bobby, and he was immobilised. The crude splint chaffed his leg. They carried him into the creek to bathe his leg and re-bandage it. Each time they improved the splints and straps, he became a little more mobile. The day they ate the last bananas, Milly saw his head bop past the hut window. 'Bobby, are you walking?'

'No, Missus. I'm wheeling my leg.' He disappeared, his broken leg supported by Bea's pram, his other leg hopping behind. They celebrated his increasing mobility but he still couldn't sneak up behind unsuspecting animals. He could pull his body into the bush and hide. Sometimes he hid all day, unmoving, waiting for an animal or bird to pass by.

Milly and Caro tried several times to find more bananas, but every time Milly attempted to drop down into the valley at the red tree, her stomach emptied itself. On their third attempt she sat, head between her knees, willing her body to behave. Frustrated, Caro stormed down by herself. Hoey begged to go with her but Milly made him come back. *Lord, please settle my stomach. You did it the day I rescued Bobby.*

Yes

Well, please do it again.

Let My peace guide you, Milly

A thought flashed through her mind. Her stomach didn't have the peace to go. *Okay, Lord, I see. You don't want me to go.*

Milly sat near the red tree all day waiting for Caroline. She emerged from the bush on dusk, empty-handed and exhausted. 'I got to the dead country. The grass, the bushes—everything's brown and withered. The smell's disgusting. I saw dead animals and rotten bananas. There's no good food and nowhere to go.' She climbed up to Milly and burst into tears. 'What will happen to us? Whatever will we do?'

Milly wrapped her arms around her but her own heart was cold.

'I've been counting.' Ky yanked up her loose pants and sat beside Milly.

'Counting what?' Milly frowned as she tried to fix a hole in their fishnet.

'Days and supplies. I think we've been here about twelve or thirteen weeks. The supplies have lasted much longer than we expected but, short of another miracle, we don't have much longer. We need a plan.'

Milly ran behind a tree and emptied her stomach again.

'That's another thing. You should eat more often. When we had the bananas, you weren't as sick.'

'I must be close to three months, Ky. The tummy should settle soon.' She wiped her mouth with a rag. 'How much longer will the food last?'

'I've reduced the allocations again. Maybe three weeks, maybe two. Depends on the hunting.'

'Hunting is getting harder. I don't think there are many animals left around. Now I understand why aboriginal people were nomads. They moved to find more food. But we can't go anywhere.'

Ky reached out and held Milly's hands in hers. 'God. We need rescuing, we need food. Please show us what to do.'

As Ky prayed, a picture of Pete's penthouse flashed through Milly's mind. She shuddered.

El Shaddai

'What is it, Milly?'

'Nothing.'

'You saw something.' Ky shook Milly's arm. 'Look at me. What did you see?'

'The cave. Pete's cave.'

Ky dropped her hand. 'Sorry, Hon. I thought God must have given you an answer.'

'Maybe God will send Dan or Mal. I don't understand why Dan hasn't come, unless...' Milly straightened her back, as though the action would stall the thought. '...he's dead.' She buried her face in her hands and wept. *God, it's all too much. I can't bear it. Why, oh why, have You done this to me?*

She felt a soft touch. 'Lily loves you, Mummy.'

She dried her eyes. *My children!* She must find an answer for all the children.

Bobby returned with an empty pram. Nothing for dinner. They loaded the family into the car and went to the oasis early. While the children played the women searched for anything edible. They discussed roots and water weeds but ended up arguing, frustrated by their lack of knowledge. 'Let's ask Bobby.'

Bobby lay on the sled with Hoey pulling him close to the water. His leg no longer gave him pain. He asked Milly everyday if he could remove the splints. She pleaded with him to wait one more week to be sure.

The boys were excited and digging in the ground with a stick. 'Mum. We need the shovel, quick. Grubs, Mum. Hurry.' They were digging with their fingers, throwing white witchety grubs onto the bonnet of the car, their little faces beaming.

'Bobby says they're good tucker. If you get the spade, we can dig more.'

She hated the idea, but ran to get the spade. Hunger overcame scruples. Back at the hut they feasted on fat, roasted grubs and a few small fish. As usual Ky gathered them together and prayed. 'Father, we thank You for being so faithful. Please continue to provide us with food, protection and wisdom. Please look after our daddies and show us a way to go home.'

Caro looked bored. She caught Milly's eye. 'God, if You're listening, we need vegetables.'

Had Caro challenged *her*... or had she challenged God?

The next morning when Milly woke, Bobby had disappeared. She shrugged, rolled over and went back to sleep. Maybe he'd gone hunting early.

Hoey woke her. 'Mum. I found these in the pram. Where's Bobby?' He held up the splints and dirty old bandages.

Bobby didn't return. Without him they dug a few more grubs and caught one fish. Ky cooked more pasta to add to the sparse dinner, but it reduced the number of days they could survive. Worried, Milly offered her food to Hoey and Johnno. Ky's hand shot out. 'No, boys. You've had your share.' She glared at Milly. 'You eat, Milly. Please try.'

'We need vegetables.' Caroline had been lying in the car all day. It had become her refuge, even though they couldn't find any radio stations anymore. 'I asked God for vegetables. I don't see them here.'

Hoey glared at her 'God will answer, Caroline. He answers me. But sometimes He's dreadful slow.'

El Shaddai

Milly pulled him into a hug. 'I didn't see you hunting today, Caro.'

She pushed her hands through her messy hair. Her green eyes lacked their usual fire. 'There're no animals left. What's the point?'

'What's the alternative, Caro?'

'I've counted the bullets. There's plenty. One for each of us and leftovers.'

'Caro!' Ky grabbed her shoulders, swivelling her around. 'Don't give up. There'll be a solution.'

'I've searched every corner of this stupid dumb plateau. There's nowhere to go. Bea's whimpering all the time. She needs more food. It's hopeless.' She dropped her head onto Ky's shoulder, her body racked with dry sobs.

Milly slipped away to the hut. She gathered all the bullets and wrapped them in a plastic bag. Behind the hut she found a hole in a fork of a tree. Pushing them well down, she covered the package with leaves. *Please God. My God. Please. We need a way out.* Once again, Pete's penthouse flashed through her mind. Sighing, she lifted her head. *Lord, I can't go back there.*

In front of her flashed an open panorama, not bright but darkened. Where had she seen it before? As the vision faded, she remembered. It was the open country she saw the first time she navigated the path into Pete's cave. Bile rose into her mouth. She spat and chewed on a gum leaf to refresh her breath before returning to the family. *I can't, Lord. I can't.*

Ky still held Caro. The little girls were crying.

'Come, kids. Let's all sit on the bed and I'll tell you stories.'

As Milly led them into the hut, she searched her mind for a story she could tell them.

Tell them about Me

Jesus. She'd talk about Jesus. Gathering them together under her arms, baby Bea in her lap, she began. 'Once there were lots and lots of hungry people. Jesus had been telling them stories. The people were tired and hungry. Jesus's helpers were worried. "The people need food. Send them home," they said. But Jesus loved the people. "Let's ask them to stay for dinner," He said. His helpers whispered in his ear. "We can't. We don't have any food." Jesus laughed. "I'm sure there's enough food for everyone. What have we got?" The helpers sighed because He didn't seem to understand. "We don't have any. We don't even have any for You except for one little boy's lunch. He gave it to us for You. Look. Five itty bits of bread and two tiny fish." Jesus jumped up, excited. "Ask everyone to sit on the ground." The helpers were confused. Jesus danced around, as though he had a secret. His helpers thought he must have ordered pizza. He picked up the lunch box and broke the itty bits of bread. He handed it to his helpers. "Go and give it away." One of the helpers, Peter, turned and gave a big man a tiny bit of bread. He felt mean so he gave him more and more. Then he gave some to the next person. There was always more. For every piece he gave away, more seemed to appear. They all had dinner and there was more left over then when they started.'

Milly lowered the sleeping girls onto the bed. Johnno lay at her feet, asleep also. Laying Bea between the girls, she wriggled off the bed and sat on the chair. Hoey climbed on her knee. 'It's a true story, isn't it, Mum?'

El Shaddai

'Yes, Son.' She nestled her chin on his thick blond hair and held him close.

'Are there any other stories in the Bible like that one?'

'Jesus stories?'

'No. Food stories.'

'I think Jesus fed crowds of people twice.'

'Two times! Wow.' He sat up and looked her in the eye. 'It must mean He really can do it.'

'Yes. I guess it does.'

'Let's ask Him to do it. Let's Mum, let's.'

'But...' Milly didn't know what to say. 'Jesus did those things, not us. It's bedtime now, Hoey. Hop up on your bed and go to sleep.'

'But, Mum. I want to sleep with you or you'll be lonely.'

Milly snapped at him. 'Hosea. Go to bed now as you're told.' She turned and ran out of the hut into the dark.

The house stood old and rambling. The chimney on the red roof released a thin line of smoke, trailing straight up. It was surrounded by casual, untidy gardens. Hiding behind the shrubbery, Milly snuck closer and peered through a window. The room hadn't been decorated for about thirty years. Deep comfy couches beckoned her. She longed to go in, but turned into the vegetable garden, knowing where to go as if she'd been there before. She put out a hand to grab a juicy red tomato...

She woke. It was a dream. She still lay under a purple towel on the hard ground. Her stomach growled.

How much of their precious rice would Ky allow them this morning? Maybe Hoey was right. She screwed up her eyes and tried to conjure up enough faith to multiply food. It didn't work. Although she'd seen bananas appear, and seen God supply food, the multiplication of their meagre supplies was too hard for her to believe. *Sorry, God.* Going into the hut she stirred the cold ashes and set the fire.

Ky sat in the chair feeding Bethie. 'Milly, whatever are you doing?'

'I thought I'd cook breakfast.'

'But Milly...'

'What's wrong, Ky? I can cook, you know.'

'Milly. You must be feeling better. Usually I cook and you throw up.'

Milly stopped, a log of wood in her hand. Her stomach was asking for food instead of rejecting it. 'Ky, I feel better. Today I'm going hunting and I'm looking for Bobby.'

Straight after a mouthful of rice, she took the rifle and retrieved a few bullets from the tree. The old gun made her palms clammy. She'd never used it before, but desperation made her carry it outside, holding it, barrel to the ground. Alone, she drove to the waterfall. Hiding herself in bushes, she loaded the gun, rested it on a rock, and waited. In her conscious mind, she watched for a wallaby to come and drink. In her heart, she monitored the path to the cave for any signs of human life.

Maybe she should check out the cave. Her heart raced and she broke into a sweat. Pushing the thought aside, she concentrated on wildlife, edible wildlife. To practise, she aimed the gun at a mark on a tree. The gunshot sent a lizard scuttling under a rock. The sharp noise shocked her too. Her shoulder booted back. Maybe the sound would bring someone from

El Shaddai

the cave. She shrunk further back among the scrub, willing her hands to stop shaking.

Deep breathing calmed her nerves. When her pulse slowed, she determined to try again. The second bullet hit closer to her target and she breathed a little easier. She would wait and pray. *God, please help me.*

She about to give up when a wallaby hopped along the path from the cave, making her heart race. It paused to sniff the air. She lifted her shaking hands and, steadying the rifle on a rock, pulled the trigger. Once again it booted her backwards. Scrambling to her feet, her eyes scanned the path. The wallaby lay on the ground. Shocked, she dragged the animal towards the car. She wanted to be excited and thankful. They had enough food for days. But she wept. *Lord, I'm a murderer. First a man, now a kangaroo.*

The fire was lit and meat set to roast. The family watched until Ky declared it cooked. She sliced pieces from the outside and returned the rest to the oven. They ate until they couldn't move. Milly had been ravenous. Her stomach welcomed the food but she missed Bobby. She worried about him but reminded herself that he'd always returned.

In the afternoon, the women sat at the table surrounded by raw meat. Ky was determined to preserve it. Some they cut into thin strips to dry on the roof in the sun. With the help of the axe, they chopped up larger portions and submerged them in salty water. The remaining parts of the carcass hung under wet bags awaiting a hearty breakfast.

Milly and Ky sat together in the camping chairs under the stars. Caro reclined in the car. The children all slept.

'Ky.'

'What is it, Milly?'

'I don't want to leave here. I know we need food and clothes and all sorts of things, but...' To her horror, tears poured down her face. '...if I think of leaving, think of meeting another man, any man, my heart shrinks. I break out in a sweat. My heart pumps like mad and I want to hide. I know we must find a way out of here. I even think God may be showing me, but I'm terrified. I blamed the morning sickness, but it's over. The terror isn't.'

'I'm sorry, Milly.'

'And I wish Dan would come and then... then I'm terrified. What if he comes?'

Ky wrapped her arms around her, rocking and humming. Milly hung on, as though her friend was a lifeline. Grief and fear fought within her for supremacy. She groaned. Maybe the earth would have mercy and swallow her. Ky tightened her hold on her thrashing body. Words emerged out of the humming. 'Rock of ages, cleft for me. Let me hide myself in Thee.'

'Sing with me, Milly.' But the groans continued.

'Just try to sing the word, *Jesus*,' Ky urged.

'*Jesus, Jesus.*' It didn't sound like singing, but as she focused on His name, the battle eased. The enemies retreated. She lay on the ground, exhausted. Ky held her head and stroked her hair. Slowly, she relaxed and slept.

El Shaddai

The house stood old and rambling. The chimney on the red roof released a thin line of smoke, trailing straight up. It was surrounded by casual, untidy gardens. Hiding behind the shrubbery, Milly snuck closer and peered through a window. The room hadn't been decorated for about thirty years. Deep comfy couches beckoned her. She longed to go in, but turned into the vegetable garden, knowing where to go as if she'd been here before. She put out a hand to grab a juicy red tomato...

'Milly. Milly. Wake up.'

She opened her eyes, her mouth watering for the tomato.

Ky sat beside her on the towel. 'Milly. Look.'

She pulled herself up. Her backpack lay near her feet. A massive bunch of wilted silverbeet stuck out the top. She rubbed her eyes. Was she still dreaming?

Ky grabbed the bag, pushing her nose into the leaves as if it were a bunch of fine roses. 'Mmm. Lovely.'

'But where? How?'

'Who cares? As far as I'm concerned, God did it.'

'Or Bobby?'

'Does it matter who God used?'

Milly jumped to her feet. 'Bobby? Where are you?'

'Missus.' He lay under his tree, his dark frame hidden in the early morning shade. 'Sorry I took so long, Missus. Sorry veggies are limp. Had to go the long way. I walked very slow. Sorry, Missus.'

Milly ran and hugged him. 'Bobby, you're amazing. Where did you get these things?'

'El Shaddai.'

'Yes. God has provided again. But, where, Bobby, where?'

'Boss's house, Missus.'

'Milly, look.' Ky had taken the bunch of greenery out of the pack. She pulled out carrots, dirty sweet potatoes and tomatoes. Not red and juicy, but firm and pink.

Milly sat stunned. Her dream had fallen into her life. *Lord. What is going on?* She felt His grin. *That's no answer, Lord. What are You doing?*

Answering the prayers of the little ones

'Tuck...' Bobby struggled to speak. 'Tucker under the tree.'

'Bobby. Does the boss's house have a red roof?'

His response was laboured snoring.

A sleepy Johnno pushed the hut door open. 'You woke me up, Mummy.'

'Johnny. Good morning, darling. Look what God has given us today.'

The little boy rubbed his eyes. 'Wow. Caro's veggies.'

'And a chicken.' Milly retrieved a large white hen from the base of a tree. 'Today we'll have a party. God has rescued us. We'll celebrate and honour Him.'

The family gathered under the trees to feast on roast chicken and vegetables. Milly called Bobby to join them. When he didn't respond, she went and shook him awake. He followed but collapsed on the ground near her. Sitting cross-legged, the family held hands. Bobby's hand rested in Milly's, but his fingers hung limp. His hand was burning.

'God, we love You.' Ky's voice wavered as she spoke. 'Thank You so much for this food. Thank You for protecting us and providing everything we need.'

El Shaddai

'Thanks for the vegetables, God.' It was the first time Caroline prayed. 'I didn't believe You could do it. Now, can You please get us out of this hole?'

When Lily released Milly's hand, she turned to touch Bobby's forehead. He had a raging fever. 'Please, Missus, I go back to sleep.'

She nodded. 'You're too hot, Bobby. I'll get a towel.' She dipped the towel in a bucket of water, laid it over him dripping wet and returned to the festivities.

'Ky, you're a genius in the kitchen.' Caroline loaded her fork. 'I've never tasted better in a restaurant.'

'Well, thank you, Ma'am.' Ky bowed. 'I used my secret ingredient.'

'What secret ingredient?'

'Food.'

The boys rolled on the ground, laughing.

'There must be more where this came from. There must be a garden.' Caroline's eyes scanned the group. 'Where's Bobby?'

'He's not well, Caro.' Milly looked at him, lying still on the ground. A cold shiver slid down her spine.

'Wake him up and ask him. He's been sleeping all morning, lazy boy.'

'Caroline.' Ky's voice cut the air. Every child's eye jumped to attention. 'You apologise this minute. He walked all night carrying this food. How dare you?'

'Sorry, Bobby.' Caroline lowered her eyes, child-like under the rebuke.

'Thanks. Can you help the boys to clear up? I'm going to put the girls down for their nap.'

'Ky, is there any paracetamol?' Milly sat at Bobby's head with a rag and a bucket of water. He needed a doctor. So far, they'd managed to treat themselves without professional health care, but this frightened her.

She lifted the towel and fanned it over him. The towel was hot. He was hot. The day was steamy. Ky joined her and they sponged his body over and over. 'Why is his skin so dry, Milly? Is it usually?'

'I don't know, Ky. I'm frightened.'

He woke, groaning. 'I need leaves from blue bush.' His eyes pleaded with Milly as he tried to stand. She helped him to his feet. His slight body leaned on her.

'Blue bush. It makes sickness better. Mum told me.' He doubled in pain.

Ky passed him a tablet. 'Take this first, Bobby.' She offered him a water bottle. He drank the bottle dry before collapsing.

'Dead land. Dead land made Bobby sick.' He curled into a ball, shaking and groaning.

'Is Bobby going to die, Mum?' Hoey peered over Ky's shoulder.

'He's very sick.' Ky jumped up and steered both boys away. 'We need more water. Can you ask Caroline to take you boys to get water? We need it now. You can go back for your swim when the girls wake.'

She emptied all the containers into the metal tub, and handed the empties to the boys. They ran to the car, knowing Caroline would be there.

Bobby started to drag himself along the ground. Every movement squeezed a groan from his parched lips.

'Bobby. Let me get it. What do you need?'

El Shaddai

'In cave.'

'What you do want me to get from the cave? Which cave?'

'I must get to cave.'

'Okay.' Ky took charge. 'First, we will sit you in the bath. It will make you stronger so you can walk.'

Together the woman carried him and placed him in the water. Milly felt so useless. 'The skin cools, but the fire inside rages.'

'Cave. Cave.' Bobby wafted in and out of sleep. 'Please, Missus.'

They lifted him out of the tub and lay him on a dry towel. Using it as a sling they carried him between them, as they did when he broke his leg. 'Bobby.' Panic squeezed Milly's heart. 'Bobby. Does the boss's house have a red roof?'

Did he nod? 'Is the boss home? Anyone home?' They laid their burden gently on the ground.

'That bush.' He pointed. Ky rushed to pick leaves for him. She handed them to him and ran back to the hut to get more water. He crawled off the towel and lay in the dust in the cave, pushing the leaves into his mouth. 'You go now, Missus.'

Milly sat on a rock. 'What are those leaves, Bobby?'

'I'll die quick. Stop the pain. Please go.'

Urgency gripped her heart. 'Bobby. Do you know Jesus?'

'He's Pete's God.' He shuddered.

'No. Pete talked bad about Jesus. Pete worshipped the devil. Jesus is my God. He will take you to the Father in heaven.' Within her heart, Milly screamed. *Why am I talking this way?*

'Jesus. Okay.' He tried to lift more leaves to his mouth, but his hand fell to the ground. By the time Ky returned with wet towels, he lay still.

Ky led Milly back to the hut. Grief flooded her, sapping her strength. She collapsed on the grass. Ky sat beside her, holding her. 'Did he mean the dead land near the bananas, Milly?'

Milly shrugged her shoulders. 'I don't know and I'll never know. He's gone.' The vision of his thin frame curled in the cave shook her. 'Ky, what will we do?'

'We must bury him as soon as possible, but the ground is so hard. And we need to be careful of contamination. Do you think he was contagious?'

Milly pushed herself up and grabbed the crowbar and an old towel. 'I'll do it.'

'Not alone, you won't.' Ky grabbed the shovel and followed.

'What about the kids?' Milly looked at the hut.

'They'll be okay. Look. Caroline's back. I'll ask her to mind them for once.'

They lifted Bobby on the towel. They placed him under a ledge at the rear. Milly covered him with the towel and, using the crowbar, they levered five large rocks up against him. Puffing, Ky left to check the kids. Alone, Milly moved smaller rocks to close the gaps, tears dripping off the end of her nose. Soon a rock wall hid his body.

Panting, she paused at the entrance to his cave. 'I honour you, my little friend.' She wiped her face with the back of her dirty hand. 'You are the bravest person I have ever met.' As she spoke, the truth of the words impacted her.

Yes, Milly, and I love him

What, God? Where were You? Show up now? Why didn't You heal him?

El Shaddai

♪ You didn't ask ♪

Milly stopped, stunned by the thought. She hadn't prayed for him. Why not?

♪ It was his time ♪

But, Lord ...

♪ I love you, Milly, I'm so proud of you. You are doing so well ♪

It doesn't feel good. It feels lousy.

She marched back into the hut, with the crowbar over her shoulder and determination in her heart. Fear had stopped her long enough. No longer. She would use everything Bobby had taught her. Even if she had to go back to the penthouse, she would find food and lead all of them back into civilisation.

Chapter 10

KY RAKED HER FINGERS through her curls. 'Please, Milly. Take a day to recover. We need a day to mourn and… and regroup. Stay for me.'

Milly gave her a quick hug. 'Sorry, Ky. I'm going while I have the courage.' She hitched her shorts and tied a rope through the belt loops. 'I dreamed of the house with the red roof again. I know it's there.'

'I'm frightened for you. It's only a dream.'

'So was the tidal wave.' The old, familiar horror flooded through her. 'This dream shows good things, Ky. For all of us.'

'But, Milly…'

'We can be at home there. Cook food. Keep warm. Summer will be over soon.'

'Can I go with you?' Both women spun. Caroline was tying her belt of string.

Milly's heart sank. She didn't feel like company. 'I don't think so, Caro. We can't leave Ky with all the children.'

'I can manage the children. And I'd feel happier if you went together.'

'I'll grab my shoes and water bottle.' Caroline turned back into the hut.

'Ky. How could you? You know she'll drive me crazy.'

Ky grinned and patted Milly's arm. 'You worked well as a team when Bobby broke his leg. And two are better than one. The boys and I will fish today. Be home in time for dinner.' She turned, tears in her eyes.

'Ky, it may take two days. Bobby didn't get back in a day.'

'Two.' Ky didn't turn back. 'Okay. But no more. I think I can handle it, but can Caro?'

They walked towards the waterfall, the only sound the slap of their feet on the familiar path. Milly made herself remember Bobby's sick body and the wall of stones. She needed the emotion to fuel her determination. But the Bobby she saw in that moment wasn't sick. He stood on one leg with his foot on his knee. 'Bobby.'

Caro jumped. 'What, Milly?'

'Nothing.' She rubbed her eyes. The image had vanished.

'Why did you say "Bobby"?'

'I thought I saw him, but it must've been a strong memory.'

'Maybe he's leading us?' Caro grabbed Milly's arm. 'He knew where to go. We should follow.'

Milly flicked the hand off her arm. Caroline was right, but to follow meant entering Pete's cave. Her stomach churned. The vision flew past her eyes again. She ran through the bush, away from the cave. *It's not fair, God. I need Bobby with me.*

Follow Me

El Shaddai

Milly stomped on, pushing through the scrub.

Bobby's way

But I can't go back in there, Lord.

Go forward. Leave the past behind

Turning, she stamped back through the undergrowth. Caroline jumped to her feet. 'Feel better now?'

Milly ignored her. But it wasn't as easy to ignore God.

You have a destiny, Milly. A future. Remember

Milly retied her rope around her pants. *Whatever, God. Look at me. I'm useless.*

They stopped at the familiar oasis and filled their bellies and bottles with fresh water. Caroline stretched out her arms, lifting her face to the sky. 'You can nearly touch God in this place.'

'You feel it? I didn't think you liked God?'

'We've had a few conversations here. He says He likes me.'

'God likes everyone, Caro, even you.' The words were mean, but she didn't care.

'Yes, Milly. He even loves you.'

Milly jumped up. 'Try to keep up.' But her bravado deserted her at the narrow path leading to the cave.

'We're not going on that path, Milly. It's too dangerous.' Caroline's voice quavered. 'Don't be crazy.'

You were scared too the first time

God, I'm scared now. She dropped onto a rock and tried to calm herself, staring at the path. A wallaby appeared. Seeing her, it bounded over a rock, towards the water. Behind her, Caroline screamed.

Milly raced back. The woman cuddled the rock face, her body shaking. The wary wallaby sipped from the waterhole.

Caroline slid down the face of the rock and sat on the ground. 'He frightened me half to death.'

Milly shivered at her words. Death was too close, just around the rock to be exact. But hope lay past the site of her horror.

It's the way to freedom

Isn't there another way, Lord?

Freedom comes by way of facing our regrets

But, Lord. I've confessed it all.

And I've forgiven you

So why must I go through the shadow?

I had to go through Golgotha

She shivered. *Isn't there any other way to get food?*

'Milly?'

Milly blinked and lowered herself to the ground beside Caroline. 'Maybe we've done enough for today.'

'Are you going to give up because of me?'

Milly shrugged. She didn't want to go in the cave, and the path from there was unknown. 'I'm not giving up. But I don't know how far we have to go to find help or food. I've wasted a lot of the morning fiddling around. Let's go back for the gun and try to get the wallaby. I'll leave early tomorrow morning. You can drive me this far and I'll be underway as soon as there is enough light to see.'

'How did you know to go down the path, Milly?'

'It's where I found Bobby. I kept seeing him standing in the cave at a certain spot.'

'The cave?'

'There is a cave behind this rock. It opens up to the west. Bobby came through it.'

'Wow. God showed you?'

'Yes.

'Let's go a little further, Milly. We can return. Let's explore a little more.'

'You'll have to walk the path.'

'Is there no other way?'

'No.'

'Well, you can help me.' Caroline got to her feet. Startled, the wallaby jumped back onto the path and skittled past the rock and out of sight. The stones he dislodged ricocheted down the valley. Caroline gulped. 'How far down is it?'

'I don't know. I haven't been game to look.' Milly pulled herself to her feet. 'Walk behind me. Put your right hand on the rock and hold the strap of my backpack with your left hand.'

'Are you frightened? Your hand is shaking.'

'Look, Caro. Are you coming or not? I'm not coming back for you.'

'I'll shut my eyes.'

'Whatever, but keep close to the rock.' Milly crept forward, feeling the gentle pressure on her backpack. Eight steps and they were in the cave. 'Open your eyes, Caro.'

A forest lay at their feet. Beyond the trees were rolling hills, fold after fold as far as she could see. Hope swelled in her soul.

'Wow. How wonderful. There must be people out there who can help us. Where's the track, Milly?'

Without a sideward glance, she led Caroline past the pile of rocks. They dropped over the edge of the cave and slipped down a steep track. Caroline screamed and laughed. 'This is fun.'

Milly dropped one level at a time. *What about the return journey?* Bobby had tried to take the easier way but found it blocked. There was only one way back to their children. As the track levelled it became less distinct. Animal tracks came in from the sides. Neverending lines of tree trunks stretched to the right and the left. They paused to sip from their water bottles. 'Don't drink too much, Caro. We don't know where the next water is. We don't know where anything is.'

'Do you know where to go, Milly?'

Milly shook her head. 'I do know if we want to get home tonight, we'll have to turn around soon.'

Look for tracks

'Caroline, we need to watch for tracks.'

'There's lots of kangaroo markings.'

'Yes. But is there any evidence Bobby came his way?'

'Milly, it was weeks ago.'

'He brought the vegetables yesterday.' It felt a lifetime ago. Milly walked a little further along the most distinct path, intently studying the sandy soil. In many places leaf litter covered the sand. In other spots it looked to be swept by the wind. An occasional drag of a marsupial tail or prints of birds and animals indicated plentiful hunting. *God, please show me.*

'Milly, look. What's that?' Caro pointed.

Off the track, under some shrubs lay an old wheelbarrow, covered by a sack. Milly lifted the bag. Sweet potatoes, eggs, tomatoes and some wilted carrots. She blinked. 'Bobby? Do you think Bobby used it to carry stuff?'

'And he left here what he couldn't carry up the hill.' Caro rubbed a tomato on her shirt and bit into it.

El Shaddai

Milly took another. Delicious juice filled her mouth. They packed tomatoes, two sweet potatoes and two eggs and continued on the track, following the wheel marks from the barrow.

In the late afternoon they walked out of the trees. A wire fence marked a boundary, as though God had drawn a line in the sand. In front of them stretched open grasslands. Milly dropped her backpack and stared. Shading her eyes from the afternoon sun, she surveyed the scene. Golden grass stretched as far as the eye could see, dotted with an occasional tree. She couldn't spot a house of any description, with or without a red roof. Caroline paced up and down the fence line, like a penned cattle dog.

Where, God? Where to now?

Be still

Be still

When had she last heard those words repeated? Her whole body stiffened as she remembered. The day she had gone looking for water, before she pushed her way through the scrub, the Lord had three times said, 'Be still.' In her haste, she'd ignored the quiet thought. It had cost her. Her push through the bush was sheer pigheadedness. *Sorry, God.*

She retreated a little into the forest and sat, leaning against a tree in the shade. She allowed herself a sip of water and polished another tomato. It was soft due to its ride in the backpack, but she relished every savoury drop.

Ah, God. It's like the nectar of heaven. Thank you.

He smiled. *Be still*

Caro's screaming woke her with a start.

'Milly! Where are you?' Caroline raced past her.

'Caroline.'

But Caroline kept running and screaming.

~·~ *Be still* ~·~

God, she's frantic.

~·~ *She'll be back in a minute* ~·~

She pulled herself to her feet and waited by the fence in the sunlight.

'Milly. Oh, Milly. I thought you'd gone.' She fell into Milly's arms, panting. 'Why did you hide?'

'Hide?'

Caroline shoved her away. 'It's not funny, Milly.'

Pointing her back into the shade, she offered her a drink and a tomato. 'Sit, Caro. I was resting in the shade. Look at you. You're so hot.'

'But why did you hide?'

'I'm sitting beside the path where we stopped. Why did you go away?'

'This is the path?' Caroline looked around. 'Oh. I see. I couldn't find it anywhere.'

'Good point. We need to mark the entrance to the forest or we won't be able to find our way back tomorrow.'

'Tomorrow!' Caroline sat bolt upright. 'We're going home today.'

'Look at the sun. If we started back now it'd be dark before we get to the mountain. We could never climb it in the dark.'

'But we can't stay here.' Tears ran down Caroline's cheeks.

'Well, let's keep going. If there are fences, there must be people somewhere.' She recoiled at the thought of meeting

El Shaddai

anyone. She hoped to find the house empty and its veggie garden full.

Caroline brightened. 'I found Bobby's wheel tracks. It's that way and a long way, still on this side of the fence.'

Dead land

'I don't think it is the right way.' Milly pondered the thought. 'Bobby said he tried another way but the land was dead. Then he had to go back to the hard way. I don't think we should follow the tracks anymore.'

Caroline looked at her as though she'd gone mad. 'But Milly, where will we go? What will we do?'

Milly picked up her bag and stood by the fence line. 'I think we should go to the top of the hill. Maybe we'll see more from there.' *God, was that Your idea?*

His silence and her peace pushed her forward. They dragged a couple of dead sticks and leaned them on the fence as markers for their return. Squeezing between the strands of barbed wire, they walked into towards a huddle of gum trees not far from the top of the hill. As soon as they reached the shade, Caroline slumped to the ground and grabbed her water bottle.

'Have a tomato, Caro. Save the water.'

'But they're bruised.'

'They're moisture. They won't keep. The water will.'

Milly left her and walked through the shade to the other side of the trees. Rolling hills were dotted with a few cows. Fences marched through valleys and over hills. Her heart sank. *No house, God.*

Look closer

Sighing, she turned back. What did He mean her to see? There was no house, no buildings of any description. A spur of the hill hid a valley on her right. All the fences seemed to run into the valley. Was that significant? She walked further up the hill, noting rows of trees in the valley. *Maybe an orchard?*

She called Caro and they followed a cattle-track down the hill. A sense of excitement swelled in Milly's heart. She ran down the last incline and into the orchard. They couldn't identify the trees, but God's presence pushed against Milly's heart. They were walking under boughs that held hands above their heads.

I met her in the vineyard

Father, where are You taking me?

Home

They walked out of the orchard into a grove of orange trees. Abundant fruit hung from the branches, but it was not yet ripe.

A land flowing with milk and honey

Tears coursed down her face as a sense of absolute safety flooded her soul. Beyond the orange trees stood the house, exactly as she had seen it, complete with faded red roof and shrubs to the side. She ran through the backyard to the window. Standing on tiptoe, she could just see the dusty lounge reflected her dream.

'Milly.' Caroline sounded scandalised. 'Don't peek. Knock on the door.'

'There's no one here, Caro. But find the front door and knock anyway.'

Caro crept towards the front door. Milly heard her knock but turned away to find if the vegetable garden was there. It was beautiful and well-kept. With a grin in her heart, she ran to the back door. It swung open. Leaving her shoes outside,

El Shaddai

she padded through the deserted home and opened the front door. 'Come in, Caroline. Welcome.'

Caroline squealed. 'Milly. How did you get in there?'

'Through the back door. Come, let's explore.'

There were bedrooms opening off each side of the front hall. Beds were crisply made with bedspreads tucked under the pillows and falling neatly to the floor. The rooms were tidy, but covered with thick dust. A few broken ornaments lay on the floor. 'No one's been here for a long time.' Milly ran her finger through thick dust on the dressing table. 'Maybe years. I wonder what happened?'

The hall opened into the living room Milly had seen in her dreams. Caro flopped into an over-stuffed chair. A cloud of dust enveloped her, making her sneeze. Milly righted a lamp on the floor and walked to a closed door. 'Another bedroom with twin beds. The boys'll enjoy this one, I think.'

'Milly.' Caroline sneezed again. 'You sound as though it's ours.'

'It is.'

'What? You can't walk into any old house and claim it's yours.'

'God told me it's mine.' She moved through the large room. 'C'mon, Caro, we're running out of light.'

Caroline flicked a switch on the wall. 'No power.' She pushed open another door.

Milly walked through to the kitchen. Old fashioned but clean, it lay under a thin layer of dust. A coffee cup, bowl and spoon waited in the sink. The stove was huge. She opened the fire box. The cold ashes of the last fire waited for attention.

'Milly, there's running water and a proper loo. It even flushes.' Caroline burst into the kitchen. 'Can I have a shower? There's shampoo and conditioner.'

Milly laughed. 'Better hurry. There are no lights.' The bathroom door slammed causing the dust to slide down the walls. The last door opened off the back landing. She pushed it ajar. Her hand flew to her mouth. 'Oh, God. What happened?'

A pair of men's pyjamas lay crumpled on a large unmade bed. Long khaki dungarees hung over a chair. Someone left one morning and never returned. From the appearance of the house, he lived alone and hadn't been in the front rooms for years. *Why did he disappear?*

Finding wood piled near the kitchen door, she set about making a fire. In the fading light she searched cupboards, looking for candles. Flinging one open above the bench, three coffee cups fell and smashed at her feet. 'The earthquake. No-one's been here since then. That's why it's tidy and yet disorderly.' She opened the next cupboard a crack and pushed back a whole row of glasses. There were no candles under the sink or in the cupboards. There must be a pantry somewhere.

Where's the honey, Lord? She grinned at her own impudence.

Going to get more wood, she found another door. The door opened to a whole room lined with shelves. Unable to see much, she groped in the dark. Her hand fell on a box of matches. She lit a match, holding it high. Beside the matches an old-fashioned lantern waited. Taking it outside to the fading dusk she lit the wick. It burst into life.

El Shaddai

At the table, they held hands before they ate. 'Thank You, Lord, for bringing us to this lovely place. Thanks for this food and please, please send your angels to guard Ky and the children tonight.'

They feasted on tinned tomato soup, poached eggs, sweet potato and peaches. Working by the light of the lantern, they cleaned the two front rooms. They wiped down every surface, swept and mopped the timber floors. The bedspreads were carefully folded to contain the dust and Milly carried them to the laundry.

On the way back to the bedroom, she spied an old telephone in the lounge. A landline. *Dan.* She grabbed the handset, heart racing. *What if he doesn't answer? What if he rejects me because of the baby?*

'Milly. Is that a phone?' Caro snatched the handset from Milly and started dialling. 'I can ring Mum.' She put the phone to her ear. 'Why isn't it ringing?'

Milly took the handset back and jiggled the phone. 'The line's dead.'

Caro turned in silence but not before Milly saw her wet lashes.

Milly showered, hot tears blending with shampoo and the cool water. 'When can I find Dan, Lord?'

I love you, Milly

But, Lord…

Everything I have is yours

Caroline pushed the door ajar. 'Here, Milly. I found some clothes. I'm sure the lady who owns them won't mind.'

Thankful for anything clean, she pulled on a soft, white nightie. It fell to her ankles, floating as she spun. Back in the front room, she slipped into crisp sheets. No stars above, no dew in the morning. Instead she had a soft pillow, sheets and clean clothes. It overwhelmed her.

When she stirred in the night, the moon threw dim shadows on the wall. Without thinking, she rolled over to cuddle Dan's back and jolted awake as reality crashed in. *God, I want Dan. I need Dan.*

You have Me

I want Dan too. We promised to love and cherish each other. Where is he? God, where is he? How will he ever find me here? Her tears turned into sobs. She pressed her mouth into the pillow, hugging it to her. *What about all Your promises, Lord? Promises of us ministering together.*

Come with Me

Holding the pillow close, she padded through the house, lit by the moon. Leaving the door ajar she wandered into the orchard. Her tears still fell. It was dark under the trees. Something whooshed past her head, flapping wings beating the air. Jumping to one side, she squealed.

It was only a startled owl. C'mon. Not much farther

She shook her head. What was she doing? Where was she going? She didn't know. Up ahead the trees parted and moonlight bathed the short grass. Stopping in the middle of the pale blue light, it surrounded her in the shape of a heart.

Will you dance with Me?

In the middle of the heart, she lifted her face to the moon. Breathing in the beauty of the halo of light and the heavy scent of the orchard, calmness seeped into her soul.

El Shaddai

I wanted to share the beauty with you. You are My beloved

She stretched her arms wide and started to turn, watching each treetop glide past her vision. Her long, white nightdress billowed away from her ankles. Caught in the love, light and the magic of the moment, she turned faster and faster. The trees spun around her. She felt light, as though she could lift off the ground. Closing her eyes, she gave herself to the wonder of the moment.

I love you. I love you. I love you. You are Mine. If you run to the highest mountain, I will be there. If you go the deepest depths, I will be there. I am yours and you are Mine

'Milly!' Caroline stood over her, hands on hips. 'You're impossible. A soft bed and what do you do? Go back outside to sleep. You'll be all wet.'

Milly lifted her arms and stretched out her legs. A delicious feeling of peace permeated her whole being. Opening her eyes, she watched the shadowy shapes of the trees starting to colour.

'Milly!' Caroline stamped her foot.

'Good morning, Caro. Isn't it a wonderful morning?' She pulled herself to a sitting position, curling her legs under the beautiful nightie. 'What are you doing up so early?'

'Boobs are sore because there's too much milk. I need my baby. Is it time to go?'

'Must be.' Milly's brain kicked into gear. *Babies*. Her babies were still back with Ky with scant food while she'd been dancing under the moon. She jumped up and jogged back through the trees beside Caroline. 'I'll get dressed. You find us something to eat and fill the water bottles.' She held the door open and followed Caroline in.

I am yours and you are Mine

Smiling, she pulled on her dirty clothes. *Lord, can I get everybody back here before dark tonight?*

We can, My lovely

El Shaddai

Chapter 11

'Now?' Ky's UNKEMPT CURLS fell over her face. 'No, I can't leave now.'

'Ky, there's a house waiting for you. Beds. Shower. Proper loo. And food... did I mention a full pantry?'

'But why not tomorrow or the day after? Lily's not well and Bea missed her Mum and...'

Milly forced herself to stop rushing. 'Hard night?'

'Have you ever tried camping with five kids by yourself?'

'No. I'm sure I couldn't do it. I'm sorry, Ky.' When had Ky got so thin? She needed food. They'd carried some food back for breakfast but it was all devoured.

'C'mon, Ky. You can do this. The kids need the food.' Milly was desperate to get the family on the road. It had taken them four hours to return to the hut. They needed every remaining minute of the day to get the little ones the distance. Maybe she should wait and leave at first light tomorrow. But an urgency in her spirit pushed her on.

Be still

But God, why this urgency?

~ *Be still* ~

She led Ky to a chair and sat beside her. Opening her pack, she handed her a big red tomato.

'Oh. How lovely. It will help with dinner tonight.'

'Eat it, Ky. Eat it *now*. You need it.'

Ky looked shocked.

'Let me guess? The children have all eaten this morning, but you haven't?'

Ky nodded.

'Eat it, Ky. And sit still.' Entering the hut, she found Caroline packing. 'Only take kids' clothes, Caro.'

'But...'

'There is lots of stuff in the house. You and I can come back to get things. Today you need to carry Bea.'

'But the pram... oh... we can't get it down the hill.'

'We'll carry the babies in slings. Let's store all the tools and stuff inside.' Without further bidding Caro called the boys to help.

Behind the door she picked up all the rope she could find. She had no idea how they were going to get the little ones down, but they must.

'Ky's asleep.' Caroline returned, a frown creasing her forehead. 'And hot. Maybe we shouldn't go today?'

'I'm worried about her. But we must go now. Can you make sure the kids are dressed and wearing shoes? Load the car. I'll put Ky in the front.' She glanced around the hut. It had saved their lives. Opening the cupboard to grab a tin of beans, she gasped. Bare shelves. One packet with a few pasta shells, the flour bag drooping sadly on the shelf, almost empty.

El Shaddai

Time to go, Beautiful. Trust Me

But... She backed away. *But God didn't protect you.* The voice in her head mocked her. She started to shake. *God. You didn't protect me from Pete. Why should I believe You now?*

I have always been with you, Amalya. Come

She squashed the voices down and straightened her spine. This wasn't the time to fight with God. Squaring her shoulders, she walked to the door. *Okay, God. I don't have another choice. Please get us there.*

Outside, she knelt in front of her sleeping friend. 'Wake up, Ky. We're going.'

Startled eyes tried to focus on her face. 'Going?'

'Yes. Everyone's in the car.' Caroline waited to fold Ky's chair. Milly ran her hand across Ky's forehead. Burning hot. Returning to the hut she emerged with two wet washers and covered Ky's forehead and neck. Bobby had taken the last paracetamol.

Father. Please heal her.

Rise up and go

She pulled Ky up and led her to the car. Caroline didn't say a word until they were filling the water bottles by the creek. 'Milly. How are we going to do this?'

'I don't know, Caro.'

'Why are we going today then?'

'There's no food left. The cupboard is empty.'

Caroline shook a bottle up and down and tipped the water out on the grass. 'What about the pass into the cave? Problem number one.'

'You must be confident there, Caro. If there's no hesitation from us, the others will follow.'

'But what if one of them falls?'

ༀ I will command My angels concerning you so you won't hurt your feet upon a rock ༀ

'Let's all pray together before we leave.' She whistled and the kids came to her. Johnno led Bethie by the hand. Caroline took Bea from Hoey and sat on the ground.

'C'mon, Ky.' She still sat in the car. Something told Milly Ky must start under her own choice. 'We're all here and waiting.'

The car door opened. 'I can't find my bag.'

'We have all the bags here, Ky. We just need you.' Milly stood and met her halfway. She gazed around the little group. They looked back at Milly, waiting. With a start, she realised how skinny they were. Some of the little faces had black circles under their eyes. Did she wait too long to find this path?

She plastered hope on her face. 'Today is a big adventure. We're going on a big, long bushwalk and you might get tired but at the end there will be a lovely house and lots of dinner. There are taps with running water and a proper toilet.'

Lily clapped her hands. 'Can I have a big bath?'

'Yes. And you too, Bethie. There are gardens and fruit trees.'

Ky sighed. 'You make it sound like the land flowing with milk and honey, Milly.'

'We looked for the honey last night, didn't we, Caro? Now listen. This is important. The track is steep. We must help each other. Caroline will carry Bea. I will carry Bethie and hold your hand, Lily. Hoey, can you help Ky? She's not feeling well. Johnno, Caroline needs you to be her helper.'

Big eyes looked back at her. 'Now Caroline will lead the way with Johnno. Then Ky and Hoey. The girls and I will go last. But before we start let's hold hands and pray.'

El Shaddai

Ky always prayed but today she sat silent. Milly squeezed her hand. 'Lord, thank You for a new home. Thanks for strength to make the trip. Please send Your angels so we won't hurt our feet against a rock. I ask You to lead us every step of the way.' She caught Caro's eye over Johnno's head. 'Okay, Caro. You lead the way.' She stood and strapped Bethie's slight body to her own with Ky's sling. Heaving her backpack over her shoulders, she walked behind the group towards the track to the cave.

Okay, Lord. Let's go.

Hoey turned to glare at his mother. 'You said we're not allowed to go here. Cause it's dangerous.'

'You're right, Hoey. But this is the only way. It is not dangerous when we're together. But Mummy needs you to listen carefully. You must keep one hand on the rock wall. All the time.'

Like little soldiers they followed Caroline, each one reaching out to touch the wall as the path came alongside the rock. As the ground began to fall away to their left the procession slowed. Milly sensed Caro losing courage.

God… help.

March

'Let's pretend we are God's army. We will be soldiers and march.' Caro's eyebrows were nearly in her hair. 'Attention!' The boys laughed. 'Okay. March. Left, right, left, right…'

As the boys joined her chant, Caro squared her shoulders. 'Stay close to the rock and follow me, Johnno. I need your help with Bea.' She disappeared out of sight marching around the corner.

Milly sighed with relief, but she kept yelling, 'Left, right…'.

Ky screamed. 'Johnno's gone.'

Caro's voice echoed from the unseen cave. 'He's with me, Ky. He's fine. Follow us. It's easy.'

Hoey's fear-filled eyes sought Milly. He grabbed one of her hands. Lily snatched the other.

Ky spun around. 'Bethie?' Her eyes were scared and feverish, her face drained of colour.

'Bethie's fine, Ky. Snug and happy. Now turn around and follow the path. Right hand on the rock. Stay close to the wall. In a few steps you'll be with Johnno.'

Ky looked over the edge of the looming precipice. 'Milly, I can't. It's too dangerous.'

'There's no other way, Ky.'

'C'mon, Mummy. Johnny did it.' Johnno's little voice rang from the other side of the rock. 'Do you want me to come and help you?'

'No, Johnny. You stay.'

For a few heartbeats the world seemed to stop. Milly cried out to God.

Trust Me with your children. Put them behind you and go help her

She gulped. Squatting down to her children's height, she looked them in the eyes. 'Mummy must help Ky. I want you to follow close behind me. Hoey, hang onto the strap on my backpack and hold your sister with your other hand.' Lily's flash of rebellion faded under her mother's stare. 'Lily, hold Hoey's hand and touch every bit of the wall. Pretend you're painting a long line with your fingers.'

'Paint Mummy?' She brightened.

El Shaddai

'Pretend paint today, Lovely.' She ruffled her dark hair. 'Do you know what to do, Hoey?' He nodded. Milly took a deep breath and turned to Ky. 'Hoey, pull the strap so Mummy knows you are holding it.'

Her shoulders yanked back. 'I'm strong, eh, Mummy?'

'Sure are, my big boy.' She calmed her mind and summoned her faith. As Milly moved closer to Ky's frozen back, Caroline's face appeared from behind the rock. Her baby sling hung empty. 'Give me your left hand, Ky. Hold the rock with your right.'

'I'm going to hold you from behind, Ky.' Milly put her hands on Ky's waist and pushed gently.

'I can't, Milly. I can't.' The desperation in her voice grabbed Milly's heart.

'Close your eyes, Ky. Keep them closed. Can you imagine our beach near Bullhead Rock? Can you hear the waves? Can you smell the salt? Remember the day we walked beside the rock.' She felt Ky's body respond to Caroline's gentle tugging. 'Walk with me on the sand, Ky. Keep your fingers rubbing alongside Bullhead Rock.'

'Wow, Mummy. Look.' Hoey's excited voice broke the stillness. 'You can see forever.'

Ky froze. Milly pushed her back and she took two more steps.

'You did it!' Johnno sounded excited. 'Open your eyes now, Mummy.'

Milly rounded the end of the path to see him sitting on a rock that marked Pete's head, his arms squeezing Bea. Not knowing whether to laugh or cry, she pulled her two children to herself. 'What wonderful listeners you are. Mummy's so proud.' She reached out and tousled Johnno's hair. 'You're all such good children.'

And Me?

You, God? Always. You're good by definition.

Smiling, she turned her attention back to Ky. Like Hoey she stared enthralled by the endless rolling hills beyond the forest. Her eyes looked a little brighter.

'Milly, I don't like it here. It's smelly and dirty.'

'Though we walk through the valley of the shadow of death we will fear no evil, Ky.' As the quote fell unbidden from her lips, she shuddered.

'But there's no way out.'

'Yes, there is.' Caro nestled Bea tightly in her sling. 'Do you still want me to lead, Milly?'

'Sure do, Caro. Let's go.'

Ky looked frantic. 'But where to?'

Caro chuckled. 'You've done the hardest bit, Ky. But you will need to keep your eyes open for this stretch. Ok, Johnno. Let's go.' Using a root as a handle she dropped over the edge and onto a rock below and lifted Johnno down.

'C'mon, Ky.' Hoey took her hand. 'I'll be your helper.'

Milly turned to look for Lily. She had run to the back of the cave. 'Let's go, Lil. We have a hill to climb down.' With Bethie strapped across her tender belly, the descent was difficult. At every drop, she lowered herself and the toddler and then lifted Lily down. Overwhelmed, she stopped in front of a big boulder. This morning she'd found the monster hard to conquer with no children. The others were nowhere to be seen. She needed help. 'Caro. Wait up.'

El Shaddai

'Turn left around the big boulder, Milly.' Caro's voice carried through the forest. 'We couldn't get over it, so we pushed around it. It's a squeeze but we're all through.'

Lily ran between the rocks and disappeared from sight.

'Hoey. Can you help Mummy?' His eager face appeared between the rocks. She released Bethie, passing her to Hoey. 'Take her to Ky, Hoey.'

Lowering her pack, she managed to push it through the opening and squeeze through herself. A track led her to the left. The others were well ahead. 'Caro. This track goes the wrong way.'

'I spied this track from the top of the big rock. It's longer but it joins the other one. It's an easier walk for the kids.'

God?

There was silence.

Why aren't You showing me? How do I know it's right?

Trust Me

How can I? We're off-track.

You gave the leadership to her

But God, I don't trust her. She barely knows You.

Even My lambs know My voice

Milly hurried after Hoey. He was carrying Bethie on one hip and leaning under her weight. They rounded a corner and found Ky sitting in the leaf litter.

'I can't do any more, Milly.' She put tired arms around her little girl who snuggled on her lap.

Caro yelled from the track ahead. 'Just a little further, guys. I can see a great place to rest. Keep coming.'

Milly pulled Ky to her feet. 'C'mon, Ky. You can do a few steps more. Bethie, you hold Mummy's hand and help her.' The toddler's bottom lip quivered and she clung to her mother.

'Mummy hasn't seen you walking in the forest like a big girl. Can you show her?' Milly breathed a prayer. With a giggle, the little girl toddled down the path. She tripped and fell face down into the leaves. Ky leapt to her feet. Bethie giggled, scarmbled up and ran towards the others. Her mother followed.

Thanks, God. But how can I get this sick woman the rest of the way?

⁓ᴓᴓ⁓ *One step at a time* ⁓ᴓᴓ⁓

They sat on two logs to rest. 'I'll wait here. You can come back for me later.'

'No way. Up you get.'

Caro left, leading the others down the track. Milly strapped Bethie to her chest. She cried for her mother.

'Leave her with me, Milly.'

Pretending she didn't hear, Milly walked on, patting the fretting toddler. Lily followed, but she dawdled, slowing the whole group. Milly had no way of carrying her too. To her relief the track turned back to the right. She hoped they'd meet the other path soon.

The boys ran on ahead. Lily tried to follow but her little legs were too tired. Caro waited for Milly. 'Ky's a long way back. I'm worried about her.'

'She'll come because her kids are here.'

'I'm hoping it's not far to the wheelbarrow.'

'I think we're close. I'm hoping Bea will lie in it.'

'It won't be Bea. It'll be Ky. And Lily.'

El Shaddai

When they found the wheelbarrow, they stopped to rest. Lily curled up on the grass and fell asleep. Milly stretched out beside her. Her whole body ached and soon she had to push a wheelbarrow. *Lord, I don't think we can do it. We need help here. It's long past midday.*

Rest a minute. Be still. All is well

She closed her eyes and allowed herself to relax.

'Milly. We fell asleep. We must go.' Caro strapped Bea to her body. Milly blinked, trying to get her bearings.

'Ky. Come.' She felt her friend's forehead. It was burning. She retrieved a washer from her pack, wet it from the water bottle and damped her down. 'Sit in the barrow, facing me.' When Ky's hot eyes just stared at her, she coaxed. 'Come on. Just try. Sit right in the middle.'

Ky settled herself on the bag in the barrow. Milly passed her Bethie and lay Lily between her feet.

'You'll never be able to push it, Milly. Leave me behind and take the children.'

Ignoring her, Milly heaved at the handles. 'Lean back further, Ky. Let's work at getting a balance.' The barrow lifted and the load started down the road. Once they'd started, the pressure on her arms eased and they moved faster. Milly wanted to get as far as possible before her strength gave out.

'Does the forest go forever, Mum?' Hoey trotted beside his mother.

'Did I tell you about the house where we're going, Hoey? It's got lots and lots of trees. There's a special room with two beds. I thought you and Johnno could have your own room.'

Jo Wanmer

When she felt she couldn't go any further, Ky opened her eyes. 'Milly, my legs are cramping. Maybe I can walk for a bit.' She climbed out and Johnno hopped in to hold Bea. Bethie rode at the front, while Caro pushed. Milly strapped Lily in the sling and linked her arm through Ky's. She talked about the house to keep her walking.

By the time they saw the barbed wire fence, it was dark and gloomy. Ky was leaning heavily on Milly. Once out of the trees, Milly gasped. Towering black clouds threatened them. 'C'mon, everyone. We're almost there.' She held the wires apart and ushered the family through the fence. 'Hurry. It looks like rain. Ky, take the children towards the trees.'

She helped Caro heave the barrow over the fence and they ran to catch up. Ky collapsed under the biggest tree. 'I can't go any further. Not another step.'

Strapping Bethie to her front, Milly dropped her backpack at Ky's feet. 'I'll be back. It will take me about half an hour. Don't move, okay?' She turned to her children. 'Hoey and Lily, your turn in the barrow. Johnno, can you run with me?' Pushing the barrow, she set off down the cattle track, as the first bolt of lightning cracked the sky. Caroline clutched Bea to her chest and raced towards the house.

They burst through the back door, the kids frightened by the approaching storm but still dry. Milly sat them at the table and gave them a cup of water each. Caroline rummaged in the pantry and emerged with the lantern and a packet of biscuits. Raindrops pelted on the roof.

Milly waved from the door. 'I'll get Ky. I'll be as fast as I can.'

El Shaddai

'Wait.' Caro pointed. 'There's rain gear behind the laundry door.'

'Ky.' Her voice was dampened by the driving rain. *Oh Lord, where is she?*

She ran back and forth under the tree. Lightning hit the top of the hill. Milly's scream merged with a clap of thunder. She threw her backpack into the barrow and ran from the tree. *God, where is she?* She stood in the downpour, scanning the hill in every flash of light.

Be still, Milly

Be still, God? It's pouring. Ky's lost. Kids are crying and the best You can offer is 'Be still'? She upended the barrow and plonked down on it. The orchard and the hill were visible when the lightning flashed, but not Ky. Pulling the second raincoat over her head she waited. *Still enough?*

I love you, Amalya

If You loved me, You'd still the storm. If You loved me, You'd have healed Ky today. If You loved me... Her tears mingled with the water dripping from her hair. Every muscle in her body ached. *Why the urgency, God? We should have waited until tomorrow.*

You are My beloved daughter, and I'm pleased with you

She sat in the rain, angry and resentful. Dan's voice rang in her memory: *Don't harden your heart, Amalya.* Why did she get cross so easily? *I'm sorry, God.*

Turn around

The rain eased a little. She spun around hoping to see Ky, but there was no sign of her. In the west, the storm lifted like a stage curtain, revealing red, gold and purples. As if orchestrated, the rain stopped and the sun dropped below the clouds, suspended between the earth and the storm. She gasped at the riot of colour. Rays of light turned wet stalks of grass into gleaming blades. The leaves on the tree radiated gold. *Lord, it's wonderful, but where's Ky?*

Come with Me

Leaving the wheelbarrow, Milly followed the voice of her heart. Maybe Ky hid somewhere. In the golden light, she climbed along the ridge, higher than she'd been before. Her body felt exhausted and yet her spirit leapt at the same time. The whole world gleamed with water diamonds sparkling in the late afternoon sun. Turning back, she could see the house. Her heart skipped a beat. Her dream and the view collided. The lighting was the same. The faded roof presented crimson in the evening light and smoke from the chimney tracked upwards in the post-storm stillness.

Look wider

Beyond the house lay a series of farm buildings. A cottage, about twice as big as the hut they'd left, stood a short distance from the sheds. She stretched her tired body. Was it only this morning? It felt like a lifetime ago.

Cattle yards lay unused to the left of the sheds. From her vantage point, the orchard's trees were standing with military precision. The light on wet leaves emphasised the different foliage, forming a patchwork quilt in green. Fences fanned from the stockyards in several directions.

Yours. All yours

El Shaddai

Thanks, God, for a dry home, for food for today, for comfort.

You will eat from trees you didn't plant

Thanks for getting us here safely... Wait. Where's Ky?

Live in houses you didn't build

The golden light began to fade. Milly scrubbed the crazy thoughts from her mind and ran down the hill. 'Ky. Ky.'

'Milly. Did you see the sky?'

She spun around. Ky was walking towards her, leaning on the arm of a short dark-haired man. Her wet curls stuck to her head and her saturated clothes clung to her skinny body, but her face glowed. 'It's so beautiful, so full of promise. I love our new home, Milly. Thanks.'

Am I going crazy? Maybe the whole scene was a vision, but the man pushed out his right hand. 'My name's Cheng, Ma'am. Pleased to be at your service.'

Stunned, Milly took his hand and looked into kind, slanted eyes. 'Is this your home?'

'Shi, Ma'am.' He nodded his head up and down.

Embarrassed, Milly's cheeks flamed. 'I'm... I'm sorry. The house seemed deserted.'

He chuckled. 'Shi. I don't live in the big house. I live in the smaller house. Big house is the boss's. He's gone.'

Ky's legs gave way and she crumpled towards the ground. He grabbed her, holding her up. 'Lady's sick. She needs a dry bed.'

Milly ran to get the wheelbarrow and they lowered her in. She walked beside him as he pushed. 'My wheelbarrow's back. Ah good, very good. Thank you.' He dipped his head again.

'We found it in the forest. I've pushed Ky in it for hours.'

'Bobby promised to bring it back. Strange. Bobby always keeps a promise.'

'You knew Bobby?'

'He's the boss's boy.'

'I'm sorry… but Bobby died a couple of days ago.'

He stiffened beside her.

'Sorry, Cheng.'

They walked through the orchard in silence. A million questions ran through her head, but the man remained silent. In the dusk, she tried to absorb his features. He was a little shorter than her, his long hair was tied back and he could push the barrow with little effort. And she felt no fear. He caught her eye. 'Nearly home, Ma'am. Fire going. Cheng get hot bath for lady… and then for you.'

El Shaddai

Part 3

The Refuge

Chapter 12

MILLY PULLED KY from the bath and dressed her in the long white nightie. She rolled her into the bed she'd vacated in the morning. Ky tossed and turned, moaning. 'No further…'

'You're home, Ky. Rest now. I'll find you some food.'

'It's dark. Why's it dark? Where's Bethie?'

'I'll bring her to you as soon as she's bathed.' Milly felt her way to the door.

'Don't leave me.'

'I won't be long, Ky. Jesus is here. He's with you.' She slipped from the room, following the noise to the bathroom. The boys were lying in the bath, eyes half-closed, tired and exhausted. The girls sat on the floor rolled in towels.

'We need another light, Milly.' Caro's voice showed her strain. 'I can't move anywhere without all of them following. And we need clothes.'

'Leave them naked, Caro.' Milly scooped up Bethie. 'C'mon, little one. Can you look after Mummy for me? Lily, I'll be back for you in a minute.' She felt her way to the bedroom and slipped Ky's baby in beside her.

She'd just picked up Lily, when there was a soft knock on the back door. 'Ma'am?'

'Coming, Cheng. Come in.'

A soft light pervaded the whole house. 'Another light for you, Ma'am. Okay?'

'Wonderful, Cheng.'

'Did you find the medicines?

'No.'

'I'll get them. Lady needs medicine. She very sick. Come.' He headed for the larder and pulled a stool from behind the door to reach the top shelf. 'You carry the light, please, Ma'am.' Back in the kitchen, he lifted the box onto the table. 'You'll find medicine in there. Cheng will get herbs in morning.' Bowing three times, he turned, then paused. 'Will I get dinner for you?'

'You would do that for me?'

'Shi... Shi.' He bobbed up and down. 'Cheng would be honoured.'

'Thank you.' Sitting Lily on the table, Milly peered into the medicine box. Moving a sling and bandages, she found paracetamol lying on top of bottles and tubes.

Cheng lit a wide red candle from the fire in the stove. Placing it on a saucer, he handed it to her.

'Come, Lily. You can be my helper.' The little girl dragged her towel up the hall as Milly carried the candle to Ky's room. It glowed crimson, reminding her of blood. 'Jesus, thank You for Your blood that heals our diseases. Ky needs Your touch, Lord.'

Milly woke in the night to Ky's moaning. By the light of the candle, she wrung a washer out in a bowl of water. After sponging Ky's feverish body, she headed towards another candle in the kitchen, stopping to check the children. The sleeping girls lay beside their big brothers in the room with twin beds. Her heart missed a beat. They were safe and had food. Wiping a tear away, she headed to the kitchen.

She added a log to the fire in the stove. Cheng's soup simmered on the top of the range. Taking a little, she carried it and more tablets back to the bedroom. 'Wake up, Ky. I've bought you soup and some pills.'

Ky tossed and moaned. 'No, Mal, no. Must feed the children.'

'Must feed Ky.' Milly sat on the bed and pulled her up. For the fourth time that night she dribbled soup into Ky's mouth. When it ran out of the corner, she scolded her. 'Ky. Wake up. You must eat.'

Ky swallowed a few mouthfuls, including the pills. Milly sponged her again. Her dry skin stretched over her bones. When had Ky stopped eating? Milly tried to remember. She ate when they had meat, but always busied herself serving. She'd pray and rush off to do something else. Why hadn't she eaten? Whatever the reason, that was changing now. Milly flopped down beside her on the bed, exhausted.

Milly woke to a room flooded with light and Caro washing Ky down. 'She's too hot, Milly. I'd put her in the cold shower but she won't get up.'

'Mal, no. No, Mal, no.' Ky mumbled over and over, tossing on the bed.

'What will we do, Milly?'

Jo Wanmer

'First, we pray, then I explore the medicine box and we continue to cool her. Do you want to be Mummy or nurse?'

'I'll do the kids. I'm not as good at it as Ky, but I can feed them and watch them.'

Bringing medicine box back to the bedroom, Milly started to dig for antibiotics. Maybe she'd find a packet with a few leftovers. She sorted box after box searching for a drug name she recognised. She didn't know what most of them were. If only she could ring the Help Line. *Lord, I am so ignorant.*

Open the packets

Of course. Read the paper tucked around the tablets. She'd never read them before. On the sheet in the third packet, the word 'Antibiotic' leapt out of the page. It also promised to reduce fever. After praying over them, she persuaded Ky to swallow one of them.

Later in the morning, Cheng presented Milly with oranges. 'Earliest oranges. Not sweet but good for sickness.' He bowed his head. 'Will Cheng make more soup? Chicken soup?'

Milly hadn't seen any chickens. 'Are there enough chickens, Cheng?'

'I grow plenty chicken. I bring one when I bring the milk. Okay?'

'Milk? Chicken? You're a wonder, Cheng.' She shook her head. Would this miracle disappear like one of her dreams?

Ky's fever raged. Milly spent the day sponging her, spooning in small amounts of soup and administering tablets. *Lord, I'm trusting You. I don't know what I'm doing.*

Her mind kept throwing up images of Bobby, but she refused to dwell on them. This time she'd prayed. Ky must get better. After the kids were asleep, Caroline crept into the room with the red candle. 'Go and sleep, Milly. I'll wake you when I get tired.'

With relief Milly kissed Ky and left the room. At the kitchen table she found a bowl of soup, full-bodied and delicious. *Where will I sleep, Lord?* She decided to stretch out on the couch.

Wait

What's wrong with the couch?

What's wrong with your room?

In her heart, she knew he referred to the main bedroom. The door hadn't been opened again. Of all the rooms, she felt most like a trespasser there. Frozen in time, it waited for the return of its master. *It's still his room, Lord.*

He is no longer. I've chosen it for you

Taking a deep breath, she pushed open the door. She picked up the discarded pyjamas, their odour tickling her nose. They smelt a little unclean, a little of deodorant, but all masculine. One side of the king-size bed was rumpled, sheets left open by its previous occupant. The other side lay smooth and untouched. Slipping her clothes off, she crawled in the unused side and embraced the luxury.

⟡

For three days they fought a survival battle of a different kind. They revelled in the luxury of shelter, a bathroom and plenty of food, but still Ky tossed in delirium. Caroline took the children on adventures, keeping the house quiet. Milly nursed, cooked and worked at getting the house clean. She dribbled food into Ky six times a day and treated her with tablets from the box and Cheng's herbal teas.

On the third day, Milly couldn't wake Ky. Sobbing, she knelt beside the bed and cried. 'Lord, I lay my hands on Ky. I speak healing as You spoke healing when You walked the earth. Thank You for getting us here, so I could nurse and feed her. But now please heal her.'

I love you, Milly

I know, Lord. Ky?

I love her too. She is the delight of My heart. One more day and she would have sacrificed her life for the family

Milly's tears soaked into the sheets, but she felt at peace. Ky would get better. She was sure of it. Climbing onto the bed she lay beside her friend and watched. The girls played in the front garden.

She woke with a start when someone touched her. Ky reached out. 'Milly. I'm hungry. Is there any more soup?'

Next morning, Caroline's eyes sparked at Milly across the kitchen table. 'I'm going and that's that! I'm leaving early tomorrow. The old car's running and ready to go. I filled it from the big petrol tank.'

'Caroline. Be reasonable. You don't even know where you are going.' Milly's stomach turned.

'Reasonable? You went exploring whenever you liked at the hut and left us behind. Now it's my turn.'

'I was looking for a way for us to survive.'

'I'm looking for my parents, and a hairdresser.' She pulled at her hair. 'I must get my roots done.'

Roots! How could she still be concerned with trivialities? Milly banged dirty dishes together, disgusted.

'And we need more supplies.'

'Like what? We get fresh milk from the cow every morning.' Milly waved her arm at the table. 'Cheng brings fresh vegetables most days. There's an abundance of chicken and eggs. Now we've got the kerosene freezer going, Cheng's going to help us butcher a calf.'

Caro crinkled her nose in disgust. 'My point exactly. There has to be somewhere to buy real meat, and bread and newspapers. And the kerosene will run out eventually.'

'I thought you said there was two years' supply?'

'A wild guess to keep you happy.' She pushed back her chair. 'I don't care what you say. I've got the car working. I'm going.'

'Okay, Caroline. Do whatever you like but you will, of course, take Bea.'

'What?' Caroline banged her hands on the back of the chair. 'How many times have you left your children and asked us to mind them? Huh?'

Milly held Caro's angry gaze. 'You're going on a shopping jaunt, Caro. You have a car. She's your child.' She took a deep breath and lowered her voice 'Or is there another reason, Caro? I think you're looking for a man.'

For a moment she feared Caroline would lash out at her again. But the crimson drained from her face. 'And what's wrong with that? We could do with more male help around here and besides...' Pink flushed her cheeks again. 'I'm itchy for a man. Aren't you?'

'Caro!'

'C'mon, Milly.' Her eyes sparkled. 'Even you must miss romping with Dan in the sheets. Me? I'm still single and free. I don't have to wait for any man to reappear. So I'm going to find one. Do you want me to get someone for you too, or are you determined to believe Dan is still out there somewhere?'

Milly flew to the stove and banged the kettle over the firebox. The diversion didn't work. *Lord, where's my Dan?*

Soft arms encircled her from behind. 'I'm sorry, Mil. That was thoughtless of me. How about I try to find Dan?'

'Find Dan?' Ky's voice was shaky voice as she clung to the doorpost. 'What are you girls arguing about?'

'Ky.' Caroline rushed to her side. 'You're up. Here... sit down. Milly's about to make a cuppa.'

Ky sank into the chair. 'I feel as though I've been asleep for weeks.' She looked around the room. 'Nice kitchen.'

Relief flooded Milly. Ky was up. Weak and still pale, but standing, walking, talking. A load rolled off her shoulders. The mother to them all was back. She carried the teapot to the table, and poured three mugs of tea.

'Can I have milk, Milly? Do we have any?'

Milly chuckled. 'There's lots of milk.' She added milk and sugar and stirred the cup.

Ky took a big gulp. 'Ah. Tea, sweet milky tea. It's like heaven. Okay, girls, I'm waiting.'

'For what?'

'For the answer to my question. What were you girls fighting about?'

Caroline grinned. 'There's a car in the shed, Ky. I got it going. It's running like a charm.'

'Wow. You're so clever, Caro. But that's not what you were arguing about.'

'I'm going shopping tomorrow.'

'Shops. Are there shops?'

El Shaddai

'Of course there are shops.' Caroline threw her hands in the air. 'I intend to find them.'

'And you're happy with this, Milly?'

Milly shook her head and Caro rushed on.

'Milly is being selfish as usual. She says she won't mind Bea. Can you mind her for me, Ky? I shouldn't be gone too many days.'

'Days?' Ky caught Milly's gaze.

A steely determination darkened the younger girl's eyes. 'Well… it takes time to get some of the things I'm after.' Her eyes shot daggers at Milly.

'Who's going to feed your baby, Caro? Since I've been sick, I'm dry, bone dry.'

Caroline gestured to the milk jug on the table. 'There's plenty of milk. You said so yourself, Milly.' She flounced from the room, slamming the door behind her.

Next morning, Milly stood on the stool in the pantry. Furious, she pushed jars aside as she searched each box on the top shelf. In the background she could hear Ky's soft voice trying to comfort the screaming baby. It was madness looking for a baby bottle, but this house seemed to have everything else. A quick check of the shed this morning had confirmed her suspicions. Caro had left before the family woke.

'Milly.'

At Ky's call, she jumped off her chair and returned to the kitchen.

'Let's try solids. She's eight months old. Can you boil some sweet potato?'

Fifteen minutes later, Ky dribbled the potato and milk slurry into the angry little mouth. Bea gagged and swallowed. The next spoonful went in before she could draw breath to scream. Through dry sobs, she accepted the food. But when she'd had enough, she turned and nudged Ky's breasts. 'Sorry, little one.' Within a minute Bea fell asleep and Milly returned to continue her search.

'Mummy? Will this help bubba Bea?' Lily offered a lidded cup. Milly blinked. It had a sipper spout on the lid.

'Where did you find it, Lily?'

'In the cubby.' She ran back outside.

Milly followed. 'What cubby?'

'Cheng fixed it for us.' She pointed to a rough shed, a little larger than a chicken house. Inside a rickety table balanced against two plastic chairs. Old plastic kitchenware lay everywhere.

'Oh, Lily. How wonderful. Aren't you a lucky girl?'

'I'm making a cake, Mummy.'

'Okay, Darling. When you're ready, come in for breakfast.' Milly returned to the kitchen with a sipper cup needing to be sterilised.

Four days later, Milly sat with her tea, enjoying the quiet of the early morning. *Lord, I'm tired.*

Be still

And who is going to do the stuff while I 'be still'?

You are troubled about many things. Spend a day with Me

And what will I do with five kids? Put them in front of the television and let them watch DVDs? Send them to day care? Tell them to find their own food? As if on cue, Bea started to fuss from the bedroom. *And where's Caroline? She's been gone for days. Has she abandoned Bea for a quickie in the hay somewhere?*

Don't harden your heart, My Milly

Rising from the table, she chopped sweet potato and dropped the pieces in boiling water. Bea would demand her breakfast soon. Pouring milk into another saucepan, she added rice and pulled it over the heat. Creamed rice was the new favourite family breakfast.

Just one day, Milly

She threw her hands in the air. *Okay. You make a way and I'll do it.*

Deal

Somehow, she felt He did a little skip. Turning from the stove, she went to get more wood, reminding her they needed to find more firewood and kindling. A squeak of the barrow wheel announced a visitor. 'Mornin', Ma'am. Cheng at your service.'

'Good morning, Cheng.' Milly stood amazed as he started to fill her wood box from the barrow.

'I thought you'd be nearly out of wood. You must tell Cheng what you need.' His head bobbed up and down. 'Miss Caro's gone but she told me what to do. She said you don't want help. But you're the boss. You ask. I'll do it.' Dark, honest eyes gleamed at her. 'You need more wood in fire?' When she nodded, he grinned and rushed to stoke the fire. 'You need the lever this way now.' He pointed to a black bar below the firebox. 'Not cooking? Goes this way.' He started stirring the rice and then pulled the boiling potatoes off the increased heat. 'Miss Milly. Have you been bolting back door at night? It's very important.'

'I... I didn't feel it necessary, Cheng. Why?'

Cheng wrung his hands. 'I tell Miss Caro. I tell her to bolt door.'

'Sorry, Cheng. I didn't know. We will bolt the door.'

'Shi, Shi.' He bowed and then smiled. 'You want eggs for breakfast?'

Stunned, Milly grinned, feeling ridiculous.

'You go. I call when breakfast ready.' He waved her away from the kitchen.

When he called, she gathered the family to a table set with crockery and cutlery. Cheng served creamed rice, scrambled eggs garnished with leafy herbs, and fresh tomatoes. Glasses glowed with orange juice. Cheng hovered over them, unable to hide his boyish delight. 'Long time since I've served a family.' He bowed again. 'Cheng at your service.'

'Wonderful breakfast. Thank you.' Milly leaned back, sipping her coffee. 'Cheng. Do... do you mind children?'

He beamed and bowed. 'Maybe boys can help Cheng dig potatoes? They're ready for harvest.'

'Can we, Mum, please?'

She nodded. God chuckled in her heart. Ky pushed her out of the house. 'I'm strong enough to watch the girls. Go, Milly. Go and explore. Take some lunch. Don't forget your hat.'

Thanks, God.

This way, Milly

El Shaddai

At the shed she wandered past a couple of tractors and unfamiliar implements, stopping at a quad bike. The key waited in the ignition. *Can I? Would I dare?*

'I'll show you, Ma'am.' She turned to see Cheng and the boys. In a matter of minutes, she rode out of the cattle yards, leaving the boys to shut the gate behind her.

The property stretched into the distance. Logic told her to follow fence lines. Her heart pulled her down a rough track. It dropped into a grove of eucalyptus trees. After she passed the second windmill, she realised the track connected watering troughs for the cattle. *Not much water, Lord? I guess that's why the kangaroos do the hill climb past Pete's penthouse.*

I'm glad you raised the topic

What topic?

Pete

She twisted the handle on the quad and roared up the hill, leaving the track and God behind. Cresting the hill, she dodged a few fallen logs and gunned the machine down the other side. The air stung her eyes but she didn't care. Waves of revulsion crashed through her. Skidding to a halt, she jumped from the bike to empty her stomach under a tree. 'I hate him, I hate him. I hate him.' She pummelled the innocent gum tree. *And, God, where were You? Why didn't You protect me?*

But God wasn't there to answer the charge. She'd left him behind. *I want Dan.* At the thought of her husband, she slid down the trunk and buried her head in her hands. Even if Dan walked up now, alive, how could she talk to him? Could she look him in the eye again without reading his pain and disappointment in her? Pulling her knees to her chin she hugged her legs, feeling her tightening stomach. Filth seemed to invade her. She needed to scrub again. Shuddering in disgust, she remounted the bike and came across an animal track. It led her to a creek. A trickle of water lapped around stones, but there was a waterhole big enough to bath in. Sitting naked on a rock, she scrubbed and scrubbed with sand. Her tears flowed downstream with the water.

Dressed, she mounted the bike. The dirtiness remained and loneliness engulfed her. Even if Dan came, would he ever take her back? *God, what will I do?* Her heart question was met with silence. Feeling sheepish, she retraced her journey back to the spot where she had lost her temper. *I'm sorry, God, for being so childish. Will You please forgive me?*

Forgiveness is yours... as always

Can You cleanse me from all unrighteousness? Like the Bible says: 'He is faithful and just and will cleanse you from all unrighteousness.'

You mean all unrighteousness, or only the bits you give Me?

Lord, You're talking in riddles again. The ache in her heart was suffocating. She restarted the quad.

Can I come this time?

Does that mean I'm cleansed?

It means I want to come. Where are we going?

You tell me. She followed the track, devoid of emotion and enthusiasm.

Want to go back to the creek? We could lunch there

Do we have to? Is there a different spot? The farm track forked. She took the less-used road and drove in silence while

El Shaddai

her mind grappled with the fact He'd avoided the question about cleansing her. How could she trust the Bible if God Himself was side-stepping it?

When the track dipped to cross the tiny creek on a pebble causeway, she heard God chuckle. So, He still led her. She stilled the quad beside the water. On a whim, she lifted the bike seat. A well-worn blanket waited for her. Spreading it on the ground, she sat to eat her creamed rice and preserved apricots, packed by Cheng. Satisfied, she slept.

Her hands were dirty. Stained. It didn't matter how many times she scrubbed them. They were still dirty. She went for a manicure, but the technician refused to treat her hands. She went to the doctor, but he shook his head and said they'd always be the same. She soaked them in bleach. They peeled, but the new skin was still stained and dirty. She ran down endless streets, trying to hide her hands, but people pointed at her and mocked her.

Exhausted she crested a hill and threw herself into a pool of blood below a Cross. Looking up, she saw Jesus. Gentle eyes met hers. 'You are cleansed.'

She woke, drenched with sweat and gasping for air. The creek gurgled at her feet. All was still and calm, except for her heart rate. It was only a dream. She looked at the clouds moving above her. What did it mean? Holding up her hands, she turned them over and back. Her nails were chipped and worn and her hands rough, but they were pink and clean. *But, Lord. These hands killed a man.*

Yes. But I forgave you, remember

Y... Yes. Milly closed her eyes to think. God seemed to be saying He'd forgiven her but hadn't cleansed her. She didn't feel cleansed. In the dream she was covered in His blood. She shuddered at the thought, but basked in the sweetness of His pronouncement of cleansing. She pushed herself to her knees. *Lord, I come to You. I confess I killed Pete. Please wash me in Your blood so I may be clean.*

She waited. Or was He waiting? *God?*

Anything else?

I confess my anger and unforgiveness towards Caro.

And

I've been impatient with the kids, short with Ky.

And

I get cross with You.

I love you, beautiful one

So... am I cleansed?

Do you feel cleansed?

Slipping from her knees, she considered the question. *No. Yet Your word promises it and the dream said it.*

I can't cleanse unless you bring it to Me. It's called confession

I've brought it, Lord, brought it all.

All except the big one

The big one?

You won't talk about the big one, the one that eats you up inside. Bring it to the light, Milly

She curled into a ball. *It's not my sin, God. It's his sin. I carry the dirt... and his baby. I can never be clean again. I've tried and tried.* Her sobs shook her frame.

He waited. When she calmed, she could hear His still voice again.

Cast everything upon Me

She jumped to her feet and screamed. 'God. He violated me. His filth courses through my body. He forced himself on me again and again. He nailed me to the ground. I carry a hole in my being to prove it.' Hot tears from deep in her belly erupted and flooded the ground. She felt like the woman brought to Jesus, the woman caught in adultery. 'I'm an adulteress. Lord. I'm unclean.'

Lift your face to Me

I can't, Lord. How could she lift her eyes? The shame invaded her. She wanted to run and hide. An unseen finger pushed under her chin and lifted her head to the sky.

Open your eyes, Milly. Let Me look into your eyes. Please

He pleaded with her. God pleading with her? But still, it was hard. To open her eyes was like opening her soul. He would see everything.

C'mon, Milly. You can do it

She forced her eyes open wide. Light flooded her, from the top of her head to the end of her toes. In an instant. Light crept into every dark corner and hidden crevice. The black rushed out. Yes, she felt clean. Then she glimpsed His hands and saw a hole. Two holes. He too was nailed.

For you, My Milly. I did it for you

Thank You, my God.

I love you, My Milly

Her tears dried. She lifted her clean hands and danced with Him by the running stream, under a cloud-streaked sky. He didn't speak again until she headed home on the quad.

You will have a son. His name will be Joshua

But God... He is the son of a devil.

I created him for My good purposes

Chapter 13

MILLY SPREAD A BLANKET over a log that formed a garden edge. Leaning back, she watched the house darken as Ky turned off the lights.

Thank You, Lord, for the power. But it would have been good a month ago.

You didn't ask Me then

Milly sighed. Worried about the cooler nights, she'd asked God for a heater. The next day, in the shed, she eyed the generator. Maybe, just maybe, it was the answer. With Cheng's help, a bit of oil and a tank of petrol, it burst into life. It took all her strength to crank the handle but when she got it going, the whole house lit up. Once the batteries were charged, Cheng demonstrated the electric start. Life changed that day, but lights had stolen the quiet, dark evenings.

Ky carried a tray with two mugs and a single candle across the grass and sank down on the rug with a long, contented sigh. 'I've missed this: our chats around the fire, the deep blue of the sky, God close enough to feel. Those months in the hut were hard, but there were precious moments.'

'Yes, but mostly it was hard, Ky. I'm thankful there's a light switch and a comfy bed just over there.'

'True. But we learned so much. The important became paramount and the unimportant seemed ridiculous. What a precious revelation.'

Milly rolled Ky's comment around her mind. So much she had considered important had been relegated to the 'so what?' basket. Things previously taken for granted had pushed to the front. 'Yes. Food and shelter became critical.'

'And things that used to consume our thinking became trivial. Once we worried if our kids didn't have the latest fashion. Now we know naked is beautiful. We learned to rely on each other for survival.' Ky leaned in to give Milly a hug. 'My kids and I owe our lives to you, my precious friend.'

'It's worked both ways. We've each helped the other. I wouldn't have made it without your prayers, Ky. We've learned to use our own strengths and trust each other in theirs.'

'You found this place, Milly. And somehow you got me here, just in time. Another day and I think I'd have died.'

'You can thank Bobby and God. I don't know how I managed to get you here. It was God's strength... and His insistence.'

Empty mugs discarded, they watched the stars, enjoying the deep quiet, lost in thought. 'I've never thanked you Milly for...' Ky's voice trailed off.

The silence stretched until Milly broke it. 'You've just been thanking me.'

'Yes... You rescued me and my kids from more... much more than a tidal wave. You've given us life and hope.' Ky snapped a twig in half. Then in half again and threw the pieces on the grass. Her fists clenched in a knot. 'The morning of the earthquake was bad at our house, really bad. I feared for Johnno. Mal was so cruel to him. I'd learned to live with the torment, but I didn't want to let him abuse my kids. So... so... I asked God to rescue us, to remove us or get rid of Mal.'

'Is that why you don't talk about Mal much?'

'And why I didn't want to leave the hut.'

'And why you stopped eating?'

'I don't know. Maybe. The less I ate the longer we could stay, I guess. And I don't mind if we never leave here.' Ky rolled over and opened her fists one finger at a time. 'Enough about Mal. How long have we been here, Milly?'

'Two months or so. I marked an old calendar I found in my room.'

'How long since the earthquake?'

'I'm not sure. Six months? It was spring and now it feels close to winter. It's hard to figure how long we were in the hut and we left in such a hurry I didn't count your marks on the wall.'

'Well, your morning sickness stopped before we moved. Do you know when the baby is due?'

'Pretty much. I tried to mark it on the calendar. I reckon I'm over six months and he's wriggling plenty. He'll be born in the winter. Thank God there are plenty of rugs to keep him warm. I worry about clothes for him. I worry about clothes for all the children now it's getting colder.' Under the blanket, she rubbed her hands down her oversize pyjamas. 'And I'm thankful for a man I've never met who left clothes big enough to cover my expanding belly.'

Ky chuckled. 'And I'm thankful we found a few dresses in this house for me. One of them will fit you after the baby's born, Milly.'

'There's still storage boxes we haven't explored...'

'Maybe Caroline will bring us clothes for the children, but she doesn't know about the baby, does she?'

'Caroline. Really, Ky, she's gone.'

'She'll return for Bea. I'm sure of it. She loves her.'

'Loved her enough to abandon her! Bea won't even know her if, I repeat, if she returns.'

Ky's voice broke. 'Don't be so harsh, Milly. We don't even know if she's alive. What if she drove into some hole like Dead Man's Gully?'

'More likely fallen into someone's bed, Ky, and she took the only car with her. Not that I want to go anywhere. I could hide here forever if Dan would join me. If anyone but him drove up the road, I'd have to face real life. If you're happy minding Bea, I don't mind if she never comes back.'

'Wasn't Bea cute today? She's trying so hard to walk.' Ky's pride was audible.

Milly took the hint and left Caroline out of the conversation. They always fought when they talked about her. 'Ky, when's Bea's birthday? It's time for a party. We've missed several birthdays. Hoey would be six now and Lily must be close to three.'

'A party. A first birthday party with a candle and all. Let's do it, Milly. What fun!'

Lying together, cocooned in blankets, they talked late into the night. Milly must have dozed. She woke with a start. 'Ky. Can you hear that noise?' It sounded like a motor, a soft purring engine. Pins and needles raced up her spine.

Ky sat up. 'Is it the quad?'

'No. Wrong type of motor.'

El Shaddai

'One of the tractors?'

'No. Could be the truck, but it's not coming from the shed. It sounds as though it's coming from the road.'

They stood and crept across the yard, hiding in the dark shadows of the trees. Milly's heart pounded as she listened to the soft throb of the engine. 'It's climbing the hill. It'll be here any minute. Let's get the stuff in the house. No lights, Ky. Not even a candle.' Inside, Milly shoved her heart-pounding fear aside and grabbed a coat from her room. She pulled it on over her pyjamas.

'Ky. Bolt the door behind me. Don't open unless I knock like this.' She rapped her shaky fingers on the table.

'Milly, don't go. Stay here.'

'Ky, you take this gun and guard the kids.' Grabbing the bigger gun and a handful of bullets she slipped out the door. 'If it's a man, he's dead.' She ran through the orchard, heart belting against her chest wall.

The unlit vehicle stopped outside the machinery shed. Staying under cover, she crept through the shed, moving in the direction of the back door. Through a crack she watched a tall man walking towards Cheng's hut.

Milly dug into her pocket. Hands shaking, she loaded a bullet in the rifle. She hadn't used one since killing the kangaroo but figured she could frighten the intruder. She rested the repulsive weapon on the protruding door lock and pointed it at Cheng's roof.

The man leapt onto the landing of the hut. 'Cheng.'

She strained her eyes. Palms sweating, her finger moved to the trigger.

He banged the door and rattled the door knob. 'Cheng! Wake up. Let me in.'

The soft glow of a candle lit the hut. 'I'm coming.' The door opened a crack. 'Jamie.' It opened wide. 'What you wanting at this hour of the night?'

'Grub and a cuppa for a start.' He pushed through the door and pushed it shut behind him.

Milly lowered the rifle. She'd heard or seen the name Jamie somewhere. At least there was someone else alive on the earth, but why sneak in at midnight? Without thinking she slipped through the door and, staying in the deep shadows of the shed, she crept towards the car. *God, are You coming?*

Wouldn't miss it

Why do You always sound as if everything is an adventure? Leaving the shadows, she crouched low and, circling to the back of the hut, she huddled down under an open window.

'I'm thinking I'll drive into the dead country. He won't follow there.' The deep male voice sent a shiver down her spine.

'Dead country?' Cheng rattled plates. 'What is *dead* country?'

'Power station blew up. Radiation killed everything in the land.'

Milly shuddered, thinking of Bobby.

'Chicken stew. Good man. Knew you wouldn't fail your favourite.'

'Why you sneak in?

'Don't want to wake Dad.'

She glanced down at her attire, embarrassed. *Am I wearing his father's pyjamas?*

'Think I'll drop in on Zach. You seen him lately?'

'Nuh, nuh.'

El Shaddai

'Since when?'

'Long time.'

'Seen him after the big quake?' There was a moment's silence.

'What wake, Jamie?'

'No, Cheng, quake. The day the ground shook and moved.'

'Shi, Shi. Very scary.'

'Have you seen my brother since then?'

'Nuh. Long time. Strange.'

'Probably taken out to sea in the wave. Lucky I wasn't in Wamberoo when the quake hit.'

'Cup of tea, Jamie?'

'Thanks, Cheng. I'll leave as soon as you've packed some grub for me. I'll fill the car while you get it.' His chair scraped the floor.

Move

Milly ran like a hare past the car and back to the shadows of the shed. She pressed herself against the wall as the door opened.

This way

She eased herself around the corner. Her gun clanged against the downpipe. She froze. Heavy footsteps strode towards the shed. 'Who's there?'

In here

She ducked in behind a couple of empty drums.

'Cheng.' Jamie bellowed from the side of the shed. 'Who's here?'

'Here?'

'There's a noise in the shed. I heard somebody.'

'You nervy.' Cheng chuckled. 'Since when is Jamie frightened of possum in shed?'

The boots receded. She heard the car door slam.

'Shhh, Jamie. You're being quiet, remember.' The car crept towards the tank mounted on a tall metal stand. The boys loved to climb it in the daylight. Milly was relieved they were tucked up in bed. She watched until Jamie waved to Cheng and the car crept along the drive.

Back home, she tapped on the back door. The lock belted back and Ky threw it open. 'Milly. I've been worried sick.'

'He's gone now.' She replaced the rifle and emptied the bullets into their box.

'He? Who?'

'Jamie.' She paused. 'I think I'm wearing his father's pyjamas.'

Next morning, Cheng arrived, carrying fresh milk.

Milly waved him to a chair. 'Please sit down and have a cuppa with us.'

'Busy, Ma'am. Need to get veggies.'

'They can wait, Cheng. I want to thank you for protecting us last night.'

The colour drained from his face. 'What do you mean?'

'We heard the car last night. I'm sorry, Cheng, but I listened at your window.'

His eyes opened wide. 'You were in the shed?'

'Yes. And I let the rifle hit the downpipe.'

'You had a rifle?'

Milly grinned at him.

'It was only Jamie. He's okay. Not like Zach.' He shuddered. 'Cheng hopes Zach never come back, but you still must bolt door, okay?'

'Who are they, Cheng?'

Cheng sat on the offered chair, his hands clamped together. 'Boss's sons. Two of them.'

'There's more?'

'There was.' He dropped his head. 'Sad story.'

Ky leaned forward. 'Please tell us, Cheng. Someone has supplied us with a home and we want to know who to thank.'

'It's your home now.' He stood and bowed. 'Cheng at your service.'

Ky waved him back to his chair. 'How can it be our home? It belongs to your boss.'

'Boss'll never come back. He died... in Dead Man's Gully. Earth opened up and swallowed him. No boys home to tell. I didn't know what to do. I asked God. He said he'll send a new boss. But instead… He send two women.' His eyes twinkled. 'God said new boss's name is "Man". But I'm happy you came. You're good bosses.'

Milly patted his clasped hands. 'Where's the boss's wife? What about other children? Won't Jamie want to live here?'

Ky poured three mugs of tea. 'Please tell us the whole story, Cheng.' She passed one mug to him. 'How long have you been here?'

'I was born here. My father came from China. He worked for Alice's daddy as a gardener. We were kids together, Alice and I, the two of us.'

Ky touched his arm. 'Wait a minute. Who is Alice?'

'Ah, Alice.' His eyes brightened. 'Most beautiful girl. But she married Boss. He was okay, I guess, but nasty in the end.' He shuddered. 'They lived away for some years. Told me I needed to get out into the world. But why? This my world. She was my girl. I never wanted to marry anyone else so, when dad died, I become the gardener.' He paused. 'When Alice's daddy died, she came back to watch the place and care for her mum. Boss came with her. He ran the farm. Good farmer... not good father.'

'Father?' Ky leaned forwards on the table. 'Jamie and Zach's father?'

'Shi, shi. Alice had four babies. Zach first—strong, chubby baby. Boss thought he was the best baby in the world. Baby rode horse before he walk. Even before William was born, we knew Zach would take over the farm.'

'William?'

'William. Delicate baby. Named after Alice's daddy. Boss didn't like him because he wasn't strong. He a keen little gardener, and good with chickens. Ah, I loved that boy. Boss busy with Zach, Alice had baby Jamie, so I looked after William... lots.' Cheng wiped away a stray tear. 'They were good days. Boss worked hard with sheep and cattle. He bred good stock. He put cows in the big shows, won trophies. Everyone thought he was a clever farmer. But Alice was unhappy. Big man around town, bad man around home.' The long ponytail shook from side to side. 'Alice was a good mumma. Boys loved her. She taught them about God, but it made Boss angry. He shouted lots, lots. But he told me you have to let her know who's boss. Women must do as told. Anyway, years later, Alice had baby girl, Hannah Rose. Boss loved her... treated her like little princess. Boys doted on her. Tragic. Real tragic.'

Cheng sat in silence for some time. In Milly's bedroom hung a picture of a beautiful, dark-haired little girl. It reminded her of Lily. She retrieved it to show Cheng. 'Hannah Rose?'

El Shaddai

His eyes watered. 'Shi, shi. She was about three there. When she turned four, Boss took her to a show with the cows. Alice didn't want to let her go. William begged to go. There was a big fight. Boss left in truck with both William and Hannah. We never saw her again.' He wiped a tear away. 'Poor Alice. Broke her heart. Poor William. Boss blamed William, but wasn't his fault. Boss never went to show with cows again. No more ribbons. People stopped coming. He didn't like people any more. Zach grew up angry—William sad. Jamie, he tried to stay out of trouble, keep the peace. Zach and Will were always fighting. One day the boss took the boys shooting. William shot—dead.' Cheng sat in silence for a long time.

Milly touched his arm. 'I'm sorry, Cheng. How awful!'

'Boss came home. He was angry, furious. Jamie ran home, yelling for help, but too late. Zach said Will's gun went off while he was climbing through a fence. Jamie didn't see anything… he said. Police come. They say it was an accident.'

'But you don't think so?'

'Zach and Will fight, I reckon. Shot went through heart… close range. Didn't look like accident to me. Boss made up stories for police. Nobody believed it. Boss sent Zach away. My poor Alice!' Cheng shook his head and pushed his chair back. 'I need to garden. Many mouths to feed and one more coming.' He bowed at Milly's swelling belly. 'Cheng is happy to have children here and soon a baby.' The door clicked behind him.

Ky gathered the mugs. 'How sad! I wonder why Jamie hasn't been here. What happened to Alice? And where's Zach?'

'Cheng thinks Zach perished in the earthquake.'

'Why does he think we own the place, Milly?'

Milly threw up her hands. 'He talks to the same God. And God told me He was giving us this place. He's told me a few times. I don't understand, but I'm grateful for it right now.'

'Milly, we're squatters. Any day Jamie or Zach could walk in and order us out. We don't have a lease or even an invitation.'

'Yes. That's our legal position. However, according to God, we own it. I'm trusting Him to work the rest out.'

Ky raised her eyebrows. 'I'm not sure if that's trust or naïvety.'

'I'm living one day at a time, Ky. If I look too far ahead, I panic.' Her hand pushed a little foot poking into her ribs. 'How good are you at delivering babies?'

Ky backed away. 'No, Milly. You know my story. Two caesareans. I've never even seen a baby born. We need a doctor.'

'How? I've wondered about trying to get to a town. Do I go in the truck and leave you here alone with five kids? Or I take my kids and leave you behind? Or we all pile into the truck and go? We have no money so no way of getting petrol once the tank is empty, unless my credit card still works.' Ky sighed. 'Jamie must have come from somewhere. What's down the track?'

'I've been down there on the quad. It leads to a road. I check occasionally but I've never seen a tyre mark on it. There's a letterbox but no evidence of a mailman. I think the road goes Wamberoo and that means it's cut at Dead Man's Gully by the earthquake. There could be landslides or gaping holes further west.'

'But Jamie got through.'

'Yes. That does change my thinking.'

'You think the road may be open?'

El Shaddai

'Open enough to worry him. He's concerned someone might follow him. I wonder if he's running from the police.'

'I'd welcome the police.' Ky grinned.

Milly shivered. *What if they come looking for Pete? What if they arrested us for unlawful entry? What if they told me Dan's dead?* Her whole body shuddered. No, she wasn't ready to re-enter society.

'I wish I'd bought my mobile phone from the hut.' Ky interrupted Milly's thoughts. 'I've been thinking about going back to get it and my Bible. And the rough journal I wrote in.'

'Go back to the hut? How, Ky?'

'Walk.' She chuckled. 'I can walk now, you know. You went from here and back in a day and carried me half the way. I must be able to do it by myself.'

Let Ky go? The thought terrified her. 'But could you pull yourself into the cave?' She shuddered. 'Then what about the narrow track along the precipice?'

'What?'

'The track where Caro pulled you forwards and I pushed from behind. You had your eyes shut.'

Ky gasped. 'Did that really happen? I thought I dreamt it. Did we go past dead Pete?'

'Right beside him.' Milly nodded. 'Still want to go back?'

'Isn't there another way?'

'Do you think I would have gone through the cave if I knew of another?'

'Milly, how did you make yourself go back in there?'

'God, Caro and six hungry mouths behind me. I thank God every day for leading me here.' A thought bubbled to the surface from deep inside Milly's mind. She pushed it aside but it burst through with sudden clarity. 'Ky. If Pete hadn't forced me into his cave, I'd never have found the way. God used him to show me the path. Yuk.' She shuddered. 'I don't think I will ever fathom God's ways.'

As she left the kitchen, she remembered Ky's handbag. She'd grabbed it from the car, but she knew she hadn't carried it through the cave and down the hill. What had happened to it? *God, Ky would like her Bible. I think it would have been in her handbag.*

A week later, Milly gathered her courage and they loaded all the children in the truck. The two boys sat on the tray, leaning on the cab behind Milly. The three little girls screamed with excitement as Milly drove and Ky tried to contain them. They stopped at the letterbox. Jamie's tyre tracks came in from the left but turned right as he departed. Milly shuddered. He'd turned towards Dead Man's Gully.

The boys raced up and down the road, yelling and pretending to shoot each other. 'Boys.' Ky grabbed Johnno as he raced past. 'How many times must I tell you not to play with guns?' She held out her hand. Johnno handed her the flat bit of timber he'd been pointing at Hoey. He ran off, shooting Hoey with his finger.

Milly couldn't stop the chuckle. 'Boys! Don't you love them?'

'Sometimes they drive me crazy.' Ky turned over the board. 'It's an old sign.'

Milly peered over her shoulder. *'El Shaddai!'* Same as Dan's red mug. 'Do you think it is the name of the property, Ky?'

'And red lettering to match the roof.'

Milly's memory swung back to her old kitchen. Dan was speaking. 'God Almighty, *El Shaddai*, is still in control, Honey. We can trust Him.'

Ky looked up from the sign. 'What did you say, Milly?'

'Nothing, Ky. Let's load the kids and drive that way.' She pointed to the left with the *El Shaddai* sign, then dropped it at her feet in the truck. They chugged west, driving slowly to keep the boys safe.

They passed another letterbox. Ky jumped out to inspect it. It had been taken over by spiders. Further on, a little-used track forked to the south. 'Can't see any wheel marks.' Ky slammed the door after her inspection. 'The gravel is solid. I'm not sure a car would leave any tracks. Should we check?'

Milly's heart fluttered. The thought of driving up to a stranger's house sent shards of fear through her body. 'I don't think there'll be anyone there. It doesn't look as though the road's been used for a long time. Let's keep going.'

A little further, they rounded a bend. Milly braked hard. A pile of boulders, rock and dirt blocked the road. They unloaded the kids and inspected the blockage. The boys climbed the rocks like mountain goats. A long, open scar in the hill bore testimony to the savagery of the earthquake. They picked their way over the rubble until they could see the road emerging from the other side.

Ky shaded her eyes from the dropping sun. 'There's no sign of tracks on the other side. No one's come this far and turned around.'

'Makes you wonder if there are more landslides further down. Well, I guess we have our answer. No way of finding a doctor now.' Milly whistled the children and led the way back to the truck. 'Luckily I birth easily, Ky.'

Ky shuddered. 'I don't like it, Milly. I'm going to pray God does something.'

They turned and headed home.

The next morning, Ky rushed into the kitchen. 'Milly, look.' She held up her handbag. 'I found it pushed right back under the bed.'

'Is your Bible there?'

'Yes, and my notebook and phone.' She turned and rushed out of the room.

I do answer prayer, Milly. Be still

El Shaddai

Chapter 14

CONTRACTIONS WOKE HER in the middle of the night. *It's too early, God. It's not my time.*

⁓ Be still ⁓

Not a time to be still, God. Obviously, You've never given birth.

⁓ Doesn't creation count? ⁓

You birthed creation? A gripping contraction distracted her. As it faded, she climbed from the bed and wrapped a blanket around her shoulders. In the kitchen, she shut the door and flicked on the light. It shone a pale yellow. Fading embers glowed in the stove. Shivering, she added kindling to the coals, praying it would flare and warm the kitchen. Leaning on the kitchen table, she breathed through the next contraction. *They seem close, Lord. Is my baby ready?*

⁓ Be still ⁓

Milly stopped pacing. *Be still. Why do You say that at the most ridiculous times?*

⁓ Be still in your soul. Calm your worries and fears, your anxiety and questions ⁓

Not my body?

~ Your body will move of its own accord. When I created you, I programmed the birthing process in you. Allow your body to do its work. Focus your mind on Me ~

Milly added a log to the fire and went to the laundry for more chopped wood. After the next contraction, she collected some towels and the 'birthing bundle' Ky had helped prepare. Back in the kitchen she straddled a chair through the next wave of pain.

She yearned for Dan, yet… *he's not the father.* When Dan found her, *if* Dan found her, the evidence of her shame would be in her arms. Would he ever love her again?

Maybe she'd birth a monster. This baby she was forcing into the world was fathered by a monster. But Joshua didn't feel like a monster—as he'd grown within her, so had her love for him.

~ Be still ~

Her eyes fell on Ky's Bible. How excited they were when she found it.

~ Ask and you shall receive ~

Yes, God. You answered that prayer.

~ And ~

Milly opened the Bible at the beginning, but struggled to concentrate. Skimming the page, her eyes fell on 'greatly increase your pain when you give birth.' She blinked. *Increase my pain?*

~ I didn't create you to suffer in childbirth ~

Well, why did You increase it? She must look a little closer. The contractions were getting strong. She gasped and bit hard on a rolled towel.

El Shaddai

Returning to the passage, she read the previous verses about the disobedience of Adam and Eve.

The consequence of man's decision to choose knowledge instead of relationship with Me

I thought mankind sinned?

That's what I said

The next contraction began building. She bit down again, longing for the gas she'd used when she birthed Hoey and Lily. In a flash, she understood. This extreme pain is because of Adam and Eve's disobedience. But Jesus crushed the enemy. The Devil was defeated on the cross. *Why does this consequence remain when others don't? I'm saved from hell. I'm no longer banished from Your presence, Lord.*

And you don't have to suffer this pain, either

What? It sure feels as though I am. As the next contraction began, she remembered Ky's excitement when her handbag came to light. She had asked. *God,* she gasped, *You died to take the pain. Please take it.* Grabbing the back of a chair she lowered herself to ease the pressure. She felt it go through her body, doing its work to open her so this baby could come forth. But the searing pain wasn't as severe. *Wow, God.*

Well done. You are listening well, My lovely

She walked and straddled the chair and walked again, flicking through the Bible on the table. Contractions came and went. The more she claimed His promise and asked for help, the easier it became. The pressure through her body continued, but the intense pain wasn't there. In the middle of a contraction, her body started to push. She panicked. Nothing was ready. She needed Ky, and a bed.

Be still
Be still
Be still

There was a warning edge to the interior Voice.

Her eyes flew to the Bible. *'They crouch down and bring forth their young.'* The next contraction came upon on her and advanced with intensity. She pulled the towels and the kit to the floor and crouched. Her body responded. She caught her tiny son in her hands as he rushed into the world.

When Ky walked in, Joshua, like Jesus, lay wrapped in bits of worn-out sheet. Milly still sat on towels on the floor. The placenta lay to one side and a fluid mess surrounded her. 'Ky, look. He's so beautiful.'

'Milly. Oh, Milly. Are you okay? Why didn't you wake me? Let me clean you up. Goodness, he is beautiful, and so small.'

Together they laughed in the sheer joy of birth.

That, My child, is how I felt at the birth of the world. I saw it and it was good, very good

Thirty days later, Cheng bustled around the kitchen. He had declared it a feast day. The children danced with excitement. The boys had been whispering with him all morning and were busy with secrets they refused to share with Milly. Lily, fascinated, watched the baby. Often, she lay on her tummy and stared in awe. 'He is so special, Mummy. Can we keep him?'

'Yes, darling.'

'Forever?'

El Shaddai

'Until he is a man.'

Her eyes opened wide. 'Will he be a man?'

'Yes, and a big man, I think. And you will be a beautiful lady one day.'

'I bigger than him.' She cocked her head on one side. 'He a baby. I a girl.' She turned her attention back to the object of interest. 'Mummy. He makes funny faces.'

'Yes, and nasty smells.' Once again, she longed for disposable nappies. Babies were so much easier with modern conveniences. *Sorry, God. I don't mean to be ungrateful. It's just the edge pieces of old flannelette sheets aren't very absorbent.*

Have you asked?

For disposable nappies?

For your heart's desire

Seriously?

Ask, according to your faith

That's the catch.

He chuckled. *Milly, you are such a delight to Me. One glance of your eyes and I'm undone*

Stop talking nonsense. She couldn't help herself. She laughed out loud.

'He pooped, Mummy. It's not funny.'

She kissed Lily's dark curls. 'Do you think we could ask God for better nappies?'

Her serious eyes met Milly's. 'Yes... and better clothes.'

The little girl squeezed her eyes tight. 'God. We need softer nappies for Josh. And he needs proper clothes and little socks for his feet. Thank You, God. Amen.'

And a little child shall lead them

She picked up her smelly baby. *You want to change this one, Father?*

I'll go with you if you like

She dealt with the mess in the bathroom, surrounded by a cloud of floral perfume.

⁂

Ky pushed her empty plate away. 'What a wonderful meal. Thank you, Cheng.'

'Yes, delicious.' Milly held Josh close, glad of the warmth from the kitchen fire. 'Tell us why the feast was held today, Cheng.'

'My mother taught me. Always celebrate baby on day thirty. Always with red eggs.' He waved to the basket of eggs which he had boiled in beetroot juice. 'Even number means it's a boy. It speaks of good life and marriage one day.' He turned and nodded to Hoey. 'And there must be presents.'

Hoey ran to the pantry followed by the other children. Bea stayed curled on Ky's lap, her thumb filling her mouth.

After a lot of whispering the children returned, each carrying a gift. Bethie held out two chubby hands, each one holding an ear of corn. Lily followed with a bouquet of flowers. The boys each offered crudely wrapped parcels, one small and one large.

Milly kissed each of her precious children, blinking to clear her eyes. 'Corn, Bethie, how wonderful. And, Lily, I love the flowers. Hoey, if you can reach the vase in the pantry we can put them in water straight away.'

Hoey ran to the pantry, returning with the vase half-full of water. 'Mummy, can you open our presents, now?'

El Shaddai

'Bea and I have one too.' Ky pulled a little box from her pocket.

'But, where? How?'

Cheng rose from the table and bowed. He returned from the pantry with an old shoebox tied with a piece of blue ribbon. 'Cheng welcomes baby Joshua. May he live a long and prosperous life.' With two hands, he slipped the box in front of Milly.

Milly's heart faltered. Both laughter and tears caught in her throat.

'You can open them now. Start with youngest.'

She swallowed. 'Can Lily help me?' Her daughter's fingers were hovering over the string tying the brown paper.

At Cheng's nod, Lily ripped at the paper. 'Mummy! Look. God did it.' She pulled out a pair of blue baby socks.

'Th... thank you, Johnno.' Wiping her eyes, she looked at Cheng. 'How?'

You've seen nothing yet

Cheng bowed his head. 'More to open.'

Lily ripped the string from the next one. Hoey waited, fidgeting, his anxious eyes on his mother.

'Only towels.' Lily wrinkled her nose and looked for the next parcel to open. Milly grabbed the parcel. 'Lily. They are nappies for Joshua. Towelling nappies. Hoey, how wonderful!'

His worried frown cleared and he rushed to his mother for a big hug. 'Cheng helped me, Mummy.'

Milly caught Cheng's eye across the table. His head nodded up and down. 'More gifts yet.'

A delicate gold ring with a single red stone sparkled from Ky's little box.

'But how, Ky?'

'I found it at the back of a drawer in my room. I'm guessing it's okay for you to wear it.'

Cheng jumped up. 'Red! Perfect gift for new baby.' He peered at it, turning it from side to side. 'My mumma's ring. It belonged to Alice, but went missing. Boss never liked it.'

Milly held it out to Cheng. 'It's yours, Cheng.' He accepted it with tears running down his face. He stood and passed the shoe box to Ky. 'You give this gift... please.'

Ky hesitated. With an uncertain grin and worried eyes, she passed the box to Milly. 'I do hope you like it.'

Milly chuckled and undid the string. She lifted the lid. Her heart leapt into her throat. Her hands covered her mouth. She looked in wonder at a knitted layette. Yellowed with age it boasted embroidered pink rosebuds. Lifting the bonnet, she found a little jacket, some knitted leggings, singlets and more socks. She tried to swallow the lump in her throat to speak, but instead she held her baby and cried.

Lily clapped her little hands. 'God did it.'

'How, Cheng? How? Ky and I looked everywhere, but we didn't find any baby clothes.'

'God did it.' Cheng bowed towards Joshua. 'I felt so sad that such an important baby has no clothes. So… I asked God for baby clothes. Yesterday, I went to boss's storeroom looking for seeds for the garden. Lots of boxes in there. It's not my business so I never touch them. Yesterday one caught my eye. I felt bad but I looked and... wonder... I found baby clothes. There's more in the big box in pantry, Ma'am.'

He put up his hand to stop Ky who rushed to explore. 'Wait. I also asked God for a gift, a special gift for a special

El Shaddai

occasion.' His voice broke and he paused, gripping the edge of the table. 'You see… fathers give their daughter a special gift when she gives him a grandbaby. Red gift, like red eggs.' He stood and bowed before Milly. 'As a sign of my high esteem, I present this ring to you, my beautiful daughter.' Tears streamed down his face. 'My grandfather gave this ring to my mother when I was born. My mother gave it to Alice when Zach was born. Now I give it to you, to celebrate birth of Joshua.' He bowed and went to step back, but Milly threw her right arm around his neck and pulled him close.

She kissed him on the cheeks, first the left, the right and the left again. 'Thank you, Father, from the bottom of my heart. I will wear this ring with pride.'

He stood, wiping tears from his beaming face.

Hoey pulled at Milly's arm. 'Mum, Mum. I can hear a car. Maybe Dad's coming.'

'Shush. Listen.' Milly's stomach contracted. *It can't be Dan, can it?*

Silence fell like a blanket. A vehicle was approaching. 'You stay here.' Cheng moved faster than Milly had ever seen him move before. 'Cheng will check.'

Ky jumped up. 'Milly. There must be other people. Maybe shops and phones. I'll go and ask.'

'Wait, Ky. What if there is danger?'

'This car isn't sneaking in, Milly.' With a little skip she followed Cheng. The boys jumped up to follow.

'Boys.' Milly winced at the sound of her own voice. The boys stopped in their tracks.

'But I wanna go with Mummy.' Johnno's clenched his little fist.

'Come with me.' She led them all into the sitting room and pulled back the curtains. They watched as a dusty four-wheel drive navigated the track leading to the shed. Before it went out of view, Milly thought she saw long blonde hair. *Caroline?* A deep unease unsettled her being. God.

I'm here, as usual

What now?

Follow Me

'Boys, go and clear the table. We might have visitors. Lily, you can help. Bethie, you stay here and watch Bea.' Holding her sleeping baby tight, Milly kissed him. In Ky's room she placed him on Bea's little bed on the floor. 'Sleep, Bubba. Sleep quiet.' Pulling the door behind her, she joined the children in the kitchen.

The table was soon cleared into the sink. All evidence of presents and party was stored in her bedroom. Lily was putting the flowers in the middle of the table when they heard voices. Ky burst through the door. 'Milly, look who's here!' She flung her hand towards the door. 'Caro!'

Caroline smiled, but her eyes were uneasy as they scanned the room. Her hair, once again bleached blond flowed in shiny waves over her clean t-shirt and snug new jeans. 'Milly.' Leaning forward, Caroline kissed her on the cheek. 'It's lovely to see you.'

Ky's eyes danced. 'I told you she'd come. She's brought a friend.'

Caroline beckoned a tall solid man through the door. Dark eyes surveyed Milly's. Her stomach turned. Visions of a big smelly man with similar dark eyes flashed through her mind.

Steady. Be still

El Shaddai

'George, this is Milly.' Caroline turned to Milly. 'I'd like you to meet George. I told you I'd bring a man to help.'

His hand swallowed hers, his stature towering over her. 'It's good to meet you, Milly.'

'Come and sit. Would you like a cup of tea?'

Throwing his felt, wide-brimmed hat on the floor near the door, he grabbed a chair and turned it around. The room seemed to shrink, dwarfed by his size. His ironed, monogrammed khakis screamed class. He straddled the chair and met Milly's eye. 'Coffee would be great, thanks.'

Why did she feel as if he was challenging her… as if she was in a battle she didn't understand? 'Sorry. We have tea or I can offer you some of Cheng's herbal brew.' Her hands shook as they held the kettle under the tap and put it on the heat. *It's just a man, Milly. Not all men are like Pete… even if their eyes make me fear a trap.*

You are Mine, Milly

Cheng stood in the doorway and caught Milly's eye. He shook his head from side to side. *Is there a warning in his eyes?* He too was nervous.

'Caro!' Hoey and Johnno raced through the door and threw their arms around her.

'Hello, boys.' She disentangled their arms, and ruffled their hair. 'Look how tall you're both getting! Come help me find some coffee in the car.'

As they left, Bethie and Bea ran in giggling, followed by Ky and Lily. In Bethie's rush, she tripped Bea. Her wail as she fell face down reverberated in the closed room. George winced and followed Caro out the back door. Cheng moved to the stove and removed the singing kettle. 'Not good, Milly.'

'Who is he, Cheng?'

'Boss's nephew. Don't trust him.'

Lily pulled at Milly's arm. 'Where's Caro? Ky said she was here.'

Milly picked up Bethie and took Lily's hand. 'They've gone to the car. Let's go and find them.' Ky followed, still cuddling Bea.

Milly glanced up just in time to see George disappear into the shed. The girls ran towards Caroline, screaming and giggling, except for Bea, snuggled into Ky's shoulder. Caroline leaned into Ky's ear and whispered. Ky spun. Her eyebrows raised, red tinge in her cheeks. She lowered Bea to the ground to toddle after the other girls.

'Milly, Caro says we're not to let George know Bea is hers. But that's not right.' The red spots on Ky's cheeks deepened. Milly turned to Caroline, raised her brows and waited.

'George is wonderful. He wants me to marry him as soon as it's appropriate. He's standing to be elected as mayor soon, so needs a wife. I'm experienced in local government so I'm perfect. But Bea complicates things.'

'So just pretend she isn't yours?' Ky snorted.

'She loves you, Ky. You'd be a much better mother for her.' She held up a large bottle of instant coffee. 'Look, coffee! Come back inside and have a cup.'

Cheng sat on the bottom step, eagle eyes roaming everywhere. 'I'll mind the girls. You ladies talk.'

'What about George?' Milly walked towards the shed. 'I'll tell him coffee is ready.' She paused at the door, allowing her eyes to adjust, and calming her fears. There was no sign of the man anywhere. The storeroom door was ajar. Unusual, as

El Shaddai

Cheng was very thorough. She peered in. George wasn't there but several things had been moved. *What does he think he's doing?* She circled around the shed towards Cheng's cottage, without sighting him. *Lord, what is he up to?*

The devil prowls around

Great! Are You saying he is a devil?

Cheng's hut door was open. Surely, he hadn't left the girls and returned. But no. George was in the living area, pulling open drawers and rummaging through them.

'What do you think you are doing?' At her bellow, he spun, dropping a sheaf of papers from his hand. 'Get out of Cheng's house.' She shook with fury.

Gathering the papers up, he walked to the door, dark eyes holding hers. 'Milly. What Carrie didn't tell you is my surname. It is McLaughlin.'

'I don't care if your surname is Windsor, it doesn't give you the right to go through other people's belongings. Now put them down and get out.' She stood below him. He was bigger, but no one dared to touch Cheng. He was her hero.

He dropped the papers and glared, walking towards her like a tiger on the prowl. 'Who do you think you are? I said I'm a McLaughlin. You're a squatter... no more. I've a good mind to get the coppers out here to run you off the property. I'm the heir apparent to Mac's place. All this is mine...'

'George!' Cheng appeared behind Milly. 'You talk rubbish.'

'Face the facts, Cheng! Mac drove into the gully... dead. Zach was partying in Wamberoo the day of quake... missing, presumed dead. Jamie's at the bottom of Dead Man's Gully too... dead. Only me left, old man, so don't you dare challenge me again.' Even though he spat the words at

Cheng, he jumped down the steps and stormed off. 'Treat me with respect or you'll be gone!' He reached his truck, yelling, 'Carrie! We're leaving!'

Caro ran across the yard. 'Not yet, George. I want to stay and talk.'

'Now, Carrie!'

She stopped, her eyes challenging him over the black shiny cab of his truck. 'George.' Her voice softened as she walked around to his door. 'Honey, why don't I stay here for a few days?' One finger ran down his face. 'Milly has a new baby I haven't met yet and I've missed the kids. You're busy for the rest of the week anyway.'

His eyes swung to Milly. 'You have a baby? Where? Who?'

'In the kitchen... and it's none of your business.'

Turning, he slammed the car door and advanced. Milly winced, but it was Caroline he grabbed. He kissed her, long and rough. 'Remember, you're mine.' She tottered when he let her go. From the back seat she yanked out a bunch of shopping bags. The driver's door slammed and George roared down the road, covering them in a cloud of dust.

'A month old? But he's so tiny, Milly. Bea was never that small.' Caroline sat in the lounge and held Joshua as though he was fine glass. 'I didn't even know you were pregnant and I've not been gone that long!'

'Remember all my sickness at the hut, Caro?'

'Oh!' Her eyes lifted. 'Did you know then and not tell us?'

'You had enough to be worried about. And I wasn't sure... no pregnancy tests...'

El Shaddai

Caroline lifted the baby, kissed his dark hair and passed him to Milly. 'Can he live... being so tiny and all?'

'He's doing fine. I've been feeding him every couple of hours. The kitchen scales say he is gaining weight.'

'Coffee!' Ky stood at the door carrying a tray and sniffing the cups. 'I've never known coffee to smell so wonderful.' She put a cup beside each chair. 'Now, Caro. Start talking. You drove away early one morning...'

'The track led to a dirt road. But it was blocked with rocks. I turned back and went up the only other road. I thought I was going to have to come back without finding the shops. Anyway, the track led to a farmhouse like this one. The old farmer, Joe, told me how to get to the nearest town. When he found out I hadn't eaten, his wife cooked me breakfast. They are lovely people.'

'Hang on.' Milly lifted her eyes off her feeding baby. 'How far away are they, Caro?'

'Not far. Fifteen or twenty minutes.'

'Did you tell them about us?'

'N... not exactly.' Caro's blond mane fell over her eyes.

Milly felt her anger rising so returned her focus to the little life in her arms. He couldn't afford for her to get upset. He needed a calm mother.

'Caro, what did you tell them?' Ky put her mug down.

'The truth. I just didn't tell them there were others with me. They asked why I was driving Zach's car. I told them I'd found it abandoned, worked on it to get it started.'

Ky sighed. 'The truth, but not the whole truth. Go on.'

'Just before we were finished breakfast... can you believe it? They even had bacon... this truck roared into the yard.

Daph cooked another breakfast and George joined us. It was my lucky day! Handsome, gorgeous and heading into town. By the time we got to Blue Rock, I had a dinner date. He dropped me in the main street, at the hairdresser and promised to pick me up at five. The colour wasn't up to city standards but the cut was okay. She also did my brows and lashes, waxed my legs and bikini line. Wasn't I lucky she was having a slow day? I shopped for clothes and perfume and...'

'And what did you buy for us, Caro?' Milly stared at her. 'You didn't ask for anything, did you?'

Ky reached out and patted her arm. 'No. We didn't, Caro. So… you went for dinner?'

'Steak and pepper sauce... it was delicious. And red wine. And dancing. Oh, it was a magical night. We sat on a lounge in a dark corner and talked and ordered martinis. At closing time, he took me back to his place. I've been there ever since.'

'Why didn't you come back for Bea? Why didn't you send someone to get us? Or at least try to ring Dan or Mal?' A fire stirred in Milly's belly.

'I was going to after a few days. I needed to party for a while. We didn't leave the house for three days. George declared it was time to go to town when he ran out of condoms. He took me to the library and we discovered that my... my...' Tears ran down Caroline's cheeks. 'Mum and Dad are both dead. I collapsed. George took me to the chemist. They gave him something to help me with shock and we went back home. I spent the next days in bed... I'm not sure how long. George was wonderful. He cared for me and even went to a solicitor to find out about Dad's affairs.' She gulped.

El Shaddai

'He came home one day with roses and asked me to marry him. I'll always remember it... he's so sweet. We can't plan a wedding until after the mayoral election and he can't have anyone know I'm living with him. It would be bad publicity. So I stayed home when he went out on business or to work. I wanted to come to see you, but I didn't have a car and he was carrying my credit cards.'

'It's been over five months, Caro. I don't understand why you didn't miss Bea.'

'I did... but I only cried when he was out. He's a wonderful man. So strong and sure of himself. I'd never argue with him.'

Milly frowned. *You almost sound bewitched, Caro.*

A tap sounded at the door. Caroline shoved her clenched fist in her mouth.

'Cheng, Ma'am.'

Pulling back the bolt, Milly opened the door. Her stomach sank. Cheng stood with a bedroll over his shoulder and a bag in his hand. *Is he leaving? Has George scared him away?* 'Cheng.' She felt like dropping at his feet and begging. 'Please don't leave. We need you.'

'Milly.' Cheng put his hand on her arm. 'Cheng never leave you. I'll stay with you until God comes for me. I hope the one named "Man" is here to help before then. I asked God to send "Man". But not George. God will send a good man.' He dropped his bag and turned to bolt the door. 'Cheng will sleep here from now on. Keep guard. Good night.' He disappeared into the pantry.

A week later, Milly wandered through the sheds with Cheng, clipboard in hand, listing supplies they needed. 'This farm was very well-stocked, Cheng. Was the boss rich?'

Cheng chuckled. 'Boss never looked rich and he was never generous. But he kept plenty of fuel and food. Last year he bought lots. Said he'd had dream, scary dream. So, he prepared for anything. Like he knew disaster was coming.' He walked over to the kerosene drums, kicking them to see if there were any full ones. 'Funny. Ever heard of dream like that, Milly?'

'I had a similar dream, Cheng. I kept seeing a wall of water coming and snatching Hoey out of my arms.'

Cheng's eyes widened. 'And then tidal wave come.'

'Yes. Because of the dream, I'd driven to the mountains. If I'd stayed home, we'd have drowned. According to the news, my whole street disappeared.'

He shook his head. 'Sad. So sad... thank God He saved you. And He told my Boss to buy supplies.' He threw his long hair over his shoulder. 'We need kerosene, Ma'am.' He moved on and unlocked the storeroom. Milly followed him. It was an unexplored vault. Cheng checked bags of fertiliser and garden sprays. There were trays of dried seeds, a bag of seed potatoes, and empty preserving bottles. Boxes of vegetable seeds were examined and bottles of poison tidied. Milly recorded everything he said.

Wide shelves lined the full length of one side of the room. Stacked storage boxes waited to be explored, each labelled. *Main bedroom, Wardrobe 1, Wardrobe 2, Bedroom 1.* 'Cheng, what's in all these boxes?'

El Shaddai

He shook his head. 'Boss started putting them here after Alice left. Baby clothes were in one with Alice's writing. It said, "Maybe?"'

'I wonder if there are any kid's clothes. We need them. This list says we need lots of supplies so I don't think there will be money for clothes. Do you know how to get to Blue Rock, Cheng?'

His pony tail swung from side to side. 'Cheng never need town.'

'I have another problem, Cheng. We don't have much money. How do I sell some cows?'

'A truck always comes and gets them. Boss brings them into yard on quad. Driver loads them.' He looked up. 'But I don't ever remember seeing a truck driver give the boss money.'

Cheng couldn't help her. Milly sighed. '*El Shaddai*. Why is this property called *El Shaddai?*'

'How do you know its name? Not called that anymore.'

'It's painted on an old sign we found on the ground near the letterbox.'

'Boss pulled signs down when Alice left. Yelled at God. Said he'd paint new ones. Never did.'

'Did you know *El Shaddai* means God Almighty? God All-Sufficient?'

'How do you know, Milly?'

'My husband Dan always encouraged me to trust God, to keep Him in the picture. I guess, if God has brought us this far, He will show me the way.'

They worked in silence for a time. Leaving the storeroom, Cheng caught her eye. 'You go visit Daphne and Joe. Have afternoon tea. She loved Alice. She'll love you. I send veggies from the garden. Their place isn't far. Take the truck. I get it ready for you.' As far as Cheng was concerned, the subject was settled.

Milly pondered his suggestion as they checked the level in the petrol tank. They needed to find the town Caro talked about. Although they'd settled into a surreal cocoon, their supplies were diminishing. She must face her fears and contact family. *But what if Dan has died?* A cold hand of fear squeezed her heart.

Halfway through the orchard, she paused between the trees at her heart spot. She spun around, her arms in the air, hoping to recapture the sense of beauty and love, like the first night she had worn the white nightie Ky now owned. Today she was dressed in the boss's dungarees, turned up at his boots and held up by his belt. *God. I can't go anywhere. My own clothes are worn out. The few dresses Ky found are stained. These trousers are practical and comfortable, but not suitable for a neighbourly afternoon tea.* Flopping down on the grass she imagined knocking on her neighbour's door, wearing men's clothes, with a baby boy dressed in faded pink. *It's okay, Lord. I don't want to go anyway.*

Go, Milly

You want me to go?

I have a gift for you

Each day is a gift. Every time Josh feeds at my breast, it's a gift. She waved her arms wide, indicating the ripening fruit around her. *This whole place is a gift. What do You mean, Lord?*

'Milly!' Ky's yodel pulled her to her feet. 'Bubby wants your milk.'

El Shaddai

Sipping a cup of tea, she pondered the problem of clothes as she fed Josh at the kitchen table. She couldn't even go to the shops. The door flew open and a giant box squeezed through the opening.

Cheng dropped it. 'Come. See.'

Caro opened the lid and squealed. Layers of clothes, still on hangers were folded a dozen at a time. The boss must have emptied Alice's wardrobe in a great hurry, dismissing all evidence of his wife. Within minutes, dresses hung on every protrusion. Ky's eyes shone with excitement. The girls ran in and out of Milly's room, laughing and giggling. Christmas erupted in their kitchen. Right at the bottom Ky pulled out five little girl's dresses.

Lily's eyes shone at the fairytale sight. Soon both girls spun and danced, clutching an extra dress they'd claimed. The last one Caro slid over Bea's shoulders. The skirt fell to the floor and tripped her but she clapped her hands and giggled. 'Pritty, pritty.'

Tears threatened Milly's eyes. *Yes, it's time.* Her girls deserved pretty clothes. Her boys deserved proper shoes and jumpers. Her family needed a wider world.

❦

Milly waved to Ky and Caro and drove the truck down the track. Lily sat close beside her, shifting back and forth, folding and re-folding her skirt. Josh nestled into her breast, safe in his sling. Milly's nerves were as jumpy as Lily's skirt. *It's only afternoon tea, God. Please keep me safe.*

Be still, Milly

❦

'Be still, my soul.' She spoke aloud. Her stomach continued to churn. 'Stomach. Be still.' Milly used her stern voice and then laughed at herself. She smoothed her brown and cream skirt. It wasn't her fashion choice, but fashion had become irrelevant. To be dressed like a woman was both intoxicating and strange.

Gathering her thoughts, Milly stopped at the driveway to Daphne and Joe's property. A faded sign, *Bethel*, swung from the wire gate. Taking comfort, she swung the gate open and drove through. The house and lawns hid behind trees, but she guided the truck down the most used track, stopping in front of a farm shed. *Lord. I can't stop the butterflies. I need Your peace. Mine's vanished.* Taking a deep breath, she lowered herself from the cab. She lifted Lily out and leaned over for Cheng's basket of vegetables. Lily ducked around the truck and ran down the path towards the house.

'Lily. Wait. Where are your manners?'

Running into the back garden, Lily spun and spun, her dress spreading out like a pink fairy cake. 'Look, Mummy. A fairy dress and a fairy garden.'

A screen door slammed.

'Oh Joe, come quickly.' A plump woman sank down on the steps, her right hand clutching her chest, her eyes glassed over as though she'd seen a ghost.

The door flung open. 'Daph! What is wrong?'

A bean-pole man looked first at his wife, then gasped when he saw Lily. The fairy turned and fled back to Milly.

'It's okay. Seems we have visitors.' He walked towards Milly, hand outstretched. 'Hello. My name's Joe Cavanagh.'

Milly watched Lily dancing in the front garden. She sat on the veranda with the best coffee she'd drunk since the one Ky conjured up in the hut. 'It's a lovely veranda, Daphne, and wonderful coffee.'

'Joe, fetch another, and make sure you use today's cream. And don't make it too strong or the girl won't sleep tonight.' Daphne turned back to Milly. 'Caroline came from you? She never said she had friends next door. I was concerned for her when she left with George. He was out here sniffing around, asking if we'd seen anyone from Mac's place. I don't trust him.' She pointed down the track Milly had just driven down. 'He drove that way the other day, but came back past later in the afternoon, driving like a bull chased his tail.'

Milly didn't know what to say. To her relief Joshua stretched and started making little noises.

'Oh, is he awake? Do you mind if I look? It's so long since I've seen a baby.'

Milly laughed and loosened the sling. 'Here. You hold him for a while.'

'Oh my. Oh my, oh my, oh my.' Daphne's face collapsed. She struggled to rearrange her smile. 'He's perfect, Milly.' She handed Josh back as though he'd bitten her. 'I must see what's happened to Joe and our coffee.' She almost ran down the hall to the kitchen.

What upset her? Milly slipped Josh back in his sling and called Lily. She needed to go home, but how could she leave without seeming rude? As she'd expected, this social event had proved too difficult. Yet somehow she longed to feel Daphne's arms around her, holding her tight the way she herself held Lily.

A little arm curled around Milly's neck. 'Why you crying, Mummy? Did you hurt yourself? Will Lily kiss it better?'

Milly accepted the kiss and swiped the errant tears from her eyes. The screen door flung open.

'Look at this, little missy.' The tall man squatted to Lily's height. 'Poppa Joe made fairy bread. Let's go and eat it in the garden.' The old men held the little girl's hand. She skipped down the stairs. 'Do you think we can find fairies to share it with?'

Daphne placed two steaming mugs on the table and perched on the edge of her chair. 'He's as happy as a pig in mud. It's been a long time since we've had children here. I had to do the coffee myself.'

Milly looked from her excited daughter to her neighbour who chatted as though nothing had happened. 'Did I offend you, Daphne? I'm sorry if I've forgotten some of my social etiquette. It seems a lifetime ago.'

'Goodness, no! You can't offend old Daph.' She chuckled. 'I got a shock, that's all.'

'You've had two shocks today. Lily frightened you when she rushed into your garden so rudely. I think it's time I left you in peace.' Milly stood, lowering her full mug on the table.

Daphne shook her head and stared at her shoes. Tears splashed onto her laced fingers. Not knowing what to do or say, Milly waited, studying the garden. Lily's bottom stuck up in the air as she looked under a toadstool. Maybe she would find a fairy today. It was a day when anything could happen.

'Please don't go, Milly.' Daphne blew her nose and lifted wet eyes.

Milly lowered herself on to the chair, her stomach churning, her mind fighting her feet's urge to run.

El Shaddai

'Can I ask you where got your beautiful dress, Milly?'

'Cheng.' Milly turned to the clouded eyes. 'When I left Wamberoo, I only had the clothes I wore the day of the earthquake. We've taken the liberty of wearing the boss's clothes, especially when it got cold. But today Cheng brought in a box from the storeroom. It had Alice's dresses in it. I hope she doesn't mind, but I didn't want to come visiting you, looking like a waif in giant's clothes.' Embarrassed, she dropped her head. 'I'm sorry, Daphne. It seemed a good idea at the time.'

Daphne's hand closed over Milly's. 'I'm sure it's fine. Alice would be delighted. But do you know how much you look like her? You could be her daughter. And Lily! I thought she was Alice's little girl who died so tragically. Hannah Rose. Ah, how we doted on that little beauty.' She gazed down the garden at the giggling girl who rode high on Joe's shoulders. 'It's a wonder Cheng hasn't mentioned it to you, Milly.' Daphne raised a questioning eyebrow.

'Cheng is wonderful. He treats me like he'd treat a daughter. When we arrived, he welcomed me as though he'd been waiting for me. He serves me as though I own *El Shaddai*.'

Daphne lifted surprised eyes. 'How did you know it's called *El Shaddai*?'

'One of the boys found an old sign near the gate. It's painted red like the roof. To me, it speaks of the blood of the Lamb announcing the Almighty rules. I have it in the truck and will tie it to the gate on my way home. I thought of doing it as I came, but didn't want to dirty my dress.'

'So *El Shaddai* and *Bethel* could be neighbours again. How wonderful.' Daph leant back in her chair. 'It's so nice to have you here, Milly.'

They chatted, sharing their faith and their lives. As Milly's stomach calmed and her mind settled, she revelled in the extravagance of heart-to-heart conversation. When Joshua started to cry, she noticed the sun dipping below the trees. 'Goodness. I didn't realise it's so late. I must go home.'

'Do you need to feed him first?' Daphne had been cuddling the sleeping baby on her lap. She squeezed him tight and kissed him on the cheek. 'Come sit in the lounge and feed him. Joe has Lily in the kitchen. I hate to think what he's up to.'

After settling Joshua, Milly surveyed the homely room. Framed photos rested on every surface. A large print on the end wall showed a younger version of Joe and Daphne, with a son and a daughter.

Daphne selected a picture from the piano and held it out to Milly. The similarities were striking. Alice sat with her daughter on her lap. At first glance it could have been Milly and Lily. 'There are differences.' Daphne stared at the photo over Milly's shoulder. 'But more similarities.' She dropped her gaze to the feeding baby. 'But this little one... He looks like Zachariah... and he's wearing the matinee jacket I knitted for Hannah.' She stroked Joshua's little head, sniffing back tears.

Milly chased Daph's revelations around her mind as she watched the rhythmic swallows of her son. It didn't surprise her that Daph had knitted the little jacket. *But he looks like Zachariah?* That defied logic.

Daph blew her nose for the second time. 'Please, will you come again soon? I feel as though God has handed me a precious gift today.'

'You can cuddle Joshua anytime, Daphne.'

'Thank you, Darling. But you are my precious gift. Two wonderful children are the icing on the top.'

Chapter 15

A WEEK LATER, CARO PORED over a long shopping list. Joe and Daph had offered to take Milly to Blue Rock. Milly's mind conjured up all sorts of fears, pictures of bulky men with foul body odours. She shuddered. Caro rummaged in the pantry checking how much cinnamon they had. 'How much money do we have, Milly? There are some things we must have like shampoo and conditioner, underwear, shoes and I need a hairdresser.'

'A hairdresser, Caro? What about petrol, flour and oil? Otherwise, we'll have styled hair and no way to go anywhere.'

'But my roots.'

Ky laughed. 'I could trim all the blond for you, Caro. Easy.' She turned to Milly. 'I have fifty dollars cash. But I have cards. Do you think they'll work?'

'I don't know. It must be a year since we've used them. Would they be frozen? Have Dan or Mal been using them? Is any credit left? I used half our limit on supplies the day before the quake.' She studied the page in front of them. 'How much do you have, Caro?'

'Umm...' Caroline's eyes focused on the floor. 'George has my cards. But I'll pay you back when...' A tear hit the floor.

Milly ignored her grief. 'I'm going to bed. It'll be a big day tomorrow. You girls can mark the top ten things on the list.'

Caro swiped at her eyes. 'Please let me come with you, Milly. Just shopping... honest.'

'What about the children?'

'Well, you'll take the baby and, if we took the boys, Ky would only have the three girls. It'd be easy for a day.' Her eyes sparkled with excitement. 'Please, Milly?'

'Great thinking, Caro. It would be good to take the boys.'

Caro jumped up and pumped the air.

Milly's hand fell on her shoulder. 'Steady, Caro. You have no money.' She turned to Ky poring over the list. 'You come with me, Ky. You, me and the boys. Caro can mind the girls. She just said it'd be easy.'

Caro scowled. 'But...'

Ky silenced her with her hand. 'I don't know, Milly. I'm happy here. The world frightens me.'

'It terrifies me. Let's go together.'

'Joe and Daphne will help. I suppose I could come.'

Caro looked close to tears. 'But, Ky, you are better with the girls. I've got a headache. I'm frightened here alone. What if George comes?'

Milly paused at her bedroom door. 'Good point, Caro. What if you run into George in town and he remembers your promises? You're safer here with Cheng. He'll watch you. Keep the girls inside and you'll manage fine.' Ignoring Caro's protests, she slipped through the door. 'See you in the morning, Ky.'

El Shaddai

When Milly rose next morning, Cheng had the truck waiting. 'I filled her right up, Milly. Not much petrol left now. If you get a drum of petrol and one of diesel, we be right for a month or two.' He handed Milly a list and a brown paper bag.

Milly ran her eye down the list of urgent items. 'What's in the bag, Cheng?'

'Boss gave me pay sometimes. I kept it for when I might need it. And today you need it for the family.' His head nodded up and down. 'Cheng's glad to have money for my family. If there's any left, please buy for the children.' He put his hand back in his pocket and took out an old brown envelope. 'This one is gift for you, Milly. You buy pretty dress or something.'

'But, Cheng...'

He raised his hand. 'Please, my Milly. Do it for me.' He bowed and opened the truck door. 'You drive safe. Not fast. Steering's not too good.'

When they left *Bethel*, the excited boys were belted into Joe and Daphne's car. Ky drove the truck as Milly sat beside her and fed Josh. The noisy engine contrasted with the gentle grunts of a contented baby as a cloud of dust followed them along the gravel road. Milly closed her eyes and tried to relax on the uncomfortable seat. *Lord, I need You today. Can I please find Dan?*

Today

Today's a good day. Yesterday would have been better. I miss him, Lord.

Haven't I been good to you?

Of course.

~☉☉~ Am I not sufficient? Haven't I supplied house, food, protection and clothes? Today, didn't I even supply money? ~☉☉~

Thank You, Lord. Milly squirmed under His list. *Yes, God. Your care of us has been wonderful. But Dan... well, he's my mate.* Opening her eyes, she turned her focus to Ky. 'Are you going to try to contact Mal?'

'I've been thinking about it. I dialled our home number from Daph's phone the other day. All I got was the disconnected tone. I'm thinking we should read the missing lists first. What about you?'

'I'm going to ring everyone I can. I'm hoping I can find a charger for my phone so I can retrieve numbers.'

'Do you think we should register with someone? What if our names are on the missing list? I'm nervous, Milly. We're family here. Everyone's happy. Cheng cares for us. Re-emerging into an unknown world scares me.'

'Mal?'

Ky gripped the wheel of the truck, avoiding potholes Milly couldn't see.

Lord, what's going on?
~☉☉~ Gently, Milly ~☉☉~

'Ky? You don't want to see Mal?'

'No. I asked God to rescue us, but now I'm confused. My kids need a dad.'

'It's not as though you have another man's baby on your breast.'

'Oh, Milly. What will you tell Dan?'

'The truth, of course. He'll be devastated. I dread seeing him hurt. But we'll find a way through, I hope.'

'Mal's probably remarried.'

El Shaddai

'Ky! You can't be serious.'

Ky's hands white-knuckled on the steering wheel. 'I could never satisfy him. He often told me what a disappointment I'd turned out to be. He'd be happier with someone better.'

'That's crazy. I've known you for years. You, of all women, are a model wife.'

'Sometimes life isn't all it appears.' Ky's deep breath was ragged. 'I'll check the missing lists… if I get time.'

When they arrived at Blue Rock, they stopped at a supermarket. Joe stooped to look in the truck window. 'Milly, why don't I come with you and we'll do the farm supplies? Ky, would you like to shop with Daphne and the boys?'

Relief flooded Milly. She'd be in the company of this lovely, gentle man.

Joe jumped in with Milly. 'Now show me Cheng's list.'

'Joe…' Milly was hesitant. '…we have limited money and no income. God has supplied everything we need, but I feel I should be doing more. Is there a way we can sell some cows? Could we put the money into a special account, so when the family comes back to *El Shaddai*, it will be there? In the meantime, could we use some for buying farm supplies?'

'I've been thinking about your need for money. If I call in at the bowls club this afternoon, my mate Dave should be there. I'm going to ask him some general questions. We'll talk about it again later.' He patted her shoulder. 'Let's get this list covered. We'll order the drums of fuel, but I won't pick them up until we're about to go home. Don't want them on the truck all day.'

Mid-afternoon, Joe dropped Milly at the library. Ky had gone home with Daph and the boys, so her only companions were a restless baby and a churning stomach. Waiting at the counter felt like standing at the edge of a precipice.

A woman smiled a welcome. 'How can I help?'

Milly hugged Joshua and tried to untangle her tongue. 'I'm looking for the missing person list… you know… from Wamberoo?'

The librarian waved towards a computer. 'It's all on the screen. There are three different lists. *Confirmed Dead; Missing, Presumed Dead;* and *Missing.* Each list is alphabetical.' Her tone softened a little. 'Are you looking for someone special?'

'My husband.' Should she add and *myself, my family*?

The lady's eyebrows rose a little. 'Your hubby? It's been close to a year. Haven't you seen him in all that time?'

Milly swallowed the lump in her throat. 'I've been stranded, unable to get to a town. And all my contact numbers are in my phone. It's flat and I don't have a charger, so I can't access them.'

The lady's face went from horror to sympathy. 'I've got a charger. Show me your mobile.'

Milly took the neglected phone from her backpack and passed it to the woman. 'Look. It fits.' The lady beamed as she handed the phone and charger to Milly. 'There's a powerpoint beside the first computer.'

'Thank you.' Milly took the phone. She felt like the edge of the precipice was crumbling.

'I hope his name isn't on any of those lists, Honey. That rotten earthquake has caused enough heartbreak already. Too many people gone.'

Milly nodded, unable to speak. She forced her feet to cross the room.

El Shaddai

'Give me a call, if you need a hand. My name's Laura.'

The computer poised like a crouching tiger. *God, hold me tight.*

I am sufficient

She attached her phone to the charger and turned it on. The computer screen waited as black as death. Joshua stirred in his sling. She rocked him back and forth, buying time. The saying, 'Ignorance is bliss,' made sense today. She'd prefer to imagine Dan trying to find her than to know he'd never walk in her door again.

Summoning all her courage, she shoved the mouse. The screen flashed and she jerked back as though a tiger had bitten her. Forcing her heart to slow, she perched on the edge of the stool. A smiley face on the mouse pad mocked her distress. The screen blinked. *Click on Preferred List.*

The cursor hovered over *Confirmed Dead*. She couldn't do it. She wouldn't check there unless she had exhausted all other options. Taking a deep breath, she chose '*Missing — Presumed Dead*'. 'F' for Furley.

A long list of names unrolled down her screen. *Lord, there are so many.*

She scrolled quickly, not wanting the words to turn into familiar faces. Finch, Fryer, Fullbrock, her eye ran down the list — *Furley, Dan.*

His name. It blinked at her from the screen but it felt like a pistol shot in the heart. The precipice gave way. Her heart plummeted into a bottomless pit. Maybe she read it wrong. But it stared back at her. Nothing else. No when, where, why.

Her head fell into her hands. Tears seeped through her fingers onto the keyboard.

'There, there.' The librarian knelt beside her and read the screen. 'Is your hubby on the list?'

Milly nodded but couldn't speak.

'But he's not confirmed dead, Honey. He may still be okay.'

The words chased each other around Milly's head. *Presumed dead... okay... dead... okay... dead...* She clicked another letter. Anything to get Dan's name off the screen.

'Do you have others to look for? Can I help?' Laura pulled over another stool and pushed a pad of paper towards her. 'Write the names. I'll look them up for you.'

Milly swallowed the jagged rock in her throat and managed to whisper her thanks. Her list started with Mal, Ky and their children and Caro. She added her Mum and Dad and Dan's mother and his step-dad, even though they didn't live in Wamberoo. She'd tried to ring her mother from Daphne's phone without success. At the bottom of the list, she scrawled her name with Hosea and Lily.

Her helper worked fast, searching one list at a time. She found Ky, and Caro on the same list as Dan. Swallowing the lump in her throat, Milly found some voice. 'But... but... they're alive.'

'Which proves the list isn't always right. It should give you hope for your hubby.' The librarian opened the *Confirmed Dead* list. Mal's name jumped out at her. Horror settled on Milly like a black cloud. Poor Ky. She closed her eyes to block the black but it deepened. 'Sorry, Honey. There's two more here.' The woman sounded close to tears herself. She pointed to the paper.

'My Dad! No! He wasn't in Wamberoo the day of the earthquake.' She pressed her fist against her burning eyes.

Dan's step-dad was also confirmed dead. Her head spun. She pointed to her mother's name.

The lady shook her head. 'Can't find her name anywhere, which is good news. These last names on your list are all *Missing*.'

Milly stared at her own name blinking on the screen. How could she be alive when her world had collapsed? Why did God save her and not her dad, or Dan's step-father? They were good, wonderful people.

'Are you okay, Honey?'

'Those names.' Milly pointed to the list. 'Me, my son and daughter. Can you remove our names from the list?'

Milly's phone burst into life. Her screen lit up with messages. Startled, Milly jerked back as though bitten. 'Oh. It must have coverage. I thought... I assumed it would be disconnected.'

Joshua squirmed in his sling and began to cry. 'A little bit longer, little one. I know you've been bundled up all day.'

The librarian rose. 'You'll need to go to the police station to get your names taken off the list.' She dropped her hand on Milly's shoulder. 'Anything else I can do?'

Milly shook her head. Deep, dark sadness crouched in the pit of her stomach, threatening to explode. She needed to wail, to scream and cry but she must get home first.

'Come. Follow me.' Laura took Milly's hand and led her down a corridor. She opened a door and ushered her into a small meeting room. 'You sit here for a bit. Unwrap your gorgeous baby and make a few phone calls.' She waved to a comfortable chair and plugged her phone in to keep it charging. 'Is there anyone I can contact to come and help you? I could call a social worker or a chaplain?'

'No. I don't think so. My friend, Joe, will be back to get me soon.'

'Do you mean Joe Cavanagh?' Relief flashed through her eyes. 'He'll look after you. I'll call you when I see him arrive.'

'Thanks so much. I don't even remember your name.'

'Laura, Honey.' With a sad smile she closed the door.

Cheng's special envelope lay forgotten until they were about to leave town. 'Joe. Do you know where I could buy a phone charger?'

'Show me the phone.' He frowned as she passed it to him. 'I've got one at home I don't use it. It's all yours.' A grin transformed his face. 'Daph will have dinner ready by the time we get there. You look all tuckered out. Would you like to talk, or lie down on the seat and sleep?'

'Dan is missing, presumed dead. I listened to some of the messages he left...' Hot, violent tears burst from a deep cavern and cascaded down her cheeks. Her chest heaved. 'He... he sounded so... so desperate.'

'Here.' Joe pushed a couple of parcels off the seat onto the floor. 'Scoot over here beside Joe. Can't have you crying in the corner.' He pulled her under his arm and gave her his large checked handkerchief. His big hand cradled her head tight against his chest.

A void yawned where her heart used to be as though the earthquake had sliced through her and left a gaping hole—a

El Shaddai

gaping black hole that wanted to swallow her. Joshua squirmed and grizzled. She settled her baby to feed.

Under the shelter of My wings

What, Lord? Where were You? Dad was under Your wing. You didn't shelter him! Don't talk to me... don't talk to me.

'Confirmed dead?' Ky sat still. Her right foot jiggled up and down. 'Are you sure it was Malcolm?'

'I'm so sorry, Ky. It listed his full name and address.'

'What about Dan?'

'Missing, presumed dead.' Milly's stomach convulsed, but her tear ducts were dry. She felt like a robot jerking through the motions. She'd stopped at Joe's place only long enough to get everyone in the truck. At home they'd cuddled the girls, sat as a family and eaten the dinner Daph had sent with them. The kids fell asleep. Milly lay on the lounge, a gaping hole where her heart used to be.

Caroline flopped down in the lounge chair opposite the women. 'Dead? Who's dead?'

Milly took a deep breath. 'I checked the computer in the library. It appears both our husbands are dead.'

Ky shook her head. 'There's some hope Dan's alive, Milly.'

The colour drained from Caroline's face. 'You looked at the lists?'

Milly nodded. 'Mal is confirmed dead. Dan is listed as *Missing, Presumed Dead.*'

'George found Mum and Dad but he didn't check anyone else. I only gave him their names. Are we on the lists?'

'We're all there. Caro, you and Bea are also listed as *Missing, Presumed Dead*.'

'What! How dare they? That's ridiculous.'

Ky rose and put her arm on Caro's shoulder. 'Steady, Caro. No one has heard from us since before the earthquake.' She looked at Milly. 'Are we all on the same list?'

'You, Bethie and Johnno are. My kids and I are listed as *Missing*.'

'Why aren't you presumed dead, Milly?' Caro's hands shook. 'Who made up these silly lists anyway?'

'What's it matter? We can go to the police station in Blue Rock and identify ourselves so our names can be removed.' Deep heaviness engulfed Milly. 'Let's talk more tomorrow.' She gave Ky a hug, patted Caro on the shoulder and turned for bed.

'But Milly, wait! Can I go in tomorrow and check others?'

'Let's talk about tomorrow when it gets here.' Milly ran to her room, slammed the door and fell on her bed. Her tears weren't dried up at all. *God! Where were You?* The wind whistled through the garden, but she couldn't hear any reply. *I'm angry, God. I asked You to protect Dan, to bring him to me. I thought You answered prayer? And what about all those promises?* Beating the pillows with her fists she screamed long silent wails. How could it be that her own father was no longer waiting at the end of the phone? *Sleep...* she longed for oblivion and hoped it would never let her go.

A soft little snort on the other side of the bed snapped her back to reality. Joshua. She lay still now, willing him to stay asleep, knowing he needed nourishment. Inky blackness flowed through her and around her, submerging her, suffocating her. Easing herself over the edge of the bed and out of the room, she gulped water from the kitchen tap. *Why, God? Why? Why did You ever send the dream? What was the point? You warned me and so You saved me from the raging water... only to be overwhelmed by loneliness, hunger and...*

The memory of Pete's crow of victory hit her ears. 'Bingo.' Her body shuddered. The memories had dulled, the sharp edges blunted, the day the Lord held her at the creek. But today's horror yanked back the deep pain. *And now Lord, I'm left with a baby. Yes, he's cute but he's the son of a criminal, a moron, a god-hating filthy scumbag. What hope does my baby have? He has no future, no father, no grandfather, no prospects, no name. His mother is a homeless squatter, living a ghost of a lie, wearing the clothes of the dead. No money. No family. No hope. Maybe we're dead like Dan, Pop and Dad. Maybe we're all dead and haven't realised it.*

She swooped around the kitchen mimicking a ghost. *Maybe I'm not really alive. I'm a ghost trapped between life and death. There's no life but neither is there the relief of death. Ah, death. No more suffering. No more pain. No fear. No worry.*

Milly, I love you

Love? Is this what You call 'love'? I want nothing to do with it! Or You! Shutting off the silent voice in her mind, she slid down the door of the fridge and sat on the floor, pulling her knees up under Alice's dress. Her feet were frozen and her body chilled.

Death tempted her. No more cold. No more heat. No more torment. No more battles. No more whimpering, simpering Caroline.

The sound of Joshua gurgling drew her attention. She returned to the bedroom, wondering if she should feed or smother the unfortunate waif. She turned the idea over in her mind. Ky would assume she'd rolled on him in the night. She could leave on the quad in the morning and never return. She'd climb back up to Pete and leave his baby beside him. Serve him right. Let him suffer the loss.

Why smother him? A different whisper surrounded her. Soft, wheedling, suggestive. *Sacrifice him. Appease the gods. Offer Josh. Save Hosea and Lily.* Strange voices pulsated through her head. The idea, like tentacles, pushed through her confusion, sounding more reasonable by the second. *You have to pay… you have to pay.*

She started shoving things into her backpack. In the pantry she located Cheng's long butcher's knife. With care, she checked the blade with one thumb. Razor sharp. Wrapping the blade in a tea towel, she stowed it in her backpack.

The baby's hungry little noises increased. Exhaustion squeezed her to the point of collapse. She slipped under the covers and pulled Joshua onto her breast, casting all guidelines to oblivion. Last meal. He'd be dead tomorrow. As the familiar sweet pain hit her breast, she gave in to sleep.

Wild-eyed Pete grabbed Joshua. 'He's mine. All mine. Born to be sacrificed. Born to bleed.'

Dan snatched the baby back. 'This baby belongs to God. Dedicated to God. Born to rule and reign.'

Pete jumped Dan from behind. He grabbed the baby by

El Shaddai

one foot and threw him in the air. Dan knocked Pete over and caught the baby before it hit the ground, pulling him in against his heart. 'Child of destiny.'

'Child of sacrifice.' Pete lunged while Dan ducked and weaved, dodged and rolled. Pete's hands were free. Dan tried to defend the baby and fight at the same time.

'Give him to me.' Drool dribbled from Pete's mouth. 'He's not yours. He's mine. Bone of my bone. Flesh of my flesh. I can do what I like. The altar is waiting.'

Wood lay on top of the pyre of rocks covering Pete's remains. A flaming torch held by a black-gloved hand waited to ignite the blaze. Pete charged again.

Dan yelled. 'Mil...ly, ca...tch.' The baby, legs and arms flailing, flew through the air.

Her own scream woke her.

Ky held her. 'Milly! Milly!' Sitting on the bed beside her, she stroked her hair. 'It's all right, I'll look after you. God will protect us. He'll be a father to our kids.'

Milly's whole body shook. Her teeth chattered. She tried to focus on Ky, but in the early morning light, shadows slithered around the room.

'I light the fire, ma'am?' Cheng stood at the bedroom door.

'Yes, please, Cheng. She's very cold.' Ky picked up Joshua. Milly reached for him. Ky held him. 'I'll change him, Milly. He's sopping wet. I'll bring him straight back to you.'

Milly watched—her muscles stretched tight, ready to jump and grab her baby. He was hers and she would do whatever she wanted. At the table she supervised breakfast, but couldn't eat. After the children had stacked their plates in the sink, they donned new coats and shoes and raced outside.

Ky put a cup of coffee in front of Milly. 'Want to talk about it?'

Milly shook her head. Her thoughts were scrambled. Words were impossible to push past her constricted throat. The silence stretched. Ky rose and fetched the fresh flour. 'I thought we could have bread for lunch. We even have Vegemite.'

Under Ky's experienced hands, the dough formed and was tipped onto the table. Ky folded and pushed the dough over and over. Milly related to the dough. Pummelled, stretched, pulled, and punched—soon to be consumed. *Maybe that's all I am?* Something God was pummelling, preparing her to be consumed.

Covering the dough with a tea towel, Ky placed it near the fire. 'I'm sad for my kids today.'

Milly fiddled with the corner of the tablecloth, hiding her eyes in case Ky saw the fermenting anger.

Ky washed her hands at the sink. 'Today I know my kids don't have a father. I'm sad for them. But I find I'm not sad for me. I've lost my husband... but in a way I'm relieved. But it's tough for you, Milly. Dan's the love of your life.'

Caroline yawned as she came through the door. 'What are you girls talking about?'

'Death.' The first word Milly had spoken dropped into the room like a rock. 'Nice of you to get up so early, Caro.'

Unaffected by the sarcasm, Caro crossed the room and sat beside Milly. 'I'm exhausted from minding those girls yesterday. You were so late I thought you were lost. Why so uptight, Milly?'

Milly stood and glared. 'Dunno. Maybe the number of deaths I had to face yesterday?'

El Shaddai

Caro shrugged. 'Mal and Dan. You haven't seen them for ages, anyway. You'll get over it.'

Ky gasped. 'Caro!'

'Sorry, Ky. But she's such a drama queen.'

Banging back her chair, Milly left the room.

'What other deaths, Milly?' Caroline's voice followed her into the bedroom.

Past caring, she yelled from her room. 'My father. Dan's step-father.' She stuck her head back into the kitchen. 'And of course your parents, Caro.' Grabbing the sling, Joshua and her backpack, she left the house, slamming the door behind her.

'Milly! Wait!' Ky's frantic voice floated behind her, urging her into a run.

Chapter 16

THE QUAD LEAPT at her brutal twist on the throttle. Wind whipped her hair as she roared down the track before circling towards the forest. She didn't want anyone following. Her fist belted the handle bar, her emotions screeching along with the scream of the engine.

Joshua yelled his protest at the bumpy ride. She ignored him. Driven by a desperation to end the pain, she pushed on. 'You were born to death, Joshua. Your mother is a murderer; your father a wicked felon. Your future is miserable. We will appease the gods, you and I together. They will be satisfied. Hoey and Lily will survive. Maybe Dan will come.'

A groan escaped. She'd forgotten to say good-bye to her children. Caro had made her so mad she'd stormed off. The quad skidded to a stop as she considered Hoey and Lily's future. If she didn't return, they'd be raised by Ky, the perfect mother. Cheng would watch over them. Joe and Daph would lavish love upon them. They'd live on *El Shaddai* in peace and comfort. Yes, they'll be fine.

But should she go back to say good-bye? The quad wandered in circles, Milly's progress reflecting the confusion in her mind. It took her several minutes to decide. *No.* She'd leave and never return. She turned the quad towards the forest. Dan dead. Dad dead. She too must die. Murderers must die.

The trees seemed to stretch forever. Milly wove through them at speed. She stopped the bike at the spot where they'd found the wheelbarrow. Ahead the trail rose steeply around rocks.

Milly

She spun around and peered through the trees, her heart pounding. 'Who's there?' Her ears were tuned to every little movement of the forest. She shuddered. This is Pete's country. Maybe he had a brother? The hair on her arms jumped to attention.

Milly

Grabbing Josh, she hid in a bush, pulling its branches around her.

Why are you hiding?

Sitting on the ground, her whole body shaking, she covered her eyes. *I didn't invite You, God. This is a private trip.*

Can I help you?

No. You couldn't help my dad. You didn't help Dan. My children? She pushed her head between her knees.

I am El Shaddai. I am covering your children

Go away, God. Get lost. You've stuffed up my whole life. My life. You hear me? It's my life and I can do what I want with it.

Joshua's life

That's my business.

Milly

Ignoring the pain in God's voice, she turned her back. Spreading out a rug, she changed Joshua, dressing him in a dry nappy and a clean singlet. She hugged him and kissed him before clothing him in the long white dress she suspected had been Hannah's christening gown. Wrapped in a pink blanket, she held him at her breast for the last time, her tears baptising his head. She didn't try to stop them. There'd be no room for tears in the penthouse.

Thank You, God, for these precious weeks with this beautiful baby. He has been such a treasure to me.

I thought you weren't talking to Me

I'm not. I was just expressing my thanks.

You said 'God'

Consider it a generic term. 'Go away, God. Leave me alone.' Irritated, she yelled as she jumped up. 'Enough, Joshua. I hope you're ready, for this is your big moment. Hang tight while we get up the mountain.'

Strapping him to her chest, she swung the backpack on her shoulders and started the climb.

Milly!

Milly!

Milly!

Every tree and rock seemed to call her, mock her. Her torn insides felt savaged by wild dogs. Could she survive long enough to make the sacrifice? She must get there and atone for the murder, so her other children wouldn't have to pay.

I've paid the price already. Paid in full

The thought was drowned out by a drumming chant in her head. *Murderer. Murderer. Murderer.* The leaves on the trees pointed accusing fingers at her. She leapt up the rocks, ignoring scraped knees and bleeding palms. She embraced the hard way on purpose. Pain was her friend. It blocked out the clamouring, raucous noises in her head. The final ledge into the cave stopped her. There'd been two of them when she'd done this before and they'd helped each other. Now alone, a baby strapped to her breast, she couldn't pull herself up.

Balancing on a rock, she released Joshua. Bundled tight in the sling, she lifted him over the edge and pushed him away from the drop. His startled cry cut her heart. She threw her backpack in a different direction. Heaving her body, she dragged it over the ledge and into the cave. Joshua still looked startled. 'We made it, Josh. You've been on your best behaviour.' As she started to unwrap him, her hands left stains of blood and dirt.

A sacrifice must be spotless. She eased past Pete's altar. The wood wasn't in place as in the dream. Wood. She must gather wood. Determined, she turned her back and traversed the narrow way, breaking out to the familiar oasis. The baby didn't complain at being laid on the grass. Shaking, she ripped one edge off his blanket. To her relief, his long gown glistened white, unblemished. Kneeling beside the cool water, she soaked her bleeding hands. Taking the rags, she bandaged them, stemming the trickles of blood.

Joshua

What?

Joshua

She spun towards her baby. A massive snake advanced towards him, its tongue darting in and out. Her scream didn't deter it as it doubled its body over Joshua.

El Shaddai

A stick. She needed a stick. But she couldn't see any. *A rock.* She threw the nearest one at the creature's tail, but missed. *Closer.* She must go closer. The next one she drove down into the lower half of the body. A shiver vibrated through her. The snake raised its head and hissed. Joshua wailed. Screaming, she banged down the rock, over and over again. Joshua's wail intensified.

Desperation overcoming fear she stamped her boot on its head. Its tail flicked up, towards her. The movement loosened Josh a little. He drew a panicked breath and screamed. Her other foot pinned the monster's back. The tail swatted at her. With one hand, she pulled at the serpent's body. The other scooped the baby up. Losing her balance, she fell back. Horror coursed through her, but the snake slithered into the shrubbery.

Back on her feet, squeezing Joshua close, she ran to the sunlight. In the open space, she collapsed to her knees on the ground. Her sobbing and his crying echoed off the escarpment walls. She kissed him over and over, running her crudely bandaged hand over his little head. 'My baby. Oh, my poor baby. I couldn't bear it if he'd swallowed you! Oh, Joshua. Mummy loves you so much.'

She rocked him back and forth. Confused thoughts chased each other around her brain. God rescued Josh even after she'd told Him to get lost. Why would He do that? The other voice hissed, urging her to gather wood and build the altar. A soft little tongue tugged at her breast pulling at the depths of her being. She couldn't, just couldn't sacrifice him today. *Not today.* But what would happen if she didn't obey?

Milly pulled herself to her feet. There was no sign of the snake. And no car. She'd left it here. That was months ago, but even if it wouldn't start, it should be here. How strange. She'd led Ky from the car at this spot, kicking the door shut, not even stopping to check it.

Was someone else here somewhere? A shudder shook her. *Pete's family?*

A loud clap of thunder shook the ground. Black menacing clouds rolled towards her. They needed shelter. The rolling clouds mesmerised her. *Get drenched? Go back to Pete's penthouse?* But Pete's altar waited in the cave. *Run for the hut? Is someone there?* Every option sent a shudder through her. Booming thunder started her feet running across the open grass in the direction of the hut.

Like a giant ferocious beast, the storm growled at her heels. The wind howled through the gap near the waterfall, building to a roar. The blast hit her with such force she struggled to stay upright. Joshua's long white dress streamed out, driven by the wind at her back. Holding his tiny body close, she rounded her shoulders, trying to shelter him. *Lord! Please help me.* Her stride lengthened. Her feet flew faster.

The hut! It was in sight.

Big drops of water splattered around them, causing dust balls to rise from the ground. She stopped only long enough to kick the door open. Puffing, she banged it shut. It felt as though more than a storm was chasing her.

The fresh smell of rain competed with the musty odour of the hut. The shutters were down and secure. *But how?* In her rush to leave, she hadn't stopped to shut them. Fear pounded in her heart. Her eyes strained in the dim light. 'Is... is anyone here?'

Pelting rain on the roof blocked any sound but the rasping of her own throat. She laid Joshua on the bed and surveyed the dim room. His little fingers held a lock of her hair tight. She curled up beside him on the bed, facing the door. He sought her face and smiled. 'First smile, Joshua. Now! In the middle of a wild storm when Mummy is terrified.'

The shutters rattled and a piece of tin on the roof started to bang. The whole building shook in the wind. *Lord? Lord, Your word says You are a refuge and shelter in time of trouble. Doesn't it say You'll rescue me from the tempest?*

Ping. Ping. Bang. The noise reminded Milly of the earthquake. Another freight train roared towards her. *Lord, help me.* Holding Joshua close, she dragged blankets and pillows from the bed and huddled under the table. Although small, it offered the most protection if the roof blew away or caved in. Lightning flooded the room and thunder vibrated through the floor. Outside, timber ripped. The hut shook as a tree smacked into the ground.

The storm eased. Her stomach growled. She hadn't eaten all day and hadn't brought food. The backpack was still in the cave. She shuddered. There was nothing here when they'd left. Except for an empty flour bag and two matches to start a fire. Maybe there'd be enough flour to make damper, but no dry fuel to light the stove.

The rain stopped. The wind faded away to Dead Man's Gully. An eerie stillness filled the hut. Milly shivered. She tugged the door. It creaked open. Startled, she jumped back. Wet leaves filled the doorway. The tree she'd slept under so many times lay at her feet. What if it had fallen on the hut? Dull, yellowish light cast an eerie veil over the familiar. Something didn't feel right. Spikes of fear prickled her frame.

Unable to get to the tank she took a bucket from behind the door and placed it under the tree. As she shook the branches, the bucket caught enough water to give her another drink. Without food, water would help her make milk. She opened the cupboard to get a mug. A row of tins stood in the shadows. *How can it be? God. How? Who?*

A roar built from the direction of Dead Man's Gully. Had the storm turned on her? Kicking the door shut, she fastened it tight and ran back to Joshua. The gale smashed into the opposite side of the hut. It moaned and groaned. Under the table, she calmed her screaming baby with her breast. One tin she found was in her hand. Beans. Ripping the lid off she poured beans into her mouth straight from the can, easing her hunger. Water had found a way through the roof and dripped in a line across the floor, just missing her feet. Water poured onto the stove. How much longer could they stay dry?

Lord? No answer. He hadn't spoken to her through this whole time except for the warning about the snake. Her heart ached for His presence, His touch, His peace, His humour. *Lord, I'm missing You.*

Other voices clamoured. The slap of the fallen branches on the door chanted, 'Sacrifice... sacrifice.' Images ran through her mind of mad men holding babies up towards a sky criss-crossed with lightning flashes. Bring him out. Bring him out. She pushed herself tight back in the corner, as though it would help her escape the sinister voices. Unperturbed, Joshua opened one trusting eye, his little mouth still clinging to her nipple.

Bring him out. All is ready.

'No.' Her own yell reverberated off the table. 'You're not having him.'

Bring him out. He belongs to the gods. You belong to the gods.

Terror ripped through her. 'Father. God, my Father. I need You.' But the noise of the wind gobbled her cry.

God won't come. You denied Him. You're mine now. All mine.

In another flash of lightning, she saw the snake sliding towards her. Belching fear defiled her mouth. Icy cold fingers clawed at her stomach, climbing rung by rung, aiming for her heart. Each claw left a gaping hole. Frozen to the floor, backed in a corner, her panic rose. Unseen hands closed around her airways, squeezing tighter and tighter. 'Jesus, my Jesus.' She forced the whisper past her closing throat.

***

Milly

Where was she? Had she passed out? Curled on her side, she grappled to face reality. The storm had eased to gentle rain. A gentle golden light flowed through the hut, sneaking through the slats of the shutters.

The snake! Terror flooded back. She crawled out of the corner and eased onto the table, her eyes darting in every direction.

Milly

It sounded like God. She dropped her head and shut her eyes. She couldn't talk to Him, face Him. Her words replayed in her mind. *It's my life and I can do what I want with it.*

Milly

She wanted to hide, but the blankets were on the floor. She sat still, wanting to be invisible, but feeling dreadfully exposed.

Why are you hiding from Me, Milly?

You are so good, so… so… pure. Her tears splashed on the baby's dark hair.

Today I'm the same as yesterday and I'll be the same tomorrow

She gulped, mute in His presence. What could she say? She'd denied Him and swallowed the lies of other gods. And His response? He'd saved Joshua from the snake at the oasis. He imprisoned her with a tree to stop her rushing outside and throwing her baby to the storm. Somehow, He'd held the hut together. And when the snake returned, He must have dealt with it. She had no excuses and a mountain of regrets. Filth covered her soul.

Who told you you're not worthy?

I'm filthy, Lord.

Yes

She wept. Even He agreed. How could she ever dance with Him again? Shame flooded her, like a young foolish bride who had stormed off and committed adultery on a whim. Adultery? Idolatry? Is there any difference? She'd flirted with evil, deciding to sacrifice her precious baby. *I'm sorry.* The whispered words were inadequate.

You are forgiven

The thought resounded through her being.

Forgiven, Lord?

Yes, forgiven, because of the blood of Jesus

El Shaddai

But Lord, this is worse than murder. I turned my back on You. I listened to other gods.

◦◦◦ *You mean you denied Me* ◦◦◦

Worse than that.

◦◦◦ *Unfaithful—like My chosen people* ◦◦◦

Milly's brain whirred trying to recall Bible stories. He'd rescued Israel, God's chosen people and then they'd built a golden calf. Bit by bit the story returned to her mind. *Thousands died because of the idolatry.*

Milly found a dry section of the bed for Joshua. She faced the light slanting through the shutters. *I'm here, Lord. Do what You must do. I'd rather die at Your hand than walk without You.*

She waited—waited to die. It wasn't the first time she'd faced death today. It had been the most terrifying day of her life. A gentle peace crept into her being. This death was welcome. Not black and gloomy, but white and welcoming.

◦◦◦ *Milly, come. Come with Me* ◦◦◦

She bent to get Joshua.

◦◦◦ *Leave him* ◦◦◦

Visions of the slithering snake assaulted her mind.

◦◦◦ *I have commanded My angels concerning him* ◦◦◦

She couldn't see any angels. Neither could she see the snake. She wavered. Could she trust God to protect him? Wasn't it her job as a mother, to protect and defend her child? But didn't she prepare to sacrifice him just this morning? Then God had saved him.

Squaring her shoulders she kissed Joshua, swallowed her fear and walked to the door. It jerked open. With her body flat against the wall, she pushed past the fallen branches, unscathed but damp. Several trees had fallen. Branches and leaves littered the ground. She shivered. Memories of the earthquake assaulted her. Picking her way over branches and around trees, she walked towards the drop to the valley. Dan was down there somewhere, either dead or alive.

Peace, My Milly. Peace

She sighed. Peace. Death bought peace. If Dan was dead, he'd be at peace. If he was alive, she imagined he'd be tormented, not knowing if his family was dead or alive. At least she knew where her kids were. God had saved all of them.

Thick dark clouds, ripped by an odd lightning flash hovered over the valley, emphasising it as a valley of death. She hugged her body, trying to bring comfort. Without her dream, she and her children would be buried there—or at sea. *Thanks for saving us, Lord. I'm sorry for my spoilt, ungrateful attitude.*

Turn around, Milly

She paused, staring into the doom and gloom to the east.

That is the old. It is gone. The new has come

Puzzled, she turned to face the escarpment. It loomed tall and shadowed. Above the rim, sunlight forced its way between the last of the clouds. As if instructed, the clouds parted and the full force of the late afternoon sun bathed her.

I am the light of the world. Can I be the light of your world, Milly?

But I'm dead. Idolatry brings death. Are You saying it's time for me to go to heaven? Her chest tightened in panic. Until then she hadn't considered what happened after death. What if, in her foolishness, she was separated from God forever? And caused Joshua to be separated from Him.

Don't let fear deceive you

Can I still go to heaven? I don't want to lose You again. Those few hours were hell, sheer hell. Is there any way I can stay with You? I'm so sorry. Tears channelled down her face and dripped off her chin.

Grief, pain and guilt deceived you last night. They sold you a lie, and you believed it

You mean about the... sacrif... She couldn't articulate the word in His presence.

Yes... and

Lies about Joshua?

Yes

I forgot Your forgiveness, didn't I?

You were lied to, Milly. The devil is always out on the hunt. His pleasure is to rip lives apart

Heat shimmied down her back bone as she remembered long talons ripping her. *How then, Lord, can anyone survive?*

By faith. Whoever believes

Shall have eternal life?

Yes. The enemy's first step is to plant doubt. He steals away your belief in Me and My power, My grace, My everlasting love

The sun stood still, as though the Lord had paused, overcome with emotion.

He will tell you My grace isn't big enough for your sin; My power can't defeat him, and My love won't stretch as far as you

How can I withstand him? Today's been horrifying. I lost my ability to think or make decisions.

Always believe. Believe the truth

Jo Wanmer

The sun dropped over the mountain and the pinks of sunset crept across the clouds. She turned back to the valley. Golden light flooded it. The clouds were now painted orange, pink and gold, filling the valley with luminescence. *God, it is so beautiful, so amazing.*

My glory will always triumph

The colours spread up and over her. She stood captivated by a canopy of the glory of God. Barely able to breathe, she marvelled in wonder of her Creator. *God... thank You.*

A gift for you, My Milly

Bubbles of joy pushed their way through her being, like oil bathing her wounds and then pooling in explosions of happiness. Her laughter echoed through the trees, increasing her joy. As the sky darkened, she turned back to the hut. *Thanks, Lord. I've had a wonderful time. I hope the baby-sitting angels have minded Joshua well.*

Milly

She stopped amongst the ravages of the storm. *Yes.*

Am I sufficient for you?

Yes, Lord. She lifted her face to the sky. *You are more than enough for me. You satisfy me, You are my friend, my mate. You are my redeemer and restorer of my soul. You are my only hope.*

Will you be My bride? I will love you forever. Every time I look at you, I am undone. You are the delight of My heart. I will honour you and cherish you. Everything I have is yours

Heat flushed her neck. Lord... *Your love is so pure.*

Can you love Me, Milly?

The God of gods waited on her reply. From the back of her memory a fragment of Scripture came into focus. She grabbed it. *You alone know, Lord.*

Do you want to?

With all my heart, yes. But what if I disappoint You again?

Just believe, Milly. I will look after the rest

I... I believe You, Lord. A deep contentment crept through her being. In the deepening dusk she pushed past the wet leaves and shut the door. Opening the windows, she embraced the evening air. *I love You, Lord.* Joy flooded her. *I love You, Jesus.*

No longer do I call you 'servant'. You are My beloved

You are my God. Heat, like warm oil, flowed from the top of her head to the tip of her toes, seeping through every part of her. Her heart missed a beat and her breath caught in her throat. *God?*

I give you the Holy Spirit as a taste of what is yet to come

Holy Spirit? Like Dan's El Roi?

Clothed in warm peace, she curled around her baby under the doona and welcomed sleep.

Light slanting through the shutters woke her. *The hut?* Confusion gave way to the horror of her battle. Then the wonder of God's love brought her to tears.

El Roi. She breathed his name. Joshua woke, nuzzling, seeking food. As he sucked, she sang soft praises to her Saviour. Though she had fallen off the precipice and tumbled down into a bottomless abyss, somehow Jesus had saved both her and Joshua. And poured His love into her heart.

Her father was still dead. Dan was still 'presumed dead' but today felt different. God was her Father. Jesus was close and El Roi her friend. As the sucking eased, she pushed her finger to ease the baby off her breast, anxious to get home. Ky would be frantic. Climbing off the bed, she surveyed the room in daylight.

Everything was ordered, except for the things she'd used last night. The tools lay stacked in their proper place. Pillows were tidy. The clothes and towels they'd left piled in the corner were gone. *Has Dan been here, Lord? Those tools are stored his way.* Her heart leapt with hope. That would explain the food. Last night she wondered if she was crazy.

A red mug sat on the back corner of the table. Turning it around she read, *El Shaddai.* Dan's mug? Surely not. There would be others the same, wouldn't there? Rolled sheets of paper rested inside. Hands shaking, she spread them on the table.

Dear Milly

Dan's handwriting! Her heart flipped. He was alive. Alive! He'd been here. He had come. He hadn't abandoned her. She wiped her eyes with her shirt so she could read.

Dear Milly,

I'm heartbroken. I finally found a way to get to you, and you're not here. I guess that's better than finding you all dead. If your marks on the wall are counting days, I missed you by a few weeks.

I can see you were out of supplies and water, though I did find the car at the spring. I could see footprints running here and there. The tracks seemed to end at the edge off the ravine. My fear is you've all fallen.

God help me, I won't, I can't believe it's true. I must believe you found a way I haven't yet discovered.

She stopped, tears blurring the words.

It took me two days to hike in. I've left some supplies in case you return. Not much, but all I could carry on my back.

I'm tormented without you, Hoey and Lily. I need you so badly. With God's help, I will search for you until I find you. If you get this letter, you can contact me through Mum. Dad died trying to rescue the trapped.

All my love for ever and ever.

Your loving husband, Dan.

Her Dan. She wanted him—now! After re-reading it, she folded the letter and pushed it into her pocket. Her heart raced with joy. *Thank You, Lord. He's alive.*

Paper! She needed to write a reply. There was none. Frustrated, she opened the firebox of the stove. With a lump of charcoal she scrawled 'Blue Rock' on the table. The red cup sat with it. If he returned, she hoped he could decipher her message.

The car waited on the track leading to Dead Man's Gully. 'Dan. Dan.' Her shouts reverberated back off the escarpment. He was alive but they were still separated.

She drove to the waterhole, dodging trees and sticks from the storm. Searching the car, she found a dirty pair of socks and an empty chocolate wrapper. Retrieving the saturated baby blanket by the creek, she used the bits and pieces to mark a trail to the narrow way. The storm left a path of destruction. Walking tracks were gouged out by angry water rushing towards the creek and the ravine. 'We'll need to watch our feet today, Joshua.' Her baby, oblivious to the world's challenges, lifted his eyes to his mother, a little grin playing around his lips.

He trusts you completely, Milly

Without reason. I betrayed him yesterday.

Unless you come as a little child

Oh, I get it. You want me to trust You, El Roi, the way Joshua trusts me.

Lean not on your own understanding

Lord, help me. Please take me home to my children and El Shaddai. Please protect me as I walk through the cave of death.

My rod and My staff will comfort you

What does that mean?

My power, My authority. Rest in them, Milly

She headed to the narrow path, then stopped. The path had vanished. A gaping hole yawned between two rocks where a torrent had rushed down the escarpment. Her heart sank. Collapsing on a rock, she stared. *O Lord. How can I get home now?*

A breeze whispered in the trees. The waterfall, full and fast, crashed onto the rocks, reflecting how she felt. If she stayed at the hut and hunted, she could last for a week, maybe a fortnight. Dan might come but what if he didn't? He hadn't been back for months.

No turning back

Yes, Lord. But how do I get forward?

A wallaby turned from the waterhole and hopped down the path. At the washout it hesitated. Then in one bound, cleared the gap and disappeared into the cave. *God, I'm not a wallaby, and I have a baby.*

She did too

I'm trying to believe, but I don't think I can jump that far.

Can you jump from there to there? He seemed to indicate two rocks near where she sat.

Yes.

That's further than the gap

But the fall?

What fall? Who's going to fall?

Oh, God. Help my unbelief. She looked at the gap from all angles. She could jump it, but if she missed her footing the crash down the mountain meant death for them both. Yesterday she climbed up, expecting to die, but today life was too precious to risk.

'Milly!'

Yes, God.

'Milly. Milly. Cooee!'

Was someone there? She jumped up. 'Cooee!'

'Milly, my Milly. Where are you?'

'Cheng. Is that you?' She tried to locate the voice but the echo confused her. 'I'm at the waterfall. Where are you?'

'In a cave. I hear water but can't see a waterfall.'

'Are there big piles of rocks?'

'Shi, shi.'

'Come to the edge of the cave and look around the rock.' She rushed to a spot where she'd be visible.

'Ah, Milly. You okay? Baby okay?' He looked from her to the broken path. 'How did you get there?'

'Yesterday there was a path. The storm washed it away.'

'Milly, we were worried. Ky frantic. I must get you home.'

'I'm so sorry, Cheng. I've been an idiot. I want to come home, but I'll have to jump.'

'Ooh, no.'

'There's no other way.'

'Wait.' He disappeared from sight. She could hear him moving rocks.

Her heart leapt to her mouth. 'Don't touch the big pile of rocks, Cheng. Please.'

'Shi, shi.'

He emerged, struggling under a boulder. Dropping it into the gap, he returned for more. Some rocks crashed and bounced their way down the ravine, chilling her to the bone. But then one wedged between the rocks, and then another. Copying him, she dropped in a few smaller ones from her side, trying to find sizes and shapes that would lodge between the existing ones. Every time one crashed down the mountain, her stomach turned.

'Good, good.' Cheng's voice echoed from deep within the cave. 'I found a rope.'

He threw her one end. 'You tie it close to rock wall. Find a strong tree or firm rock, waist high. Tie tight.'

Looping it over a rock protruding from the escarpment, she tied it firmly, pulling the rope to test it. 'What now, Cheng?'

He disappeared into the cave. The rope pulled taut. 'Tight this end, Milly.' His beaming face appeared around the rock face. 'Now you have a hand rail. We pray and then you come to Cheng. And we go home. Okay?'

She swallowed the lump in her throat and whispered, 'I believe, God. I believe.'

El Shaddai

'Father God, help Milly and keep her safe. Thank you.' He beckoned her. 'Come now, Milly.' It felt like a command, not a suggestion.

'Hang on, Joshua.' Kissing his head, she faced the rock wall and grasped the rope with both hands. Her left leg waved over the edge and located the first rock.

'Keep your eyes on the next rock, Milly. Good. Another step.' Cheng's calm voice steadied her. The next rock moved under her feet. She screamed. Her knuckles gripped white on the rope.

'It's safe, Milly. A bit wobbly. Keep going. Only two more steps.' With that, Cheng pulled her into the cave. 'You're safe, my Milly. I can't bear to lose you.'

She clung to him, shaking, waiting for her heart to slow. When she opened her eyes, she saw the pile of rocks. For an instant she saw a fire blazing on the pyre. She blinked and it disappeared. 'Let's get out of this cave, Cheng.'

Without a word, he shouldered the backpack and helped her down the track.

***

That afternoon, Milly sat on the front veranda with Ky, Caro and Daphne. The kids were playing. Cheng had asked Joe to go with him to the shed. 'Okay, Milly. We're waiting.' Ky's red-ringed eyes reflected anger. Or was it disappointment?

'I'm sorry I frightened you, Ky. It's hard to explain. I was just so upset about losing Dad and possibly Dan. Voices started bombarding my head. I felt so guilty, upset, hopeless... I listened to a lot of lies of the enemy. I've been...'

Caro threw up her hands. 'Stop talking in riddles, Milly. Where'd you go? You met a man, didn't you? Where's he now?'

'Caro, I met Jesus.'

'What?'

'Yes. Jesus proposed to me last night, asking me to love Him for the rest of my life. First, He protected us in the storm. I thought the hut was going to be blown apart.'

'You went back to the hut alone!' Caro stamped her foot. 'Did you pick up my mobile?'

'Sorry, Caro. I didn't pick up anything.'

Caro stormed off the veranda. The screen door slammed behind her.

'Don't be hard on her, Milly. It's been difficult for her since she learned her parents died.'

'I can't judge anyone, Ky, not after leaving you.' Milly took the letter from her pocket and handed it to Ky. 'I found this in the hut, in Dan's red *El Shaddai* cup. Read it aloud so Daphne can hear.' She closed her eyes, letting the words wash over her.

As Ky finished reading, she jumped up and hugged Milly. Daph reached over and took her hand. 'Milly, that's so exciting. But you still haven't told us why you went back to the hut. Or how your hands got so torn.'

Milly dropped her head. How much could she tell them?

If you confess your sins to one another

Raising her eyes, she took a deep breath. 'I listened to a lie and let it consume me. I had a dream and I followed its instruction. That's why I returned to the cave.'

Ky reached for Milly's other shaking hand. 'The nightmare? Tell us.'

El Shaddai

'It said to the only way to get forgiveness was to sacrifice Joshua on the altar in the cave.'

Ky gasped. 'That's crazy…'

Daph patted Ky's knee. 'It's all right. Obviously, she didn't do it. Go on, Milly.'

'Voices called me, mocked me. The worst part… I abandoned God and followed them. It felt like talons were ripping me apart. I didn't care about my hands or our safety when I was climbing. I reached the cave, but I couldn't offer a clean sacrifice with dirty hands. And there wasn't any wood on the altar.' Her voice faded. The talons were coming for her throat again. The icy claws were stabbing her gut. She began to shake.

'Jesus!' Daph jumped to her feet. 'Jesus is sovereign over this home and these women. Devil. Be gone.' Her arms held Milly's quivering frame. 'I should have warned you about the darkness that claimed *El Shaddai*.'

'Go on,' Ky whispered.

'I took Josh to the oasis and laid him on the grass on a blanket. I didn't want to dirty his dress. I left him to wash and bandage my hands. When…' Her fingers covered her eyes. The stare of the snake's eyes bored into her soul.

'Tell us, Milly. Bring it all out.' Daph squeezed her hand.

'The light. Jesus bathed me in light.' It was a relief to change the picture. But the snake's eyes held her spiritual gaze. She jumped from the chair and ran inside.

Two hours later, she sat in the car beside Daph. Lily snuggled under one arm and Josh slept in his sling. She waved to Hoey swinging on the gate with Johnno. *Lord, I feel like a prisoner.*

As though she could read Milly's mind, Daphne patted her hand. 'You need a break, Milly. Stay with us for a few days.'

'I thought I could trust you so I told you the truth, but now I feel as though I'm being punished.'

'You've been through a shocking spiritual attack. There will be spiritual backlash. Let Joe and me support you for a few days.'

'There's something you're not telling me.'

'Cheng found the butchering knife in your bag.'

'So… you don't trust me?

'I don't trust the devil.'

'What about God? He rescued me. I trust Him.'

'And He's asked Joe and I to be His hands and feet, Milly. Come and rest. Let us protect you.' She smiled. 'You can try to contact Dan from my place.'

Milly brightened. Maybe Dan's mother's phone was still connected. She closed her eyes. She was so very tired.

Chapter 17

'JOSH IS LOOKING for his mummy again.' Daph stood at the bedroom door rocking the baby.

Milly pushed through the fog of sleep. 'How long have I been out, Daph? I'm sorry. I should be helping you.'

Daph sat beside her on the bed. 'I'm fine. I love minding the little ones. You were exhausted. Three days of rest and you can still sleep hours in the afternoon.'

Milly sat up and took charge of her squirming boy. 'I was close to the edge, wasn't I?'

'I'm glad you've rested. We're expecting visitors soon. The police have found some human remains. They want to ask us all some questions.' She turned and left at the sound of knocking at the front door.

Milly's heart beat out a tattoo in time with Joshua's sucking. *Lord. You said You'd be my husband. Where are You now?*

Right with you, Milly

Well, stop the police nosing about. I'm scared.

Be still, Milly

Don't say that. She felt like stamping her foot.

∼∞∼ I didn't come to manipulate and control the world. I came to walk with you in it ∼∞∼

Well, send Your angels if You can't handle it.

∼∞∼ Together we will handle it one day at a time. I am El Shaddai. I am sufficient ∼∞∼

She huffed. *Not happy, God. Not happy.*

∼∞∼ What happened to the trust and belief? ∼∞∼

She closed her eyes, her thoughts racing back to the evening at the hut. Trees had covered every part of the block, except the hut. He'd rescued her. He'd been her refuge and shelter. She had ridden out the storm because of His faithfulness. *Will You keep me out of jail, Lord?*

∼∞∼ I will never leave you or forsake you ∼∞∼

Daph pushed her head around the corner. 'Milly, they're here.'

In the kitchen, she shook hands with two policemen. The group sat around the table chatting. There was an easy repartee between the three men. 'Mrs Furley, Joe tells me you escaped Wamberoo. Well done. Do you have any identification on you?'

'Shall I get your purse, Milly?' Daph disappeared without waiting for a reply.

'When I sight your ID, we can remove your name from the missing persons list. We've already been to Mac's Place and spoken to Kyogle and Caroline, so we've heard most of your amazing survival story.'

'Mac's place?'

'The house where you are all living. Belongs to Mac.' He perused her licence. 'Cheng tells me you are his guests at um… *El Shaddai*, as he called it, pending the return of a McLaughlin family member. It's unusual but we live in unusual times and no one has charged you with trespassing. I can confirm Mr McLaughlin has been found deceased in his vehicle in Dead Man's Gully. We have been trying to locate Jamie McLaughlin to notify him of his father's death.'

Joe interrupted. 'It's all so tragic. You think Jamie is still alive? What about Zach?'

'It appears Jamie is still alive. Cheng had a visit from him some months ago. He's a little vague about the timing. We found human remains a couple of days ago. The autopsy is still be finalised, but we have reason to believe it is Zachariah.'

Daphne gasped. 'Oh no!'

'The body is in an unmarked grave. The location is confidential police information at the moment.' He turned to Milly. 'Now, Mrs Furley. Did you see any other people in your months on the mountain?'

'Yes. Two.'

'Who were they?'

'Bobby, a dark-skinned boy. Maybe in his early teens. He lived with us for a couple of months before he died.'

'What did he die of?'

'I don't know. He was very sick but we had no access to a doctor. He said he went into the dead country. His temperature soared and we couldn't get it down. It was very distressing with no medical assistance. Didn't Ky tell you this?'

'Yes. I needed to hear you confirm the story. Where would we find his body?'

'It's in his cave.' In response to his raised eyebrows, she rushed on. 'His camp before he stayed with us.'

'Can you tell us how to locate it?'

Milly explained as best as she could. Her head hurt.

'You said two people.' The sergeant turned to a clean sheet of paper. 'Who was the other one?'

She paused, checking her heart.

I'm here. Tell the truth ~~~~~~

'The other one... he raped me.' Tears, unwanted but unstoppable, coursed down her cheeks.

'I'm sorry, Mrs Furley. Can you describe him? Do you know his name? We will do what we can to charge him.'

'He... he said his name was Pete. He lured me into his parlour, as he called it. He was crazy. He told me he'd asked God for a wife, and God sent me. He claimed... claimed we would re-populate the earth like Abraham and Sarah.' Milly tried to shut out Daph's shocked face. Having never been asked about the baby, she'd never told this story. She held Joshua close, her tears bathing his head again.

'We'll need more details. What happened after the rape?'

She paused, studying a stain on the kitchen floor. 'Sergeant, may I talk privately? This is embarrassing for me.' As Joe and Daphne rose to leave, she decided to let Joshua go. Kissing her little boy on the head, she wondered how long it would be before she saw him again. *Lord, are You sure? I'm frightened.*

Warm peace crept back into her heart. She took a quick breath and rushed on before she changed her mind. 'After he raped me, I killed him.'

'You overpowered him?'

El Shaddai

'Not exactly. He was a broad man. Too strong for me. I kicked and fought and bit, but he still held me down on the dirt and... and...'

'It's okay. Let's take it steady.' He waited for her to calm. 'First things first. Had you encouraged him at all?'

Milly jumped up, enraged. 'What are you implying?'

'Did you run away or hide? Did you talk to him, go swimming with him?'

She clung to the kitchen table. Her body shook. Her legs turned to jelly.

The sergeant stood and held her arm. 'Please sit down, Mrs Furley. I'm sorry to have to ask you these questions. But we must get a clear picture. You say you killed a man. I must ascertain your motivation.' He eased her back to her chair. 'I'm sorry I don't have a female officer with me. I can ask Daphne to come back in.'

'I'm sorry, Officer.' She tried to pull herself together.

They were interrupted by a knock on the door.

'Come in.'

Ky rushed in. 'You okay?'

Milly didn't reply. *No, I'm not okay.* Except for a corner of peace in her heart, she was terrified.

Ky looked at the sergeant. 'Can I stay?'

He indicated a chair beside Milly. 'Now, as I was saying, did you have any interaction with this Pete before the rape?'

Milly swallowed. 'We had run out of water at the hut. So I explored further than I'd been before, looking for a creek, a well, anything.' In a monotone she related the story of finding water. Both men listened in silence until she related taking her clothes off to bathe her body.

'You swam naked when you knew he was there?'

'No. I called out. He didn't answer. I assumed he wasn't there.'

'Why did you swim naked?'

Ky grabbed Milly's shaking hand. 'Can I explain something, Officer?' At his nod, she went on. 'We hadn't had enough water to drink, let alone wash, for days. We'd take sponge baths, using the same water we used to wash our filthy children. When you are that dirty, you need a bath with no clothes. The next day when Milly led us to the water, we all bathed naked.'

As both men stared at her, blank looks on their faces, she shrugged. 'I guess you wouldn't understand unless you'd been in the situation... and were female.'

'My job, ma'am, is to get facts. Not to understand.' He turned back to Milly. 'I have noted your desperate need to clean your body, and hence discard your clothes in a public place.'

'Public place!' Ky exploded. 'We were marooned on private property, isolated from all civilisation and you call it a *public* place?'

For a moment Milly thought the sergeant would send Ky from the room. A red flush flooded his ample neck. He loosened his collar. 'Maybe I will come back and do this tomorrow and bring a woman officer.'

Milly couldn't bear the thought of another day. 'No. I'll tell you the rest of the story.' In her frustration, she related the story in graphic detail. 'What choice did I have, Officer? Stay there and suffer ongoing abuse and leave the others without water? Run away and have him track me back to the hut and put everyone at risk?' She folded her hands and waited, pulse racing.

Both men wrote in silence. The younger man, who hadn't yet spoken a word, looked at Milly. 'What date did it happen?'

'You don't get it at all, do you?' Ky glared at him. 'We were marooned. No calendar, no phone, no radio. And you want a date?'

He had the grace to blush. 'Sorry, Ma'am. I didn't think. Somehow, we must try to get an approximation.'

'It's all right, Ky. I can answer. Joshua is seven weeks old. He was smaller than my other babies. Maybe born at thirty-five weeks? Work it out from there.'

The sergeant looked stunned. 'Are you saying this baby is a result of the rape?'

'Of course. I thought you'd have worked that out.'

He shook his head. 'Mrs Furley, I'm sorry for having to make you relive such a horrendous event. You have my sympathy. We have more investigation to do. Please don't leave here until we talk again.'

Milly's stomach turned over. 'Can I go back to *El Shaddai*?'

'Yes, but don't leave there.' They gathered their papers and left.

Milly held her head in her hands. The whole world seemed to be spinning out of control.

'Why did you tell them, Milly?'

'God told me to tell the truth. I have to trust He will protect me, Ky. He promised to be my husband.'

Back at *El Shaddai*, the days dragged on with no more word from the police. Milly felt hemmed in and insecure. Part of her was desperate to find Dan but his mother hadn't answered her calls. The other part was relieved, as she dreaded having to tell him about Pete and Joshua. Waking early one morning she snuck out of the house, leaving Joshua asleep. *Lord, please send Your angels to watch him. Will You meet me in the orchard? I need to talk.*

As she walked through the first section of trees a breeze played with the leaves. They danced and twirled in front of her, catching the early morning light. A flock of tiny robins sang in the orchard, their chorus conducted by a lone magpie, dressed in his best morning suit. *Wonderful floor show, Lord.*

I'm glad you like it. I do a different one each morning

And no two are ever the same?

Every morning is new, like My mercies

I love this place, Lord.

I knew you would. I prepared it especially for you

She wandered past the area where they'd danced in the moonlight. Leaving the trees, she leaned on the rail of the stockyard. How much longer can I stay here at El Shaddai?

I have given it to you. It is yours

The papers say it belongs to the McLaughlin family.

Not on My documents

But, Lord, it's easy for You to say. I live in a world full of rules and regulations. There are laws. I have no legal rights.

Not that you understand

But, Lord. It's crazy. I can't just behave as if I own it.

Open a trust account. Call it El Shaddai His laughter seemed to bubble from deep within her. *Then*

I'll own it. It will be under My name, and what is Mine is yours. Now, come and dance with Me ～ɘɘ～

Laughing, she climbed to the top rail. With arms held wide to keep balance, she walked around the yards.

～ɘɘ～ *Can I walk with you?* ～ɘɘ～

She paused on top of a post and one foot after and other raced to the next one. Exhilarated, she felt as though she didn't have a care in the world. Reaching the large corner post she spun, embracing the first rays of sun, her face lifted to the sky. *Lord, help me not get dragged down by the cares of the world.*

～ɘɘ～ *Your choice, My Milly. I can only carry what you give Me* ～ɘɘ～

Well, have it all. She flung her arms in the air.

Later that morning, she sat on the office chair in the bedroom. She'd never before touched the boss's private desk. The filing drawer didn't respond to her tug. She'd need a key to access the contents, but the top drawer slid open. The contents were tidy, like the rest of the property. The pen tray sat high in the drawer. Lifting it she found a large writing pad. Under it were stacks of different envelopes, stamps and invoices.

Fuel was the biggest expense. There were payments to trucking companies, Telstra, the hardware store in Blue Rock. At the back of the drawer she discovered a black pouch, closed by a red drawstring. *Is it gold nugget, Lord?* She chuckled, opened it, and tipped the contents onto the desk. A pile of keys winked at her, each one labelled. The key for the filing drawer turned the lock and it slid open. She looked over her shoulder as though Mac's ghost watched her. *Is this okay, Lord?*

꧁ Let's look together, Milly ꧂

Her fingers followed the file labels, until she found *Legal Documents*. She placed the file on the desk. *Okay. Let's see if we can find my name anywhere.*

Near the bottom of the folder, she found the property deeds. *Alice McLaughlin!* The deeds were in Alice's name. Mac's name wasn't anywhere.

His will held no surprises. His entire estate was bequeathed to his sons or, in the event of their deaths, their sons. No mention of daughters. The will named Benjamin (Jamie) McLaughlin as executor and, in the case of his death, Joe Cavanagh. As she returned the paperwork, she spied another key in the bottom of the legal folder. The faded paper label said, *El Shaddai*, written in a flowing hand. She twisted it over in her hand, heart fluttering.

꧁ Now you have the key to El Shaddai ꧂

I have no idea what you mean, Lord. Wandering around the house, she checked the locks on the doors. The key didn't match any of them. It was the only key in the pouch that puzzled her. The others were all labelled: *storeroom, petrol tank, post office box.* Should she keep this special key in her purse? After all God led her to it.

꧁ Everything is yours, Milly ꧂ His soft presence took her breath away.

🪶 🪶

Daph carried a tray to their table on the veranda. Milly visited often now, trying to ring Dan's mum or her own mother, without success. Joe flopped in a chair, having just returned from a visit to Blue Rock Legal Advisors.

He spread jam on one of Daphne's scones. 'There's nothing I can do. Alice still owns *El Shaddai*. The solicitor says we will have to wait until Jamie is located. He should be able to claim the property.'

Milly listened but something seemed wrong. *What are we missing?* 'I need to find Alice's will. It isn't in the drawer with the boss's. Maybe it's in the storeroom.'

Joe wiped jam from the corner of his mouth and reached for another scone. '*El Shaddai* is crying out for attention. The stock need care. Some of the water points need maintenance and then there's weed management and fences to fix. Mac's been gone more than a year. I want to do something, but my hands are tied.'

'Can I do some of the work, Joe?'

'Maybe you could spray, but you'd have to leave Joshua behind. Cheng tells me you are out of chemicals.'

'God told me to open a trust account called *El Shaddai*, and run the business through it. Could you be the trustee?'

'Interesting idea. Then we could sell some cattle, deposit the money and buy what's needed. If the books were well-kept and audited...' Joe sipped his coffee, a faraway look in his eyes. 'I'll go back to the solicitor.'

Early next morning Milly left Joshua with Ky and went for a walk. The first rays of sunlight turned the orchard into a glittering wonderland. *It's beautiful, El Roi.*

Let's go out on the quad

I'm trying to conserve petrol.

Why? There's plenty

Jo Wanmer

But we could only afford a month's supply.

We? I'm not limited by petrol supply

But, Lord...

Nor am I limited by money

I try to understand, but it's hard for me to grasp.

Did you ever go hungry in the hut?

It got mighty lean towards the end.

Which forced you to overcome your fear and find El Shaddai

Leaning on the rail, Milly turned the thought over in her mind. It was true. Desperation for water had pushed her out, led her to the spring and waterfall. Lack of supplies had sent her on a hunt for the garden and house. *Yes, Lord. But it's hard for me to ignore the world's restrictions.*

The quad? Let's ride

Once away from the yards, she opened the throttle and sped down the track, relishing the wind rushing through her hair. Just her, God, and wide-open spaces. *Where to, God?*

Back to the forest

I don't want to go back there. It's embarrassing.

Embarrassing?

It's where I nearly... I'm not saying it God. You know.

Nearly, Milly. But you didn't

Thanks to You.

At the edge of the forest, she stilled the motor. The soft glow of the Lord's presence encouraged her to go further. She walked among the towering trees. The sun hadn't yet penetrated the canopy to dispel the gloom. No mocking voices in her ears this time, just wind in the treetops and her own pounding heart. They wandered down the path, a sense of expectation bubbling in her.

Milly, do you love Me?

Yes, I love You, Lord. Have You bought me back to the place where I denied You? This is reminding me of the day You met Apostle Peter on the beach.

He chuckled. *I love you so much, Milly. Don't leave Me again. Don't let another love come between us*

She leaned against a tall tree and considered His words. What did He mean?

I will never, never leave you, Milly. I may turn My face in anger, but My love will never fade

How should she respond? *You alone know My heart, Lord. As well as I can, I will always love You. Please help my love.*

It's all I ask. I love you, Milly

It felt as though God had closed the conversation. She turned to go. Plenty of jobs awaited her. The watering spots needing checking. She'd swing past them on the way. The joy in her heart erupted into singing as she marched back through the trees.

'Milly. Is that you, Milly?' A male voice rang through the forest.

She stopped, frozen. It sounded like Dan. *Could it be?* Her heart beat a crazy tattoo. *But this is Pete country.* In silence she slipped behind a bush.

'Milly. Milly.'

The voice arrested her. 'Who's there?'

'It's me, Milly.' Footsteps crashed through the bush. 'Milly, I've found you. By the grace of God, I've found you.'

Heart in her mouth, her feet flew towards the voice. 'Dan… this way.' Her heartbeat pounded in her ears drowning out his voice.

Then he came. Racing to her. She froze. *What if I'm going crazy again?* He grabbed her. His arms pulled her in close, her head pushed against his chest. His heart beat as loud as hers. 'Milly. Oh, my Milly.' His tears fell into her hair. Hers washed his t-shirt. Her legs collapsed under her, but he held her tighter. 'Never again! Never again will I leave you. Hoey? Lily? Are they okay?'

She nodded, wiping her tears on his shirt. 'They'll be so excited. Oh, Dan. How did you find us?'

'I tried to track you from the hut through the forest, but I lost the trail. Yesterday I wandered through endless long grass without seeing anyone. I decided I'd have to go back to the hut. But before I fell asleep, I asked God to bring you.' He lowered her feet to the ground and sought her eyes. 'And this morning, I'm woken by your singing.'

With her shoulder tucked under his arm, she took him towards the quad. She turned, nerves quelling her excitement. How could she tell him about Joshua? She stared back to the trees.

'Milly? What's wrong?'

As usual he could read her every mood. He lifted her chin. 'There's so much to tell you, Dan.'

'And?' His hands rubbed her shoulders.

His closeness thrilled her and yet her insides were in turmoil. 'Dan, I want to hear what's happened to you.'

El Shaddai

'There's something bothering you. Something is stopping you taking me to the children.' He shuddered. 'Is there another man, Milly?'

'Only Cheng.'

He stepped back. 'Cheng? Who's Cheng?'

'He's the gardener. He's been so good to us.'

Dan frowned. 'Did you think I'd never be back?'

'No. I was sure you'd find us somehow. And then I found your name on the *Missing, Presumed Dead* list. It broke me.' She lifted her gaze from the trees. His eyes were filled with pain. 'What, Dan?'

'Why then, did you take another man?' His voice was a tearful whisper. 'What's his name again? Bing? Bang? Bung?'

Milly spun him to face her. 'Dan. Cheng is like a father to me. Don't talk crazy.'

'But you said...' He stopped, his head tilted. 'I'm confused, Milly. Please tell me whatever it is.'

'I... I was raped.' Shaking, she hid her eyes in his chest. 'I'm sorry, Dan. I'm so sorry.'

He stiffened. Every muscle went taut, but his arms tightened around her. 'Milly... oh, Milly. Who...when?'

'Not long after we were stranded. A rough violent moron.' She took a deep breath. 'There's more, Dan. He… he left a permanent legacy with me.'

'Did he hurt you? You look fabulous, Milly, even in those unusual clothes. What are you talking about?'

'I... I.' She swallowed. 'I have another son. His son. I'm sorry, Dan. But when I get home, he'll be looking for a feed.'

'A baby?' He cupped her head and looked into her eyes. 'You have another baby? A baby is fine. Another man I'd have to fight. Is he in jail?'

'I... I...' She couldn't say it.

'Milly?'

'He's dead, Dan.'

The tension left his face. She saw him pull himself together. Then a smile, for her sake. 'So, you and I are good. Nothing coming between us?'

She wondered what dark valleys he'd been through in the past year that he was so readily accepting of her news. 'Never, Dan. Except for one of the cutest babies you've ever seen.'

'Let's go, then. I've got three kids to hug.' He settled behind her on the quad, his arms around her waist.

They sped back towards the house. Milly's heart sang. Dan was home. Everything would be fine. He'd look after them as he always did.

'Who owns this place Milly?' Dan's question whistled around in her head as the wind rushed through her hair.

'We're not sure.' She laughed. 'But we're living here.'

'I've seen it... as though I've been here before. I've dreamt... of land like this.'

She peeped the horn, hoping Hoey would come. Cheng emerged from the shed door. 'Milly...' He stopped, startled by the man clinging to her waist.

'Cheng. This is my husband, Dan.'

Part 4

The Recompense

Chapter 18

CHENG'S FACE WAS DRAWN. It was obvious he was disturbed. 'Milly...'

Milly jumped from the quad. 'Cheng, What's wrong?'

'Milly.' The sergeant strode from the shed. He acknowledged Dan's presence with a brief nod. 'Please accompany me.' He led her into the shed to a bench. 'Milly, do you recognise any of these items?' Unwrapping a cloth, he waved her towards it. 'Please don't touch them.'

Cheng's red ring blinked at her. She'd lost it... she didn't know when but suspected it was on that dreadful climb back to Pete's cave.

Beside it, lay a gold band, very like her wedding ring. She hadn't had it since the hut.

'The ring with the stone looks like one Cheng gave me. I lost it the other day.' She swallowed before she could talk about the other one. 'I would need to check inside the gold one.'

'What would be inside?'

'Dan loves Milly.' She turned met Dan's startled eyes behind her.

'Exactly.' The sergeant cleared his throat. 'Amalya Furley, you are charged with the murder of Zachariah McLaughlin. I must now place you under arrest and ask you to return to Blue Rock Police Station for further questioning.' He continued, rambling on about her rights, but her mind was too scrambled to listen.

Dan grabbed the policeman's arm. 'What's going on?'

The sergeant turned and glared. 'Who are you?'

'Dan Furley. Milly's my wife.'

'Ah. Caught you out of hiding.'

'What do you mean? I found her this morning, about an hour ago. I've been searching for her and my kids for nearly a year.'

The younger policeman grabbed Milly's hands and yanked them behind her back. Cold steel bit as he jammed her wrists into handcuffs.

'Milly?' Dan's voice broke. 'What...?'

The sergeant pushed past him and grabbed her arm. 'Car's this way.'

'Mummy, Mummy...' Hosea stopped under the trees, confusion in his eyes.

'Hosea.' Dan ran to him.

'Daddy. You came.' He jumped into Dan's open arms. 'What are they doing to Mummy? Make them let her go.'

Milly's heart shattered as they dragged her away. 'My baby. Sergeant, I need my baby.'

He pulled her towards the car. 'Kid's been in the car waiting for ages. I told you not to leave Mac's Place.'

'I didn't.' Behind her Lily cried. In front of her Joshua screamed, strapped in a car seat. The constable shoved her

El Shaddai

into the vehicle. The door slammed. Before she could right herself, the car drove away.

The barred cell offered no privacy. Not that it mattered. No one had been near her for hours. Three times the sergeant had started to interview her. 'Can you explain why your wedding ring was under the body of Zachariah McLaughlin?'

'I've never met the man,' she insisted, cradling Joshua.

The door burst open and a constable yelled. 'Drunken brawl at Wallace's place. The old girl out there is frantic.'

The sergeant had shoved her straight back in the cell. Three times—the same sort of interruption. *God. I want Dan. First You bring him, and then rip me away from him. It's harder than if I'd never seen him.* Hot anger boiled.

Be still, Milly

How? I'm in jail. Accused of a murder I didn't do.

But I'm here

Well, fight for me. Dan tried to fight for me.

And legalists stopped him

Yes. What are You saying, God?

There always is a battle to claim Promised Land

God, I'm too tired for riddles. The bare bulb glared at her from the roof. She wriggled on the bench. Memories of sleeping outside the hut flashed through her mind. It seemed a lifetime ago. *At least when I slept on the ground there were stars. Is there any end to this battle? You say to come to You and You'll give me rest. Is this the best You can do?*

Milly sat on the thinly padded plank that doubled as a bed. Joshua squirmed, wanting to sleep. She turned the sling into a cradle and laid him against the wall.

Get ready, Milly. Strap Joshua in

Was it her imagination? Even with God's presence in the room, a foreboding shimmied through her body. As she tied the sling around herself, she heard the front door open. Someone crept through the station. Every hair on her arms stood to attention. Where could she hide?

Under My wing

It's not feeling safe, Lord. She crouched in the corner. Doors opened and shut, one after the other.

'Hah! Bingo.' The familiar, whispered voice made her shudder.

Lord, I trust You. Well I... I'm trying.

'There you are, Milly.' George leered at her through the bars. 'We meet again.' The keys rattled in his hand. 'I'm trying to let you go before the pigs get back. Do you know which key?'

She pulled back into the corner. 'I'll stay here, thanks.'

'Bingo!' The door swung open. 'C'mon. Hurry up.'

Milly didn't move. 'Don't be stupid, George. You can't break into a police station.'

He grabbed her arms and yanked her up. 'Do you want to walk, or will we do it the rough way?' He glared. 'Either way you are coming with me. Now!'

'Let me go.' She snatched up her bag and marched out. If she could get to the street first, she'd run. But as she reached the front door, a hand grabbed her and a rag covered her nose.

When she woke, she was lying, on her side, jammed into a small space. Her brain was foggy. Joshua screamed, squashed

El Shaddai

against her, still in his sling. As she tried to push herself up, she realised she was on the back seat of a speeding car. The world spun.

'Shut the kid up.' George poked her in the ribs. 'You can sit now. We're well out of town.'

'Stop being a moron, George.' It took Milly a moment to realise there was someone else in the car. The driver looked older, maybe Joe's age. 'I said I'd help you get her, but don't you dare you lay another hand on her.'

'Just me eyes, mate. Told you she was good eye candy.'

'My car's here.' The driver pulled off the road. 'You look after her well.'

The car stopped and the man jumped out. Dread overwhelmed Milly as George jumped into the driver's seat and adjusted his rear-view mirror so he could watch her. 'Kid locks all on, so don't try anything fancy.'

Under the cover of the sling, Milly fed Joshua. 'Where are you taking me?'

'I got a little place. Not fancy, but the pigs won't find you there.'

'Why? What do you want with me?'

'Not you… though you could be a bit of fun. My beef isn't with you but with the little fella there. I need more information.' He swung the car off the bitumen and they bounced down a nearly invisible track.

Joshua? What's he want with Joshua?

The trees parted. In the glare of the headlights, she could see a shack. The car braked at a crude entry. He leapt out and reefed open her car door. Gripping her arm, he yanked her up the path and shoved her into the hut. Her bag hit the floor beside her. 'See you later, Darling. Got a party to go to.' The door slammed, leaving her in the pitch-black room. She heard the click of a deadlock. The car engine roared away into the distance.

Her nerves boomed in her ears. She rocked Joshua and blinked, willing her eyes to adjust to the dark. *Lord. Are You here, Lord?*

Always. Be still, Milly

As if I have a choice. What's going on? Where were the angels?

Be still, Milly

Milly stamped her foot. *Be still... be still... I'm over it. I'd like action. You said You'd be my husband.*

You said you'd trust me

The pounding in her veins dissolved in tears. She moved towards a bed-shaped shadow in the corner. Kicking off her shoes, she crawled under a doona. Her crying baby settled back on her breast. Dry sobs shook her body until sleep claimed her.

Joshua woke her. Her bed smelled masculine and musty. *God, where am I?* The craziness of the previous day rocked her. George had somehow staged those interruptions at the police station so he could get a chance to abduct her. *No. Not me. Joshua.*

Her gaze swept the dim room. Two doors, one secured by a deadlock last night. Putting the baby over her shoulder, she crossed to the second door. A gush of cool air hit her face as it opened. Her heart leapt.

El Shaddai

She was looking into a crude outdoor bathroom with a hand basin and shower. The slatted floor allowed water to fall to the ground below. Past the shower was another shut door. Pushing it open, she recoiled at a putrid smell. A board with a rough-edged sawn hole covered a drop toilet. The foul-smelling room had no ventilation or window. Her hopes plummeted. She held her nose, and retreated.

Back inside, she checked the windows. All were covered with heavy bars behind faded curtains. *God, there's no escape. But I remember somewhere in Your word it says You'd make a way out. So, I'm asking for it. I want to get back to Dan and the kids.*

I am the Way, Milly. Breakfast

The kerosene refrigerator and pantry were well-stocked. At least she wouldn't starve, but her heart flipped. Did he plan to keep her for a long time? Eating cereal at the bench, she made sandwiches and filled her backpack. If any chance of escape opened, she'd be ready.

Joshua gurgled on the bed, his arms and legs waving as he smiled. 'I'm glad you find it funny, little man. Mummy's not amused.' She smiled back. 'You think Mummy should be still, don't you? But I can't sit here and do nothing. You wait on the bed. Mummy is going to check every board and nail in this place until I find something loose.'

After a while she sank into the old recliner near the windows. *Nothing, Lord. Nothing. Not even a loose nail.*

The bathroom tantalised her because the ground was visible below her feet. Maybe she could lift floor boards. All she needed was a hammer. George must have some tools. Where would he keep them?

Starting with the kitchen drawers, she went through all his possessions. A desk with three drawers sat diagonally opposite the bed. A couple of plastic boxes with blue lids were beside it. She started at the top drawer. Pens and pencils lay with a couple of rulers and a tape measure. In the third drawer, she pulled out a manila folder. The name scribbled on the tab arrested her. 'Mac's Place.'

Is there something here, Lord? The warmth of His presence touched her, catching her breath. She laid the file on the desk. *God, please help me to see what You want me to see and to hear Your voice.*

The top piece of paper was a copy of the boss's will, the same document she had found in the desk at *El Shaddai*. Another sheet was attached behind it, with a red paperclip. It listed the deaths of Alice, Hannah and William, each entry highlighted by a big red tick.

At the bottom, written in red, he'd scrawled. 'Only two? to go.'

Jamie DEAD?	No kids known
Zach DEAD. Lost in earthquake	Kids? A couple in Wamberoo. Mother never let him close. They don't know their dad. Girl in Blue Rock — girl. OK. Milly's bastard?????
Robert? Disappeared	His squawking mother is with Zach.

Below the table he'd scrawled, 'ALL MINE.'

What did it mean? Milly's bastard? Joshua? The hackles rose on the back of her neck. Why would they be on this list? *El Roi, I see but I don't understand. Does he think Josh stands in the way of him inheriting El Shaddai?*

It belongs to you, Milly

Not according to this.

I've staked a claim on your behalf

She tried to order her muddled thoughts. One by one she turned over sheets of paper, trying to understand. She found a copy of the police report on the boss's death, declaring it accidental. Red pen circled the word and also circled the DNA report confirming his identity.

Multiple pages of maps were clumped together with an orange paperclip. Studying them she recognised *El Shaddai*. All the watering places and fences were marked. The property spread much further than she'd realised. Some of the maps were marked by crosses, with scrawled comments. 'Twenty paces NW from red gum.' 'Marked big rock with a cross.'

Sorry, God. I don't get it. Is this where he hides drugs? Or guns? Or buries his victims? She shuddered and checked the rest of the drawer. Below random receipts and bills was a file of newspaper clippings. She stopped at a headline, *Bull Tramples Rose*. Her eyes scanned the report of Hannah Rose's death.

Lord, why would he keep such a report? There's more, isn't there? But what if he finds me reading his stuff?

He's been detained

Milly shook her head and tried to make sense of the papers. They confirmed George's determination to own *El Shaddai*. Had he killed anyone who stood in his way?

After reading a report on William's accidental death, she found a clipping about Alice. Old man McLaughlin requested a death certificate for his wife, stating she'd been missing for five years. 'Alice McLaughlin was last seen when she left the homestead at Mac's Place to go and live with her son, Zachariah McLaughlin. He presented an affidavit, stating he had never seen his mother. Neighbours presented statements saying her disappearance was out of character.' The court had granted the death certificate declaring her deceased, whereabouts of body unknown.

There were some old family pictures taken on the front steps of her house. Milly pored over them, trying to identify people she'd never met. George stood in the front row, circled in red. Hannah looked about three, reminding her of Lily. Lily. *God, I've got to get out of here and back to my kids.*

Keep learning, Milly

Turning over a cattle sale report, she gasped. *Pete!* His filthy face leered at her from the page. 'WANTED. PIRATE PETE.' The tattered poster looked like it'd been ripped off a wall. It offered a reward for any information leading to his capture, dead or alive. The sergeant needed to see this.

But how? The danger of George returning increased by the minute. She pushed the desk, wedging it up against the door. Puffing, she settled back on the bed to feed Joshua.

Be still, Milly

What is it, God? Her nerves jangled on edge. Was something about to happen?

A car? She strained her ears.

A car stopped outside the front door. The motor stilled. Milly waited, nerves jumping. She checked the desk. It was solid but she leaned against it to be sure. A door slammed. A key turned the lock. *George! Only he'd have a key!*

The door didn't budge. The key turned the lock a few more times. Another car door slammed. There were two people. The driver who'd helped George abduct her?

'Let me try.' The voice was male but muffled. The lock turned and she heard a strong shoulder hit the door. It moved her blockade a little. She shoved the desk back.

'It's jammed. You won't get in there. C'mon, let's go.'

'But, Dan. Have one more go.' Milly recognised Caroline's best wheedling voice.

'Dan!' Milly tried to pull the desk back but it was wedged tight. 'Dan, don't go!' She banged the walls, yelling.

Caro screamed. Car doors banged. Dropping Josh in the middle of the bed, she pushed back the desk and yanked at the door. It opened. They'd left it unlocked. She ran down the track, yelling and waving her arms. The car accelerated into the distance. It was the car Caro had used to leave *El Shaddai* a few days after they arrived. Her heart sank as it disappeared. Dan had come but he'd left when she called. He must have heard her when she banged on the walls. *Surely.*

Tears coursed down her face. How could he? Did he hate her because she'd been raped? He'd been too quick to accept Joshua. Was he now rethinking? And why was he with Caro? Her devastation turned to anger. She ran back to the hut. Picking up her screaming baby she strapped him to her chest.

No longer captive

Of course. I'm free. But for how long?

Slipping both folders into the backpack, she filled a couple of water bottles and left the shack behind, door pulled shut, furniture all over the place. But where would she go? Where could she go? Nowhere felt safe.

She jogged down the track until she heard a car. Ducking behind a bush she hid and peered through the foliage. *Is it George?* The vehicle roared past. A public road. Should she hitchhike? But where to? Back to the police? Home to confront Dan? Hopelessness suffocated her. There was no answer. She sat under the bush, knees under her chin. *I'm waiting for You, Lord.*

Several cars went past. She had no idea what to do. A vehicle passed the track, then braked hard. Had the driver had seen her? The car turned and eased onto the track. It wasn't George.

Dan! When she stood, he skidded to a stop, and ran from the car. 'Milly. Milly, it is you! We thought you were dead.' He squeezed her, twirled her and kissed her.

'Dan.' Was she excited or angry? She didn't know. 'Get me away from here. Now.' He bundled her into the car and turned it towards *El Shaddai*. 'Dan, we should go to the police station.'

'No station to go to. It burned to the ground last night.'

'What?' She shivered and moved closer to his side.

'I went in this morning to try to get you. The whole building is a charred mess of ash and twisted metal. They told me they'd left you locked in the cell to attend a call out. Firemen are still there. They're assuming you died in the fire.' Tears ran down his cheeks. 'To have just found you and to lose you was... was...' His shoulders shook. 'Caro was driving me home and she decided to call in to get something from that place. I was upset and angry. I didn't know how to tell the kids you were never coming back.'

'Why did you leave?'

'Caro freaked out. She thought she heard a ghost. It took me a while to realise it could be you. Then she wouldn't turn round and go back.'

'A fire.' Milly's brain whirred. *George!* 'Dan, do you think God rescued me before the fire? And I've been so angry with Him.'

He turned onto the road past Daphne's place. 'I'm taking you home to *El Shaddai*. When we're ready, we can ring the police and sort the false charges out.'

'But Dan...'

'Yes?'

'I did kill a man, but not Zach.'

Chapter 19

WHEN THEY ARRIVED AT EL SHADDAI, Joe and Daph were in the kitchen with the family. After Milly hugged her kids, everyone gathered around the table. Her head still spun. Was it only yesterday she found Dan? Nothing that had happened quite made sense. 'Caro, why do you have a key to George's shack?'

'He used to lock me in when he went to town. One day I found the key and hid it. He was livid but he had another copy. He never locked me in again.'

'Why go back today?'

'Some of my stuff is there. We saw George being arrested in Blue Rock, so I grabbed the opportunity to raid his place.'

Milly blinked. 'Arrested?' *Is that what You meant by detained, God?*

Ky offered Milly a cup of tea. 'Well, I'm very glad you're alive. I don't understand why George would kidnap you.'

'He wanted Joshua and more information.' She looked at Daph and Joe. 'Does it make any sense to you?'

Daph shook her head. 'My poor brain is so muddled.' Joe looked thoughtful but he also shook his head.

'I found some interesting things in George's shack. I brought them with me.' She reached for her backpack and retrieved the folders. 'He won't be happy when he finds they're missing.'

Cheng nodded. 'I'll sleep in the pantry tonight. He's dangerous.'

Milly spread the will, papers and maps on the table. Joe grabbed the sheet with the will, staring at George's list of family. 'He really is after *El Shaddai*. This implies he's willing to murder to get it.'

'And always says *El Shaddai* his.' Cheng pointed to a cross one of the maps. 'I saw him here years back. He got very angry. Said next time I followed he'd shoot me.'

'But what does he want with Milly? With Joshua?' Dan's arm tightened around her shoulders.

Taking the second folder, Milly paused, nervous butterflies fluttering in her stomach. *Are there clues here, Lord? Should I leave this one?* 'You have a look, Joe. There's lots of photographs and newspaper articles.'

Joe and Daph poured through the pictures, exclaiming over photos of their old friends. Cheng looked over their shoulders. 'Why the circle?'

Milly turned to Daph. 'I thought one of them looked like George. Who is the other one?'

Daph pushed a few across the table. 'This is George and the other is Zach. And again in this picture and this one. Look at Alice. That wasn't long after Hannah died. There's so much sadness in her eyes.'

El Shaddai

Joe selected another picture. 'This one is clearer. It's the two of them. They were close as boys.' As he held it up, Milly saw writing on the back.

'Let me have a look.'

Dan read the faint red writing aloud. 'This day I, Zachariah, solemnly declare I will equally share *Mac's Place* with my blood brother George. This day I, George, declare I will never betray Zachariah.' He looked up. 'It's co-signed.'

Milly shivered. 'Do you think it is written in blood, Dan?'

Caro giggled. 'A bit melodramatic, Milly. It's just a kid's playground deal.'

Dan shook his head. 'It's only dated a few years ago. And yes, Milly, it looks like blood to me. We should photocopy it before it fades completely.' He dropped it on the table. 'I'll get an envelope for it.'

Milly turned it over to look at the picture and dropped it. The pulse in her neck banged like a drum in her ears. *Surely not!* But those eyes, the face.

Ky reached out to steady her. 'Milly, are you okay?'

'Joe.' The tremor in her voice betrayed her panic. 'Please pass me the bottom piece of paper in the folder. Be careful. It's tattered.'

As he pulled it from the pile, Daph started to cry. He looked at it, swallowed and placed it in the middle of the table.

'Who is it, Joe?'

Joe pulled Daph in close. 'It's Pirate Pete. We believe he killed a precious girl who worked for us for years. We loved her very much. The police offered a reward, but they never caught him.'

'But who is it, Joe?'

'He looks a lot like Zach. We have sometimes wondered if it was him.'

Cheng was shaking with anger. 'It's Zach. He was a wicked man. He took innocent Mary. He took my Alice. Thank God he's dead. He can't hurt anyone anymore.'

Dan put the picture and the poster side by side. The resemblance was obvious. Milly's emotions flooded through her, out of control. She shook, teeth chattering. *Pirate Pete. Of course.* A memory of his guttural 'arr' flashed into her mind.

'Oh, Milly!' Ky jumped to her feet. 'It's Pete, isn't it?'

Milly nodded, tears running down her cheeks. The man she'd killed was Zachariah MacLaughlin, after all.

'Of course it is, Ky.' Caro eyes sparked. 'Why all the drama? I don't understand.'

Ky pinned her gaze on Caroline. 'Pete raped Milly. He's Joshua's father.'

All eyes at the table turned to Milly, shocked. Dan banged his fist down on the leering face again and again, until Ky rescued the frail poster. 'Milly may need this.'

Every eye in the room focussed on Milly. Heat flooded up her neck to her face. Now they all knew of her shame.

'You killed him, my Milly? You killed him?' Cheng sought her eyes with his wet ones.

'I... I'm s... sorry, Cheng. I was hurt... and scared... for me and the family.'

'Then you're a hero, my hero.' His eyes met hers. 'And Joshua is really his baby?'

Milly nodded. Her head spun.

Cheng bowed. 'That's why I love you so much. You bring me a little piece of my Alice.'

She lifted her eyes to his. 'But I still killed a man. Zachariah McLaughin apparently. I'm still under murder charges.'

Daph wept in Joe's arms. He looked over her head, his eyes wide. 'So... Joshua will inherit *El Shaddai* unless Jamie shows up.'

'What?' Dan and Milly sat bolt upright.

'Well, if he is Zach's son and the other sons have died...'

'What about other grandchildren?' Dan's voice was weak.

'George has checked it out. Because George has no claim unless everyone else is dead.'

Dan slumped back in his chair. 'That explains why he's after Joshua. And Milly.'

Daph wiped her eyes with Joe's chequered handkerchief. 'Joe, there's still Bob.'

'Who's Bob?' Milly asked. 'I've never heard of him.'

Cheng shuffled to stand near Milly. 'Another son of boss. One day Boss brought home indigenous girl to help Alice. That's what he told her. He used her, used her bad in shed most nights. He'd say, "Nail 'em to the ground, Cheng, so they know who's boss." Nasty man.'

Milly buried her face into Dan's shoulder. Caro started wailing. Ky held her. Daph sobbed again. Joe nodded. 'It was one of Mac's disgusting mantras.'

'Mantras?' Daph's eyes were wide. 'Joe, you never told me!'

Caro shuddered. 'George was so cruel. I'm still frightened. What if he finds Milly here? He knows she's still alive. When the coppers let him go and he finds she's gone, he'll come straight here to get her... and me.'

Dan shook with anger. 'Did the scumbag nail you, Amalya? I'd like to get my hands on him.'

At Dan's defence of her, Milly felt a measure of calm push back the horror. 'I smashed a rock into his head when he came at me the second time.' Her gut spun over and over. 'Now I'll go to jail for it.'

Joshua started to cry in the bedroom. She rose from the table. 'Excuse me. I'm going to feed the possible heir. Then I think I should to return to Blue Rock.' As she fed Josh, Dan sat behind her and supported her back as he had done with their other babies. She leaned back, basking in his closeness. 'Dan, how did you survive the earthquake when Mal and Caro's parents didn't?'

'Your dream warned me. The minute I felt our office shake, I ran. I tried to get others to follow me. They laughed. I raced down the stairs and drove out of the underground car park. The whole world shook. Cars were being tossed all over the road. I managed to bounce through them without hitting anything. I had to get to you. I'd promised to meet you at the hut, if the earth moved.'

She could feel his body trembling behind her. 'Thanks for trying.'

'The road was cracking. I kept going up different back streets, trying to find a way to the lookout. It became impossible. There were cars all over the place. Houses were collapsing. People screaming. Massive hill slides. I left the car below the lookout and ran up the hill, praying I wouldn't get caught in a landslide. When I finally made it, you weren't there. I hoped you'd managed to get to the hut. All I could do then was help the ones in front of me and trust God to help you.'

Milly lifted her baby to burp him. Satisfied little lips remained in a pout.

El Shaddai

Dan turned and sat cross-legged on the bed. 'I want to do everything I can to help you, Milly. I feel as though I've failed you… didn't protect you… didn't provide for you.'

'We survived because of you.' She nodded as his raised eyebrows questioned her. 'You organised the hut for me, Dan. You told me to get supplies.'

He stood up to pace the room. 'Milly, I don't understand why you sat here at *El Shaddai* for months without contacting me. Whenever I could access a computer I checked the bank, desperate to see you use your credit card…' He gripped the bedrail, his knuckles white. 'Why didn't you at least try to ring? I was going out of my mind and you were sitting here doing nothing.'

'Your phone was disconnected. Why couldn't I reach your mother, or mine?'

He spun around. 'Mum had to move after dad's death. I lost my phone trying to help rescue people. When I got a new one, it was a different number. I messaged my new number. And Mum's.'

'I didn't get any messages until I got to Blue Rock. My phone was flat and I had no charger. When I did access it, my message bank was full.' Her pain exploded into tears. She fled towards the door. He grabbed her. She pulled away but he held her tight. She twisted, banging her fists into his chest. 'You abandoned me. You abandoned me. I wanted you, needed you… but I was scared of finding you. I felt so ashamed, so dirty. And I… I… was carrying another man's baby.'

He pulled her close and she calmed as he stroked her hair. 'I hate seeing how you suffered. Knowing a moron has hurt you makes me furious, but not at you.'

'I guess I settled in a bubble, Dan. I didn't want to face any man ever again. In the time here, God has healed me, bit by bit.'

He pulled her away from his chest and lifted her face. 'Open your eyes, Milly.'

She shook her head and turned her face away. The shame threatened to choke her.

You looked at Me, Milly

Yes… but You're God.

And I healed you. Shame has gone

'Amalya.' Dan kissed her hair, softening her heart with butterfly kisses. 'I love you. We promised to love each for better or worse, didn't we?'

She nodded and lifted her face. 'Do you still love me, Dan?'

'More than ever, Amalya. More than I could believe possible. More than the day I married you.' His eyes confirmed his words. 'But can I keep you now or are you going to slip away again?'

'I must go and ring the police.'

He took her hand and led her back to the kitchen to find Joe and Daph had already gone. She hugged Ky and Caroline, and Dan loaded his family into the car. 'Cheng will mind you girls, Ky. If George comes, Cheng will tell him we've gone into hiding.'

As they drove out the *El Shaddai* gate, Milly wondered if she'd ever return. She sat in the back seat with Lily and Joshua, willing her insides to be calm.

Dan turned into *Bethel*'s driveway. 'I like Joe, Milly. He's a decent bloke. I'm looking forward to a great friendship with him.'

'You sound as though we're staying.'

'This is our land, Milly. God said it. I believe it. And even the legalities are lining up now.'

'There're a couple of problems, Dan. The land is still in Alice's name. And no one has a copy of her will. And Jamie is alive.'

Daph welcomed them at the gate. 'Joe is in the yards. You can take Hoey and Lily to see the cows if you like, Dan.'

'What do you think, kids? Cows?' Dan led two dancing children past the shed and towards the yards. Milly's stomach settled a little as she followed the older woman into her kitchen. This was a safe place.

'Phone, Milly?'

She nodded and placed Josh in Daph's waiting arms. 'I don't want to ring, but I must tell the police I'm alive.'

'Talk to them in the lounge.'

Milly stared at the phone. She had used it many times before, trying to get through to her mother and Dan's mum. She had never managed to get connected. Taking a deep breath she dialled 000.

When she returned to the kitchen, Daph was spreading butter on bread for sandwiches. 'Josh is asleep on my bed.' She passed Milly a cup of tea and lifted an inquiring eyebrow.

'They'll send a police car for me when they can. But they don't have anywhere secure to hold me, so they're threatening to send me to Brisbane. It's too far away.'

'What about George?'

'I told them he abducted me. He was charged with drink driving this morning but they've released him.'

'Are they going to arrest him again?'

'They can't until they've taken my statement.'

'Maybe they won't take you back into custody. I'll tell the sergeant I'll keep an eye on you.'

'But Daph, I did kill a man and it seems it was Zach.'

'In self-defence and to protect your family. I'm sure the court will see it that way. I'm still shocked. How could Zach stoop so low?' One lonely tear traced a path down her soft cheek. 'Poor Alice. I'm glad she's not here to experience such shame.'

'But Daph, if I stay here, I'll be putting you and Joe in danger. I'm sure George will come after Joshua.'

'We will trust God to take care of George. I hate what happened to you, Milly, but out of such evil, God has brought amazing good.' She wiped away another tear. 'Alice would have loved you, Milly. Somehow, I believe you are the answer to all her prayers.'

The door burst open as the kids ran in. The men followed. Joe pulled shut the kitchen curtain. 'Make yourself scarce, Milly. There's a car. Not sure who it is.'

Dan hustled Milly and the children from the room. 'Okay, kids. Time to play hide and seek. Daphne will help you hide. Then you must be very quiet until Daddy comes and finds you.' He squeezed Milly's arm and returned to the kitchen.

Daphne ushered Milly into her bedroom. 'Get Josh and go into my walk-in robe. Move whatever you want to.' The bedroom door clicked as she left.

El Shaddai

Fear belched into Milly's mouth. Hoey tried to keep Lily quiet, but his young voice betrayed his nervousness. 'Will they take you away again, Mummy?'

'I... I hope not, Honey. Now let's go down the back.'

'You hide behind me, Mummy.'

'Shhh. Listen.'

A voice in the kitchen sounded like George but she couldn't be sure. Heaving aside a couple of storage boxes, she slipped in behind them. Lily crawled into her lap beside Joshua. 'I be very quiet, Mummy.'

The voices in the kitchen got louder.

Lord. Protect us. Send Your angels.

Anyone who comes against you will have to surrender to you

What?

It's My word, Milly

What are You saying, Lord? Is this an instruction or a promise?

Both The warmth of His presence flooded her.

Do You mean he has to surrender to me, Lord? Really?

'Hey, Mum.' Hoey's loud whisper sent shudders down her spine. 'Look. A gun! Can I hold it in case the bad man comes?' He pointed at an ancient shotgun behind the door.

'Hoey. Leave it and come here.' She slipped out of the hole and sat him in her place. A cold determination pushed down the fear. 'You hold Joshua and look after Lily. Quiet. Be very quiet.'

In response, Joshua gurgled.

The voices were loud now. George was yelling. 'I know she's here. Get her and the baby or I'll shoot Joe in the foot.'

'George.' Daphne yelled. 'Get out of my kitchen. Now!'

Milly grabbed the old gun and closed the robe door with sweaty fingers. The weapon, although unloaded, boosted her confidence. She leaned against the wall beside the kitchen door, willing her jellied legs to hold. George dropped his voice to a low threatening tone.

There were sounds of a scuffle. Daphne screamed. The door flung open and Daph ran past Milly. George's shadow fell across the doorway. His back was towards her. He held a pistol, pointing it back into the room. Anger rose in Milly. *How dare he invade this house of peace?*

Furious, she went to the door, shoving the shotgun barrel in his back. 'Drop it, George.'

He froze, but didn't move. Dan lay on his face on the floor. Joe sat in a chair, the revolver trained on his forehead. Milly gulped. *Father, You said…*

Courage

'I mean what I say, George. Drop your gun. Now!' She jerked her gun against his back.

His revolver fell. Dan rolled and grabbed it. In one swift move he was on his feet, the hand gun aimed it at George. 'Sit!'

Milly increased the pressure on the shotgun rammed in his back. She pushed him towards a chair. Dan held George's own pistol at his forehead. Joe grabbed packing tape from a drawer and tied him up.

Milly's legs gave way. She flopped onto a stool.

George turned in his chair to glare at her. 'I hate you. I hate your bastard son. He will die. I have cursed him to death. Cursed him, hear me? *Mac's Place* is mine. The covenant has been cut. Nothing can stop it. Not even you, you stup...'

Joe shoved a tea towel over his mouth and tied it tight with another one. 'Sorry, George, but that's no way to talk to a lady.'

Milly's whole body started to shake. Stumbling through the kitchen door, she collapsed into a lounge chair.

Dan held the phone at his ear. 'We've been attacked by a gunman.'

She didn't want to listen. Pulling herself out of the chair, she discovered Daphne lying on her bed. 'Daph, I'm so sorry.'

'I'm alright, Milly. Just a black eye and a few bruises. Are the men okay?' Daph's face had taken a king-hit. Milly's fists clenched. She thought of marching back to George and taking revenge.

Steady, Milly

'The men? Joe?' Daph's voice broke.

'They're fine. Joe has George tied to a kitchen chair and is guarding him with his own pistol.' Milly squeezed Daph's hand. 'I'm so sorry to have bought such violence into your home.'

Dan strode into the bedroom, turning drama into a game. 'Now where are my children hiding? Are they under the bed?'

Lily giggled and Dan rushed to retrieve all three children. He ushered the older two down the hall, away from the kitchen and into the garden to play. Milly followed to the front veranda, reclaiming Joshua. Dan dropped beside her on the front steps. His hands were still shaking. 'Milly, when did you learn to use a gun? And since when did you rush into a room and confront a criminal? This is not the girl I married.'

'I guess I'll never be the same again, Dan. I've had to do things I never dreamed I could do.' She held up quivering hands. 'But I still shake… and my stomach churns.'

'Me too.' He put his arm around her and pulled her close.

She relaxed on his chest. 'The fear triggered by the dreams seems miniscule now compared to the fear I've faced in the last year. But George makes my blood boil. He came to *El Shaddai* to claim it a while ago. He gave me the creeps. But today God said George would surrender to me. I guess His word gave me enough courage to challenge him.'

Dan moved back from her, looking in her eyes. 'I think I'm liking this new Amalya.' He stood. 'You check Daph and I'll back up Joe in the kitchen.'

Milly sat beside Dan in the lounge room, exhausted. The late sun slanted through the window. The sergeant had to finish taking Joe's statement before coming back to Milly. She felt as though she'd been talking all day. She'd given statements regarding George's violent visit to Daphne's kitchen and the abduction from the police cell. Her only comfort came from the knowledge that George sat in a paddy wagon on the way to a cell somewhere.

Daph dropped back in her chair, re-applying an ice pack to her face. 'Have the police talked to you about the murder charges, Milly?'

She shook her head.

'Have you talked to them about the folders you found in George's shack?'

'A little. But I don't think they get it.'

'Don't get what, Milly?' The sergeant lowered himself in the seat opposite her. Lines of exhaustion marked his face.

'George's determined plan to own *El Shaddai*.'

El Shaddai

The policeman ran his hand through hair. It already stood on end. 'Which case does that refer to? The murder, the abduction, or today's assault?'

'Which murder are you referring to?

'How many murders are we dealing with? I was referring to your murder charge.'

'How many bodies did they find in the cave, Sergeant?'

'The cave? I didn't tell you we found a body in a cave.'

Milly tried to shake the fog from her head. Hadn't they found Pete's body? Whose body was it?

'Is there something you need to tell us, Mrs Furley?' His tone changed, lost all compassion.

'Whose murder have you charged me with?' Her voice wavered.

'How many have you murdered?'

She sighed, raising her hands in frustration. 'The first day you interviewed me I told you I killed Pete, the man who raped me. I killed him in self-defence. He is the only man I have ever harmed.'

Dan fetched the folders from Joe's office. 'This picture is of Zach and George. Joe can confirm it.' Dan passed the WANTED poster to the sergeant. 'This is Pete.'

The sergeant scrutinised one picture, then the other. 'I will need to take these to be examined. Is there anything else?'

Dan reached for the folder but Joe's raised hand halted him. 'Nothing else today, Sergeant. You will receive any other information through Milly's solicitor. Why would we assist the police in their investigations without an offer of immunity? You haven't even been able to protect her. She's been hijacked from a cell in an unmanned police station, conveniently declared dead by police when, in reality, she was abducted and imprisoned. Then she had to capture her tormentor herself.' Joe stood to his feet. 'Let's call it a day, Sarg. You go back to Blue Rock. You have my word Milly will be here, should you want to ask any more questions.'

Joe moved to the kitchen door and waited for the policeman to collect his papers. The Sergeant eyes were cold. 'You must come with me, Milly. You are still under arrest. There has been no parole hearing.'

All air left her. She tried to grab a breath to be able to argue. 'I've done everything I can do to cooperate with you, Sergeant. My baby needs a break. I'll come in tomorrow.'

'No. You are under arrest. And we can't accommodate the baby. I have bottles and formula in the car. You will leave him behind.'

Panic exploded in her belly. 'But… you can't take me from my baby.'

'I have checked. I can.' He moved to her and took her arm. 'Are you going to come quietly, Mrs Furley?'

Chapter 20

THE CONSTABLE USHERED MILLY into a tiny cell at the back of the court house. 'Sorry about the accommodation. It's the best we've got since the police station was torched.'

The gate clanged behind her. Her heart dropped. A straight-backed wooden chair stood in the corner. It was accompanied by a metal bucket. One bottle of water, topped by plastic tumbler, stood on the chair. Two sides of the rectangle were bars. No bench. No privacy. No baby. No belongings. One naked bulb swung from the ceiling.

Ignoring the chair, she slid down the wall and curled into a ball on the old grey linoleum. How much more could she handle? Her heart felt broken. And anger spewed from her belly. *Lord? How could You let this happen to me? My poor Joshua!*

Her breasts were uncomfortable. Her baby would be looking for a feed. Who had him? His trusting little eyes floated before her. Pushing up, she paced, like a caged tiger. *Lord, help Josh feed from the bottle. Comfort him.*

She dropped back to the cold floor. Increasing pressure in her breasts marked the passing of time but with no window or clock she became disoriented. Had ten minutes passed or two hours? Would the light burn all night? She was thirsty, but only took tiny sips from the plastic bottle of water. Liquid would help to make more milk and increase her need for a bathroom.

A key turned in the lock of the outer door. It opened and slammed shut. A woman pushed a trolley past her cell. Lifting a tray of food, she disappeared out of Milly's sight. Her heart flipped. Was there someone in another cell?

'Tell Sergeant to get me a mattress and a blanket, or else.' George's gravelly voice growled at the woman. Prickles of horror raced down Milly's spine. She wanted to hide but there was nowhere to go. *He's here…* on the other side of one flimsy wall. But he couldn't see her. The woman returned to the trolley and pushed a tray through a trapdoor into her cell.

Milly walked to the bars, her voice a hoarse whisper. 'Thank you very much.'

The lady stopped and turned, wide-eyed. It was the librarian. 'Laura. Why are you delivering meals here?' Milly's words were barely a whisper.

Laura's mouth opened and shut. 'My husband works here. He asked if I could help. I didn't expect to see you.' Pink flooded her cheeks.

'Laura, they've taken my baby.' Tears escaped her defences. 'I need a breast pump. I'm about to blow up. Can you request one for me?'

El Shaddai

Laura's eyes darted around the room, as though checking for eavesdroppers. 'I've got to come back for the trays. I'll see what I can do… I know someone…' She left in a rush.

Milly tasted the sausages and mash, but her stomach was too unsettled to eat. The Sergeant burst through the outer door, unlocked Milly's cell and threw in a bedroll.

'Thanks, Sergeant. Please can I have a Bible, pen and paper?'

'What? This isn't a hotel, you know.'

'A Bible, pen and paper are basics. And I need a bathroom.'

'Laura will take you to the bathroom when she returns.' He spun on his heel, clanged the door shut and picked up a second bedroll.

George must have been able to see him. 'Sarg, don't forget the pen and paper.' His growl came from behind the concrete block wall. She shuddered and retreated to the far corner.

With a loud sigh, the policeman left the room. A few minutes later he returned with two large yellow notepads. He shoved one through Milly's bars and dropped a pen on the floor. He did the same at the cell next door. Its lock turned, a door opened and clanged shut. The sergeant and George began talking in hushed tones. Fragments of the conversation teased her ears. 'Not me. She threatened me.'

Curious, she held the plastic tumbler to her ear, placing the shut end on the wall. After a while her ears adjusted to the echoed conversation. She started to pick up threads, shocked at what was being said.

'Address me properly.'

'…sorry, Sir.' The sergeant seemed to be grovelling.

A key in the door announced Laura's return. Conversation stopped. She went to collect George's tray. 'Leave it, Laura.' The sergeant sounded back in control. 'I'll bring it when I've finished the cross-examination.'

Laura turned to Milly. She pushed a parcel through the trapdoor, her finger to her lips. Milly opened the packet and pulled out a power cord. Laura shrugged and searched for a power point. There was one on the back wall outside the cell. Retrieving the cord, she plugged it in. It only stretched about twenty centimetres into the cell. 'Thanks, Laura.'

'I'm sorry, Milly. I'll try to improve it in the morning.' Laura's eyes darted. 'Don't use it until the Sarg goes.' She threw in two government-issued towels.

'Wait.' Milly spoke in a loud voice. 'Sergeant said you would take me to the bathroom.'

The sergeant confirmed the request in an impatient voice. Laura collected his keys and unlocked the cell. She ushered Milly out the door and down the hall. 'Milly, why are you in there?'

'I killed a man in self-defence while we were isolated after the earthquake. They've charged me with murder. I'm hoping I'll be out on parole in the morning.'

'How dreadful! Do you have a solicitor?'

'I don't have any money.'

'Then ask for Legal Aid. You must have a solicitor, Milly. Things are not as they seem here.' She pushed open the door to the ladies. 'Can I ring someone for you?'

'I don't think so. Joe and Daphne know I'm here. Joe spoke about a solicitor. Thanks so much, Laura.'

El Shaddai

A few minutes later the cell door clanged shut behind her again. The sergeant had gone. Laura turned out the lights as she left. The flicker of hope in Milly snuffed out with the light. She collapsed on the bed roll on the floor. Back in the dark, Lord.

I am the light of the world

I don't see much light.

I love you, Milly

You've got a funny way of showing it. Her eyes began adjusting to the dark. The fire in her breasts drew her to the pump. Because of the short lead, she knelt at the bars and attached it to her breast. Her knees ached. The pump hurt but she welcomed the pain. Anything was better than the horror of being jailed, separated from her baby, unable to talk to Dan. When her knees couldn't hold her any longer, she curled up in a ball on the thin bed roll. The rasping snores from her unwelcome neighbour jangled her nerves, making it impossible to sleep.

In the dark, she pondered the conversation between George and the sergeant. Something about it was strange. *Lord, I need further protection. Is there any hope of justice when the police and my enemy are working together?* She tossed and turned on the thin mattress. Her breasts, though eased somewhat, were still burning.

Your feet aren't in stocks

Of course not. What's that got to do with anything?

Peter's feet were in stocks

Pete is dead. I killed him, remember?

My Peter. How I love his passion and faith

Oh. You mean the disciple Peter?

ᥱᥱᥱ My apostle Peter went to jail too ᥱᥱᥱ

Once again Milly tried to remember her Bible. Why hadn't she'd paid more attention to it when it was available? Why was Peter in jail? How did he get out?

ᥱᥱᥱ They sang songs to worship Me ᥱᥱᥱ

Will that get me free tonight?

ᥱᥱᥱ It will free you from one prison ᥱᥱᥱ

I don't feel like worshipping You, Lord. I'm locked up and they've stolen my baby.

ᥱᥱᥱ Sing, Milly ᥱᥱᥱ

Sing? What could she sing? Only one song came to mind. *'Jesus loves me'*. At first only a whisper stirred the air. Then a little more strength came. Over and over, the words quietly drifted around until peace overwhelmed her.

Next morning George's solicitor spoke with George in his cell. Milly listened through the wall. 'We'll try to get the charges dropped, George. But the evidence is compelling.'

'…her word against mine.'

'She did disappear from a police… burned down… returned from the dead.'

'…she escaped… don't know how...'

Milly grabbed her pad and pencil and started recording the conversation in shorthand.

'I'm not sure… get the charges dropped today… to delay the hearing until tomorrow, we may… find some more alibis.'

'There'd better be alibis. Everyone was...' She couldn't catch every word.

'Yeah, yeah. I know. But some... watertight.'

El Shaddai

'Bail?'

'I can get it today.'

Bail? Milly's stomach turned. He'd have another go at Joshua. 'Good. What time?'

'Eleven. There may be conditions on the bail.'

George growled. 'Conditions! There better not be… replace my solicitor…'

Milly heard the solicitor laugh in the cell next door. 'Now that would be interesting… only blood member who is a solicitor. Another solicitor would find...'

Milly's scribble stopped. *Blood member.* Whatever did they mean?

'Don't take the bitch's case. She should… detained for several days. She's trouble...'

Several days! Shaking, Milly stopped her notes.

'Did you nail her while you had her?'

Nail? Milly shuddered. Her gut turned at the thought.

'No. Didn't have time… I told Sarg to accidentally leave the cell doors unlocked last night, but he...'

'…asking for trouble. You're not above the law… If the detective who arrives today gets a hint Sarg is involved, we're...'

'Why… detective coming? We have an agreement.'

'…no police station… calls go to head office. They decided… needed help. Definitely no playing with prisoners...' The solicitor's chuckle sent shivers down Milly's back. '…I thought Pete nailed her.'

Milly was shaking, but made herself continue her shorthand notes.

'The evidence pointed to such... there is a baby… tests will confirm… he then allowed her to murder him…

absolute failure! And she's still not toeing the line... even with the curse...'

'Then we either nail her again... dispose of her.'

Milly almost dropped her pen. *Father... please save me.*

'Now... other urgent matters. I... start the court action... *Mac's Place.*'

'...still missing a will.'

'I fixed it... done. No one... get eviction notices... squatters as soon as possible.'

'Cheng?'

'Harmless old coot. Organise... unit at the old people's home... good will.'

Hearing movement, Milly stuffed her pad under the mattress and pulled the rough blanket over her head. She lay, motionless on the outside, confining all the shaking inside. She didn't move until George was taken out of his cell.

The day dragged on. She used the breast pump every time her breasts demanded it, always fearful someone would walk in on her. A female constable offered her a cold hamburger for lunch. At Milly's pleading she escorted her to the bathroom. On the way back Milly requested a tooth brush, hair brush and clean underclothes.

'Sorry. No personal belongings allowed.'

'I'm asking for hygiene items.'

'Sorry.' *Did fear just flash through her eyes?* 'I can't help you.'

'I thought my husband would have come.'

'No visitors. We don't have enough security.' She straightened her shoulders and turned on her heel.

El Shaddai

'Wait. I believe I'm allowed to make one phone call.'

'You'll have to ask the sergeant.' The door banged shut. She was alone again.

Milly rattled the bars, frustration burning hot. No windows, no natural light, no space and worst of all, no baby. She started pacing again. Three short strides, turn, six little shuffles back. Fear and confusion traced a similar pattern in her head.

∽ Take every thought captive ∽

The quiet thought stopped her in mid-stride. Rolling up her bedroll she tidied the small space. She would not allow them to defeat or demoralise her. Nor would she submit to George's lies and fear tactics. Using an imaginary skipping rope she started to skip, counting the jumps. *One hundred, one hundred and one...* she panted, her heart raced, but she didn't stop. At least she never missed a jump. She pushed herself to do two hundred, then collapsed on the chair.

Her brain felt clearer. The dark hopelessness a little lighter. Grabbing her yellow pad, she transcribed her notes from George's session with his solicitor. *How did they know Pete nailed her?* And what was 'the line' they expected her to follow? What was the curse?

Taking the shorthand page, she folded it and put it in her bra. With no way to dispose of the pages of notes she shoved them under the mattress.

Father, I need Your protection.

∽ Always ∽

I'm being targeting by a group of lying madmen, bent on destroying me. Please, Lord. I don't think I can survive being raped again.

~ℯℓℯ~ I will command My angels concerning you ~ℯℓℯ~

And I want to go home... We're being evicted from El Shaddai. I thought You said it was my home.

~ℯℓℯ~ For you and your children and your children's children ~ℯℓℯ~

We have no claim. It belongs to Alice, and Jamie is alive. And George scares me.

~ℯℓℯ~ Many things you can't yet see ~ℯℓℯ~

God! I can't even see a way out of jail, let alone a way to stay at El Shaddai.

~ℯℓℯ~ There is a way. A narrow way ~ℯℓℯ~

A narrow way? Like the path into Pete's cave? So narrow I needed a rope and Cheng to get me through? Cheng? She paused. *Is he a key?*

~ℯℓℯ~ Be still, Milly ~ℯℓℯ~ ~

Is Joshua okay? Please send Your Holy Spirit to comfort him.

~ℯℓℯ~ I sent Ky ~ℯℓℯ~

Ky. Lord, thanks so much for Ky. Tears slipped down her face again. She wanted her children and her family and Dan. But her whole body ached for her baby.

~ℯℓℯ~ I understand ~ℯℓℯ~

I didn't even ask You.

~ℯℓℯ~ I hear the cry of your heart. My heart hurts with yours ~ℯℓℯ~

How can You understand? You haven't nursed a baby.

~ℯℓℯ~ I've nursed many. Lean into Me and drink of Me, Milly. I will give you strength and sustenance. My arms ache to hold you ~ℯℓℯ~

She sat on the floor, rocking from side to side. Little by little the searing heartache eased. After a while a song rose from within and crept out of her mouth. *Trust and obey, for there's no other way, to be happy in Jesus but to trust and obey.*

The other verses escaped her so she sang the lines over and over. Without realising it she changed the lines. '*There's no other way to have El Shaddai but to trust and obey.*' Lifting her hands, she rocked on her knees, her voice gaining strength. On her feet she danced on the spot, singing now at the top of her lungs. *Am I going crazy?* She didn't know, but a joy bubbled from deep inside. They could take her baby, her solicitor, water and food, but they couldn't steal her joy. *I feel better, God. Thanks. I need more water. And food. No one's been here for hours.*

Come to Me, all you who are thirsty

Okay, God. I'll trust You.

Returning to her chair, she headed two fresh pages. 'The defence case for Amalya Furley' and 'The narrow way to *El Shaddai*.'

Was it night? Was it morning? Milly couldn't tell. Had she missed dinner? *Breakfast?* The bare bulb burned, never turned off. She tipped the chair over her bedroll and covered it with the towels. With her head in the shaded area, she managed to sleep a little.

Waking, she stretched her aching bones and moved her head into the glare. *Lord. I need more strength.* Pulling herself across the floor, she leaned on the bars of the cell and applied the breast pump again. Every time she produced less milk. What if she dried up and couldn't feed Josh again? Fighting back tears, she tried to comb her hair with her fingers.

Her imaginary skipping rope turned at a sedate pace, but she decided to do at least one hundred, even though there would be no water when she'd finished. On her fifty-third jump a key turned in the door. A sharp-suited man entered and the door clicked behind him.

'Amalya Furley?' He stretched his hand through the bars. 'Robert Roundup, solicitor, at your service.'

She shook the offered hand and blinked. He looked so out of place. She must look a mess, her borrowed dress crumpled. She'd slept in it for days. 'Sorry.' Dragging her eyes up from the floor, she looked at him. He was pulling up a chair and sat near the bars, indicating she should do the same.

'Umm... Mr...'

'Call me Robert.'

'Robert. Can you find me a drink of water, please?'

His eyebrows shot up as he glanced around the cell. 'No tap? No toilet facilities?'

She shook her head. The odour from the bucket in the corner filled her nostrils. 'No toothbrush. No deodorant. I apologise.'

He jumped to his feet and banged on the door to the hall. When no one responded, he beat it with both fists. Pulling out his mobile phone he dialled, tapping his foot as he waited. 'This is Robert Roundup, solicitor. I am visiting Amalya Furley. I wish to speak to the Sergeant... *now*.' He waited. 'He's not available? Tell him I will go straight to Channel Nine.' He shoved his phone in his pocket.

'I'm sorry you have suffered this way, Amalya.' His sympathetic words nearly broke her. Footsteps raced up the hall. The door swung open and the constable stood to one side. 'The inspector will see you now, Mr Roundup.'

'Good. I expect him within two minutes.'

'He's waiting in his office.' She waved down the hall.

'Well, you'd better tell him to get here. And bring a bottle of water.' He didn't bother to lower his voice. The startled woman scuttled down the hall, leaving the door open behind her.

Thirty minutes later Milly sat in an interview room with Robert. She had showered and changed into fresh clothes left by Dan two days earlier.

'Eat, Amalya.' Robert waved at the plate of sandwiches. 'We've only twenty minutes before we're due before the magistrate.' He shuffled his papers. 'The last two charges are ridiculous. I have enough information from Dan to see them thrown out by the judge. But I need help with the murder charge.'

Milly unfolded the yellow page, headed: 'The defence case for Amalya Furley'. She handed it to him. He read the detailed report she had prepared.

'I think it is enough to get bail, but I would like to see the charges dropped. Is there anything else you can think of?'

'Did Dan show you the poster of Pete the Pirate?'

'No. He said he gave it to the police. It was lost in the fire. But I don't see the relevance.'

'It was Pete who raped and threatened me. He looks like Zachariah McLaughlin, but I have no proof. A reward is offered for any information leading to the capture of Pete the Pirate. Does that help?'

Robert grabbed his phone. 'I need any information you can find on Pete the Pirate. There is or was an offer of a reward.' He turned to Milly. 'Do you have any idea of a date?'

She shook her head. 'I got the impression it was some years back.'

He passed her a bundle of papers. 'Please check these statements.'

She flicked through them. There were still two more to read when they were called to court. The cheese from her sandwich threatened to make a second appearance as she was ushered into the dock. *An accused criminal.* She sat on her hands to stop them shaking.

My strength, Milly

A line of a psalm returned to her head.

We don't trust in horses and chariots. We trust in the Lord

Okay, God. I don't trust in solicitors and judges. I trust You.

She lifted her head and looked the judge in the eye as Robert began. 'Your Honour. Can we begin with the lesser charges?'

As the proceedings continued, she tried to follow the legal jargon while her heart repeated the promise over and over. *I don't trust in solicitors and judges. I trust in the Lord.*

Robert's skilful representation reduced most of the charges to nothing. As each charge was dropped, the sergeant's face got a little redder and he pulled at his collar. The judge shuffled his papers and peered over his glasses at Robert. 'The next charge is for first degree murder. My understanding is Mrs Furley has confessed to this murder.' He turned to Amalya. 'How do you plead? Guilty or Not Guilty?'

As though a spotlight blinded her, her throat closed up and her voice failed her.

'She will be pleading not guilty, Your Honour.'

'Not guilty? We have a signed statement saying she killed Zachariah Peter McLaughlin.'

Her brain swam. Zachariah *Peter*? Now Pete the Pirate made sense. But… she had never signed such a document. She looked down at the papers, now crushed in her hand and spread them on the bench. Yes, it looked like her statement and her signature at the end. She glanced through the document, heart in her mouth. The name jumped out at her. On the bottom of the first page was his name, Zachariah Peter McLaughlin. The original name had been covered and his name typed below. Without thinking she spoke aloud. 'I didn't sign here.'

'Out of order. Please wait to be addressed, Mrs Furley.'

Robert reached over and took the paper from her hand. 'This statement has been tampered with, Your Honour.'

'Not true, Your Honour.' The sergeant jumped to his feet. 'It has a countersigned adjustment.'

'Not on this copy.' Robert walked towards the bench.

The judge sighed and held out his hand. He perused the paper, comparing it with the paper on his desk. 'My copy is countersigned.'

He passed it to Milly. 'Is this your signature, Mrs Furley?'

The scribbled initials were a good copy. 'No. I did not countersign.'

The sergeant stood. The judge nodded, giving him permission to speak. 'This is a stenographer error in the copying process. I apologise, Your Honour. However, the defendant has admitted to murder. I suggest we move on and stop wasting the court's precious time. I ask she be committed to trial and held in custody. Her violent behaviour deems her unsafe to be released.'

Milly gasped. *Held in custody?*

ܥܠܠ *Don't trust in horses and chariots* ܥܠܠ

The judge turned to Robert. 'Mr Roundup?'

'Your Honour. My client admits she killed a person called Pete in self-defence. A murder charge could not be proved. Are you familiar with Pete the Pirate?'

'Do you mean Pirate Pete?'

At Milly's nod, Robert continued. 'I believe he is a renowned criminal and there's a reward for his capture.'

The sergeant jumped to his feet. 'Your Honour. This is not the place to be running down rabbit trails.'

'I concur, Sergeant. Your point, Mr Roundup?'

The door at the back of the court banged open. Everyone in the court spun as Caroline rushed in, waving a paper in her hand. 'Here it is. I've found it.'

The Judge banged his gavel. 'How dare you interrupt my court hearing!'

Caroline stopped in her tracks. Her cheeks went bright red. 'Sorry. I didn't mean to offend. I had to get this to the solicitor as soon as possible.' She handed the paper to Robert and fled.

'My apologies, Your Honour. Permission to approach the bench.' At the judge's nod, Robert stood and held out the

El Shaddai

paper. The sergeant pushed him aside in his hurry to get the best vantage spot.

The judge studied the paper and passed it to Milly. 'Is this the man you murdered, Mrs Furley?'

Robert interjected. 'Objection.'

Pete's leering gaze shot the familiar foul feelings through Milly's body. She shuddered.

'Mrs Furley?'

'This is the man who raped me, Your Honour.'

He passed it to the sergeant. 'Do you have any evidence Mrs Furley murdered Zachariah McLaughlin, Sergeant?'

'Yes, Your Honour. We have her statement.'

'Which is disallowed.'

'And her wedding ring was found under his body. Another ring belonging to her was found in the near vicinity.'

Robert jumped in. 'Which is where they were living at the time, trapped by earthquake destruction.'

'Mr Roundup.' The judge fixed his eyes on him. 'The sergeant requests Amalya Furley be committed to trial and opposes bail. What do you say?'

'Your Honour, there are no grounds for first degree murder and limited grounds against my client for the manslaughter of Zachariah McLaughlin. If the man in question is indeed Pirate Pete, then in my understanding of this reward, she has immunity. To commit her for trial on the given evidence would be unjust.'

'Agreed.' The hammer came down on the bench. 'Amalya Furley, you are free to go.'

Milly slumped back in her chair, every nerve tingling.

The clerk of court stood. 'All stand.'

As Milly struggled to get to her feet, the judge paused at the dock. 'Mrs Furley, I wish to apologise for the conditions under which you were detained.' He nodded and left.

The minute the door closed, Dan jumped the dock and threw his arms around her.

'Dan! Where? How?'

'I've been sitting up the back.'

'Joshua?'

'Outside, waiting for you with Ky. Go. I'll talk to Robert.'

Finding new strength, she rushed to get her baby.

They all jammed into one booth in a coffee shop. Joe and Daph sat on one side with Caro. Dan, Milly and Ky faced them and Robert sat backwards on a chair at the end. Ky kept one eye on the children racing around a playground.

'Coffee!' Milly sniffed her cappuccino. 'I haven't had a cappuccino since the day before the earthquake. Am I the same person? Doesn't feel like it.'

'Hmm. Totally different person, I'd say.' Dan had his arm around her shoulders and squeezed her. 'But I love what I'm seeing. Now… to try to stay together for a while.'

Everyone laughed. But Milly held Joshua closer. 'We need to talk about that. While George is free, I'm not safe. The legal system in this town has some sort of vendetta against me and Joshua.'

Robert's eyes sparked. 'Tell me. Sounds interesting.'

She glanced around the coffee shop. 'There are too many ears here.'

'I don't have an office in town. Is there somewhere we could hire a professional room?'

Dan raised one eyebrow. 'Are you sure we still need a solicitor, Milly?'

She nodded. 'Do you have time, Robert? I know Dan is concerned about your fee, but if you help me claim the reward for Pirate Pete, it will be covered.'

Robert stood and shook her hand. 'Deal. Besides, I'm fascinated. Some strange things occurred in the courtroom today.'

'More than you know.' Relief flooded through her. Someone would help her. However, her thoughts seemed like spilled spaghetti. 'But first I need sleep.'

'Question is... where can we go?' Robert looked at Joe. 'Any ideas?'

'Would you be happy to spend a night at *Bethel*?' Joe asked. 'We can work together to get to the bottom of this mystery.'

Chapter 21

'FREEDOM! TO BE FREE to move, to make my own choices, to feed my baby... it is so wonderful!' Milly's heart flipped as she watched Joshua sucking her breast. He opened one eye and looked at his mother as though checking she didn't disappear. 'Thanks for caring for him, Ky.'

'I'm amazed you can still feed him.'

'God sent an angel to bring me a breast pump. If not for her, I think I may have exploded.'

The door opened, admitting a burst of cool air and four noisy children followed by Dan. 'Visitors are here. I think they're looking for coffee.' He ushered in Daphne, Joe and Robert.

Joe sat on the chair Ky offered him. 'Hope we're not too early, girls. We want to get to the bottom of this craziness. I want to ensure you're safe, Milly. At the moment I'm not confident.'

'Me, either. Dan slept across the bedroom door last night. Cheng in the pantry. They had a gun each. We can't live like this for long.' Milly looked around the room. 'Hoey, Johnno.

Please run and ask Cheng to come.' The children disappeared out the back door, leaving Bea wailing in frustration.

Ky scooped her up and offered her a muffin. Robert leaned on the wall looking more like a farmer than a solicitor. His presence helped to calm her racing heart. No corrupt sergeant could attack her today. But George roamed free somewhere, plotting their destruction.

Robert dropped onto the chair beside her. 'Milly, I'd love to hear your story. Daph says you escaped Wamberoo. Where have you been since then? How did you end up here?'

As she told the story, the others settled around the table. Dan, close to her other side, rocked Joshua. Caro and Ky served muffins and coffee, interjecting their perspective into the story.

'And this house was empty when you moved the family to *El Shaddai*.'

'Empty, neglected and dusty. Yet the pantry was stocked. We were hungry and desperate.' Milly paused, trying to assess Robert. Did he understand spiritual things?

Can you truly tell this story without talking about Me?

'God led us here. He told me this property was a gift to me. God and I have had many arguments about it. I still can't see how it can happen, but it's been an amazing refuge for us.'

'Who owns it?' Robert directed his question at Joe.

'Interesting question. For the last several years it's been known as *Mac's Place*. Mac and Alice lived here with their four children. George, Mac's nephew, visited often. Alice disappeared about twelve years ago. Her body has never been found, but the courts have issued a death certificate. After the boys left, Mac

El Shaddai

only used these two rooms.' He waved around the kitchen and pointed to Milly's bedroom. 'He and his car were swallowed by Dead Man's Gully in the earthquake. Cheng has always been here but he has his own quarters behind the shed.'

As though on cue, the children arrived with Cheng. Ky handed the children a muffin each and ushered them back outside.

Cheng shook Robert's hand. 'Cheng at your service, Sir.'

As Cheng sat, Joe continued. 'George thinks he has claim to *El Shaddai*.'

'How? You said there were four children.'

'Two passed away years ago. Zachariah, you know about. Jamie is missing. George thinks he's dead.' Joe opened the file in front of him and passed George's chart. 'This explains George's plans.'

Robert pursued the chart and whistled. 'Aggressive.' He frowned. 'Who is Robert?'

'He's dead, too,' Cheng said. 'Milly told me the day she arrived.'

Milly's brain swirled. *What did he mean?*

Daph started to weep. 'Robert was Mary's son. We assume Mac was his father.'

The solicitor threw up his hands. 'Hang on. I'm confused.'

Cheng explained. 'Robert was the son of boss and Mary. Or maybe Zach's son. They both, um… used her in storeroom. They'd sneak in at night. When we could see a baby in her, Alice got very angry. One night they had a big fight. Boss beat Alice badly, very badly. Next day Zach took my Alice away. I never saw her again.' Tears ran down his face. 'My poor Alice.'

Joe pulled Daph closer. 'Do you think Mac killed her, Cheng?'

Cheng shrugged. 'Don't know. They fought about Mary. Alice was kind to her.' He shook his head and cleared his throat. 'Mary had her baby in shed, alone. I tried to help but... I know nothing about...' He wiped his eyes. 'I was so angry I put a lock on her room. Told her to lock it at night. But Boss still got her sometimes. Seemed like he put a spell on her. Or a curse. I told her to run to *Bethel*, but no...'

'Where is she now?' Robert had started to take notes.

'Zach came back. Said he'd look after her. Took her away. She was excited 'til he made her leave her boy. After that I looked after Bobby.'

'Bobby.' Milly's heart dropped. 'My Bobby?'

'The one who bought us vegetables?' Caro's eyes were wide. 'But he was indigenous.'

Daphne pulled a handkerchief away from her mouth. 'Yes, Mary was indigenous. Zach used to come and visit her. I should never have allowed her out with him.'

Caro's broken voice interrupted. 'But once he'd nailed her, she had no choice. She would have had to go with him. I know. It's what happened to me. George was charming and wonderful. He promised me everything I'd ever wanted… proposed to me and used my credit card for a hotel room. I felt like a princess. But he was rough, cruel and violent. He said... I now belonged to him so I must obey. If I didn't...' Her voice broke. '…he'd nail me again, until I toed the line.' They waited until she blew her nose.

'Toed the line!' Milly turned to Robert. 'Do you have those notes I gave you?' He passed them to her. She flicked through them, searching. 'That's what George said to the sergeant. I listened to their conversations. He was just in the next cell.

This is what I took down.' She passed the yellow sheets back to Robert. 'You can read it out. I guess the others want to hear.'

When he stopped reading, the table sat silent, as though stunned.

Dan broke the silence. 'Pete nailed you, Milly?'

'He said his god had sent me. He expected me to live with him and have his babies.'

Caro wiped her nose. 'But you're different because somehow you escaped, Milly. I know what you mean about that spell, Cheng. It felt like that. I couldn't get away, and Mary couldn't. How did you?'

'I killed him.'

'But how? I couldn't have. It was...' She dropped her head into her hands. 'It was impossible.'

Milly could just hear her whisper. That explained why Caro didn't return for Bea.

Caro lifted wet eyes to Milly. 'How, Milly?'

'He was, um, compromised. And God was with me.'

'That's why!' Cheng slapped his hand on the table. 'I see now. George become upset if you don't toe the line, do what he tells you. The brothers practised cursing. Their witchcraft controlled Mary, but it can't get you, Milly. Our God in you is stronger.'

'But Cheng...' Daph wiped her eyes. 'Alice knew God. Why could it hold her, destroy her?'

Cheng started to weep again. Joe reached across the table to the distressed man. 'Cheng, I'm sorry. I never realised. I should have stopped it years ago. But it seemed harmless. I've been so blind.'

Daph gasped. 'Joe, what are you saying?'

'Mac invited me to join a secret club years ago. The idea was we'd work together, as mates, and help each other. It sounded good, so I went to a couple of meetings. But I never joined. They insisted on cutting and sharing blood. I struggled with the idea. Jesus shed His blood so I don't need to. When Mac taught the group the importance of nailing our women, I left and didn't return.'

'Joe! You knew it happened to Alice.'

'I knew Mac believed it but it wasn't my business. Since they trapped Mary, I've been praying God would expose the wickedness. And now He has. Cheng's right. It's a form of witchcraft.' He pointed to the yellow sheets. 'I never thought it would spread into our justice system. The question is: what do we do now?'

'And how do we keep Milly and this baby safe?' Dan stroked Joshua's dark hair.

The jigsaw was falling into place in Milly's head. The club Joe described made sense. 'Now I understand why you didn't come back, Caro. You couldn't.'

Ky held her hand. 'That's right, Milly. But, when Caro did come back, George couldn't control her against the combined power of God in you and Cheng. The enemy had to surrender to you. No wonder George hates you.'

'Caro, where'd you find the poster of Pirate Pete?'

'In George's hut. I thought he was still in jail. But I passed him on the road about ten minutes after I left. Scared me half to death.'

Ky chuckled. 'Just like God to get you out in the nick of time. Milly, Caro and I prayed a few days ago. We broke the soul ties between her and George. After that God helped her remember seeing a poster in the hut. She knew you needed it.'

'Well, I'm thankful, Caro.'

'I picked up a couple of other things, too.' She passed a couple of sheets of paper to Robert.

He perused them with narrowed eyes. 'Alice MacLaughlin's will. She leaves everything to her sons or nearest living relative. Why would he have a copy of her will?'

'Is it the real thing?' Joe reached out for it.

Robert passed him the document. 'Looks real, though the paper doesn't appear aged enough to match the date. Hasn't her estate been finalised?'

Joe looked at the paper and put it on the table. '*El Shaddai* was left to Alice by her parents, but not to Mac. He was furious, but he couldn't do anything about it legally. No one has ever been able to find her will.'

'Solicitor?'

'She used one in Wamberoo, instead of the local one. Mac contacted him with no success.' Joe's eyes flicked open wide. 'Maybe she knew the guy here, the one Milly heard the other day, was part of the brotherhood.' His face dropped. 'He does all my legal work. I'll need another solicitor.'

Daph handed the will back to Robert. 'Not her signature. It's not her writing.'

'Do you have anything with her writing on, Daph? A letter, or card?'

'I don't think so, but I'll look when I get home.'

'I have some of her writing.' Milly's heart raced. From her room she retrieved the little key, meticulously labelled in

Alice's handwriting. As soon as Cheng saw it, his face paled. He pushed back his chair and rushed outside.

Robert examined the key. 'If that's her writing, this will has been signed by someone else. It won't be hard to contest.' He looked at Joe. 'Do you have a copy of Mac's will?'

Joe pushed his file across the table. 'It's in there… with the other stuff Milly brought from George's place.'

Robert digested the folder, one sheet at a time. 'Have the police seen this?'

'No. I thought it better to show a solicitor first.'

Dan nodded at Joe. 'Your wisdom saved us there, Joe. If I'd given everything to the sergeant the other night, it would all be lost in the fire.'

Quick footsteps announced Cheng's return. He sat a small wooden box in front of Milly. 'Does your key fit the lock, Milly?'

Milly ran her fingers over a skilfully carved box. The lid was engraved with the words *El Shaddai*. 'This is beautiful, Cheng. When I found this key, God told me it was the key to *El Shaddai*. I didn't realise He meant a box. Whose is it? What does it hold?'

'I made it for Alice before she married. I don't know what's in it. She gave it to me few days before Zach took her. She gave me key too, but I made a mistake. I hid box but left the key on a hook. One day the boss grabbed it and asked where the box was. I told him I didn't know. That I found the key in shed.'

Caro's eyes sparkled. 'Open it, Milly. Maybe it's treasure.'

Milly's hands shook as she pushed the key into the lock. It fitted. The lid swung open. Chairs scraped the floor as everyone crowded around. A gold chain with a cross lay across a bed of

El Shaddai

folded money. Each bundle was held by old rubber bands. No one spoke. Milly lifted the bundles out. An envelope lay at the bottom. Caro grabbed the money and started counting. Cheng stared at the box, waiting.

Milly opened the unmarked envelope. Two sheets of paper slipped out. Her hands shook. *Is this the real treasure, Lord?* His warm presence enveloped her.

She handed the sheets of paper to Robert. 'Ah. Alice McLaughlin's will. Again.' He flicked to the second page and chuckled. 'And it's signed two days after this false one.'

'Good.' Joe sounded relieved. 'What does it say?'

Robert whistled as he read. 'It leaves all her possessions, including *El Shaddai*, to Cheng Song.' He turned to Cheng. 'Is that you?'

'Yes… but you must read wrong.' Cheng's hand shook, his eyes wide.

'That's what it says, Cheng. It goes on to say Mac has three months to vacate the property.'

Joe shook his head. 'Extraordinary! Does she mention the boys?'

'She says she loves them, but their inheritance is with their father.'

Daphne shook her head. 'Alice said that! I don't understand.'

'Maybe this will explain.' Milly pulled out a second flat envelope, addressed in Alice's tiny writing. *To my dear Cheng.* She passed it over the table. Cheng shook his head, and pushed it back. 'Do you want me to read it?' Milly's head was buzzing, trying to keep up.

He nodded.

'Here? Now?' A stick of dynamite lay in her hand.

'Please, Milly.'

She slit the envelope with a knife, smoothed the pages and began to read.

My dear, dear Cheng,

I write this knowing I won't be with you much longer. That's okay. My life has been hard and I'm ready to go to my Lord.

I have taken the liberty of bequeathing El Shaddai to you. I hope you don't mind. I trust God will bring the right people to help you. I can't leave it to Mac and the boys. My parents entrusted me with their property and their dream. Mac will never use it for any other purpose than evil.

You understand Dad's vision and share it. May God guide you as you take over the management of this place we have always called home. May He send you the help you need to establish the retreat centre we have always dreamed about.

The cash is to help you to start as I'm sure Mac will take everything he can. It's not much, but it's all I could get.

Cheng, thank you for loving me all these years. I do not deserve your unending devotion. You have never stopped loving me in spite of my betrayal. You've always displayed the heart of God.

I would like to explain what happened all those years ago. I ran away from El Shaddai because I thought I was pregnant with your baby. I was frightened and couldn't bear to disappoint Mum and Dad. I met Mac one evening. He was charming, bought my dinner and offered to drive me home. Then he raped me. He told me I would always be his and said he would marry me. I felt I had no option. And I've been powerless to make my own choices ever since.

El Shaddai

Yes, my dear Cheng, Zachariah is your son. I don't think Mac ever worked it out, though when he belted him without mercy, I wondered. He belted all your sweet nature out of him, until he made Zach like himself.

I'm so, so sorry. I have failed you in every area. You are the only man who has loved me and I repaid you with lies and deception.

Remember a few months ago you prayed with me? You led me to a deeper relationship with God. It is so sweet. I haven't told Mac, but he doesn't have the same control over me anymore so he's angry. Zach wants to take me away, but I don't know if it is the right thing to do. If I go or if I stay, I fear for my life.

I didn't want to go anywhere without getting my affairs in order and telling you how much I love you.

Maybe we can spend eternity together. You, me and the beautiful Hannah Rose. I'm so glad God took her before she suffered as I have done.

I love you, my darling
Yours eternally
Alice.

Milly lifted her wet eyes to Cheng.

He raised his head. Tears streamed down the wrinkled face. 'Again.'

'You want me to read it again?'

He nodded.

As she read, Alice's sweet presence seemed to invade the room. No one moved. Daphne wiped tears from her cheeks. Ky had her arm around Cheng's shoulders and wiped her own eyes with his sodden hanky. As Milly closed the letter, Dan squeezed her shoulder and scraped back his chair. He carried Joshua around the table and stood behind the old man. 'Cheng, you might like to nurse your grandson.'

'My grandson?' Cheng wiped his eyes and held out his hands. Josh woke as Dan lowered him into Cheng's arms. His eyes opened wide and Milly feared he would scream. Instead, he smiled at Cheng.

A bubble rose from deep within Milly. It somersaulted its way, leaving a trail of joy in its wake. It burst forth, turning her tears to laughter—loud boisterous laughter. Soon the whole family were dancing around Cheng and the little boy. The big man held the little man close. 'Lord, thank You, thank You. You said You'd pay back the stolen years, but my own grandson? I'm holding a little bit of me and my Alice.'

El Shaddai

Chapter 22

'Excuse me. Robert gathered the documents together and rose from the table. 'I need to make a few phone calls.'

'And I have holes to dig.' Joe stood, his hand on Daph's shoulder. 'Dan, would you help me?'

Milly spun toward Joe. 'Holes? What holes?'

'The maps. I want to see what's under the crosses, assuming you don't mind us digging on your property, Cheng?'

Cheng dragged his eyes from Joshua. 'Dig, dig. I will help.' He passed the baby to Milly.

Milly kissed Joshua's head, eyes on her husband. 'Dan. Be careful. We don't know where George is.'

Joe paused at the door. 'We have guns. I've left one in the pantry for you, Milly.'

She watched the men walk towards the shed. Robert held his phone to his ear. With shaky fingers, she shut the door and pushed the bolt in place. *Lord, are You still here?*

I'm here with you and I'm riding with the men
I need Your peace.

Caroline restacked the money in the box. 'Forty-five thousand dollars, Milly. Can you believe it?'

'I'm struggling to grasp any of it, Caro.' Her hands shook as she slid the key in the lock. It turned smoothly. As Milly's hands stroked the lid, she remembered. *Lord, You did indeed give me the keys to El Shaddai. I just didn't know You meant a box.*

Yes. The box is the token to remind you

His presence flowed over her, bringing goose-flesh on her arms. Peace calmed her churning stomach.

'Milly?' Caro sounded tentative, unlike her normal self.

'Yes, Caro.'

'Thank you.'

Milly's fingers stopped. 'For what Caro?'

'For... for loving me. I've been so selfish, such an idiot.'

'It's been a tough walk, Caro. And you didn't sign up for it. Don't be too hard on yourself.'

'There! Exactly what I mean. You are always nice to me.' She paused, eyes on the floor. 'And... I'm so sorry for the time I beat you up.'

Milly blinked. *Am I hearing straight?* She put her hand on Caro's arm. 'It was all caused by fear and grief.'

'Uncontrolled fear and grief. But all of us were suffering the same horror. I've no excuse.' Caroline studied her nails for half a minute. 'I've been wondering... how can you and Ky always be so calm and loving? Then, when you returned from George's hut...' She sniffed and lifted wet eyes. 'I've been locked in that hut. Even when I found a key, I couldn't run from it. Something...' She lifted her hands and shrugged.

'I don't know what it was, but it stopped me. Maybe I was brainwashed. I just couldn't leave. When you went back to jail, I asked Ky what you have that I don't.'

God, help her to say what she needs to say. Milly waited.

Caroline's eyes closed as she took a big breath. 'Ky said Jesus lives in you. I prayed and asked Him to be my God. I'm a bit braver now but not much. When we realised the fire had destroyed Pete's poster, something inside me told me to go to the hut and find another copy.'

'And you were able to.' Milly's heart warmed.

'Yes, but it was the scariest thing I've ever done in my life.'

'Courage, Caro. Thank you.'

'Courage? Felt like fear.'

'That's what courage is. You feel the fear and do it anyway. If there's no fear there's no need for courage. See, you're breaking free from George's power, because you're being filled with God's Spirit. It's always stronger.'

'If God is so strong in you, how could George even kidnap you?' Caroline paused, eyes studying an invisible spot on the table. 'Why could he lock you up? Why didn't God look after you in jail? Why could Pete rape you? How come God wasn't stronger then?' She lifted confused eyes to Milly. 'I'd like to trust God. I can see He has lessened George's power over me. But I just don't get it.'

'Whoa! Big questions, Caro.' *God, I need Your wisdom.*

Open your mouth and I will fill it

'Remember the arm wrestle contest we had a few weeks ago?'

Caro smiled. 'The babies were so cute. It was the funniest thing watching Bea and Bethie trying to arm wrestle.'

'And Johnno and Hoey had such a struggle, but Hoey won in the end. Why did Hoey win?'

'He's bigger, of course. It wasn't really a fair contest.'

'But he had to fight to win. Johnno put up a strong challenge.'

'What's your point, Milly?'

'God is stronger every time. But we still have to fight to get victory. Our opponent is strong, wily, sneaky and deceptive… charming and often attractive.'

Caro's eyes clouded. 'Like George?'

'He charmed you, deceived you by pretending to love you when it was only a ruse to get you into bed, to get control over you.'

'Yes. It was all to get sex, power and control. But isn't that what Pete did to you?'

Milly took a deep breath and let it penetrate her pain. She released her tension with the air. 'I fought Pete, the same way you and I battled in the arm wrestle. I fought him with all my strength. I kicked, struggled, punched and bit him. But he was too strong for me. It appeared I'd been beaten. I felt annihilated.' She smelled his stench in her nostrils. 'He stank so bad, Caro. I wanted to die. I hurt, and I felt ripped inside and out. He was so confident he'd trapped me, he went to sleep. I ran to the waterfall and tried to clean myself with sand. I returned to get my clothes, planning to escape but, when I got back, he grabbed me again. I picked up a rock and drove it into his head.'

'What if you missed? He'd have made your life hell.'

'Stop fighting? Never! God and I won the battle. Even though I was wounded, together we were stronger.'

Caroline sat in silence for a minute. 'I didn't fight, did I?'

'Only you know the answer, Caro.'

'I went looking for sex, Milly. You know that.'

'And it made you an easy target. But God is bigger. He's still able to take George's evil plans and use them for good. Already He's used you to get the poster, for my good.' Milly lifted Joshua and he rewarded her with a drunk, milky smile. Her heart skipped a beat. 'The plunder from my battle is this beautiful baby.'

'But his father is a violent rapist, an outlaw. Doesn't Joshua remind you of him?'

'At the beginning I struggled with those thoughts. They plagued me and drove me back to the hut. I fought a massive battle that day. I nearly gave up. But when I ran out of strength to fight, God took over. Evil was beaten.' She paused, listening to her own words. They were true. Evil was defeated on the mountain. 'Then I knew my baby was a gift from God. Do you know why I named him Joshua?' The little boy grinned at his name.

'Because you liked it?'

'I do like it. But when we first arrived here at *El Shaddai*, God told me I was having a son and to name him Joshua.'

'He said that?'

Milly nodded. A revelation exploded in her brain. 'Obvious… now I think about it.'

'What do you mean?'

'In the Bible Joshua led the people of Israel into the Promised Land. My Joshua has brought us to *El Shaddai*.'

'We found *El Shaddai*, Milly, long before Josh was born.'

'Yes. But we can stay because of Joshua.'

I know the plans I have for you. Plans for good, not evil

Lord, You are amazing, just amazing.

In the afternoon Milly heard vehicles coming in from the front gate. *God! Where are the men? I'm alone again.*

Alone?

Sorry, El Roi.

We make a formidable team, you and I

Okay, God. Let's go and see who's here, though I'm sure You already know. She peered out the window. Two police cars. Her heart dropped into her boots and tears sprang to her eyes. *Not again, Lord.*

Be still, Milly

She unbolted the door, gulped a mouthful of air and strode forward to meet them. A large, jovial policeman offered his hand. 'Inspector Grimm. I'm looking for Mrs Furley.'

She pushed out her shaking hand. 'I'm Milly Furley.'

He pumped her hand, grinning. 'You're my newest hero, or should I say heroine?'

'Pardon?'

'You caught Pirate Pete. I've been trying to trap that bushranger for years. But no, God gives him into the hands of a beautiful woman.'

'You're not going to arrest me?'

'Arrest you!' He laughed, then sobered. 'No. We've given you a hard time, haven't we? I'm sorry.' He turned and introduced her to the other four men. 'We've been in phone contact with Robert Roundup. He says they've found human

El Shaddai

remains on the property. We were hoping you could guide us to the site.'

Milly's head swam. 'Human remains?'

The inspector grabbed her arm. 'Steady. I should have taken this a little slower.' He guided her towards the steps.

'Sorry. I didn't know they'd found anything.' She glanced at Ky, waiting at the door, Bea on her hip, questions in her eyes. 'The police want me to go with them.'

Ky's face fell. 'Oh, no! Not again.'

The inspector jumped forward and introduced himself. 'We need her help. We need to find the place where your men are digging.' He nodded at her. 'Do you mind if I leave two of my men here, Ky? They won't bother you. I'll ask them to watch the road.'

'Are you worried George might come?'

The inspector nodded. 'We can't find him and we believe he's desperate.'

'I'd be very relieved to have them here, Inspector.'

The front seat of the four-wheel drive was better than being locked in the back of a police car. Milly guided the inspector through the property towards the area marked on the map. Soon she was in unfamiliar terrain. There were no visible tracks from the truck or the quad. She was lost. 'Can we stop, so I can try to find my bearings?' When the vehicle stopped, she stood in front of it, trying to match the landscape to her memory of the map. *Lord, please show me where to go.*

There was no audible reply but a dead gum drew her attention. She climbed back into the vehicle. 'It may be over the hill, I think. That dead tree was marked on the map.'

As they crested the hill, they saw the men clustered around little mounds of dirt in the valley. Robert greeted the inspector like a long-lost friend. 'Gary, I thought you'd send a team. I didn't expect you.'

'I didn't come to see you. I came to meet this heroine.' He waved his arm at Milly.

Robert chuckled, then sobered. 'Come and see. We've dug in several places. It's a bit crude. We only had a posthole digger. But we've found evidence of bones in three places. The maps have been very helpful.' He led the men towards the digs.

Dan took Milly's hand and guided her away. They sat on a log under a gum tree. She leaned into his embrace. 'Bones, Dan? How dreadful.'

Dan shuddered. 'They weren't down far. At the last one we uncovered quite a bit of the skeleton.' His arm tightened on her shoulder. 'Cheng has told me *El Shaddai,* all this, will be Joshua's and therefore ours.' Milly nodded her agreement, but Dan misunderstood her. 'He's serious, Milly. He didn't ask me to help him, or even manage it. He says we must treat it as if we own it.'

'I'm not surprised, Dan. He always claimed God sent us. The only difference was your absence in the beginning. God told him he'd send a man. Instead, he got three women and a gaggle of kids.'

'My lucky day.' Cheng appeared and grinned at Milly. He lowered himself beside Dan. 'This morning, I understood what God said. Now it's clear. God said, "I send Dan." I thought he meant "man", but all the time God knows it was Dan.' Tears trickled down his cheeks again. 'God didn't say you'd bring my grandson too. God, He is so good, so good.'

The sound of vehicles roaring up the hill brought Milly to her feet. Dan grabbed her. 'Get down.' He pulled Milly and Cheng to the ground behind the fallen tree as the inspector and the others raced for the four-wheel drive.

Milly turned and watched over the top of the log. 'It's George.' Fear exploded in her belly. His truck slid out of control as it came over the hill and swerved to avoid the four-wheel drive. A police car roared over the rise in pursuit.

A cloud of dust covered Milly. An explosion of ripping metal rent the air. Dan covered her with his body. 'Stay down.'

Car doors slammed. Motors stilled. The dust settled.

When Dan released her and helped her up, the police were pulling George's wrists into handcuffs. The back of George's truck was slammed against a gum tree, bent and buckled. They dragged George over to the inspector.

'I'm Inspector Grimm, Mr McLaughlin. I appreciate you dropping in as we need your help. Come with us. I'm hoping you can assist us identify bones these men have found. We have your maps. Maybe they will jog your memory.'

Milly's heart made a curious flip. It went out to him. He was trapped by evil, but still a man. On the way to the first dig, the men paused. It seemed George was pleading. They allowed him to walk to a bush, not far from her log. He snatched a big bunch of leaves with his cuffed hands and began stuffing them in his mouth, chewing like he hadn't eaten for months.

The bush activated a memory. She'd seen it before. *Bobby!* He ate leaves from the same bush just before he died.

'Cheng?' Her hand shook as she pointed. 'What's the bush behind George?'

'It's not good. Stay away from it. It's poisonous. Very poisonous. Mary wanted me to get its leaves when she had the baby. She told me it kills you quick.'

'Inspector Grimm!' She waved at him. 'Those leaves George ate are poison.'

The inspector's eyebrows lifted to his hair. 'How poisonous?'

'I don't know but Cheng says they act fast.' Milly gulped. 'Last person I saw eat those leaves died…'

George fell, thrashing to the ground in his own graveyard, wrists still locked in handcuffs. Cheng ran to him, dropped to the ground, praying. Milly turned away, her hands over her face, trying to block out the scene.

Dan's arms held her. 'George will never bother you again.'

'But, Dan… what a wasted life.'

Dan shook his head. 'Killed multiple people, yet too cowardly to face the consequences.' He led her towards the quad. 'Let's go home.'

El Shaddai

Chapter 23

THREE DAYS LATER Joe and Daph arrived in the late afternoon. They gathered on the front veranda where they could watch the girls play. Joe had been to town. Everyone wanted to hear his news.

'The sergeant has left Blue Rock. He's on leave, pending a trial. Someone tipped off the mayor, saying the solicitor had hired a large paper shredder. The town's business people barricaded his office. They saved all our important documents, and uncovered evidence of foul play.' He turned to Milly. 'The town owes you, Milly. I want to thank you for exposing the corruption.'

'But Joe…'

His raised hand stopped her. 'God used you, my girl, and we are thankful.'

Ky turned from watching the littlies play. 'What about the bodies, Joe? Have they identified anyone?'

'One is the body of a constable who disappeared about six months ago. Another was a young lad who used to work here. They think he died over ten years ago.'

At Joe's pause, Milly pushed for more information. 'And the third? Is it Jamie?'

'No. And it isn't Alice or Mary. They know it's a man but they haven't identified him yet.'

Daph's hands turned in her lap. 'It's surprising. We thought the bodies would be Alice, Mary and Jamie. They are going to dig further. I hope they find Alice.'

'I know where Alice and Mary are buried.' As the words burst out of her mouth, Milly wondered why she hadn't realised it before. Every eye turned to her. 'They're in Pete's cave. I assumed the police found them when they found Pete.'

'What makes you think that, Milly?' Dan reached out to grab her hand.

'Bobby told me. He helped me cover Pete with rocks, but wouldn't let me take rocks from two large heaps. He said one pile of rocks covered Pete's mother and the other, his wife. I didn't realise who they were until just now.'

Joe whistled. 'So… Zach killed them?'

'Bobby thought so. He said Pete buried ladies in the cave, but fed men to the dingoes.'

A gasp spread around the veranda. 'Milly, are you sure?' Joe leaned forward, his arm around his wife.

'That's what Bobby said. Not until now did I realise one was his mother. He was terrified of Pete and was relieved he was dead.'

The whole group sat in silence, stunned. The quiet was broken as the door opened and they heard Cheng's shuffle. 'Milly. Can we talk outside, please? And Dan.'

They rose and followed Cheng down the hall and out the back door. A man stood deep in the shadow of a tree. Cheng

El Shaddai

reached out his hand and drew him forward. 'Milly, Dan. Meet Jamie... Jamie McLaughlin.'

Dan shook his hand, but Milly, stunned, looked at him open-mouthed. 'Jamie. You're not dead.' She tried to slow her racing heart. 'I'm sorry. My comment was very rude. Can I try again? I'm very pleased to meet you, Jamie, and to see you are alive and well. Come in.' She paused, embarrassed. How could she invite him into his own home?

'Wait.' Jamie sounded hesitant. 'I'd like to say something before we go in.' He lifted his eyes from his feet. 'I know this is your home now. Cheng has told me everything. Please don't feel bad. This was never a happy place for me. I couldn't return before because I was on George's hit list. But now he's gone, it's safe for me to come to visit Cheng.'

Milly took his arm. 'I was on his hit list too so that must make us brother and sister. Please come and join us.'

She led him in through the house. Joe and Daph jumped up and embraced him and then introduced him to the family.

⁕ ⁕

Milly leaned back on the bedhead and fed Joshua. Dan sat rubbing her feet. 'Dan...'

'You can tell me, Amalya.' Her heart flipped at his insight.

'Tell you what?'

'Whatever you were thinking about, whatever is coming between you and me.'

She swallowed and started to talk, but stopped. What if he rejected her?

Trust Me, Milly 'Trust me, Milly.'

Her heart did a somersault. 'Dan, you just said the same as God, at the same time. I think it will be okay after all.'

'Of course it will be okay.'

'The morning you arrived, before I heard you, I... I had to let you go. The Lord asked me to give Him all my devotion. He had proposed to me before, asked me to accept Him as my husband, to trust Him, to love Him, to rely on Him. It felt like He wooed me. He called me out of bed at night and asked me to dance.'

Dan ran his fingers up and down her ankles, sending goose bumps up her leg. 'Go on...'

She moved Joshua to the other breast. 'In the forest, just before you found me, God questioned me. It reminded me of Jesus talking to Peter by the lake. "Do you love Me?" So... I promised... I promised...'

Dan lifted his eyes and looked into hers. 'What did you promise El Roi, Amalya?'

'I'd never let another love come between God and me again. I meant it. Then, in a moment, you were there.' She lowered her eyes and gathered courage. 'Now you're here I don't know what to do.'

Dan took Joshua and laid him on the bed. He pulled Milly into his arms, squeezing her so tight she wondered how she could still breathe.

Be still, Milly

She relaxed in Dan's arms. He kissed her hair, her face, her mouth. 'I love you, you gorgeous girl. God loves you. You love God. Do you love me?' He stopped and leaned over her seeking her eyes.

For a second she looked into his depths. Overcome with the love shining in his eyes, she dropped her gaze to his chest. 'Yes, Dan. I love you so much it scares me. That's the problem.'

Dan lifted her chin. 'It was the hardest thing God ever asked me to do.'

'What?'

'I had to let you go, release you, you and the kids, to God, and devote myself wholly to Him.'

'You, too?'

'Yep.' He tucked her head in under his neck.

She snuggled in. 'So does that mean we are three?'

'Looks like it to me. A cord of three strands isn't easily broken. And this little guy? He's the bonus blessing.' With one hand he scooped up Joshua, kissed him and put him down on his blankets on the floor. Stripping his shirt off, he pulled Milly close. She stiffened. 'Amalya?'

'Dan, I'm...' How could she explain his touch triggered images of Pete's violent aggression. 'Dan, I'm sorry. I need time...'

He softened his hold and let her go. 'Of course, Milly. I should have thought of that. I can wait... with El Roi's help.'

Chapter 24

WHAT WOKE HER? Milly sat up and listened.

Come with Me

God, did You wake me up?

Come, Milly

The blankets were cosy, enticing her to lie back down. Yawning, she replayed her conversation with Dan and rolled over to hug his back.

Milly

Lord. It's the middle of the night.

Is it? I'm awake

Milly stretched and giggled. *You never sleep. But I need sleep.*

I'm sufficient for you

Feeling the pull in her heart, she wrapped her new blue dressing gown around her shoulders. As she turned the door handle, Dan sat up. 'Wait for me, Milly.'

Is it okay if Dan comes, Lord?

Awesome

They crept out of the house and ran through the garden, giggling like children. 'There, Dan. Over there.' She pulled him into the middle of the moonlight under the trees.

'It's a heart.' Dan spun around in the centre of the light.

I love you both. You delight My heart. I have called you

Milly heard the words in her racing heart. She repeated them aloud to share with Dan.

Dan nodded and grabbed Milly's hands. 'We want to follow Your plan, Lord.'

You won't always find it easy, but My ways are perfect

'You are faithful, Lord. And always with us.'

Will You shelter the broken, the hurt, the poor, the arrogant

'The arrogant?'

The abusive, the addicted, the demonised

'Lord?'

All are lost souls who need My love. Some will reject it. Some will accept it and be restored but My love is free. Will you?

They looked at each other. In the moonlight, Dan's eyes asked her the question. Could they do as God requested?

Her heart raced, spreading heat through her whole being. All she could do was nod.

He spoke on their behalf. 'We are willing, Lord, but we'll need lots of help. Where You lead, we will follow. We will shelter those You send. We will feed the hungry, clothe the poor and hug the broken-hearted. We will love those You love.'

El Shaddai

Did the moon get brighter? Milly didn't know but joy ran through her like warm oil. Dan started to chuckle. 'Give us more of Your Spirit, Lord.'

He grabbed his wife and started to dance in the moonlight. The Spirit of God swirled around them, between them and through them, pulling them closer and closer together until, in peace, they all became one, on the blue dressing gown in the middle of the moonlight heart.

Epilogue

MILLY AND CHENG LED their visitors through the front garden and past the line of trees. She hadn't been to this hidden spot until a month ago. A few weeks after the police had recovered Alice's body, Cheng showed her this place. In this sheltered corner, there were three gravestones. The larger one marked Alice's parents' remains. The two other graves were marked by smaller plaques. One said *Hannah Rose* and the other *William*.

Today she'd left Joshua with her mother in the house. He was sleeping and her mother, overjoyed at recovering her two grandchildren and an extra, loved to mind him.

She held Cheng's hand tighter, trying to settle the butterflies in her stomach. 'You doing okay, Dad?'

He rewarded her with a smile. 'Yes... only 'cause God gave you to me.'

They stopped beside the first of the three gaping holes. Dan and the children came up beside her. The others gathered around them. Jamie sidled up near Cheng on the other side. The others huddled around Joe and Daph. They had formed a close-knit family. They watched as the funeral directors wheeled five coffins into place. An old friend of Cheng's stood to speak. Milly tried to gather her thoughts and focus.

'Here today we come face to face with evil. There is no point pretending otherwise. The devil has had a field day with this family. But God has prevailed. He always wins. And as we lay these bodies to rest, we recognise He's answering Alice's prayers and those of her parents and our spiritual warrior, Cheng.'

They lowered Mac first and then placed Pete's coffin on top. Milly still couldn't think of him as Zachariah. Within the safety of Dan's arm, she watched as the neighbours filed past to pay their last respects. She couldn't move. Nor did she shed a tear. Everything she ever wanted to say to Pete had been spoken in the cave.

Mary and Bobby were buried together under a tree. Jamie and Dan walked with Cheng as he paid his last respects to the woman he'd tried to protect. Once again Milly stood still and watched. She had buried Bobby once—and once was enough. This time though, her tears, cleansing tears, flowed down her cheeks. She was glad he was reunited with his mother.

Farewelling Alice was the most difficult. Everyone in the community had loved her. Milly held Cheng in the curve of her arm as they lowered her between her mother and Hannah Rose.

He let out a big sigh, swiping a tear away. 'She said she loved me and that's enough. May she rest in peace.'

As they moved out of the hidden graveyard, silence hung like a heavy blanket, broken only by the children's whispered voices. The front lawn beckoned them. Caterers had prepared a feast and tables were piled high with food.

'Milly.' Laura grabbed her and gave her a big hug. 'It's good to see you. Thanks for inviting me. What a day! Sad, and yet exciting.'

'I know. Somehow it seemed right to close one chapter and open the next at the same time.' They accepted drinks from an offered tray. 'Thanks so much for helping me when I was in jail, Laura. You're a hero.'

'They wouldn't let me go back in. I came with dinner the next night and they said you'd already been fed.'

Milly stared. 'They did it on purpose.'

'What?'

'They didn't give me anything to eat or drink for over twenty-four hours. By then Dan had found a solicitor. He was furious.'

'I was indeed.' Robert grabbed her from behind.

Milly spun around. 'Robert. I'm so glad you're here. I didn't see you earlier.'

'I just arrived. I thought better of doing the burial thing. It saved me spitting in a couple of graves and thereby embarrassing myself.'

Her face feigned horror, but the comments warmed her.

Caroline grabbed Robert's arm and rushed him away. Milly found Daphne. Together they made their way through the crowd, Daphne introducing her to their new neighbours. With each tray of food, the mood lifted. Music played from the house. Kids played and squealed. People began to laugh. Daph whispered in Milly's ear. 'It's working. Joy is replacing fear. Look. Joshua is awake.'

Milly's mother carried him through the crowd and joined them. Joshua held out his hands to Milly so she took him, kissing his cheeks. He giggled.

Daphne touched her arm. 'I think Dan's about to start.'

Milly's heart swelled as Dan stood on the veranda and called the crowd to attention. There was nothing imposing about his appearance, but peace and a quiet confidence attracted the people's respect. The crowd quietened. He waited while mothers grabbed children and others found chairs. 'Thank you so much for coming. My name is Dan Furley. My wife, Amalya, is the beautiful one.' He waved towards her as the people laughed. 'We asked you to come and celebrate the rebirth of El Shaddai today. Many of you have known it as Mac's Place, but that chapter closed this afternoon.' He looked at the crowd and paused. 'Firstly, let me introduce Jamie McLaughlin. He would like to say a few words.'

Milly squeezed Daph's hand. *Help him, Lord.*

Jamie stood, an old felt hat spinning in his hands. 'I won't keep you long. I just want to say... sorry. My father and my brother have done a lot of dreadful things. They were trapped in the devil's ways and caused a lot of hurt and grief. I was nearly caught myself but God rescued me. Can you please forgive me and my family for... for our violent, wicked ways?'

He ran down the stairs and spun to leave. Joe grabbed him and hugged him. Someone began to clap. Another joined in. He sobbed on Joe's shoulder in the middle of neighbours eager to show their forgiveness.

Dan held up his arm to restore quiet. 'I now ask Robert Roundup, our solicitor, to explain some of the legalities pertaining to El Shaddai.'

As Milly listened to Robert review the history of the property, she marvelled again at God's work. Alice and Cheng's prayers had called her family to help. The vision, planted as a dream in Dan's heart combined with her tsunami nightmare, had rescued them and positioned them at *El Shaddai*.

❦ Just as I said ❦

I'm so overwhelmed with Your ways, Lord.

Dan called Cheng as the final speaker. He offered the paper in his hand to Dan, asking him to read his speech. Dan shook his head and waited, standing to one side. A hush fell over the crowd. Cheng tried to speak but nothing came out. He looked at his paper and glanced up. 'My... my Milly. Please come.' His eyes pleaded with her.

With shaking legs and racing heart, she mounted the stairs, carrying Joshua. Cheng pulled her close beside him with his arm. The notes were crumpled in his other hand. 'This is my Milly. My God told me He puts the lonely in families. He always promised me a daughter. The minute I saw her, I knew. This is her, my special girl. I didn't know then, but she brought my grandson.' He stroked Joshua's soft head. 'Before Milly, I only ever had one love, my Alice. But the devil stole her. All these years she's been so close... yet so far. She's in peace now.' He breathed, long and slow. 'Alice had a dream for *El Shaddai*. Her parents' dream. *El Shaddai* was established to be a place of peace, safety, rest, restoration. Mac never understood. All my hope shrivelled. The dream seemed impossible. When Alice disappeared, even the name, *El Shaddai*, died. But God. He never forgets. He brought Milly to me, and her beautiful team.' He nodded his head at Ky and Caroline. 'Milly has suffered bad... bad things, and yet the Lord has healed her. God taught her how to help people who hurt. They will come to *El Shaddai* and shelter under Jesus' wing.' He smiled. 'God told me he'd send a man to help. Instead, I got three women.'

The people pushed their tears aside and chuckled.

'Dan took a long time coming. But he's here now.' He dropped the crumpled notes and pulled Dan to his side. 'Dan is the man. As Robert explained, Alice said *El Shaddai* belongs to me. But it's too much for me. I'm just a gardener. So today, I give *El Shaddai* to Milly and Dan.'

'Cheng.' Milly gasped, but the voice of God stopped her argument.

My ways, Milly

Cheng searched the crowd until he found the face he was looking for. 'Robert. You will make it happen?' At Robert's nod, Cheng turned and hugged Milly and Dan, tears running down his face. 'New beginning, my children. You will say yes?'

Dan turned and faced Cheng. 'Milly and I have given everything to our God, *El Shaddai*. He holds our life and our future. We will walk together with you, our father.'

Arm in arm, the three of them, with Joshua, went down the stairs to celebrate with their friends and neighbours.

El Shaddai

Author's Note

THANK YOU FOR READING about Milly, Dan and their relationship with El Shaddai. It started with a crazy idea to write a novel with God as a character. He seemed pleased with the concept. It's taken a long time as it felt presumptuous to write God's words… what God was communicating to Milly. But with a lot of encouragement, I pushed forward with the story. And God said the craziest things. In faith I wrote the faint ideas that came to mind and let Him lead. The result is the book you have just read.

God also wants to talk to you! And He is doing so, but often we are not tuned to His voice. Rarely does He talk audibly. His voice is a soft impression in our spirits. We need to tune our spiritual senses to Him. Ask Him to help you turn on your spiritual sense of hearing, seeing, touch, taste and smell. Stop and ask Him to show you more when a whisper of an idea flies past. Pay attention when a sweet fragrance wafts by or different taste grasps your attention.

God communicates with those who are expectant—that

Jo Wanmer

is, those who, in faith, are waiting to hear. The other way to hear His voice is through reading the Bible. When a verse or phrase catches your eye, read it again. Meditate on it. Be still. God will show you wonderful revelations, or give you direction.

God loves you. There is nothing you have done that has stopped Him loving you. God loves you so much that He sent Jesus to take the punishment for everything you've done wrong. So you can be forgiven and free... *if* you will accept it.

It is simple. Just say... 'Jesus. Thank You for loving me, taking all the consequences I deserve and setting me free. I want to hear Your voice and follow You.'

And I pray that the Lord will release a blessing to each and every person who reads this book.

About Jo Wanmer

JO LIVES IN MORETON BAY CITY, an emerging community north of Brisbane. She has always been a Queenslander. She and her husband Steve live busy lives filled with God, business and family. Their family has grown astronomically, now embracing nine beautiful great-grand children who fill their home and garden with noise and laughter.

Jo never saw herself as a writer, but God moved so graciously during years of family trauma that she wrote her first book to tell what he had done. *Though the Bud be Bruised* won a CALEB award and was published twelve years ago. Encouraged, she found a love of writing stories, especially stories that bring a message of hope and redemption. Many of her short stories are published in anthologies, but twelve years passed before this, her next novel, was published.

El Shaddai is the first of a series of titles. You can follow their progress of publication on www.jowanmer.com.au or her Author page on Facebook:
https://www.facebook.com/profile.
php?id=100066475044806

Though the Bud be Bruised can be found on Kindle or you can order it direct from the author:
jowanmer@gmail.com

Milton Keynes UK
Ingram Content Group UK Ltd.
UKHW020057271124
451585UK00012B/1297